His^3

His^3

BRILLIANT NEW FICTION BY GAY WRITERS

edited by Robert Drake and Terry Wolverton

Faber and Faber, Inc.
An affiliate of Farrar, Straus and Giroux
New York

Faber and Faber, Inc.
An affiliate of Farrar, Straus and Giroux
19 Union Square West, New York 10003

Distributed in Canada by Penguin Books of Canada Limited
Printed in the United States of America
First edition, 1999
Pages 279–280 constitute an extension of this copyright page.

Library of Congress Cataloging-in-Publication Data
His^3 : brilliant new fiction by gay writers / edited by Robert Drake and Terry Wolverton.
p. cm.
ISBN 0-571-19963-1 (alk. paper)
1. Gay men—United States—Social life and customs—Fiction. 2. American fiction—20th century. 3. Gay men's writings, American. I. Drake, Robert. II. Wolverton, Terry. III. Title: His three.
PS648.H57H562 1999
813'.5408092066420—dc21 98-33107

Grateful acknowledgment is made to the following: *p. 55:* The University of California Press, Berkeley, for permission to excerpt lines from "Who Am I?" by Nazik al-Malaikah, from *An Anthology of Modern Arabic Poetry,* selected, edited, and translated by Mounah A. Khouri and Hamid Algar, copyright © 1974 by the Regents of the University of California. *p. 202:* Allen Grossman, for permission to use an excerpt from his poem "The Recluse." Copyright © 1965 by Allen Grossman.

To Ciarán

Contents

His³

World Without End

ROBERT ORDOÑA

Pentecost Sunday: Early in the morning, Quinn is in the bathroom, in front of the mirror, doing up the buttons of a velvet shirt—Quinn, who always tries so hard to dress for the occasion, but who always manages to get it wrong. The shirt is a bright red—perhaps it's too red, perhaps he looks silly. Once he went to Mass (had it actually *been* St. Patrick's Day?) wearing a new lime-green T-shirt and green jeans, and when he stood for the opening antiphon, a young nun sitting in the pew behind him burst into laughter.

Quinn plucks at his collar and stares at his reflection from different angles. At last, despairing, he turns toward the window.

Outside, Leager is sunning his long, sick body on the patio. His latest drug cocktail seems to be working finally. He's gained some weight and color. Still, Quinn notes the parts of his lover's body that remain tired and shriveled: his eyes, especially, and his penis.

Mrs. Chung from next door leans across the overgrown hedge and whispers in Leager's direction. Her words travel to Quinn through the hot, still air. "Mr. Peele, please. *Pssst* . . . do cover up."

Leager answers the woman by turning over on his lounge chair and flashing her with his red, bony ass.

Mrs. Chung presses her fists to her cap of white hair and waddles back indoors.

"Ahk," she cries. "Ahk, ahk, ahk."

Quinn steps out onto the patio with Leager's swimming trunks. Even this early in the morning, the soles of his feet burn against the tiles. He steps back inside and grabs Leager's sandals.

"Here," he says, dropping the clothes beside the lounge chair. Leager twists his head around and grins smugly.

Quinn says, "Sure, you're victorious now, but later you'll remember all of this and feel sad." Maybe Quinn will find him in the bathroom, in the middle of the night, staring into the full-length mirror and sobbing.

Quinn flings the trunks onto Leager's scaly red back. "For goodness' sakes, Lee. Put these on."

Leager covers his ears. He squeals, "Ahk."

"Stop that."

"Ahk, ahk, ahk."

"Lee—"

"Ahk?" Leager looks up and smirks.

Quinn sighs and shakes his head. He opens his mouth to say—what? What could he possibly say? He feels a stirring inside him, and for a moment he doesn't recognize what it is. He frowns and coughs. And then the stirring overtakes him—he's laughing before he can get hold of himself.

Leager, obviously pleased, closes his eyes and settles back in his chair.

Beyond the hedge, in the Chungs' back doorway, Mrs. Chung gestures frantically in their direction, while her husband—sweet, alcoholic Mr. Chung—fidgets beside her. He shrugs his shoulders up and down, stiffly, like a windup toy.

Quinn watches them and clutches his gut. But even the sight of his long-suffering neighbors isn't enough to restrain him. He feels helpless. Unlike Leager, he already feels guilty.

Long ago, when Quinn was a boy at a school called St. James the Greater, anything could throw him into such a fit—a priest's lisp, a nun's wagging jowls. What did he do back then to make himself stop?

Once, old Sister Daniel (the jowly one) dragged him into the cloakroom, where there was a rusty sink. She pushed a sponge into his hand. "Get to work, giggle girl," she said, her voice deep and gravelly. And while he pushed the dry sponge back and forth over the enamel, she reminded him about dear St. Bernadette and her enormous tumor, and about the Maccabees, their eyes gouged out, then their hands cut off, then their breasts (which sister Daniel called "the fronts of them") . . .

She said, "Think of that when you get that tickle in your throat."

But now, snorting crazily on the patio, Quinn is not at all affected by these images. Instead, another memory bursts into his head: a summer evening on this patio, ten years earlier—the scent of jasmine in the air, sweet and mournful as incense. In the darkness, Leager slides his shorts down to his hard, tan calves and Quinn kneels behind him, bites the taut, muscled flesh of his ass.

"Aw, don't stop," Leager says now, from his lounge chair, his eyes still closed. "Such a pleasant sound, your laughter. Listening to it, I almost forgot what a bitch you really are."

Quinn presses his palm to his forehead.

"Hello? Quinn?" Leager's eyes flutter open.

"I'm still here, Lee."

Leager sits up achily. He covers himself with the trunks Quinn had brought him. "Listen, Kinny, will you bring me out my pipe? I think I need it."

Quinn looks at his watch. "Come inside, then. The last thing I need is for Mrs. Chung to smell the smoke and send the cops out for you."

"Let her," Leager says. "The crazy bitch."

Quinn presses his lips together and looks beyond the hedge. He remembers an autumn season not too long ago when Leager heaved baskets of tomatoes and apples from their garden over to Mrs. Chung.

"I love you," the woman had cried. "Oh, how I *love* you."

Later, Quinn comes out of the bathroom, fully dressed at last. He'll be late for Mass now. He'll have to find a place to sit way in the back of the church where he won't be able to concentrate.

"Leager," he calls out. The house smells of pot. He finds Leager, still naked, in the kitchen, his eyes heavy lidded, foggy and serene. He's lifting a jar of peanut butter off one of the cupboard shelves.

"Ah," Leager says. "Off to see the wizard?" Then he stares at Quinn's shirt and for a second his eyes sharpen. "Kinny, look at what you're wearing."

Quinn freezes and runs a hand down his sleeve. He allows himself to be hurt, but only for a moment. "I'll be back in an hour or so," he says. "What are you doing?"

Leager chews his lip and looks down at the jar in his hands. "Hmmm . . . making a sandwich."

Quinn clenches his teeth, sucks air through them. He doesn't have time for this. The taste of pot smoke, bitter and spicy, enters his mouth. The pipe lies in an ashtray on the kitchen table. He's annoyed with himself for craving a toke. "You know you can't eat yet. You just had your pills."

"I'm hungry. That's good, isn't it? It's been so long since I've been really hungry. Maybe I'll just have some bread with a little sugar—"

Quinn pulls the jar away from him and rolls it sideways back onto the shelf. He says, "You're hungry because of the pot. You should have waited."

He slams the cupboard door shut. They both jump at the sound it makes.

The sound rattles something loose inside Quinn. *Idiot,* he wants to spit out at Leager. *Are you an idiot?*

It's an odd feeling, to be angry at Leager after all this time. Five years earlier, when their doctor first told them that Leager had AIDS, Quinn thought: *Whore.* Then he was never again angry at Leager, until now. And he wonders: Why now? The anger swells in his throat, oddly, in the same way lust used to swell in his throat—how it used to gag him.

Soon after they first met, Leager turned Quinn on to poppers. He held the brown vial under Quinn's nose and the stinking vapor flooded his head. Soon, Quinn felt slow and reckless and desperate. He felt tears rushing behind his eyes, and a thin membrane rising before him, fogging his vision. He wanted to taste the skin of Leager's belly, his long toes, the fleshy line that ran down his scrotum. He wanted to suckle Leager's cock forever. Head spinning, Quinn looked into Leager's face, which was hot and moist and dreamy. He saw that Leager's eyes were foggy as well, and Quinn wanted to live behind this fog—live in the power he felt behind it.

But the high lasted for only moments. Afterward, his head pounded. He felt queasy and exhausted and ashamed. Now, in their kitchen, Quinn feels the anger draining from him just as swiftly. His head clears and he finds himself staring at the lesion above Leager's right nipple, now so familiar, and at the one below the knife-sharp basket of his ribs, and the one blooming in the hollow of his neck like a dark petal. But where are the rest? Quinn steps back and runs his eyes over Leager's body. Three blemishes where once there were so many.

Leager pushes his blond hair off his eyes, a mannerism once so familiar to Quinn. And Quinn sees that Leager's hair is growing thicker and softer, that it is once again beginning to curl, and that there is a new fleshiness and color softening the sharp angles of his face.

"Don't look at me like that," Leager says.

"Lee, baby—" Quinn doesn't know what to say. He's quiet, and then he stammers, "You're beautiful."

"No, I'm not. Why do you look so terrified?"

"Why say that, Lee?" Quinn says shakily. He takes another step back. He tries to swallow. He looks at his watch. He must get to Mass. "I'll be back soon," he says. "We'll have a nice lunch then."

When Quinn steps forward, Leager stiffens and his eyes squeeze shut. He remains very still as Quinn kisses his neck, like a good boy suffering the slow, sharp poke of the nurse's needle.

The man on the phone says to Sister Sharman Summer, "My new volunteer boy is a slut."

Sharman holds the receiver to her ear and looks out the window of the office, which is in a renovated Victorian flat across the street from St. John of the Cross.

"Oh, Gustavo. Now why would you say that?"

"Because he is. He comes in always with the short shorts and the tight shirts. And his body—it's not even that good."

"Gus, seriously—how would you know? You can't see a thing."

"He let me touch," Gus says.

"I don't need to hear all this," Sharman says. She tugs absently at the rusted window latch. "All I want to know is if he's being of help to you." Sharman's voice rises because the television in the office has suddenly become very loud. The two other volunteers are hooting at the end of a football game. Sharman covers the receiver and calls out, "Guys? Please."

"Sorry, Sister," says the man who doesn't know her very well. "Sorry, Sharm," says the man who does. They turn the television down and return to their desks and their telephones.

Gus says, "Oh Sharmie, I was kidding you. I just wanted to make you laugh."

"Yes, Gus. All right." She closes her eyes and touches her lips to the receiver. He's one of her favorites, this Gus, and actually, he can almost always make her laugh. One of the first stories he ever told her was about desperately wanting to be a nun when he was six years old, and how he had made a little habit for himself out of a bedsheet and a lampshade.

Since his lover died, she's begun calling him from her apartment, sometimes quite late in the evening. He tells her about the sixty years he and Jack had spent together. Sixty years! Almost twice her age—the enormity of it is a solid wall she can't climb. Sometimes she takes her heavy wooden rosary off its peg and holds it in her lap while she listens. She runs her fingers over the smooth, dense beads and considers that each one represents a year of Gus and Jack's life together. Other times, she listens with a glass of wine on the table beside her. She leans back and sips from the glass and after a while allows the tears to slip down her cheeks.

Now she's frightened for Gus. If his new volunteer doesn't work out, there might not be another to take his place. With the new treatments, people think the worst is over. Everywhere, she feels a surge of cautious cheer. She can picture the politicians slapping each other's backs and looking for new causes. But what will happen to her dear Gustavo, and the others, on whom these new treatments have no effect?

Sharman shields her eyes and looks down on the sunny street. She watches men dressed in sport shirts and sneakers, or scuffed, comfortable loafers, climbing the steps to church. Afterward, they'll walk in groups down to the nearby restaurants. They'll huddle together on the bright sidewalks, whooping at each other's stories, until the host calls out their names.

"Oh, Gustavo. Is there anything at all I can do for you?"

"You can take me to the ballet. No, I don't like the ballet. Was it Jack who liked it? I have no idea anymore," Gus says. Then he whispers, in a tired, serious, kind voice, "Remember, my sweet Sister, that even if I did not have AIDS I would still be a very, very old man."

Sharman laughs softly, to please him, even though she doesn't quite understand what he is trying to say. Nevertheless, she is comforted somehow.

After they hang up, Sharman looks down at her phone list. Gus's was the final name. She taps a pen edgily on her lips. She feels restless and wonders if she should hear Mass again, even though she had attended the eight o'clock. Perhaps she should walk the eight blocks down to Mission Street and window-shop, budget herself two dollars for a treat—a cup of frozen yogurt or a pretty greeting card.

Through the window, she sees a dark-haired man in a red velvet shirt rushing down from the end of the street toward church. She's seen this man before—at Mass and around the neighborhood, darting in and out of the pharmacy or the supermarket, or strolling down the sidewalk with his sick lover. Once, she went into the little Japanese restaurant on Eighteenth Street for takeout and saw them sitting at a window table. While she waited for her order she watched the lover take the napkin from his lap and fold it into a large, limp origami swan.

The dark-haired man tugged the napkin gently from out of his lover's hands, shook it out, and smoothed it back down on his lover's lap. Immediately the lover plucked up the napkin and began again to pleat its wilted corners on top of the table, and, again, the dark-haired man took it away and replaced it on his lap. Sharman sat hypnotized by this scene, which played itself over and over every few moments. It was like a child's game—the dance of their hands, the white napkin flicked between them; it was graceful as a game of cat's cradle.

Sharman cocked her head and eavesdropped on their conversation, which carried on steadily while all of this was happening.

"Have the tofu udon," said the dark-haired man. "That's easy to digest."

His lover said, "Ugh, tofu. All I want is sushi."

"You know you can't have raw fish."

"I can have crab. The crab is cooked."

"I don't know about that," the man said. "I don't know about that at all. I'll have to ask."

"Well, I want *something* wrapped in rice and seaweed. Maybe they can make sushi with tofu."

"You said you didn't want tofu. So now you want tofu?"

While the man turned to look for the waiter, the lover had time to shape his napkin into a little boat, which he proudly bobbed up and down in the light coming in from the window.

"Ah," said the waiter, who had suddenly arrived. "Can we hire you to fold all our napkins?"

"We'll order now," said the dark-haired man.

"Can you make sushi with tofu?" the lover asked.

The waiter, a young, milky-skinned Japanese man, batted his eyelashes. "Of course," he said. "Anything for someone as handsome as you."

"Are you big?" the lover asked.

"Excuse me?" said the waiter, his smiling stiffening just slightly.

"You know, big."

"We'll have two bowls of tofu udon," said the dark-haired man abruptly. "Thank you." And before the waiter could say another word, the man added, "And two glasses of water, no ice. Thank you."

As the waiter retreated, the man shook out the napkin boat and dropped it on the table in front of his lover. In a voice cool with finality, he said, "Leave it, please."

Sharman hid her face behind a takeout menu so no one would notice how intently she was listening. Of course, until that moment, she couldn't have been sure that the two men were lovers. The dark-haired man could just as easily have been a friend or even a hired attendant. But there was something in the stiffness of his jaw and the indignant flush rising in his cheeks that even Sharman knew could mean only one thing: he was jealous.

A feeling ballooned in her chest. She didn't know what it was. It should have been pity, but it was something vastly different. It was something light and hot and almost sweet. The closest word she could think of was "triumph." Here was the lover, obviously sick under his camouflage of dark glasses and baseball cap and turtleneck sweater. His bones jutted against the fabric of the sweater. The hint of a lesion bloomed in the shadow cast by the bill of his cap. His face was taut and flaky and shiny, as if covered with a thin layer of fish scales. Yet—astonishingly—the man beside him could barely sit still, so shaken he was by the perceived threat of a pretty, young waiter. Two thoughts raced through Sharman's mind, one crashing into the tail of the other. The first was: *This is love.* The second was: *Is this love?*

She wanted to ask the man this question. Sitting alone in the corner of the restaurant, she was suddenly overwhelmed by all she didn't know. She felt like an old, old woman who had traveled the world many times over, but who had learned nothing from it. She wanted the man to tell her about his love, the hard sharp teeth of it chewing at his gut.

Now, from the window, Sharman watches him hesitate before climbing the steps to the church's entrance. She watches him absently straighten the collar of his shirt and square his shoulders. As he disappears inside, Sharman cannot calm the rush of curiosity she feels about this stranger—yet another ridiculously proud man whose world she so desperately craves to know.

Why do you look so terrified?

The church is full by the time Quinn arrives. The opening hymn is coming to a close. He dips two fingers into the glass bowl by the entrance and hurriedly touches the water to his chest and forehead. He takes the program that is held out to him and fans himself. He cannot stand in the back of the church today. He needs to focus. He moves cautiously down the side aisle. He feels as though everyone is watching him. He keeps his eyes on the worn maroon carpet.

He stops when he's almost to the altar and looks around desperately. To his left, a large man with long, braided white hair smiles at him. Quinn whispers, "Please, may I sit? Is there room?"

The man turns toward his companions and Quinn sees that there are already three other people crowded into the short pew. The woman sitting on the other side of the man shrugs, embarrassed. But the man pulls Quinn in beside him. There's bumping and rustling as they all try to adjust themselves.

"Thank you, thank you," Quinn says to the man and his friends. A little boy in the pew in front of him turns around to see what the commotion is about. "Thank you," Quinn says to him.

Father Tom booms his opening remarks. Father Tom, whose voice is usually such a rich, low hum. Maybe it's impossible to celebrate the feast of Pentecost without sounding a little hysterical, like a hillbilly preacher. The priest makes a joke that Quinn doesn't quite catch, something about the congregation being very much like the Apostles, except that everyone present in the church today dresses a whole lot better. The congregation roars. Quinn rubs his head. He wishes everyone would be quiet.

Father Tom leans over the altar, his voice rising and wavering. Something in the priest's voice troubles Quinn—the wildness of it, or maybe the sureness. They have never formally met, but in the past few years Quinn has become quite fond of Father Tom—of the priest's uncertainty, his humanity.

About a year earlier, Quinn visited Father Tom in the confessional. He was gulping tears; his voice shook. He had come to tell the priest that he had had sex with a stranger.

"Last night," he sobbed. "I let him take me into his car. We drove up to Twin Peaks and parked."

The priest murmured hoarsely but kindly on the other side of the screen. "It's hard, isn't it, when the urge takes hold. But did you hurt him in any way? Did he hurt you?"

Quinn moaned, "I have a lover, and he is dying."

There was silence then, except for the sound of the priest moving in his seat, and Quinn felt the sadness thrumming in the small dark place that, for this small moment, he shared with this priest, this *man.*

When the priest finally spoke, his voice was small, and it trembled as well. "Oh, my friend. My dear, good friend . . ."

But now the priest raises his arms and cries out, "Picture the Apostles huddled together in fear that night. They had already witnessed the resurrection, had seen Christ, had touched him. But think of them at that moment before the Spirit descended upon them. How minor the moment of knowing, compared to the moment of *being.*"

Quinn swipes at his forehead with his shirtsleeve, his very red shirtsleeve, redder even than Father Tom's vestments. Red is the color of the Spirit, Sister Daniel, the old bulldog, once told him. The color of wisdom and truth and power. Yet Quinn feels merely absurd and ashamed and somehow marked.

Quinn remembers the night they met, that spring evening in 1986: Leager strode through the bar—a Pacific Heights piano bar—to the shadowy corner where Quinn sat alone. Beefy, blond Leager, T-shirt and jeans hugging his body, though back then the fashion was "loose" and "layered"; Quinn thought himself so elegant—in baggy plaid trousers and a yellow blazer with enormous shoulder pads, and a big red wool sweater knotted around his throat. The hair gelled high, the polka-dotted hanky . . .

"Come join us," Leager said. Curls swept his forehead; yellow stubble burnished his jaw.

"No, I'm fine here," said Quinn, as haughtily as he could manage. In his chest, his heart whirred.

"Come."

Quinn sipped his rum and Coke. "I'll be leaving soon."

"Oh ho," Leager said. Then he plucked at Quinn's handkerchief, which flowered from his breast pocket. "You can't hope to vanish after you've tried so hard to be seen."

In church, Father Tom rattles on and on. Quinn shuts his eyes, but still he sees the wincing dance of candle flames, the deep, grave glow of stained glass. Or is it the smoky, dim lights of the piano bar? The track lighting, the gaudy gold-plated candelabra. He sees Leager's thick fingers as he pushes the curls off his forehead, his ruddy face, his dimpled grin, his eyes friendly but mocking.

Why do you look so terrified?

How could he have told Leager the truth? How could he have said that he had all but forgotten the power of Leager's beauty—how it could once press the wind out of him like a fist against his throat. Or about the relief—the shameful relief—he felt when that beauty finally withered with sickness, and how afraid he is now, to see that beauty creeping little by little back into his features?

On his cheek Quinn feels the meaty breath of the man beside him, and Quinn realizes how tightly he's pressed against the man's side, his elbow sunk into the man's soft, huge gut. "Shit, sorry," he says, and he jumps up.

The man pulls him back down. "Relax," he says, and at this moment Quinn craves nothing more in the world—to lean back against this man and accept the queasy comfort of his warm, doughy body. But he stands again. He stumbles out into the aisle. The boy in front of him twists around and stares at Quinn with blinking, wide eyes. Quinn turns and walks quickly to the front doorway. Does Father Tom watch him go? Is that why the church is suddenly filled with a close, humming silence, or has the priest's spiel just come to its natural close?

Quinn senses heads turning as he walks by. He does not look back.

You can't hope to vanish after you've tried so hard to be seen.

When Sharman sees Quinn, she is coming down the steps of the support-group offices. She's wearing a small wooden crucifix and woven sandals, and Bermuda shorts and a man's pink Ralph Lauren Polo shirt that had been in the church's lost-and-found for two years. Her blond hair, in need of a trim, is tied back with a rubber band. The wrinkles around her eyes, which she's begun just recently to notice, are covered by big round sunglasses, which she'd bought a few days earlier at a garage sale. As vaguely troubled as she is feeling, it still pleases her that she can walk out into this hot spring morning looking like a college girl.

She sees Quinn as he rushes out of the church. She watches him walk stiffly a few steps down the sidewalk and then stop. He looks around, dazed, before resting his shoulder against the church's side.

She starts cautiously across the street toward him. She had heard his lover say his name in the restaurant, but she can't quite remember what it is. It's something like Cain, though not quite. When she thinks of the name Cain, she doesn't think of the biblical figure, but of Caine, the character from the 1970s television show *Kung Fu*. Both men have the same haggard, bony, oddly attractive features, the same weary air. Though from what she remembers, the television Caine was much more tranquil. She is still pondering this connection as she comes upon him. When he squints up at her, she says stupidly, "Are you Caine?"

The man shakes his head and waves her away.

She backs up a step and says, "I don't mean to bother you. Are you all right?"

The man eyes her, and then he says heavily, "Oh, hello Sister. I know you. You once laughed at an outfit I wore to Mass."

Sharman blinks and shakes her head. "I'm sorry, I don't remember that."

"You did, you did," the man says, wagging his finger.

Sharman says, "I'm sorry if I insulted you."

The man straightens and shakes the dust off his shirt. "Oh well, I'm used to it. My lover can't remember when to take his medication, but he always notices when I'm dressed like an idiot." He says this in a joking tone, but Sharman senses something jagged in his voice.

Before she can swallow her words, Sharman says, "Oh, your shirt?"

The man turns and begins to walk away.

Sharman says, "Don't go."

The man turns slowly.

"It's a beautiful shirt," Sharman says. "Probably, all he meant was that velvet is traditionally a winter fabric." Sharman wishes she had never come over: She is a foolish, useless woman.

The man says, "For a nun, you pay entirely too much attention to fashion."

Then, because there is nothing else to lose, she takes a chance: "And for a gay man," she says, "you don't pay enough." She offers the joke with the most open, penitent smile she can manage.

The man's eyes harden, and then they go soft. Then he is laughing—a deep, hearty stream of laughter bouncing off the sidewalk and the church wall.

Relieved, Sharman laughs with him, pressing her palms to her chest. She watches a thread of saliva fly out of the corner of the man's mouth and land on his chin. She points to her own chin and makes a wiping gesture, but the man doesn't seem to notice. He's shaking his head and his laughter has turned just the slightest bit wild. Sharman steps toward him and reaches her fingers toward his face. Then, suddenly, he bends forward and before she knows it she is holding his head against her shoulder.

The laughter is like vomiting, and what he heaves from inside him into the air is fierce heat and stained glass and white braids and loose flesh and dotted hankies and ugly red velvet and old nuns and young nuns and ranting priests and bug-eyed boys and the stink of poppers and crazy neighbors and *ahk ahk ahk* . . .

The problem, of course, is that after you've purged all the dirt that had been inside you, the only thing left is a heaving pit of emptiness, a vast hunger that you don't know how to fill.

But he's not empty yet. He'll never be completely empty, because Leager remains, turning over and over inside him, in the tightest, deepest pocket of his gut.

A final fit of giggles bursts from Quinn's lips. He buries his face into the woman's shoulder and breathes in. He smells powder and sweat—a strong, sweet, motherly smell. But of course this woman is not his mother—she's a stranger, although she doesn't seem to be. He tries to lift his head, but he feels her soft palm pressed against the back of his neck.

"Tell me," she says. "What's wrong?"

"I'm fine," he says, wriggling free.

The woman steps back. "Is it your lover?"

Quinn shrugs.

"Is he very sick?"

Quinn clears his throat. He shrugs again.

"Come with me into my office," Sharman says. "It's awfully hot outside." She swings one of his arms over her shoulder. This time, he decides to accept the comfort offered by this small, sturdy body. They stumble awkwardly across the street. When they reach the other side, Quinn starts to feel ridiculous, being helped along like an invalid or a wounded soldier. "Thank you," he says, disengaging his arm. " But I'm okay now."

"You should have a drink of water."

"No," Quinn says. "Really, Leager is waiting for me. I have to make lunch."

"Leager?" the nun says. "Your lover?"

"Yes," Quinn says.

"It's a very sexy, masculine name."

It's a little disturbing to Quinn, to hear a nun talk in such terms. He says, "Well, his full name is Leager *Peele,* which I think sounds kind of silly."

"It's charming."

Across the street, the church doors swing open and organ music drifts out to the street. An altar attendant clothed in a red cassock comes down the steps, lowering his cross when he reaches the ground. Father Tom follows right behind him. Sharman waves but the priest does not see her. Quinn turns away slightly.

Sharman says, "Do you have to get back right away, or do you have time to get a cup of coffee?"

He has to shop for lunch, Quinn tells her.

He hesitates, then he says, "Listen, I'm making lunch for Leager. Would you like to join us?"

The nun pauses, then she nods and smiles, and Quinn thinks that he sees her cheeks redden just slightly.

The supermarket is crowded, and all the shoppers seem to be both anxious and giddy, piling their carts with meat and charcoal and beer, or cheese and cold cuts and soft drinks. Quinn and Sharman, each carrying a basket, walk wordlessly through the aisles. A blond boy with tattooed arms and dirty bare feet pushes between them in the deli section, a can of lighter fluid pressed to his side like a football. Sharman braces herself against Quinn's shoulder to keep herself from falling.

"Bastard," Quinn says, glaring at the back of the boy's head.

"Don't be angry," Sharman says. "Everybody is hurrying to get out into the world today. Picnic weather is so rare in the city."

She realizes that she's still holding on to Quinn. She gives his shoulder a squeeze, then quickly lets go. She's embarrassed about what had happened in front of the church, when she held Quinn's head against her. She felt Quinn trying to tug away, but she was so suddenly overwhelmed—by the feel of his coarse, sweaty hair against her fingers, his surprisingly smooth jaw, the thrumming pulse in his forehead against her cheek—that for a moment she just couldn't let go.

Over the past few years she has held dozens of men—men in the AIDS wards who were sick or dying and sometimes, then, she couldn't let go either.

Once, she was alone with a man who kept crying out for his lover. *Mac? Mac?* he screamed, over and over. *Where are you?* Sharman took him in her arms and held him so tightly she was scared she would break his fragile body.

And when Mac finally arrived, he waited at the doorway for a long time before he finally asked, "Please, may I have him now?"

When they turn a corner into the next aisle, Quinn says, "What kind of name is Sharman?"

"What? Oh, it's Old Gaelic," Sharman says. She puts a loaf of sourdough into their basket.

"Weren't you given a new name when you took your vows?"

"Oh, gosh no. My order doesn't require it. Of course, some women still choose to take a new name." She lifts a jar of mayonnaise off the shelf. "Fat-free all right?"

Quinn shrugs. "Sure," he says. "And where is your convent?"

"I live in an apartment over the hill in Noe Valley. I share it with two roommates."

Quinn laughs. "What kind of nun *are* you anyway?"

Sharman sighs, "I used to live in a convent, in St. Anne's Parish, over in the Sunset. When I decided a few years ago that I wanted to work in the AIDS community in general and the gay community in particular—well, let's just say it was mutually agreed that I move out on my own."

Quinn nods and says, "Hmmm."

"Hmmm," Sharman says, kiddingly. "Please don't get me into a discussion about Church teaching. It's always been a nonissue with me. My mother was very devout *and* she was a set designer in Hollywood. I knew lots of gay men when I was growing up."

In the produce section, Quinn picks through the tomato bin. "I'm not interrogating you, believe me. Of course, you could ask me the same questions."

Sharman rips a plastic bag gently off its roll and drops three apples inside. "Well, I'm much more interested in you and Leager. Did you meet in church?"

"Leager? Hah." He blows hair out of his eyes. "No, we met in a piano bar," he says. "Years ago."

"Was it love at first sight?"

He reaches into a bag in the shopping cart and tears several dusty grapes from their stems. He chews them slowly. He had been having quite a pleasant time, here in the market, shopping with this new, tenacious friend of his. But now he feels the old panic gripping his chest.

"Wouldn't you rather talk about Church teaching?" he says.

They met in a bar that no longer exists—perhaps all the patrons died. Back then everyone was dying, it seemed. That night, in fact, a raccoon-eyed woman wearing a limp velvet hat leaned against the piano and wailed, "Everyone is dying or already dead." Things like this happened years ago. Of course they still do, but back then it seemed there was a stool in every bar in town occupied by someone crying out such trite and helpless words.

Quinn sits in a shadowy corner. He is not dying but he is young and so very lonely, a City College student recently transplanted from a small, flat farming town called Stockton.

A man comes over and says, "Come join us." He says his name. Quinn at first thinks it's Seger, like the rock singer. The man laughs—a cocky, snorting, sexy laugh. He's wearing a tight black T-shirt and jeans. Quinn thinks he himself is so elegant, in his big yellow blazer and plaid trousers which he bought on his employee discount at Macy's, where he works nights as a stockroom clerk. The sweater over his shoulders, the polka-dotted hanky spilling from his pocket . . . But he knows in his gut that no matter what he wears, he could never be worthy of this man who has just approached him.

"I'm fine where I am," Quinn says. He feels his heart whirring.

Was it a dare that had prompted Leager to come into the shadows and invite him over? Leager's friends sit at a table on the other side of the room. They're looking in Quinn's direction and laughing. In the years that followed, Quinn would come to hate Leager's friends—all of them so polished and mean. He hated them all until they began to die.

One of Leager's friends approaches. He introduces himself as Thiu. "Short for Matthew," he says, in a scratchy whine.

He says, "Gang's leaving—this place is full of tired old trolls. It's *très* boring."

Quinn laughs nastily, on purpose. Thiu looks at him sideways.

"Sorry," Quinn says. "I just didn't realize people actually talked like that."

"Yes," Thiu says. "And people actually dress like *this*." He flicks at the knotted cuffs of Quinn's sleeves.

Thiu turns and walks back to the table. He would be the first to die: a year later, Quinn would drive with Leager through a cold winter fog to get to the hospital. He would stand over Thiu's bed and run a finger down the pale cane of Thiu's arm. The man's eyes would open and his lips would shape themselves into a slow, drugged smile. "Kinny, what is that *thing* you're wearing?"

But before all of that Quinn watches Thiu and the rest of his group push themselves up from their table in the bar. They smirk and wave at Leager, then they make their way to the door. "Shouldn't you go with them?" Quinn says.

"Why? They can make their way without me. What are you drinking?" Quinn watches Leager push yellow curls away from his forehead. He stares at the taut line of his jaw, the glint of the thick lashes in the dim lights of the bar. What do you do when someone so beautiful approaches you except wonder why. Does he want to use you? To shame you? Does he pity you? Quinn doesn't want his pity. He wraps his jacket more snugly around himself. The piano player takes a break and recorded music drifts from the speakers above their table.

Leager taps his fingers on the table. "Eurythmics," he says. "Have you heard of them?"

Quinn shrugs and listens to the singer's voice, so sexy, and so haunted. *Sweet dreams are made of this. Who am I to disagree . . .*

Leager bounces his head to the music, in and out of the bar's furry lighting, and it's then that Quinn notices the acne scars—the pale, cratered skin under Leager's chin.

"Oh," Quinn gasps softly.

Leager jerks. "What? Oh this." He touches the ruined skin. "I'm seeing a dermatologist, but he can't seem to do anything about it."

"No," Quinn says. "You shouldn't. It's not that bad." He feels his heart opening. His face tightens and grows hot. He touches his empty glass. It's still cool. He presses it to his burning cheek.

Leager smiles. His face has softened somehow, not because of the scars, but because in some way it has surrendered itself. He is more—not less—beautiful to Quinn.

Quinn puts the glass back on the table and stares into it. He could say nothing more and soon enough the man would snort and move away. But something is unraveling inside him—there is a tiny hole forming, which he could choose to rip wide open.

Finally, after a few moments, he decides: he holds up his empty glass and says, "I'm drinking rum and Coke tonight."

Later, they are on Leager's bed, in Leager's huge, sparsely furnished flat.

"Tell me," Quinn says. "Why did you choose me?"

Leager unties the sweater from around Quinn's neck. He pushes Quinn's jacket off his shoulders and lets it drop to the floor. His whisper carries the gasoline smell of gin. "You're like some feathery bird. You're like a snail or a turtle. I'm going to get to you, I'm going to crack your shell."

He pushes Quinn down onto his back and yanks his pants off. But after Quinn is completely undressed, Leager gently lays his own naked body on top of him and breathes deeply. "Tell me, my Quinn, my *Kinny,* what should I know, should I know anything about you?"

And of course what he is really asking is: *Are you infected?* But back then, Quinn had no idea about such things. At the time he thought Leager wanted him to open up, to share with him some private piece of himself.

Lying under Leager's bulk in the darkness, the scent of gin—now sweeter, somehow—blowing over his face, Quinn's mind races.

Then he says, solemnly, "I'm Catholic."

He feels Leager's laughter first, rumbling from the man's chest and stomach against his own body. And then he hears it—the deafening, mad chortling against his ear. And Quinn tries to wriggle free but he cannot, and there's nothing he can do but pray for this to be over. He thinks, if he can just make it to the morning, this will all be over.

But thirteen years have passed and it's still not over.

Quinn and Sharman go around the back of the house and through the garden. When they reach the patio, Sharman runs a hand along the back of a chair and says, "What a beautiful piece. Is it redwood?"

"It is. Clearheart, in fact. That's Leager's doing."

"He designs furniture?"

"He did," Quinn says, "and landscapes too, but of course now . . ." He sweeps a flat palm through the air, and Sharman looks out over the garden—the tall, yellowing grass, the overgrown vegetable plots, the lumpy, holey shrubs. She sees a tennis shoe lying in a puddle near a rusted spigot.

"But look at that bench," Sharman says, pointing toward a corner of the garden. "Under that apple tree. It looks like a lovely place to sit."

"It once was," Quinn says.

"And it will be again," Sharman says encouragingly. On the walk from the supermarket, Quinn had told her how well Leager was responding to his new treatment.

"Hmm," Quinn says. "Would you wait here for a moment? I want to make sure Leager is decent."

Sharman sits on the redwood chair and leans against its sturdy back. She closes her eyes against the sun and listens to the flies buzzing above her head, feels them alight on her bare arms. Her mind drifting, she begins to wonder what it must have been like for Leager—to tend this garden, to love it, to share it with someone, but then have to let it go.

She hears muffled, sharp words come from inside the house. She hears a door slam. She opens her eyes to harsh sunlight and turns her head to the hard, weedy piece of land stretching out the short distance to a graying fence. A thought hits her: what must it be like to have surrendered the garden, and then have it given back to you, in all its squalor and decay? How exhausting it would be, the thought of rebuilding. She thinks of all the people she's worked with over the past few years, who have given up careers and cashed in insurance policies and sold homes and sent away family and surrendered to drink or drugs and left lovers, or allowed lovers to leave them—only to discover that they may not die after all? How must they feel, to be given back a life that has nothing left in it?

Quinn is standing over her. He says, "Leager is not as well as I thought he would be."

"Then of course I should go," Sharman says. "We'll plan for another time."

Quinn pauses and then says, "No, I just wanted to prepare you. He's been smoking pot since I left, but it should be all right."

As they move through the kitchen, Sharman smells the marijuana smoke hanging flatly in the air. She sees a pipe lying in an ashy bowl on a round turquoise table. Then they are in the living room, where a man is sitting spread-legged on a blue-and-white-striped sofa. He is quite thin, with damp blond curls pasted to his forehead, and shriveled, stunningly blue eyes, and straight wide shoulders, and incredibly beautiful facial bones.

He is wearing a white tank top and tight blue swimming trunks. He taps the emblem on the breast of his tank top and plucks at the fabric of his trunks. "This is the best I'm going to do," he says. "This is my house and I don't think I should have to dress for anybody."

"Of course not," Sharman says. "You must be Leager." She walks over to the sofa and holds out her hand. He stares at it with wide eyes, then he blinks slowly, his head wobbling on his neck. Finally, he reaches out and their fingers graze.

At the kitchen table, now clear of the pipe and its ashes, the three of them sit before plates of fruit and sandwiches. Quinn tells a story about an old nun who once made him scrub out a sink in order to teach him a lesson about piety. The story itself is boring, but the way he tells it—wagging his cheeks and lowering his voice to a deep croak in imitation of the nun—makes Sharman giggle.

Sharman dabs at her eyes with a napkin and says, "That's nothing new. Everyone's got a crazy-old-nun story like that."

Quinn says, "It's probably the same nun. You know, like the old fruitcake joke: there's actually only one floating around the world from house to house."

Sharman laughs into her napkin.

Leager, who has yet to take a bite of his sandwich, says, "Quinn says you're a nun."

"I am."

"Are you a lesbian? I think all nuns are really lesbians."

Quinn says, "Leager—"

Sharman swallows a bit of sandwich and says, "No, I'm not a lesbian."

"I don't like lesbians," Leager says.

"Well, then, you should have no reason to dislike me," she says lightly, and then she tells her own story, about how when she was a girl, she played the little boy in the opera *Madama Butterfly*.

"My mother was the set designer on this particular production," she says. "If I hadn't become a nun I might have taken a shot at acting."

"You're joking," Quinn says.

Sharman tells them how she would nap in one of the dressing rooms until her mother came to get her. "Then I'd be brought onstage and Butterfly would scoop me up and hold me against her as she sang those tragic arias for her lost American naval officer."

Quinn says, "It must have been boring for you, at that age."

"Oh no," Sharman says. "Butterfly—the woman who played her—had the richest, saddest voice. It made me want to cry out, to comfort her somehow."

Sharman laughs. "Once, I asked my mother if Butterfly was the Virgin Mary. And she thought for a long while, that sweet woman, and she said very gently, 'Yes, I suppose she does have the same spirit as Our Lady.'"

Leager snorts. His eyes snap from Sharman to Quinn. "That church of yours—all costumes and prancing around onstage."

Quinn's voice is steady. "Lee, this is not about that at all," he says.

"And Butterfly's sailor wasn't lost. He went back to America and shacked up with a blonde bimbo."

"We know the story, Leager."

Leager turns to Sharman and says, in an eerily clear voice, "Quinn has other lovers."

Sharman looks down at the table.

"Lee, please leave now. Why don't you just go back in the living room and smoke some more."

"He goes out at night and he comes home smelling like them."

Quinn says, "Let's go, Sharman. I'll walk you down the street."

"Look at me," Leager says, "A sick, skinny dog with a shriveled dick. Of course he's going to go out whoring, who wouldn't. But you'll see, I'll be alive again. Then you'll see what I can do."

When Quinn howls, Sharman's shoulders jerk up toward her ears, and her fingers curl into fists. The sound makes her want to tighten herself into a ball and vanish.

"*Son of a fucking bitch,*" Quinn screams, suddenly on his feet. "What were you doing before you got sick? Who was the whore then? Who wouldn't come home for days at a time?" He thumps something to the table—Sharman sees that it is his sandwich, squished to a white mushy ball.

Quinn shudders and wipes his hand against his trousers, and then he turns and walks through the door, out into the garden.

Sharman stands numbly. With her napkin, she begins to wipe up the mess on the table.

Leager says, "Have you ever had a lover?" His voice is tiny and cracked, and Sharman feels him drifting back behind a fog of distance and nonsense.

Tears fill Sharman's eyes. "No," she says.

"Well," Leager says, "if you had a lover, what would you name him?"

Sharman cups her palm at the edge of the table and scoops bits of food into it. She thinks of all the men she has ever held but at this moment she can't recall any of their names.

"My friend," she says heavily, "I haven't a clue."

Once, shortly after he was diagnosed with pneumocystis pneumonia, Leager called Quinn into bed with him. He had just come back from the hospital and was still weak and racked by horrible, scraping fits of coughing.

"Are you sure this is all right?" Quinn said as he climbed in beside his lover. A week earlier, Leager had screamed at him, "Stop fucking babying me. Just get your fucking face out of mine."

Quinn was still stung by this. He had been keeping his distance.

Leager said, "I'm sorry, Kinny, for how I was to you before."

Gently, gently, Quinn put his hand on Leager's chest. He felt a sickening crackle beneath the bones.

"Will you touch me?" Leager said.

"Lee, you're still so weak."

"Go on."

Quinn reached down and took Leager's soft penis in his hand.

"Just keep it there, please? While I sleep?"

In the garden, Quinn lowers himself onto the bench under the apple tree. He presses his face into his hands and sobs. He has lost, either way—whether Leager returns to health or whether he dies after all. It's this middle ground between life and death where Quinn has been the most content, the most certain. Now, surely, all will be lost.

"It's hard, you know."

Quinn looks up and sees Mr. Chung swaying on the other side of the fence. He has a bottle in one hand and a shot glass in the other. He holds the bottle out to Quinn, who shakes his head.

"You know," says his neighbor, his voice a gentle slur, "your friend, he's crazy. Yeah, sure he is. But everybody's crazy, you know." He winks and cocks his head toward his own house.

"Daddy," Quinn hears Mrs. Chung call out. "Come inside now."

"Ayuh," the man says. "Anyway, you good boys, both of you. I know that. You are both good citizens."

Mrs. Chung, in a blue housecoat, shuffles up behind her husband. She takes his arm and leads him back to the house. But before she turns, she gives Quinn a soft look, a look of sorrow which casts the ball of forgiveness back over to Quinn's side of the fence. He raises a hand toward Mrs. Chung, and they both smile sadly.

If you had a lover, what would you name him?

Her earliest memories flood her head, a hot feverish beautiful dream: stage lights and crusts in her eyes, the white kimono, the painted ocean. The heat of Butterfly's palm against her neck, the tremble of Butterfly's breasts against her shoulders, the anguished song blooming around her. The girl's heart pounds with the enormity of it all. This is love, she thinks.

Then she grows up. When she takes her vows she is told that she is from now on married to the Church, she is married to Christ. It is never said that she is either's lover. And this has been enough. For the most part, it is enough.

But at times, she feels a desperation cutting into her like a cold sharp bone. She has never craved a lover, but she does crave that feeling of holding someone—the joy and the rage of it, and the stillness that would finally rise, calming a current inside her that she never realized existed except at those times.

In the evening, when the air has cooled, she sits alone in her living room with a glass of wine. She calls her friend Gustavo and they recite the rosary together.

. . . *As it was in the beginning, is now, and ever shall be, world without end.*

"Ah, Sharmie," Gus sighs. "I used to think that was such a comforting line. But I can't seem to say it anymore without feeling exhausted. Can you imagine it—a world without end?"

Sharman takes a sip from her glass. She doesn't know what to say. To be honest, she is jealous of Gus: only a person at peace with his life would think that forever is too long.

"Sharman, dear, are you there?"

Sharman tastes salt at the back of her mouth. After a moment, she blurts out, "I'm scared, Gustavo. I want so much to hold someone."

"Oh Sharmie, you mustn't be afraid. It's beautiful, what you want."

"But I'm afraid to hold someone. I'm afraid I won't be able to let go."

"No, Sharman, never let go." There is a long, empty silence on the line, and Sharman fears that her friend has vanished. But then he says, "After I lost my eyes, I found I could no longer touch my Jack. He was so thin and bony by then, and when I held him I felt like I was holding death itself. I hate myself now, for being that way."

Sharman cries, "No Gus, please. Don't say that." Even now, as she allows herself to wallow in her regrets, she feels her heart grow heavy and rich with all she has been blessed to witness: the astonishing heroism mixed with the saddest betrayals—and all of it so terribly, beautifully human.

"Your voice is the only touch I have left," Gus says. "Please, Sharmie. Talk to me some more."

Sharman raises her glass to her lips. She thinks back on the day.

"This afternoon, I sat in a garden," she says hopefully, and she is relieved to hear Gus's voice brighten.

"Oh? Was it beautiful?"

"It once was, I was told."

"My Jack could have fixed it up. He was the best gardener this town has ever seen. His ashes are in a garden now. He's shooting up as we speak—maybe as basil, maybe as nice green beans. Sorry, I bet I've told you a thousand times."

"Of course!" Sharman cries out.

"Of course," Gus says. "A thousand and one times."

"No sweetheart, I just remembered something."

She remembers seeing Quinn at Mass. It was on the morning Gus called to tell her that his lover's ashes had been buried in a friend's herb garden.

"In the springtime, he'll be shooting up as something lush and green and sweet."

That morning, Sharman went sadly to church to say a rosary for Gus and Jack. She slid into a pew and saw a man hunched down in front of her, praying. He was curled into a tight ball. But then Father Tom spread his arms behind the altar and as everybody stood she saw the man in front of her unfold himself—a tall, lean man dressed in green from head to toe, shaking loose his arms. And Sharman felt the keenest hope at that moment, and the lightest laughter bubbling out of her as she watched this man rise up and up and up . . .

Quinn finds Leager in the bedroom, staring at the ceiling. "Your friend is gone," Leager says. "She said that she would try to find you at Mass."

"I'll try too," Quinn says. Leager tenses as Quinn crawls into bed beside him.

"I'm sorry," Leager says.

"I know."

"You should be too."

"I am," says Quinn. He drops his head onto Leager's chest and feels the new sturdiness of his lover's body. He reaches into the waistband of Leager's trunks.

"What are you doing?" Leager says, but he does not pull away.

"Does this hurt?" Quinn asks. He's surprised to feel Leager's cock stiffen and grow.

Leager, who seems just as amazed, says, "I don't think I can come."

"No matter," says Quinn. "One day—pretty soon—you'll be able to."

As Quinn strokes, Leager smooths down Quinn's hair. "Will you stay with me?" Leager says. "Forever?"

"Yes," says Quinn. And then he says, "Will you stay with me?"

He lets the "forever" float away like a kite. Perhaps someday he'll recapture it. But for now he lets it spin off into the vast, frightened, changing world in which he lives, and which lives inside him.

Manifest White

RICK SANDFORD

When I asked Stuart why he liked watching baseball games, he said that in a life of an infinity of qualifications, a life of myriad shades of gray, baseball offered something approaching a clash of absolutes, a nearly pure exhibition of black and white. When I asked him about the meaning of life, he said I should shift the focus of my inquiry to being.

Okay.

I went to the gym by myself. As I got dressed I wondered about Stuart, about what he makes of my life. I feel like he knows something he isn't telling me. On the other hand, I wonder what I make of my life—

I go upstairs to do my stomach exercises and as I start my crunches on the Nautilus machines I notice a guy in front of me, closer to the mirror, doing his arms. He's one of those bright engaging guys with that instant kind of smile that salespeople sometimes give you, the kind that makes you want to look around and ask, "Who? Me?" As I take a breather he comes over and comments on my Springsteen T-shirt. Nice gab. More crunches: one hundred in four sets. Where'd he go? Next machine: one hundred in two. And then he's there:

"I wanted to make sure you didn't forget your glasses."

When I do these exercises I take my glasses off and place them in what I hope are safe places, since they'd slide off if I wore them. His consideration is interesting. I tell him I like the contrast: his light hair, his darker eyebrows. Mutual compliments. He's leaving, going to take a shower and head on home, am I going? "Well, my deal is," I tell him, "if I do all my stomach exercises I don't have to do the rest of my workout."

I don't tell him I haven't finished my sit-ups. Nothing is specified, the future looms vaguely before us. His name is Bob Mill, mine is Rick Sandford.

Our lockers are in different areas; I strip down and join him at his. He's really nice-looking. He's not quite the proverbial brick shithouse, but he's solid, and the soft hair on his chest defines his muscles nicely. He's just the slightest bit self-conscious getting out of his shorts. He's got a smooth dick, it doesn't seem like there's a head: he's uncut.

On the way from the locker room to the showers Bob gets waylaid by an old acquaintance. We miss each other on our various ins and outs of the showers, steam room and Jacuzzi, but we finally meet up in the sauna. I ask him if he wants to play. Yeah.

We towel off and dress, I put my gold trunks back on but I stow the jockstrap in my backpack, and we're out in the street before other considerations make themselves known. He has a lover and should be home in half an hour. I only have a bicycle and live too far away. Hmm.

"Do you know anyplace?"

We walk down the street. I muse on a blow job I gave across the street in the rubble of the Tropicana just before it was completely demolished. There's a bright, shiny new hotel there now, palm trees and neon. At the entrance to the gym's parking structure we pause.

"I didn't think I could come anyway," he says, "but I wanted to let you play with it for a while."

I open the door to the stairwell. Metal stairs ascend before us. He moves to look behind them. I discourage his interest in the current emptiness: "Too many people pass through here," but as he turns to go: "There might not be any people at the top."

We start our climb, up and around the steps. Four stories. As I climb the stairs I feel a dampness against my leg, my trunks are staining, it's sticky: my dick is oozing: he wanted to let me—

I am being accorded a privilege. No matter what—

At the top of the stairs we open the door onto the broad expanse of a gently sloping roof. There is only one car. This is great. We scout around a bit, and behind the air shaft we find a secluded place overlooking the street, West Hollywood's main drag, Santa Monica Boulevard. The air is balmy; the city lights reflect back off the atmosphere. Below us we can hear the occasional rowdy laughter of people having fun on a Friday night.

The imminent prospect of sex has me going. Exuding pre-cum I feel like I'm practically wetting my pants. His buttoned jeans are bulging. His words echo in my mind: I wanted to let you play with it for a while. Let you. Let. Let me.

"Do you want to sit down?" he asks.

"Okay."

I had sort of thought that the deal would be me kneeling before him, sucking him off and jacking my dick at the same time. But he has his towel out and is spreading it on the ground for us. We sit down, leaning against the air shaft's enclosure, and I kick my shorts off down around my feet and his uncircumcised dick is out and I'm holding it—it is smooth—and he spits in his palm and his wet hand is stroking me. Yes: he'll be generous in appeasing my dick but he isn't going to go down on me.

I'm not going to spit in my palm—

I scrunch over from beside him and I put his cock in my mouth. It's too fast—there wasn't enough eyes, there wasn't (even?) a kiss. But it's in my mouth: the privilege is manifest. It's not a choker, not yet it's not, but it has all that extra skin and I dig my tongue down in the folds. And then I look at it, and pull down on the shaft—the head gleams out from the skin: the piss-hole is glistening. That's his: that's him: that's it. And down I go.

His first words are kind of tentative, shy in the face of my slavering. He asks me how I like it, he says I'm a real cocksucker. I hold on to it with my fist and give him a couple of real good strokes, my hand and my mouth meeting each other from opposite ends of it. And then I'm up. I consider him. I'd just bought some poppers and, weighing the spontaneity of the moment against the possibility of really kicking it all into high gear, I ask him if he does them.

"Do you have any?"

"Yeah."

"Get 'em out."

So I do and we're inhaling them, me through my mouth, him with each nostril. And then I'm holding on to his dick again and eating it.

And—yes—this is real. This means something: this is being. You want black and white? If I suck this dick good enough and my mouth fills up with his stuff: that's white.

And then he starts talking, and he does it good, substantiating mindless animal over reeling intelligence. You like that. Yeah. You like sucking that dick. Don't ya? "Don't ya?"

"I love suckin' your fuckin' dick."

He pushes my head down. "Don't stop. Just answer me. You like suckin' my dick, don't ya?"

And I don't stop sucking his dick. I keep going up and down on it. But I answer him. I answer him even as he pushes my hand away—"Just your mouth"—and the head of his dick starts pushing against the back of my throat; I answer him through the salivation compensating for the assault in my mouth, the spittle lubing his dick and spreading down over his balls; I answer him as I bury myself in his crotch over and over again: I love suckin' your fuckin' dick.

"You're a goddamn fucking faggot."

More than an accusation: it's the truth. And with every plunge of my head the moral universe into which we've been born is blown apart, torn asunder with every pounding blood pulse. By virtue of the sex between our legs, by virtue of that subsequent autonomy, our rights as men lie inalienable before us, everything subject to nothing. And I'm throwing it all away, I'm abdicating. From the reckless dementia of mere acknowledgment I have fallen precipitate into the worship of another man's piss-hole.

And he knows it.

He wants to take another pass at the poppers.

I do it through my mouth and again he whiffs them, once on each side. I'm down between his legs: when that first rush comes, when the engorgement dilates it purple, my mouth is there, its wet engulfing his thrust. Yes. And then up, my tongue swirling around that piss-hole, swirling around that unprotected rim, and then back down, his dick pushing against that pharyngeal contraction at the back of my throat: Your dick's too big man—that mushroom head's not going to get through there, not without blood, but I'm a goddamn fucking faggot so what difference does it make?

It doesn't.

Membrane yields to voracity: he pushes that dick's head right on into that hole. Fuck. The muscles there start swallowing against the sides of his shaft. Fuck my mouth. And then I'm ramming it up and down my throat in a fury: fuck: me.

Yeah.

And then he pulls me up, we're breathing hard, and he's asking me, "You want to eat my dick?"

"What do you think?"

"You want to eat my cum?"

He's really asking. It's 1993. We've been flying along here without any ground rules, with nothing except the crashing of absolutes. But now he is asking, and the man who was going to let me play with it wants to know if I really want to take his cum.

I look him straight on, our eyes are flashing when they meet, we're getting naked in what we see in each other: "I want you to come in my mouth, I want you to piss in my mouth, whatever you can spit out of that dick: I want it in my mouth."

Yes.

He's grinning. Considering. And then quietly: "You want me to piss in your mouth?"

Don't say what you don't mean.

Divested of hyperbole I can only assent: gutturally: "Uh-huh."

The grin on his face is shit-eating.

I'm really asking for it.

And I want it: what I see in those eyes, his eyes, and what of me reflecting back in them, what he sees: you. And I want it in my mouth, what I see, oozing thickly, rolling warmly, over my tongue, what we see:

Us.

We take another hit of the poppers. Uh-huh. He's going to do it. He's going to concentrate on the end of his dick, the glans, on that sensation there, and he's going to pitch that feeling up and to the point where the only possible salve to that delicious ache is the utter relinquishment of self: his essence discharged into: me.

He lets me go at it as the rush overcomes us, but then he pulls me back, talking at me, calling me a faggot and, holding me back from his dick, he makes me acknowledge that thing: "That's what you want?"

God yes—it's the only thing that makes any sense out of life.

"Kiss it."

But he won't let me, it's too far away.

"Then just touch it—"

I reach my tongue out of my mouth, as far as it will go, stretching out toward his dick: erect, standing up in front of me, the foreskin partly bunched around the head.

My tongue, my taste, straining out of my head toward him, his piss-hole, and—

—glancing—

—the final delicate touching of ourselves: the tip of my tongue just touching the tip of his dick.

And suddenly the picture is so clear. He makes me see it: not a revelation of passion, just the spectacle of a man reaching out with his tongue to touch another man's penis.

"You really want my dick in your mouth?"

"God please yes."

POW!

Hot and hard and slamming up against the side of my head: it's like the sound of a seashell crashing into my ear and breaking itself. The shock can barely elicit an incredulous:

What?

He's not holding me back now. His dick is there and I can have all of it I want. Yes, good, mouth and dick, this, swallowing dick, I understand, going up and down and—no hand, just my mouth, I remember—and up and down and—

The side of my face is burning, my ear is ringing.

He hit me. This guy, this man whose dick is in my mouth, just hauled off and hit me. He hit me hard: it hurt. He hit me because I wanted to do what I'm doing. Fuck. Is he close? No, no, this isn't it. We're going to have to go again.

I pull up and look at him:

You hit me!

Yeah?

There's a little delirium in our eyes. We're really excited: looking at me he's looking into the face of someone still breathing, still alive, and yet somehow confronting his own annihilation. By putting his dick in my mouth I have already abrogated my autonomy as a man, but when that stuff starts coming up, starts spilling out of his hole, and when at that moment I start taking it in: that's when my claim to even simple humanity will be obliterated, my value as an entity become something less than shit in the street. And he can see it in my eyes, I've consciously made this decision: I have determined that his dick, that thing he expels waste with: that is worth more than my life.

And the excitement in his eyes is a dare: Say you're just kidding, back out, say you don't mean it, tell me it hurts, ask me to stop it, come on—

But he knows I won't.

I'm not kidding.

This is fucking great.

His dick is my life.

We do the poppers again.

This is it.

Fuck.

I'm back on his dick.

"You're a little pussy mouth, aren't you?"

Yeah, that's what I am—if he says it, it is—and I'm sucking his dick and moaning compliance. But he wants to hear it, and he pulls me off his dick.

"Say it. Say, 'Rick's a little pussy mouth.'"

He's really good. His hawk's eye can spot my jugular a mile away. I can offer up obsequity any way he wants it. But the true life corruption—vagina, clitoris, uterus: cunt—

We have fucking swinging dicks between our legs: our holes are coursing sperm speedways in phalli.

I hate women. I hate the way they look. Fermenting putrescence: matted pubic hair clinging to corpulent lumpen thighs, and the stink there: festering—

Just say it:

"Rick's a little pussy mouth."

"Say 'I'm Bob's little pussy mouth.'"

"I'm Bob's little pussy mouth."

POW!

WHITE.

What?

Yeah. That's right. I'm Bob's little pussy mouth.

I didn't say it like I meant it. He knows. He can tell. I was holding on to something. That's not fair. That's not the way it goes. That's why he hit me. I gotta let go. Let go. Yeah.

I'm a fuckin' pussy.

And I'm sucking this fuckin' dick and my head is ringing. But I'm holding on. I may be a pussy, but I'm a fuckin' pussy—

Volitional.

No.

I'm not a fuckin' pussy: I'm a fuckin' pussy mouth.

But the volition is too little too late.

He's not going to come this time.

He needs to know I really want it.

"One more time," he says.

I uncap the bottle and take a hit and pass it on to him. This time he inhales deeply, pulling those most potent fumes from all the way down at the bottom of the bottle, and he does it again, and passes it back to me. I take another hit. Then: screw the lid on tight: then: set it down carefully: and:

Bob.

Rick.

Our tongues are hanging out, we want to jump in each other's skulls.

He's cradling his balls and bouncing his erection: "You want this fuckin' load?"

"I want you to vomit in my mouth and shit in my face."

"Motherfucker."

POW!

Lip.

Fuck.

He really caught me that time.

He wouldn't kill me here . . .

I think I'm bleeding—

And he slams me down in his crotch.

Fuck: me.

I'm fucking myself: flying up and down that pole of his, salivating like a fuckin' dog. Fuck. That piss-hole getting rammed down this throat-hole: yes, fucker. Big fuckin' dickhead: yeah. I'm still breathing, fucker: stop it up. Come on: FUCK it, dickhead! I better be spittin' blood when you're done, asshole—

When he comes, when suddenly that moment devolves and he knows—this is it—and there's nothing he can do to stop it, his muscles tauten, his butt lifts up—really pushing it in—and lodged all the way down in the esophageal hold of my throat, he propels all those seminal exigencies out of him with ejaculations until that imminent pain at the end of his dick is transformed into an immanent ecstasy radiating out of every pore in his body.

For the duration of the subsiding spasms I hold him into my face until it's just blood: pumping from his heart, throbbing in his veins, and pulsing in his cock.

I raise up but not off, and for a moment just his dick's head is in my mouth, awash in its own semen—

It's too much. I suck off, and—

Bob.

Rick!

The shit-eating grin is on his face but the Dick, the Autonomous Man, the Fucker: he's gone. And all that's left is a boy and he is having the bestest time of his life. He practically laughs outright at the sheer overwhelming fun of it all.

I get the poppers and take another hit. I'll be way off before he's down. I spit just a little of his cum in my fist, and then start in on myself. We're both leaning back against the wall, slightly turned and looking into each other's eyes. It's too fucking good.

"Come on my dick," he says.

His pants are about his knees, and his still tumescent cock is lying there across his lap. If I did that I'd have to straddle him, and if I did that—I'd be jacking my dick and looking straight in his eyes—

He'd be grinning at me, just like he is now, not a big man anymore, just a little boy and he'd be so cute and open: innocent. Fuck. And I'd lob it in his face: the whole mouthful of cum and spit and blood. And I'd just be whaling away on my dick. He'd try to wipe his face with his hands but I'd pin them with my knees, and it'd all be dripping off his face:

Yeah, you're a big macho man, aren't ya? You hit little boys and you make them cry. And I'm shit under your feet, I'm just a fuckin' asshole faggot. Well, how about this, Mister Macho Man: you're just sitting here and I'm fuckin' jacking off on you. So what does that make you? Huh? A faggot's fucking pissing on you, asshole. So what does that make you:

Eat fuckin' THIS.

"Come on my dick." He says it a second time.

But I don't. He's being nice. And it wouldn't be right somehow: he hit me. My lip is swelling, I think I'm tasting blood, and I can't talk very well (I'm not going to swallow this stuff until I have to):

"I'm jackin' my dick off with your cum. Your sperm—I got it out of your dick. In my mouth—"

His eyes are way inside me, he knows what I'm doing, he knows what I'm talking about: "Fuck your mouth."

Yes.

Fuck my mouth.

My hand is spinning up and down my dick and I'm looking into the eyes of a boy who is happier than anyone I have ever seen in my life, I'm working it right into inevitability, and then:

I don't have to jack it anymore.

But I do: oh yes! He's willing it out of me: sucking that jism up out of my balls with his eyes: yes! Now fucker: fuck: and:

SPEW!

Out of my eyes and into your fuck-ing beautiful fucking face.

You.

Manifest: massive globules of white. Against my skin.

Yes.

That's what came out of our eyes.

Fucking white.

Afterward, when Bob and I were starting to pull ourselves together, it was very nice. Coming down from wherever we'd been there was a kind of tenderness between us that felt like something I'd never experienced before. As opposed as our positions had been—his contempt, my abjection—there was something egalitarian about us now: we had earned one another.

Bob walked me to my bicycle, and as we were parting we shook hands. The clasp wasn't quite right and when I pulled him back to me for a better grip he was right there—

Yes?

There wasn't anything embarrassing about it, it was just a simple positive reaction to us:

Rick.

Bob.

Hand to hand, with palms so recently filled with blood-engorged dicks, our final hold on one another had a real moment of affection. And then he turned and walked away.

I was leaning over to unlock my bike, and I was doing the combination, when I felt him moving back toward me. I stood up and he was there beside me again. He was a little tentative with his addendum, but imperative too: "Don't let anyone get in your butt."

I told him I wouldn't.

When I told Stuart about it later he defined what I had experienced as "intimacy." Then, after mulling it over for a while, he suddenly turned to me and said, "Why not? Why not worship a cock?"

And that night, offering obeisance to his cock, the hardest, strongest dick I have ever sucked, I had a sudden intimation of Stuart's being, his meaning: he's here.

He: is: here.

Me too.

We are.

Fucking white.

The Singing Boy

PHILIP GAMBONE

Stewart and I were sitting around one of the outdoor tables at Luna's having a Saturday afternoon cappuccino. With its wide blue umbrellas, Italian-style coffee, and earnest attempts at Western Pastry, Luna's had been, from the day I discovered it, a favorite weekend retreat. It was also a great place to pick up really cheap CDs. Lately, the cold, dry winds that signaled the coming of a Beijing winter had begun to buffet the city, but on this particular afternoon the weather was still mild and sunny, the kind of October day that back home we'd call Indian summer.

Stewart was writing in his journal. I was watching the comings and goings on Sanlitun Road. It was easy to tell the tourists from the expatriates. The tourists always seemed slightly anxious and bewildered as they scavenged for bargains at the outdoor booths and stalls. The resident foreigners—diplomats' wives, business people, the young brat packers—walked more easily through all this, most of them looking slightly bored. I wondered how I, a forty-nine-year-old American who had been living in Beijing for almost three months, came across to them—tourist or expat?

A gust of wind rustled the umbrella. As I moved my chair more into the sun, a young Chinese dressed in an open-collar shirt and sport jacket approached us. He was toting a bulging briefcase.

"CD-ROM?" he whispered.

Without looking up, Stewart waved his pen. "*Meiyou.* Go away!"

Undeterred, the young man looked at me, rested the briefcase on our table and snapped it open to reveal an enormous stack of CDs in cheap photocopied wrappers.

"Please. Take look," he invited. "Many American musics." He scooped up a handful and thrust them at me.

Back in August, when I first settled in Beijing, I had refused to buy any of this pirated merchandise. I was still willing to pass up such enticing bargains for the sake of international copyright laws. But after a few weeks I couldn't resist the delicious twenty-kwai temptations. Some days, I could even talk these guys down to fifteen kwai a disk, under two dollars, but you had to buy five or six to get a price that good.

As I began to riffle through his wares, the man walked off the café terrace and leaned against a tree at the curbside—close enough to keep an eye on me, but far enough away to seem divorced from the proceedings lest an officer of the law pass by. Stewart looked up from his journal and scowled.

"David, I wish you wouldn't do that while we're sitting at the same table."

"Here's a Pavarotti album." I held it out in front of him.

"I have it, and I paid the full, legal price," he said frostily.

"Okay, okay." I began stuffing the CDs back into the briefcase and gave the man the signal to approach. His look was so expectant that I hated to deliver the bad news.

"Bu yao." I shook my head.

Without comment, stoically it seemed, he quickly gathered up the rest of the CDs and went over to another table, where he began his spiel all over again. I looked back at Stewart; he was scribbling away.

"Writing your impressions of post-Maoist capitalism?"

Stewart put down his pen and shut his journal decisively.

"There are days when I really hate this place."

"Oh, come on, Stewart," I cajoled, but he was not to be placated.

"The spitting, the pushing, the pollution, the illegal hustling. The *ugliness.*"

I glanced back at the pirate merchant, then flashed Stewart an impish grin. "Oh, I don't know. I'd say that one was rather darling."

Stewart ignored me. "China was one of the world's great civilizations, and it's been reduced to . . ." He held out his hands, inviting me to consider the reduction. "To this. This craven, in-your-face consumerism."

Stewart rarely used expressions like "in your face." It was a sign that even his meticulous vocabulary could crumble under stress.

Our waiter came over and asked if we'd like anything else.

"Qing yi bei kafei," I said.

"One cup coffee," he repeated, translating my pidgin Mandarin into pidgin English. He looked about eighteen, though I knew he must be older.

"No, not coffee," I laughed. "Cappuccino, please." I'd been silly trying to impress him with my rudimentary Chinese.

Reluctantly, Stewart ordered a cup too. His Chinese was better than mine. The waiter nodded, smiled at me, and went back inside the tiny shop. When I looked back at Stewart, he was slumped in his chair, his arms folded across his chest, glowering at the air. Which suddenly was filled with the sounds of Chinese teenage pop music drifting on silky, sentimental currents from inside the coffee shop.

Stewart picked up a packet of sugar and began irritably flicking it with his finger.

"Lighten up," I told him. "Not everything has to be bel canto."

Stewart had originally come to Beijing to do research on Peking Opera. Back home, he was a graduate student in musicology, working on a thesis about Chinese influences on Western music. He'd arrived for the summer, then decided to take a year's leave of absence in order to stay on in Beijing. When his grant money ran out, he'd taken a job with a photocopy and printing business that specialized in brochures and pamphlets and name cards—a big deal in the new entrepreneurial China.

"Come on," I cajoled. "We all have our moments with this place. It's like any big city. Some days you just can't see the beauty of it for all the annoyances."

Three months before, soon after my arrival, I'd fallen into a similar period of disillusionment with Beijing. So much of the city was gray and grim—the brutally functional socialist housing projects, the noxious air and congested streets, the paucity of what we in the West would call style.

Then, in late September, something clicked and suddenly I'd fallen in love with the place. Buying a bicycle and getting to know my way around helped, as did the arrival of the cooler, drier fall weather. But, more to the point, it was my beginning to sleep with Chinese guys that really made the difference. There was a bar and a little park where we would meet, and sometimes I'd take them home. This increasing attraction to Chinese guys, this increasing erotic life with Chinese guys, helped turn me on to their city too. I began to see the teeming streets and dusty air with new eyes. Beijing, this ancient, shabby Mongol outpost, suddenly took on an irresistibly sensual quality. I was discovering once again the gloriously erotic nature of urban life.

Until recently, Stewart knew nothing of this. Though we shared an apartment and shopped together and ate dinner together—in short, though we were a kind of expatriate version of the Odd Couple—my forays to the discos, the cruising parks, the one gay bar had been a private affair. Only recently had I told Stewart about my sexual adventuring. His reaction was to change the subject.

The waiter came back with our cappuccinos.

"Xiexie," I said as he set down the cups and saucers.

He smiled at me again. He seemed both amused and pleased by my efforts to speak his language.

As the waiter left, I leaned back in my chair, cupped the back of my neck with my hands, and, over the teenybop music which was still perking away, warbled out, "Hey ho! Hey ding-a-ling a-ding!"

"Could you please stop that?" Stewart scolded.

"I thought you liked English madrigals," I teased.

"You know what I mean."

"Look, Stewart, if there's beauty in the world, I think it's our duty to appreciate it."

"Since when did appreciating and *cruising*"—he twisted the word, wringing it like a wet dishrag—"since when did they become synonymous?"

Stewart and I had been thrown together by necessity. I had needed a place to stay and Stewart, whose roommate had returned to the States at the end of the summer, had needed someone to share his two-bedroom apartment. The first day we met, I immediately assumed he was gay. You had only to look at some of his things—the enormous collection of opera recordings, an English bone china tea service, the leather-bound journal—to suspect that here was a big American fairy about to burst from his chrysalis. Thirty-five, unmarried, and still a graduate student, he seemed the perfect candidate for a delayed coming-out adventure. But when, during that first week we lived together, I had started talking to him as if we were riding in the same rickshaw, he told me, "Look, David, the first thing we need to settle is that I'm not of your persuasion."

"Persuasion?" I'd teased. "It's not an ideology, you know."

The wind picked up again and the blue umbrella toggled back and forth. Stewart buttoned up his cardigan sweater.

"I just don't understand why someone as old . . ." He paused. "Why someone with your intelligence and sophistication persists in flirting with these"—he paused again; it was unlike Stewart to be at a loss for the right word—"these kids."

"Stu . . ."

"My name is Stewart."

I looked up from where I'd been sprinkling a packet of sugar onto the foam of my cappuccino. "Have you ever heard of loneliness?"

"And have *you* ever heard of restraint?"

For a few moments neither of us spoke. I stirred my coffee and Stewart flipped angrily through the latest edition of the visitors' magazine to Beijing.

"I'm sorry," he muttered at last, casting aside the magazine. "I think I need a break from all this."

I picked up the magazine.

"I noticed a weekend getaway package advertised in here." I flipped through the pages. "Here." I spread it out in front of him. "Tour through Hebei province, walk along remote section of the Great Wall, visit to a typical farming village. You've been saying all fall you wanted to see the Great Wall and the countryside. Here's your chance."

From across the table, Stewart craned his neck toward the two-page layout. The skeptical look on his face reminded me of someone on a diet who has just been presented with a box of chocolates. He pulled the magazine a little closer and read some more.

"Not a bad price either, huh?" I added.

He looked up.

"It's not bad," he admitted.

"So?"

"What about you?"

"What *about* me?"

"Don't you want to go too?"

"I thought you wanted to get away from *all this*."

"David, in case you hadn't noticed, I actually do enjoy your company." He turned the magazine to face me. "Besides, the price is for double occupancy."

I shook my head. "Stewart, for a straight boy, you sure do confuse me sometimes."

"The feeling is mutual, David." Raising his eyebrows, almost as if he were mocking his own fussiness, he added, "I'm sure."

And so, early the next Saturday morning we assembled at one of the state-run tourist hotels, where we met the rest of our party. We were nine altogether: six tourists; our tour guide, Mr. Chang; the driver of the minibus; and a woman, Miss Jiao, who was either Mr. Chang's secretary or his mistress. I noticed that they'd arrived with only one overnight bag.

Our fellow tourists were a quartet of just retired Americans, two couples from Indiana, who, almost from the beginning of our outing, pretty much stuck to themselves. I wondered if they'd assumed that Stewart and I were a couple and, if so, whether we weren't being given a homophobic cold shoulder. I looked for some indication that they also disapproved of Mr. Chang's liaison with Miss Jiao, but apparently those suspicions hadn't entered their minds.

The ride out to the Great Wall took all morning and part of the afternoon. Mr. Chang explained that we were bypassing Badaling, the nearest and most frequently visited section of the Wall. "My company show you some part that is much more authentic," he promised.

We passed villages, hydroelectric plants, fields and orchards, brown in their late-autumn decay. Mr. Chang kept turning around, feeding us commentary on the passing countryside: statistics about produce, farm yields, the success of Deng's land reforms. At the dot of noon, as if to show off the efficiency of the New China, he announced that it was time for lunch.

We pulled into a bustling but shabby market town, in front of what Mr. Chang called "a typical Hebei province restaurant." In Indiana they would have called it a "home-style" place. Instead of booths and framed Bible quotations, we had large round tables for ten and a gaudy porcelain Confucius high up on a shelf in one corner.

No sooner were we seated (under the hushed gaze of every other diner in the place) than the waiters and waitresses, a half dozen of them, began bustling back and forth, setting dish after dish before us.

One of the Indiana wives asked for a fork, which caused a moment of anxious incomprehension among the wait staff. No, they were very sorry, Mr. Chang translated, but they did not have any Western-style utensils. At which point, one of the waiters leaned into the table to demonstrate the proper use of chopsticks. One by one, he gave each member of the Indiana contingent a short lesson. When he turned to me, I picked up my sticks and, smiling broadly, click-clicked them at him. He smiled back.

As we ate, Stewart tried to start up a conversation with the retirees, but he could not win them over. They kept answering his questions in single words, then returned to their food. In this way—me flirting with the waiter, Stewart awkwardly throwing out questions that went nowhere, the Indiana folks alternately picking at and dropping their bits of chicken and tofu and green beans, and Mr. Chang, Miss Jiao, and the driver carrying on their own conversation—we made it through lunch.

"What's wrong with them?" Stewart whispered to me as we waited inside the minibus for the others to come back from the rest rooms.

When I explained my suspicions to him, his jaw dropped.

"What!" he exclaimed. "That's ridiculous." He turned to look out the window, then turned back. "Of course, if you hadn't been so obviously flirting with the waiter."

"Stewart, I am not going to bury my sexuality so that other people will feel more comfortable."

"This is China, David."

"What's that supposed to mean?"

"What that's supposed to *mean,*" he shot back, "is that we are . . ." He sighed. "Why is it so important for you always to find the gay underbelly here?"

It was a good question, one I'd been trying to answer myself these last few months.

"Maybe precisely because China *is* so enormous," I told him. "Maybe finding the gay underbelly is the only way I can fathom getting a handle on any of it."

Just then Mr. Chang and the others began to climb aboard. Stewart turned away from me and sat straight up in his seat.

"Otherwise," I continued, "the whole thing would just feel like one big, thick brick wall to me." One of the Indiana ladies squinted at me. I lowered my voice. "Gay is my entry point, Stewart."

It wasn't until the driver revved up the van that Stewart looked at me again. *"Entry point!"* he scoffed.

We drove on, the land becoming ever more rugged and hilly. And then suddenly, as we jostled around a bend in the road, there it was, the Wall: low and sensuous and animal-like as it followed the contour of the land, outlining the crest of the hills.

"My, oh my!" one of the Indiana ladies exclaimed.

Mr. Chang turned around again and explained that we were about to visit a section that few Westerners had ever seen.

"Soon we stop," he said. "Must walk rest of way. No tourist facility." The minibus pulled over to the side of the road. "Please, this way," Mr. Chang directed.

We hiked through a grove of trees, bare except for a few glossy, red-orange fruits hanging from their boughs.

"Persimmons," one of the Indiana folks said. "Now that's something I know a thing or two about."

I kept my eye on Stewart. As soon as we'd gotten off the minibus, he'd moved away from me and joined Mr. Chang and Miss Jiao. They took the lead, followed by the Indiana quartet, me holding up the rear. Eventually, we all caught up to one another at the base of one of the guard towers.

"Stairway over there." Mr. Chang motioned to where we were to climb. "This very old section of Great Wall. From time of Han Dynasty emperors." He lit up a cigarette and, between heavy drags, told us the story of the building of the Wall, and how the slaves, when they collapsed from sickness or exhaustion or exposure, were discarded like so much refuse into pit graves at the base. He pointed, indicating where. Nothing but rubble and weeds and dusty soil.

"Government not restore this part yet. Must be careful where to walk."

While the others took out their cameras, I wandered off, mounting the stairs up to the walkway and along the top to a guard tower at the highest peak. There, in the parapet, overlooking that colossal river of gray brick, I sat and watched the others far below. It seemed as if the wives had finally warmed to Stewart.

As Mr. Chang had warned us, the bricks were loose here. I picked one up. A mottled, mousy gray, it was the size of a small loaf of bread, but heavier than I'd expected. I thought about what a fantastic souvenir it would make: two thousand years old, lifted from the very Wall itself. I'd be able to tell some pretty terrific stories with this thing. It felt to be about as heavy as one of those five-pound half weights at the gym, maybe a little more, something I could manage in my backpack. Taking it could be justified in lots of ways: after all, the government hadn't cared enough to restore the Wall anyway, and a country that ripped off international recording artists could hardly complain about being ripped off a little in return. I hefted the brick again. Its dusty clay felt good in my hands.

After about forty minutes, Mr. Chang called us to reassemble on the minibus. I looked at the brick one more time, then down at Mr. Chang. He was far enough away that I could hardly make out his features. Quickly, with a sleight of hand that rivaled those CD pirates on Sanlitun Road, I slipped the brick into my pack.

The sun was already behind the hills by the time we all reboarded the minibus.

"Next we visit typical Hebei province farm village," Mr. Chang announced.

It was dusk by the time we got to the village. We were met by some officials, who, with official smiles and gestures, motioned for us to follow them. We walked along the outskirts of the settlement, past walls insulated against the coming winter winds with piles of dried cornstalks. Chickens scattered from our path. Crowds of playful, giggling, children tagged along. Every other living creature—the dogs, the burros, the villagers themselves—looked at us with hushed curiosity.

"Look at those darling children," one of the wives said. "I don't think they've ever seen Americans before."

I checked my irritation with her. We all pay attention to what we can, I reminded myself.

"This way, please." Mr. Chang gestured, and ushered us through the doorway of one of the village houses.

We entered a room the size of a small American studio apartment. It was built entirely of concrete: concrete floor, concrete walls, concrete sleeping platform, under which, Mr. Chang pointed out, was a wood-burning stove. A single bare lightbulb suspended from the concrete ceiling cast harsh shadows everywhere.

The next room was twice as large. A television set was broadcasting the evening news. Here was where the family of the house had gathered. I couldn't tell whether our intrusion had been expected or not. They stood when we entered, smiling and nodding awkwardly to us, the mother bouncing a baby in her arms, the father motioning for us to take a seat on the sofa or on another bed platform. One of the Indiana wives sat down; the other stretched her arms out to the mother and infant and asked if she could hold the baby. When the mother handed over the baby, it immediately began to cry.

"The world over," the Indiana wife remarked.

Again Mr. Chang gave us the official spiel about what a model community this was: impressive increases in material prosperity, sanitation, calorie intake. As he spoke, I could feel the brick weighing down my backpack.

"Now I think we go to hotel," he announced. "Already very late."

Outside the house, a crowd had gathered: two hundred or more people whose silent, respectful air made them seem almost like mourners at a funeral. One of the officials said something to Mr. Chang and he nodded.

"I think before we go, quickly, for village people you can sing typical American song?"

We ended up muddling our way through "My Country, 'Tis of Thee." The wives had high, warbly, Sunday hymn-sing voices; the husbands sang off key. Stewart's voice was rich and clear.

As we sang, I looked out over the crowd. In the dim light, it was hard to make out faces. Briefly, I made eye contact with one young man and smiled. He hesitated, flashed me a bashful smile, then just as quickly turned to a young woman next to him and whispered something to her. She looked up at me, and I shot her a smile as well. A broad grin blossomed on her face, and she broke into a giggle.

When we finished the anthem, the villagers applauded enthusiastically. Mr. Chang made a brief speech, there was more applause, a few bows between Mr. Chang and some village official, and then we began to move toward the minibus.

All at once, there was a stirring in the crowd and a sudden hush, from which emerged, floating on the air, a beautiful soprano voice singing in Chinese. Everyone stopped and listened. Someone was returning our gift of song with a song of her own. Gradually, I was able to make out where the singing was coming from. I looked over the heads of the crowd. There, under a bare, dim lightbulb was a teenage girl, her hair cut short and wearing the baggy blouse and trousers that were the standard village attire. As she sang, she gestured with her hands and body—a delicately turned wrist, a coy tilting of the head—that seemed operatic in character. I looked over at Stewart. He was transfixed.

The villagers had gathered around the singer. Old and young, men and women—on every face expressions of respect and pride. A group of girls, about the same age as the singer, were clustered immediately behind her. I looked at the faces of the girls and then at the singer—the girls, the singer—back and forth (something was weird here), comparing their facial features, skin tone, the cut of the hair. And suddenly I realized that the singer was not a girl at all, but a boy, a young teenager whose voice had not yet changed.

The boy's song rose in intensity. His gestures became even more theatrical. It was hard for me not to think of lip-synch performances I'd seen at certain clubs during my summers in Provincetown. When the song ended, in a diminuendo of almost painfully shy sweetness, we all applauded, and the boy bowed demurely. I looked at Stewart. He was holding his fingers to his lips.

"American friends, must depart now," Mr. Chang announced. He turned to me. "Very too late." Just then, Stewart rushed over.

"Mr. Chang, couldn't we stay a few more minutes? I'd like to meet the singer."

"Not possible," was Mr. Chang's terse, official reply. "Must depart immediately. Very too late. You spend too much time at Wall."

"Mr. Chang," I began, "in America, Stewart is a musicologist. An ethnomusicologist." I pronounced the word slowly, enunciating each syllable. "He studies the music of other cultures."

"Yes, yes, but no time." Mr. Chang pointed to his watch. "Hotel planning typical Hebei banquet. Must go." He barked out something to Miss Jiao, who was already leading the others to the bus.

I looked at Stewart, ready to give him a when-in-Rome shrug, but he looked so angry that I held off saying anything.

All the way to the hotel, as we swayed and lumbered over the rough terrain, he didn't speak.

At dinner, Mr. Chang poured us all tea. "You like Great Wall?" he asked me.

"Hen hao."

Mr. Chang smiled. "You speak very well Chinese." He turned to Miss Jiao to solicit her agreement. She nodded.

"I liked the village better," Stewart announced.

The smile on Mr. Chang's face disappeared. He leaned his heavy bulk over to the lazy Susan in the center of the table and caught a slice of stir-fried sweet potato with his chopsticks.

"This county grow more sweet potato than all other county in Hebei province. Very much work."

"Don't have to tell me about farming," one of the Indiana husbands chuckled.

Stewart put down his chopsticks. "Mr. Chang," he asked, "what was that boy singing about?"

Mr. Chang glanced over at Miss Jiao, then back at his food, which he slowly began to stir with his chopsticks.

"Boy sing typical peasant love song." He pointed to the food platters on the lazy Susan. "You not try fried sweet potato?"

"But what were the words the boy was singing?" Stewart insisted.

In a hushed voice, Miss Jiao said something to Mr. Chang in Chinese and he answered back.

"Boy sing song about young man who leave village." Mr. Chang looked at all of us as he spoke, all except Stewart. "Young man go to city. Girlfriend of young man very sad he go away."

"And the young man is singing about his girlfriend?" Stewart persisted.

"No, no. Young man not singing," Mr. Chang said. "Young girl singing. She say she will miss young man very much."

One of the Indiana wives turned to the other. "You see, it's always the gals who get left behind."

The Indianans began to chuckle. So did Mr. Chang and Miss Jiao, but Stewart pressed on with his questions.

"So the young *girl* is singing," he said. "The words of the song are the words *she* is saying?"

I watched the Indiana folks shift their attention to their plates. Miss Jiao spoke again and Mr. Chang said something back to her.

"Miss Jiao say not very typical for boy to sing this song. This song typical for village girl to sing."

"I see," Stewart said. "But would it be considered . . ." He looked at Miss Jiao, then back at Mr. Chang. "Would the village people think it strange, um, not typical, for a boy to sing that song?"

"Typical for village people," Mr. Chang said, and then he consulted with Miss Jiao again. "In city like Beijing, not typical."

"I see," said Stewart. "So a city boy would not sing such a song?"

"Not such a song," Mr. Chang affirmed.

"What would happen if a city boy sang that song?" Stewart pressed.

"City people laugh," Mr. Chang said.

"I see," Stewart said. "So a country boy might sing such a song, but a city boy would not."

"Not city boy," Mr. Chang repeated. Miss Jiao whispered again. "Miss Jiao say maybe even in village that boy too old to sing like girl."

"How old was that boy?" Stewart asked Miss Jiao.

Under the table, I tapped Stewart's leg.

"Maybe that boy thirteen, fourteen years old," Mr. Chang said.

"Okay, so what if the boy was eleven or twelve?" Stewart looked at Miss Jiao again. "If he were twelve, and he sang like a girl, would city people still laugh at him?"

Mr. Chang looked at Miss Jiao.

"I think maybe yes," she said very softly. It was the first time either of us had heard her speak in English. "Because he sing girl song. This song only for girl to sing." She motioned to the lazy Susan. "Now I think you eat some sweet potato, please?"

After dinner, we retired to our rooms. While Stewart used the bathroom, I stripped down to my underwear. It was chilly in the room. The hotel had yet to turn the heat on for the season. I took a sweatshirt out of my travel bag and pulled it on.

Next to the bag was my backpack. Crouching down beside it, I lifted out the brick, still heavy and gray and powdery under my fingers. Suddenly I became intensely aware of myself, squatting there like a Chinese peasant, the pack between my legs, fondling my purloined possession. I imagined generations of Chinese smugglers before me—perhaps centuries of generations of smugglers—cutting just such a figure, hunched over the precious worldly objects they'd managed to snatch up, devising schemes to transport their treasure abroad. Smuggling was a tradition in China. I suspected Mr. Chang might even call it a typical Chinese occupation. I eased the brick back to the bottom of the pack and dusted off my hands.

"Mind if I write for a little while?" Stewart asked, emerging from the bathroom in flannel pajamas.

I told him it was fine with me. He got into bed, pulling the down comforter up close, propped his back against the thin pillow, pulled his knees up, and, steadying his journal against his thighs, immediately began to write. I got into my own bed, turned my back to the nightstand and table lamp that separated us, and closed my eyes.

For a minute, the only sound was the occasional soft scratching of Stewart's pen on the pages of his book. Then I heard him turn to me.

"Why did you try to shush me up when I was talking to Mr. Chang?"

I turned over, facing him. "Come on, Stewart, you should have heard yourself: 'So, if the boy had been eleven and a half and was a city boy but had walked from the city to the country and sang the song in a medium-high voice only to country people, but had used feminine gestures . . .' Jesus, Stewart. You were, I think it's safe to say, exhibiting a rather inordinate amount of interest in that kid."

Silence. I looked up at him. He was sitting there, his journal abandoned at his side, his hands behind his neck, staring out across the room.

"I don't need protecting, you know." He turned and looked me straight in the eye. "I knew exactly what kind of impression I was making down there."

"Sorry," I apologized, but Stewart continued to stare at me.

"Exactly," he repeated.

I let the word die in the chilly air between us. At first, I thought he was just being his testy old self. But something about the way he kept staring at me made me uncomfortable. I was the first to break our eye contact.

"It was weird, wasn't it?" I said, settling myself on my back now, gazing up at the ceiling.

"What was weird?"

"You know, how feminine that kid was. I mean, he was such a little queen."

"He was beautiful," Stewart said.

I turned over on my side and looked at him. "He was cute, wasn't he?"

"Goddammit!" Stewart snapped. "Have you ever considered that there are other kinds of beauty? The kid was brave, David. *Brave*."

"Sorry," I said. I lay on my back again. The hotel was only two years old, but already the paint on the ceiling was peeling. I decided to try again: "You're right. He was brave."

For a few moments, neither of us spoke. Then I heard Stewart chuckle.

"Okay, okay," he said. "And cute too. Very cute."

I didn't dare respond for fear I'd misinterpreted Stewart again. Instead. I just kept staring at the ceiling, waiting for something to change. Then I closed my eyes and silently practiced my Chinese numbers: *yi, er, san* . . . It wasn't until I got to seven that Stewart spoke.

"David, we're not going to sleep together, you know."

I opened my eyes, but didn't answer. "Because," Stewart continued, "even if I do have feelings in that direction, I don't think that you and I . . ."

I turned to him. "I agree."

"Good," he said. "I just wanted to make sure you understood."

"I do."

That seemed to be the end of it, but Stewart went on.

"Look, I'm sorry," he said.

"About what?"

"I don't know. I guess about not being quite ready for all this." I tried making a joke: something about me still not being ready for tourists from Indiana, but Stewart interrupted me. "Because," he said, "it's all just a little too much for me right now."

"I know," I told him. "Like the man said, it's a big, big country." I smiled. "To tell you the truth, Stewart, you're really not my type anyway." I reached across the space between us and gave him a good-buddy punch in the arm. "But I really like being your roommate."

"Thanks. I like being your roommate too." He took his journal off the blanket and placed it on the night table. "Shall I shut off the light?" I told him yes.

In the darkness, I lay there listening, first for sounds from Stewart and then to what André Malraux once called "the great silence of the Chinese night"—maybe Mr. Chang would have called it the "typical silence of the Hebei province night."

Minutes passed. There was something else that needed to be spoken.

"You awake?" I asked. Stewart murmured. "I stole a piece of the Wall today." I heard Stewart stir. Then the bedside lamp came on. He squinted at me. "A brick," I explained. "It's in my backpack."

"Why?"

"I don't know. I guess at the time it just seemed worth taking. It didn't feel like such a big deal."

"And now?" he asked.

I shook my head. "And now it feels like a big deal. I kind of wish I could put it back."

I stared up at the ceiling again. In the lamplight I could see my breath condensing in the cold air of the room.

"Can I have it?"

I looked at Stewart. "What?"

"Can I have it? The brick. I'll take it off your hands."

"Jesus, Stewart, whatever for?"

"I guess I'd like something to remember this day by. It's been a big one for me, you know."

I chuckled. "What about your journal? I thought that was your memory book."

He looked at it, lying there on the night table. "Too many words," he said. "Not enough music." There was a quality to his voice that sounded so sad.

Or maybe I should say that *sad* is how we'd describe that mood in the West. I wonder if there's a different word in Chinese. But if so, I don't know it yet.

Haram

REGINALD M. HARRIS, JR.

For John R. Keene, Jr.

The night asks who am I?
I am its secret—anxious, black, profound
I am its rebellious silence
I have veiled my nature, with silence,
wrapped my heart in doubt
and, solemn, remained here
gazing, while the ages ask me,
who am I?

—Nazik al-Malaikah, "Who Am I?"

Again The BlackAmerican gets on the train. He looks up and down the half-full subway car, searching for a seat, then moves to take the empty place across the aisle from me. The doors of the subway close, and we continue on our journey under this vile city to our homes.

I am sure this is done on purpose, his sitting there. He knows I ride this PATH train from Manhattan to the New Jersey at this hour every day, just as he does, bags from the store at my feet—filled, today, with rice and eggplant, a tin of coffee, lime and raisins, diapers, paper towels. Boxes of American cereals stick out from their tops. I have a leg of lamb for my brother's wife to cook this evening during my hours of rest and prayer before I return for the late night shift. He sits there with intent, The BlackAmerican, to torment me. He pretends to ignore me now. When I close my eyes to him, tired from the long day and many customers, he will stare, thinking me asleep. When my eyes open, he will avert his own. Slowly, we will begin to glance at each other, as we do almost every day, while the subway train rocks us like babies in a cradle to our separate destinations.

The BlackAmerican must be a student. Always he has books and papers, a black leather bag slung over his left shoulder, which he will also place, as he does now, carefully on the floor of the subway car between his feet. He takes out a newspaper, opens it, and begins to read. It is not a regular newspaper, with stories of sin and death, the latest Israeli outrage, but some other, smaller kind, filled with tales and poetry, more fertile ground for his imagination. I have seen him read this paper before, watched as his hands moved to close and open the pages in front of him as if lost in repeating prayer before its words.

I was a student once, in my country. There, I lived for knowledge, enjoyed holding a new book in my hands every day. I wished to spend my life lost in printed pages, to create stories of my own like the ones I read. No one in my family could conceive of such a life for me, however, made merely of words. My thoughts were only the foolishness of youth, they said. It had been difficult enough to send two of my older brothers to the University, my father told me. I was lucky to follow them there, and should concentrate on a more practical set of studies, one certain to lead to a lucrative profession, and I obeyed. After two years, however, I could take no more of the formulas and numbers of petrochemical engineering, and left the University entirely to join my next-eldest brother, Jabrá·, in America.

Even in this book-filled city, it is difficult to find the words of those I read in school. I must now read the hands of other men, imagining the stories they might tell. Entire novels could be written about the watches, rings, and bracelets they wear to adorn them; the way their fingers curve, sleeping on the knees of those who ride the train, or bend and dance to tie a shoelace, fix a button. The curl of hands that hold the tiny fists of children is the most beautiful of poems. The hands of those who shop in the store speak constantly to me. With fists down and mute at first to offer money, they slowly turn, rising like the sun, and begin to sing, palms open, while waiting for their change.

The BlackAmerican's fingers are long and thin. His well-kept nails carefully prick at the edges of his newspaper's thin pages. I can catch glimpses of the writing there, its jagged lines of poetry looking like the city's skyline turned sideways on the page. I glance at the American newspapers, and the one that arrives with week-old news from our country, word maps to guide me back to my home. The BlackAmerican coughs and turns a page. To what places does this paper take him, his head filled with poems? Does he know of those I read in school, perhaps—of Idris? Darwish? Bashshar ibn Burd, whose Salmá·, in a fragment of verse, had bones of sugarcane? Perhaps not. I look away from him and close my eyes.

Marriage to my Salmá· was, of course, arranged for us when we were children. Yet from our many meetings I have grown to respect my little distant cousin, and to truly love her. Time has caused her beauty to blossom, and her smooth skin and dark eyes have inflamed many men at home. But she remains faithful and waits for me. We each wear a ring as sign of our intent to marry. "This will make the women of America stay away from you," her mother said to me, pushing the gold band on my thick finger before I left. "To keep you from trouble." Each day I pray for The Most Merciful to protect Salmá· while I am so far away, making dowry enough for us to marry and she can join me here. I want our children to be born here, to grow to be good Americans, and choose with their own will the paths they wish to take in life.

My brothers have done the same before me. I will be the last of my family to be like a slave, to work and work and work, dirtying my hands only to arrive at the same place our parents were, dreams mashed down by the enormous hand of Fate. Even here, escaping, so I thought, the life of a common peddler, I remain trapped in its fist, selling brightly colored American products at Jabrá·'s store instead of the vegetables, nuts and fruits our father did, and his father before him. But not my children. They will go to school here, like The Black-American, and finish their studies, so they may later wear the White Collar, and not have to be careful of those who try to rip off, of shoplifters and holdups, and working night and day behind a counter, at the mercy of others.

Gladly I work hard, spend long hours at the store. I can endure anything for my future. It does not matter that sometimes I drift into sleep on the subway train after work. In Jabrá·'s apartment, sharing space with him, Karima, and little Fatima until my Salmá· can join me, I fall with exhaustion into a deep, dream-filled well on the same cot where Yusef slept before bringing his family to America and moving to tWashington D.C. The memory of Salmá·, her cool hands and sparkling gaze, guides me in my efforts every day.

But this country, this city, is filled with many torments and temptations.

The BlackAmerican closes his paper, sighs. Again we exchange looks before turning our heads away. He reaches down into his bag, pulls out a thick black book, and begins to read. He reaches again for pencil and paper, to make notes as he reads, juggling book and paper on his legs. His eyes continue to glance at me between his writing, like sparks flying up from a fire. I look away so he does not know I see him.

There is much gazing done by the men who ride this subway train. I expected such looking at their uncovered women, but the openness of men staring at each other here was quite shocking to me. There must be nowhere else in the world where men are so openly lustful as on this PATH subway train to the New Jersey. Perhaps I have never left the farm in our family's village, in spite of our later years in The Capital, as Jabrá· says. Such lusts between men are haram, taboo. They stare at each other, at me, sometimes even spreading their legs, an invitation to uncleanliness. Why can they not control their desires, avert their eyes, keep such things silent? No one cares what they do in the darkness of their rooms. Their kind even appears on the television set, parading down sunlit streets arm in arm. The women do it also, exposing bare flesh for the cameras, touching and kissing each other in public. Disgusting.

Such men come at all hours into Jabrá·'s store, laughing, trailing vile cologne, their voices high in imitation of women. I watch them as they enter, going up and down the aisles chattering like birds, fingering the breads, shaking boxes of noodles, dancing to the rhythms that they make. Late at night, after their nearby gathering places have closed, groups of two or three come in to buy soda and juices, sometimes a sandwich or some sweet for their journeys home together. I hear them talk about me amongst themselves, cooing like doves at the hair overflowing the collar of my shirt, calling me "sexy hot." They anger me with such words, tempting me into unholiness with their grins and winks. This is a trial I must bear, I think, some test of my resolve and faith which I must pass for the sake of my future and my family. I could do violence to them at such times, easily crush their worthless necks with my bare hands, but do not. To do so would be a greater evil. Even to say something to them would be wrong, and bad for my brother's business. I must ignore them. Their narrow hips sway like palms when they leave the store.

I knew The BlackAmerican was one of this kind the first time I saw him on the subway train. I am not certain how, perhaps from the intensity of his look. Even now he stares at me as if thirsty, and I were a cool fountain from which to drink. One day he even dared to read one of their newspapers here on the train, quite openly, as if it were nothing. Again this was done directly in front of me as some form of test. No one else seemed to notice, or to care.

Jabrá· has been in this country longer than I have, has hardened to the way things are done here. My brother says, "In America it is 'To each his own.'" He places a calming hand upon my shoulder when I speak of these creatures. "Our people are not like them, true, and we do not do such things. But let them be, Samir. Leave their final judgment to The Divine One. After six more months here, you will not notice them."

Jabrá· even has their newspapers in the store to sell—and worse. Behind the counter, away from children and dirty fingers, he keeps the books that show unclothed men and women. Their pages shine under the bright lights of the store at night as if covered with liquid glass. The men on them stare out, teasing with sweet smiles and erect genitals. Or they have their backs to the cameras, exposing smooth buttocks, looking invitingly over their shoulders. Some photos are made to look as though they were involved in some act, their heads thrown back, faces trapped in a net of ecstasy. I close my eyes to such things, turn my palms to heaven in prayer. The images continue to taunt me after I have left the store. All this is haram. We would never have such things in our country.

The BlackAmerican is not unattractive. His hands look strong yet delicate, skin the color of a pecan. His small beard is most becoming, bracketing a well-shaped mouth and lips. The hair of his head has grown longer in the months that we have been riding the PATH train together, becoming both wilder and softer. Soon, he may even look like one of us! Like one of my cousins from the South perhaps, or my friend Amín. Again his eyes, dark as coffee, glance at me and look away.

What does he think when he looks at me this way? That I would join him in some act perhaps? I would not. I must think of Salmá·. It is difficult for me to imagine The BlackAmerican doing such things in any event. He does not seem like those who come into the store, or those mentioned on the television news earlier this week, caught doing unspeakable things in the bathroom of a store in the Secaucus shopping mall. He could not be like those others, who couple everywhere as if at the haram, the baths, in The Capital. Such things took place there all the time. I would see them there when bathing to refresh myself at the end of a long, hot day, and feel uncomfortable and unclean, in spite of all my washing. Going from one to another to slake their passions—men should not do these things. They should settle down, remain with just one of their kind as men and women do, and share their lives and dreams.

Perhaps he is like the Men from Europe, who would sit in the American hotel in The Capital, fat and rich, their hair slicked back with oil. They, too, would stare over their newspapers, smiling at the local men wandering slowly between the plump sofas and potted palm trees of the lobby. One could make money there, smiling and looking back, joining these men later in their rooms, after a discreet wait so no one notices they are together, allowing them to place their hands on them. Allowing other things as well, their soft, flabby skin as white as milk and sweet like halvah. Or so I have been told.

This was a story Amín told me, which he said was told to him by someone else he would not name. He grew up in The Capital, his parents' spice shop next to ours in the marketplace. Amín and I remained almost inseparable from when we met as children until plans were made for me to follow my brothers to America. He could be a delight, gentle, the most reasonable of men when he wished to be. But also completely incorrigible as well, with little ambition, never finishing anything, constantly putting off for the sake of pleasure. Small items, watches, keys, pools of change, often disappeared around him. It was rumored he even committed adultery with other men's wives—Amín was accused of doing all manner of things. His reply to any charge was always the same, a slowly growing smile, which would get larger and brighter the longer he attempted to deny each accusation. Amín did not fully understand my love of schooling; he was always looking for excuses not to go to class, but never discouraged my interests and was always a good friend.

In the evenings, after school and my time in Father's shop was done, we would walk the streets of the Old City, dodging traffic on the twisting streets, Amín swearing at taxi drivers, on our way to one or another of our favorite cafés to meet friends. He constantly attempted to pull me into some trouble. He would see two unattended foreign women farther down the sidewalk, for example, and his hand would suddenly grow hot in mine.

"Come, Samir—live a little!" He would squeeze my fingers. "You are so stiff and formal. Where does that come from? Why are you so filled with fear? Is this what all your reading has done for you?"

It was then my turn to smile and not answer.

"It isn't right for someone big like an ox as you are to be so afraid of life. How will you ever make it in America if you do not know how to enjoy yourself as they do?"

"I am going there to work, Amín, not for fun. To make enough to help my family and take Salmá· out of this place." I stopped and looked at him. "You should do the same. Things will only get worse here. Even you must know the evenings when one can walk the streets in safety are becoming fewer. Come with me, and try to improve your lot in life."

"Yes, yes, of course my friend. I shall, I shall. But later. For now, let me enjoy myself. You go. Prepare the way for us and work. Tell me how it is there, then perhaps later we will meet again on the streets of your United States . . ." He looked into a store window and smiled. "Right now, however, come. Those two have gone into this shop. I saw the shorter one glancing at you. She wants you to speak to her, my friend, I know it! Let us both go in, and you speak to her so I can talk to her friend." And he'd drag me, objecting, into the shop and mischief.

One evening we stopped outside the American hotel, and he told me the story of the Men from Europe. Again he wanted me to go in with him, to show me these men and prove the things he said were true. But I refused.

How I wish Amín had followed me here and settled down. He continues to say. "Later, later," in his letters to me. He thinks we are like the stars, set to burn forever. I long to see his face again, to playfully pull at his attempts at a beard while laughing into his flashing eyes. We could perhaps go on another of our walks, as he suggested, I the experienced one this time, showing him around the city. Only here we could not hold each other's hands as we did at home. Here, such a mark of friendship has been corrupted.

Only those like The BlackAmerican do this, walking through their Village and along the River Hudson. To see such men there holding hands awakens a memory, a sadness in me, causing my heart to ache.

Then I am filled with anger. It is all I can do at times to not rush out and hit—the men, the women, everyone in sight—or pound my fists into a wall, turning my knuckles bloody. I despise the ease with which they touch each other, their clean, unbroken fingernails and smooth palms. It is obvious they have no ties, no family, no obligations to perform. I must swallow my anger like a bitter drink before it overflows. I attempt to avoid going to this place, not wishing to see them, to feel their eyes upon me, hear their voices, or for anyone to think as I pass along the streets that I am like them.

I can no longer stop myself.

Although younger than Jabrá·, I am bigger, and strong. Always he has packages for me to carry home. At times he loads me down like a mule, and I struggle with the heavy bags through the crowded streets. Even so, many evenings I leave early from the store, telling my brother I wish to avoid traffic. Unbeknownst to him, I walk past the gaping mouth of the subway near the store and continue on to the places where such men live and the River Hudson. The sidewalks teem with them, arms draped around one another, holding hands, sitting at tables in cafés, talking excitedly in small groups on the corners. It is both the same and different from my late afternoons with Amín and friends in our homeland. The straps of the bags chew into my hands as I walk on, past their shops, cool air from the open doors of their dark-filled bars like a kiss blown from the abyss upon my skin, to cross the wide street before the river and sit on one of the benches along the quay.

I watch them there, the younger ones laughing and dancing to strange, rhythmic music playing from large radios they have brought with them. Older ones and tourists walk by in groups, lost in passionate discussion or snapping photos. Joggers and skaters pass me on the metal bench, thumping or scratching the concrete with powerful legs, their nearly naked bodies gleaming under the lowering sun. The repeated pounding of the music beats like a racing heart and I feel myself being unraveled. Men and women of all colors, shapes, and sizes walk by, hand in hand, talking, laughing, enjoying the warm breezes coming across the water, sharing their day's adventures with each other. I must be careful at such times, remain alert. I have on occasion drifted off to sleep there, lulled by the calm air, dreaming of leaving my bags behind to join them—of walking hand in hand with Amín again under the clear American sky, watching small boats sail by as the sun quietly sets and stars rise up behind us over this city of heaven-piercing buildings. Slowly, the full Moon rises dressed in her white finery, perfect as a new bride.

At times, such thoughts overwhelm those of Salmá· and my real future. I awaken, startled, must quickly put them away and hurry to the subway. Such are the ways in which this nation is al-harath, the Hell of crushing pressure, causing me to be foolish again, to question my feelings, my true path in life. I must not think of these things.

The BlackAmerican has almost the same coloring as Amín. At times he has the same look in his eye, seems to move in the same way as he enters the subway train and searches for a seat. But he is a more serious Amín, an Amín more down to Earth than the other ever was. Perhaps that is why he haunts me so. It shames me to think of how I see The BlackAmerican's face when I lie shaking on my cot, relieving myself of the days' tensions, muffling my cries as my brother's wife rattles dishes in the next room. Then his face slides away, turning into the pearly smile of Amín as I relax and slip into a dream.

I am always returned to our last visit to the river together. How we both did not show up for work in our family's shops, like schoolboys skipping classes, and wandered along the tiny beach, watching fishermen haul in their nets filled with the flashing silver of sardines, at times dashing into the cool waters ourselves, splashing each other as we had done as children. Toward the end of the day, tired and hot, we lay down on the tiny strip of sand.

"Samir?" he said.

"Yes, Amín."

He said nothing for a while. Lightly his hand touched mine. "I will miss you, my friend," he said softly.

"As will I, Amín," I whispered. His fingers were cool against my skin. "As will I."

We lay on the sand in this way for a long time, his hand touching mine. Slowly, Amín moved to place his hand on my thigh. I let it rest there for a while, feeling the separate touch of each finger upon me, then moved my leg away, afraid of the fire it had set inside my chest. I wanted to speak, but did not. I longed to touch Amín, but dared not. We continued to lie beside each other a long time silently, not touching, until the sky began to darken and we rose to return to our homes and families.

I dream of this almost every night. Why did I move my leg away? What would have happened if I had taken Amín's hand? Would he perhaps have joined me in America if I had done this one thing? In my dreaming, I fashion for myself a new yesterday. We get up from the sand and dive into the river. The water, soft as Desire, envelops us like another skin. We return to the beach. Again Amín's fingers brush along my thigh. I turn to touch his face and smile. I dream not of the games of the flesh we played when children, but of holding Amín, placing my thick arms around his small frame while he dozes, a rabbit in the tall grass of my chest. With each passing night I imagine Amín holding me, my head resting on his shoulder as his arms close around me like the waters. My muscles loosen and relax, a pack animal unburdened of its cargo, and I drift off to sleep.

The slowing subway train shakes me awake. The next stop, Grove, is The BlackAmerican's. I look down at my tired hands. The straps from the heavy bags have left their reddened image on my palms, a thick path across the web of lines that crisscross there. I twist the band on my finger around and around and around. I have lost my way in this vile country. I must find some way to remain focused on those things that matter, my proper tasks: The store. Salmá·. The future. This other is haram. Along this way lies madness.

The BlackAmerican gathers his things and stands. I want to look away from him but cannot. I am trapped, drowning in the lake of his dark eyes. Where does he go when he leaves the subway train? Does he live with family? Alone? Perhaps he lives with another—yes, another of his kind. But not for him the pretty parrots. Some other like himself, quiet, concerned with projecting the proper look to outsiders. Together in some small apartment, they attempt to build an honorable life.

The BlackAmerican stands over me, waiting for the train to stop. His fingers drum against the metal pole next to me then tightly grips it as we begin to slow. He stares at me, a question in his eyes, and smiles. I attempt to smile back but can manage only the slightest memory of one. When we reach the platform, he nods at me, says "Good night," and leaves. I open my mouth also, but can make no sound.

I turn to look out the window as the train pulls away from the station. The BlackAmerican stands on the platform still looking at me as we move off. I watch him getting smaller and smaller, wanting to rise from my seat as the train picks up speed. Then he disappears into darkness. We enter a tunnel and the subway train goes dark. The only lights are brief flashes from the bare bulbs we pass along the damp sides of the tunnel walls. A rush of wind swirls through the train as it continues to move faster. I stare out at the blackness. I feel doomed, disowned by Time, cursed to travel on like this forever without pause. The train shudders and rumbles. We lean around a curve, and the inside lights come on again as we head into another station.

This evening I will write to Salmá·, wishing her well, sending a portion of my pay to her family, counting out the months until she arrives. Then I will write to Amín. I will tell him to forget my talk of coming to this country. I know him well. His petty crimes would expand and get him into serious trouble here. The temptations are too great. And the nights, the nights, my dear Amín, I will say, are filled with too many sounds. The winds whisper from the shadows, asking many questions. The weeping of a million people, thrown together but alone when darkness falls, fills the ears. Their crying out as he lay on his bed at night would be overmuch. Too much for him to bear.

Good News and Bad News

DAVID A. NEWMAN

A young man calls his parents to tell them he's got good news and bad news. A practical pair, they ask to hear the bad news first.

"I'm gay," he says calmly.

There is silence.

"Well what in heaven's name is the good news?" his mother finally asks.

"I'm dying."

I'm sitting across from my thirty-six-year-old sister Laney in her four-bedroom house on a man-made lake in northeast Arkansas. She wrinkles her nose—her new habit—looks down and says, "That's not funny, Kevin, it's sick."

Exactly my point, I want to tell her as she stands, sponging off the counter with wide circular motions. But her last word sticks inside me. Sick. The word that used to define me. I see it on a banner I'm holding, dripping in wet, red letters. I see it as the name of a store with a registered trademark next to it. As the name of a really bad acid metal band. I see it as just a word, the abstractness of which I'm suddenly in love with because it doesn't mean me anymore. That many words—impatient . . . graphic designer . . . living—could be used to describe me still feels impossible when two years ago I was reduced to one.

My new three-week-old niece Mary Clare, the impetus behind this Thanksgiving get-together, is passed in a gentle relay from grandparents to aunts, uncles, neighbors, even the older cousins. And, this time, me.

"She prefers men," Laney says as she drapes a spit-up rag over my shoulder.

"Who doesn't?" I place my finger in Mary Clare's wrinkled, quarter-sized grip. I nuzzle my nose against her unbearably clear skin. I'd forgotten skin could look like that. Like it's pulled from perfectly manufactured sheets, sewn taut with invisible threads. The word "sick" holds no power next to blond-haired, blue-turning-brown-eyed Mary Clare. It melts in her guileless sun, forgotten by my family and briefly by me as we sit for turkey, raise wineglasses and give thanks for our blessings.

"Look-it! I have muscles!" My four-year-old nephew Sam flexes the area that will someday be his biceps to no discernible change.

"Dude, you're huge!" I flex my biceps in return, causing a flurry of giggles to pass like hiccups through my nieces and nephews.

"Uncle Kevin has muscles again!" Laurel, my nine-year-old niece who's about two days away from discovering she's pretty, slides on purple leggings around the tiled kitchen.

My oldest sister Beth gives me a lipsticked Mona Lisa smile as we clear the mountain of dishes.

It feels like I've been forgiven for the scare I put into the children two Thanksgivings ago, before these hopeful protease times, when I slipped from "sick" to another word, a dim, gray word with no promise, no registered trademark. Back when I was dying.

I realize now my sisters must have prepped their children back then, because they did not say the things they must have been thinking. That Uncle Kevin was starting to look like a featherless bird. Like something that they'd see on the sidewalk and be confused by, something that would make their tummies ache from loneliness. I make a note to thank them, grateful for their tact. Even baby birds must have feelings, must have pride, must know on some level that they've failed the flight and worm lessons, that it wasn't supposed to end on the sidewalk, exposed, turning darker hourly by sun and atmosphere—becoming bones then stick then matter, then something less than even that.

Sam grabs my hand and pulls me toward the stairs. The rest of my nieces and nephews follow, laughing, trying to tackle me. My eleven-year-old nephew Gage roars like a monster. I roar louder. They flee and I give chase, ringing the broken grandfather clock in the hallway as I run past it to the top of the stairs and promptly miss the first step.

Dizziness has been a recent problem. I've toppled from a few Los Angeles curbs, stumbled from a friend's Honda Passport, steadied myself on a parking meter. But until now I haven't fallen anywhere, let alone down a flight of stairs crowded with small bodies. I fly forward—hands grasping for railing, boots for ground—my brain not completely comprehending this off-stage dive. It feels slow and dreamy and false, like being alive again, being here again, seeing my family when I'm vertical, when I'm working and playing and getting used to my old almost handsome face hiding the skeletal one I'd grown used to.

The stair meets my right shoulder blade and I tumble, bringing a shrieking Laurel down with me. It feels like a scribble, a mistake, like the year I got psoriasis when everyone else was covered in KS lesions. The heel of my boot hits the railing, Laurel's fingers clench my forearms, her brown hair covers my mouth. This unexpected intimate moment brings a micro flash of jet-black hair and black eyes. For a moment I am holding someone who goes by the name Will, someone with soft dark lips and cigarette smell on the tight cuffs of his vintage long-sleeved shirts. Someone who rubs my back when I say, "I'm not ready for this."

Laurel screams me back to her. I pull her closer, wrapping myself around her as we bump and fly and grunt, stopping, finally, in basement silence. Wide-eyed, the small ones stare at us in our sitting position as if we've traveled through time and landed here. Gage and Sam run back up the stairs, yelling for their parents. My niece smells of apples and bubble gum. I hold her, absorbing her sobs with repeated "I'm sorry"s, almost adding "It's not my fault" like a two-year-old before catching myself.

I hold out my hand for her to slap. "Give me the pain," I whisper, a parenting technique I learned from her father. "I'm the one who tripped"—I fake a laugh—"so I'm the one who gets the pain." Opened flat, my hand looks enormous, like a flour tortilla. My niece slaps her thin hand against mine. "Oooh!" I wince, pretending her slap hurt more than the fall. Laurel smiles in spite of herself.

In the morning, my mother and I are sent on a beverage run. The kids want juice. The moms want Diet Coke. "And wine," my workaholic middle sister Kay yells. Laurel wants a Spice Girls Band-Aid for her knee. The brothers-in-law want beer.

"Thank God for Dr. Ho," my mother says, giving me a thorough once-over in the dairy department. This is her version of a compliment.

I smile, because my mother has this habit of getting her most intimate in public, just so things won't get too sticky. "You make it sound like he's my personal physician."

"Would that he were." She picks a fuzz ball off my T-shirt as we walk toward the beer cooler. "He was *Time* magazine's Man of the Year."

"I know, Mom. I told you, remember?"

Time's Man of the Year issue hit the stands the same week I called to wish my mother a Merry Christmas. In 1996, I'd been too dying to make the trip home.

"How many?" she said, referring to my T cells, which, to her, are still the ultimate indicator of my health. I've given up trying to tell her otherwise.

"Four," I said, then shrugged as if she could see me over the phone. "I'm thinking of naming them after the Beatles."

She laughed. "That isn't funny."

John, Paul, George, and Ringo were resilient. I'll give them that. They hung on until spring when I started my combination therapy. When I had six T cells, they became the Partridge Family. Soon they were the dirty dozen . . . the fifty, nifty United States . . . ninety-nine luft balloons. After that there were too many to know personally but even now, in the middle of the crowd, I still see the Beatles, dressed in their "Please Please Me" garb: mop tops, black jackets, peg legs, slightly drunk, arms around shoulders, holding on to each other for strength.

"Watch this." My mother presses her electronic key chain as we walk through the parking lot. The side door of her brand-new van slides open automatically.

What I want to say is "Dad would have loved that." What I do say is "Impressive." I raise my eyebrows and unload the groceries.

My mom drives slowly down the right side of the unfamiliar Arkansas highway. I want to reach over and touch her, run my fingers through her hair the way she used to mine, but she's too far away. "You thirsty?" I say.

We pull into McDonald's and my mother nearly gets the van stuck in the drive-through, making it to the pickup window after three attempts. "What are you designing now?" She sets down her coffee and hands me my water, pretending not to notice as I pour my empty-stomach pills into my palm and count them.

"There's this coffee table book about heart metaphors I'm hoping to design." Of all the things I've returned to, my work is my mother's favorite topic. My dating is her least.

"Who would publish a book about heart monitors?" My mother's deaf in her right ear, from chicken pox when she was four. And I tend to mumble.

"Not monitors." I wash down my pills. "Metaphors. You know, like the heart is a highway, the heart is a spider, the heart is—"

"—a lonely hunter."

"Exactly. My rep Richard says the editors want each metaphor illustrated in edgy, unexpected ways."

My mother shakes her head. "The heart's not a spider."

"I didn't make the metaphors up, Mom. I'm just hoping to illustrate them."

"That's not a book," she says with certainty. "The heart isn't like anything else. Believe me, I know."

When I was in junior high my father died of a sudden heart attack while cleaning out our gutters. The coroner said he was dead before he hit the ground. He was fifty years old. I used to believe his soul flew to heaven as his body fell to earth. But I've never told that to my mother. Her rule is we're not allowed to bring my father up unless she does first, which she never does. Instead she drops hints like this, sprinkling the dust of my always falling father, peppering silences with him, bringing his blue windbreaker, his black-rimmed glasses, his ready smile into the van with us.

"I thought you were designing album covers," my mother says, pulling away too close to the curb.

"I am."

"Anyone I've heard of?"

"Um . . . Patti Page and Mel someone. Tormé?"

She looks at me for a second, then shakes her head. "That was a joke, right?"

"It's actually Plastilina Mosh and Jenny Please Eat."

"These are people?" She shakes her head again. "It was sad about John Denver, wasn't it?" She hums "Rocky Mountain High" and I don't stop her.

I've always loved the sound of my mother's voice, can still hear her singing "Let There Be Peace on Earth" through tears at Beth's wedding, a month after my father's funeral. She stops humming, losing the thread of the song.

"Hey Mom," I say, and she glances at me. "Let there be peace on earth . . ." Surprising myself, I begin—in a soft, low voice—to sing.

She shakes her head. "I don't sing that song anymore."

We silently pass the neither-fall-nor-winter trees and signs for Rex Spivey Realty, driving into my sister's neighborhood. My mother parks in the driveway. We inch past the biplane my brother-in-law Dave is building in his garage and enter Laney's noisy house.

It's the middle of the night. The room or me, or both of us, is at least a hundred degrees. Mary Clare's crying and I remember another joke.

"How'd you sleep?" the snoring bride asks her disheveled husband, handing him a cup of coffee.

"I slept like a baby," he says. "I woke up every two hours and cried."

It doesn't mean anything, I think, flipping on the bathroom lights, sitting on the toilet, taking no solace in the needlepointed Serenity Prayer across from me. I've always had a weak stomach, I remind myself, a teacher lecturing a slow student. According to my mother, I had constant stomach pains as an infant, and once cried nonstop as we drove across the entire state of Nebraska. "If it had been up to your sisters," she once told me, "we would have tossed you out the window."

I try to think of my life as an infant on the side of the Nebraska highway. Try to think of anything besides the pains in my abdomen, rivaling the ones I had when I was on the dreaded Norvil—a drug as resolute and severe as its name—and couldn't get out of bed. I try not to think of the seconds of dark meat and thirds of pie I inhaled. I reach over and flip on the bathroom vent to block out noise. My right leg is shaking uncontrollably, a not-so-silent protest. I refuse to let the words "side effect" enter my head. Instead I hear "sidekick." Which is what I imagine this feels like—swift, repeated kicks in the side, steel-toed boots . . . breathe, breathe, Kevin. I clench my jaw, feeling something else wind through my stomach, just below the pain. Loneliness. In my tummy. For a moment I am my nephew Sam, all emotion, crying at boo-boos. A hand towel is clenched between my teeth. I don't remember putting it there.

I want someone to make it go away, to pat me down with a damp cloth and tell me they understand. I think briefly of my ex, Arthur, who left when things got "too intense," not because he'd do these things for me, but because he absolutely wouldn't. "I gotta tell ya Kev, I didn't sign up for this," he'd say. "You know I'm an aesthete," he'd say, "and this a-i-n-t pretty." I laugh at my absurdly bad choice, filled even now with buyer's remorse, amazed that three years later Arthur still equals pain.

I hate the constant pins and needles in my hands and feet, the nausea and aches, the nonspecific kind of nonfocus I'll wake up with tomorrow. Hate my constant fear of missing a dose and thereby taking a week off my life, hate scheduling full- and empty-stomach pills, hate the zillions of pills swimming inside me like backups in an Esther Williams water ballet—Advil for aches, Odium for diarrhea, Bactrim for the fuck of it. "Hate" is not even the right word. I don't usually have the energy to muster up hate or even gratitude to science for holding me together. What I feel most is longing. I miss my old body the way I miss the seasons after a decade in L.A. Is it still called longing when it's for something you barely remember? A kick, a Jackie-Chan-flying-over-barrels-in-an-alley grand finale kick hits me, sending tears down my cheeks, stinging, then cooling them briefly.

I wipe them away wishing my hand was someone else's. Someone named Will who talks of Plato's allegory of the cave, of the Phoenix rising from ashes. Someone who claims he's a healer. Who says he's from Hawaii, swears the power of the islands sway inside him. I close my eyes, picturing black hair, black eyes, full lips. Picture telling him, "You have to leave. I thought I could do this but I can't." Will slowly gets up. I turn away, pretending not to notice how strong and fragile and absolutely beautiful he is.

"People are having side effects," my mom says the following morning, pouring herself a third cup of coffee. "There was an article in *Newsweek*."

I grunt. Although I ignore her, I admire my mother's ability to get right to the heart of the matter. "I don't pussyfoot around" is how she'd describe it, but with my health status, I intend to. What exactly is the best way to tell your mother who couldn't deal with it the first time that you're not sure but you think you just might be dying again? I feel like the boy who cried death. A faint tingle creeps through my right hand which, as it has my entire life, means only one thing: I'm about to lie to my mother.

"I guess either you have them or you don't, the side effects," she says, lingering by the toaster, pretending to search for something. It's her way of talking to me without looking at me. "How's that bump?" She touches my forehead, which I hit on the way down the stairs.

"I tripped, Mom. It happens." My hand tingles hotter, daring me to ignore it. I clear my throat. "Did I tell you I was seeing someone new?" The lie escapes. I leave out the fact that I stopped seeing someone new a month ago.

"I thought you loved your doctor."

I shake my head, more resigned than angry at this misinterpretation. "That's not what I meant."

"Oh." A light dawns. "Oh! Oh . . . okay."

I ignore her because if I don't she'll say something like "I don't know why you'd want to keep putting yourself through that" and I'll kill her for being right. My lie floats through the kitchen silence, quickly filling the room. I ignore it, flipping through my brother-in-law's *Flying* magazine, passing an article on John Denver's unfortunate crash. *Pilot error? Air conditions? Both?* the headline reads and it's too many questions for me. I turn the page and begin reading about gliders. My mother escapes into the living room and tells the army of nieces and nephews they're getting away with watching cartoons only because it's raining out.

Laney walks in with Mary Clare attached to her right breast. "The good news is it's supposed to rain all day," she announces.

I blink, confused. "What's the bad news?"

"Dave still wants to take you skeet shooting."

I pile into a huge rental van with four brothers-in-law, four nephews, an Arkansas neighbor, and his son. Until now, I'd always assumed skeet shooting was akin to snipe hunting: an imaginary activity. I find it bad form to refuse certain things: a stick of gum, dinner from a friend, a smile from a stranger. I feel the same way about skeet shooting. I may not know what it is, but I'm not missing my last chance to find out.

By the time we pull into an abandoned field, my younger nephews are asleep, their tummies Happy Meal full. I grab my wallet, assuming skeets are shot at a gallery, like a rifle range. Climbing slowly from the van, I'm surprised to see my brothers-in-law trudging through an empty field.

Laney's husband Dave holds a shotgun in each hand. His neighbor carries a silver metal tripod which, I discover minutes later, is the device that launches the skeets—clay disks painted hunter orange—into the gray and drizzling sky. I walk with Gage, my only awake nephew. "I've never held a gun in my life," I tell him, minding him to dodge cow patties. "I'm here representing peace."

"Me too." Gage nods, his attack monsters forgotten. "Can peace have two representatives?"

"Peace is in da house," I mock-rap, and he giggles.

Dave warns us to put our fingers in our ears, then demonstrates the BB-filled bullets' range by firing at a nearby pond. The pellets explode from the barrel of his gun and hail across shallow black pond water, causing dramatic ripples that quickly disappear. Fifteen minutes later, ears ringing and much less intimidated after watching my brothers-in-law miss fleets of skeets, I blurt, "Give me that gun," to the neighbor. He does, loading three bullets into the smaller, single-barrel gun before showing me how to brace it against my right shoulder for the kickback. A thin black pad of rubber is attached to the wood base. I push it against my shoulder.

"Point the barrel at the ground, Kev," Dave tells me.

"Say 'pull' when you're good and ready," his neighbor instructs from behind my shoulder. "Then shoot to kill." He laughs.

I blink. Point the shotgun at the muddy grass. "Pull," I say, calm anticipation in my voice. The skeet flies into the air. I lift the barrel, squeeze the trigger, and blow the target into a million pieces, shocked at the immediate cause and effect, thrilled by the power in my hands. My mouth hangs open. My brothers-in-law clap and holler. I smile and look down. The neighbor slaps me on the back. Behind them Gage says, "So much for peace," in a small voice.

"How'd it go?" Kay asks when we walk back in.

"Kevin's a sharpshooter," her husband says.

"Beginner's luck." I shrug, pouring a glass of water.

"What'd you think, buddy?" Beth asks her son Gage, who's still wide-eyed from his turn behind the gun.

"He's a natural, just like his uncle," his father says. "I set up a fixed target and he nailed it on the first try, didn't you, bud?"

Gage nods, thinking. "It's amazing men worked that hard to invent something just to blow each other's brains out," he finally says, setting down the skeet pieces his dad made him gather for a souvenir.

I raise my eyebrows.

"He's good at math too," his father whispers.

"Someone called for you," Beth tells me as the men leave the room. "He sounded quiet, but cute. I tried to get a name but he said he'd call back." She registers my reaction, exchanging a glance with Kay.

"Told you." Kay pulls up a chair, smiling back at Beth.

"Told her what?" I narrow my eyes.

"Just spill." Kay sips her wine.

"You owe us," Beth says.

When they were in high school, I memorized my older sisters' yearbooks and pumped them shamelessly for details on their boyfriends. They pretended to hate it, but I knew that they, like me right now, loved the attention. Too bad it has to end. "You guys remember Elizabeth Hepburn don't you?" I ask.

"Wasn't she your imaginary college girlfriend?" Kay asks.

"Whose picture you got from *Seventeen* magazine?" Beth adds.

"And who mysteriously moved to Guam the day before I visited?" Laney comes in. This time Mary Clare's attached to her left nipple.

I take a sip of water and swallow. "This new guy's kind of like that."

"You made him up?" Kay asks in a disbelieving high-pitched tone.

"Where'd you get his picture? The Internet?" Beth says.

"Funny," I say. "His name's Will." I cough. "He's a real person."

"That's always helpful in a relationship," Kay says.

"It was." I nod.

"Was?" Beth asks gently.

"I ended it about a month ago."

"So why couldn't you just tell Mom that?" Laney shakes her head in disbelief.

"Because I wanted her to treat me like a person instead of a patient, okay Laney?"

"Okay." Laney backs away. "Jesus." She cradles Mary Clare, checking to see if my barrage has somehow hurt her.

I look down, red-faced, not completely sure why I've just yelled at my sister.

Beth coughs. Kay downs her wine. Laney studies Mary Clare's breast-feeding and says, "I didn't think she was ever gonna get the hang of it, but now she's like a little vacuum."

My room still feels warm, but this time it's a good warm. I turn on the computer and call up a Quark document. Images from the Jenny

Please Eat CD appear on my screen: an illustration of a swimsuit-clad Aryan-looking couple from the fifties locked in a glorious kiss, a close-up of eyes behind old-style pilot's goggles, a pencil sketch of a bunny. "Nothing too literal," my rep Richard told me when I asked what the band was looking for. "Nothing that actually means anything." "My kind of project," I told him.

No longer wearing Mary Clare, Laney stops in. She watches over my shoulder, lightly rubbing my back. "You got a PowerBook?"

"It used to be my friend Graham's."

"That was kind of him."

"No, he died. Remember?"

"Jesus." She looks away. "I can't say anything right, can I?" She walks downstairs.

Graham was a friend from art school, a fellow designer. A month after the memorial service, his mother called to tell me he'd willed me his computer. His hard drive was called Graham's Brain and I laughed when I opened it because it was nearly empty. He'd bought the PowerBook a few months before he died. I tried to talk him out of it, but Graham was convinced he was going to Northwestern in the fall for grad school.

After that he was convinced he had dropped out and was doing the ski bum thing in Vail for a year. Then he was convinced the guy in the hospital bed next to him was hiding a dog named Thiapen beneath his bed. Then Graham told me he had directed the movie *The Indian in the Cupboard* and was redesigning Elizabeth Taylor's kitchen. For a week he thought Spielberg was coming in for a meeting and was freaked out because he couldn't find the khakis he was convinced were on a shelf above his head. For two weeks he was certain I had stolen half of a sandwich from him and would speak of nothing else every time I visited. He started calling me Fat Fat Teddy, a boy, according to his mother, Graham had beaten up in grade school. Then he stopped talking. On a Monday afternoon I brought a grape Gatorade and watched his sister spoon-feed it to him as if it was the elixir that would bring him back. By Wednesday morning he was gone.

There is one Word file in Graham's Brain. It's called *Burn Baby Burn* and I've taken to opening it, my daily secret. I can see him writing it, convinced his list was poetry, certain he had a reading with Maya Angelou, angry his khakis still hadn't turned up. Downstairs Kay pours juice for Sam. "Last glass till lunch, bucko," she says. Sam slurps from his juice cup. I open the file, still slightly spooked when Graham's full name appears on the software. Seconds later I am reading his mind.

Malibu fires.
Fevers.
Burn barrel.
Fireplace, kerosene.
Caterpillar bonfire.
Popping milk cartons.
Leaves in woods.
Kid who burnt down neighbors' house.
Blowtorch at 4th of July.
Dad burning hand at golf course.
Ovens at Auschwitz.
Which way to die?
Burn or freeze?

He wrote it one month before he died. More than anything else it makes how sick I was seem real again. More than anything else, it scares me the way the *If I should die before I wake* part of the *Now I lay me down to sleep* prayer used to when I was Sam's age. I thought Graham and I would fall into the light or the dark or the whatever together but someone combined three hopeless treatments, invented hope, and brought me back. Back to rent payments and deadlines and a sister who is still awkward around her gay brother. Back to a mother I still lie to, back to dreaming of places I've never been and all the things I used to make fun of in people's personal ads—long walks, movies, sunsets—plus little things, the smiling homeless lady at Pic 'N' Save, the days I feel almost enough like my old self to forget that I'm not, the night I finally got up the nerve to kiss Will, leaning in with my eyes closed, hoping I'd find the right spot.

"Kevin!" Kay yells up. "You got a phone call."

My heart pounds as I run down the stairs, thrilled and yet unfazed that somehow Will's found me, though I never gave him the number.

"It's him," Kay whispers hopefully, handing me the phone.

"Hey you!" I say with a smile, out of breath.

"Hey yourself. How's the family?"

"Great . . ." My smile fades. Because it isn't Will. It's Richard, my rep. "How are things with you, Richard?"

"Not bad. Listen, I've got good news and bad news."

"Of course you do." I shake my head. "Let's hear the bad."

"The heart metaphor people want to see comps on Monday."

"I got the book?"

"That would be the good news."

On our third and final date, even though we're not dating, because I can't and he knows this, Will and I go to the Museum of Tolerance. We walk through the exhibits pressed close, as if chemically connected. We hold hands, leaning on each other as we observe the prejudices-through-advertising exhibit: *ancient Chinese secret, huh?* We sing along to the Frito Bandito theme song. The rest of our tour group do their best to remain open to us—living, breathing tolerance exhibit that we are.

That night I tell him everything. I show him a picture taken while I was in the hospital. I'm thirty pounds lighter. I'm smiling. A half-empty grape Gatorade rests on the dinner tray. That night, we stare at the pattern the star-shaped metal candleholder casts over my wooden floor. Will rubs the pressure points between my thumb and index finger. A tear falls from my face and is immediately absorbed by the bedsheet. I tell him I can't do this anymore. I've never been the love 'em and leave 'em type, I explain. And I won't let him do either to me. This time he believes me.

On Sunday I take a walk with my mother, stretching my legs before my flight.

"Please let's order pizza for lunch," she says when we're out of earshot. "If I eat one more turkey sandwich I'm going to grow feathers."

I smile. It's a good kind of cold out. It smells of damp leaves and football games. My mother keeps a brisk pace.

"Too fast for you?" she asks, and I shake my head.

"I feel good today . . ." I smile at her without looking at her. A neighbor's yellow Labrador follows us with a large stick in its mouth.

"But you're having side effects," she finishes my thought, eyes frozen on the road.

I nod.

We keep walking, passing a bearded man lighting a barbecue. "Tell me about this new person," my mom finally says.

"That was a lie."

"No it wasn't." She shakes her head. "I see it in your eyes."

I swallow nervously. "His name is Will."

"Same as your father."

"He reminds me a little of Dad."

"Is that good?"

"He's quiet and kind and patient."

She nods. "Yes he was," she whispers.

I toss the stick set at my feet into the woods. The dog scampers off after it.

"How does he feel about losing you?" My mother looks at me with open eyes.

"Probably the same way you feel about losing me." I reach out and run my fingers through her short salt-and-pepper hair.

She closes her eyes and stops walking.

We stay like that in the middle of the street, me massaging my mother's head, the yellow Labrador staring up at us with steam rising from its tongue, nudging a dirty stick closer to our feet.

"Your father always knew about you." My mother speaks softly, still not moving. "He saw it in everything you drew," she says, more to herself than to me. "He saw it when I wouldn't . . ." She reaches her hand up, placing it over mine.

There are moments in your life you know better than to ruin by speaking.

"He was worried the world would break your heart." She shakes her head, finally opening her large brown eyes and looking into mine. "But I told him you wouldn't let it."

". . . Then I got into medical sales." The blond woman next to me on the plane smiles, looking up from her laptop. "Antibiotics . . . antivirals. What can I say? It's a growth industry."

I smile because I don't know whether to kiss her or kill her. "Do you sell protease inhibitors?"

"*Do* I!" She laughs. "Isn't tease a funny name for a drug?" She sips the drink she paid four dollars for. "My ninth-grade boyfriend called me the same thing!" She cackles, then whispers "I wore my cheerleading skirt shorter than the other girls . . . but never delivered." She cocks a brow. "God, those were the days." She looks past me at the white clouds slipping over the wing. "How about you? What's do you do?" She giggles at her slipup.

"I'm a graphic designer."

"What's do you design?" She flubs on purpose, flirting.

"Right now I'm doing a coffee table book on heart metaphors. You know, the heart is a chocolate-covered cherry, the heart is a box of chocolates. My job is to illustrate them in funky ways."

"Wow." She raises her wide eyebrows. "That actually sounds really great."

I smile. "It's coming out Valentine's Day. My agent says it's 'the perfect present for those with or without that special someone.'" I hate finger quotes but make them anyway. "If you think of any that don't have chocolate in them, let me know," I tell her. "I can add some if I want."

"Okay," she nods in a thinking way, turns back to her IBM.

I sneak pills from my backpack and swallow them with a quick drink of water. I'm supposed to draw the heart is an ATM machine but don't feel like it. Instead, I open the Jenny Please Eat file, take the sketch of the bunny and put the airplane goggles over its eyes. I copy it three times. I mock a metal tripod flinging a large wet heart across a wide-open field. I put rifles in the bunny's paws. It looks as if they're poised to shoot the heart. *The heart is a target,* I type at the top of the screen. I look back out the window.

The heart, like the only skeet I've ever shot, gets broken into a million pieces, picked up as souvenirs that can never again be rearranged in quite the same way. The heart, in calm anticipation, gets pulled. By family . . . by lovers . . . by dreams. "I'm here representing peace," the heart says, then proceeds to disrupt it in every possible way.

"What about the heart is a flight attendant?" The woman reapplies her lipstick. "You know, like flying all over the place, trying to keep everyone happy."

"Good one." I smile, picturing myself in a muddy field with my three brothers-in-law. I see us as we must have looked to the cars on the highway, silhouetted good ol' boys passing the time. I drag the swimsuit couple from the fifties onto a new document and place a bullet between their kiss, pressing the tip into his lip, drawing a small trickle of blood. *The heart is a bullet,* I type atop the page.

Outside, the wing cuts through the clouds, it's blinking light nearly obscured.

My heart is a bullet, nestled safely in childhood, buffered by family and friends, warm meals and memories, until it flies forward, faster than my ability to understand it, leading to places and people I never imagined, into and out of relationships I still haven't figured out, exploding when it reaches its target.

"Got one!" The woman elbows me. "The heart is a horror movie!"

I take a sip of water and swallow. "I take it you're single."

"Oh yeah." She nods. "And you?"

I shrug. "Not sure."

"Say no more." She nods, then motions to my screen. "You know, that's gonna be an awfully long book."

"Why do you say that?"

"Because the heart's not like anything else—"

"You sound like my mother."

"—it's like everything else. I mean, everything could be a heart metaphor. This airplane . . . this barf bag . . . this computer, they're all heart metaphors."

I can't explain Will's eyes when I see him waiting for me at the terminal. Old and new at the same time. Deep. He holds me. I feel like a cartoon character pushed off a cliff, headed for a certain death, who suddenly bounces off an awning and lands in a room filled with candy. It's too much to process. So I don't. I press my nose to Will's neck and smell him. Breathe him in. He massages the pressure point at the base of my neck.

"I'm so glad you came," I say when I can talk.

"I'm so glad you called," he whispers.

I feel tears well beneath my closed lids. Then I feel something else: the tip of Will's tongue, licking them away.

I open my eyes.

"Ahh." He licks his lips as if sampling wine. "You're happy," he says.

"How can you be so sure?" I tease.

"I can taste it." He takes my backpack from me as we leave the crowded terminal. "See . . . sad tears you let fall. But happy ones you have to capture."

I raise my eyebrows. "Where in the hell did you learn that?"

"Ancient Chinese secret," he says, bringing a whisper finger to his lips.

We walk down the sterile hallway of the L.A. airport. Out the window a plane escapes down the runway, growing smaller as it strains for flight. We pass a sad-eyed woman dressed in Salvation Army white and I share a smile with her, pretending I can't hear the pills in my backpack jangling in time to Will's steps.

1984

LAWRENCE REILLY

I've been going out every night this summer. And even though I'm a sixteen-year-old guy, painfully aware that there's no danger to be found on the streets of Carlisle, NJ, I still have to be home by eleven on weeknights and twelve on the weekends. It's embarrassing; Linda and Stephanie are both older than me, they both drive and talk non-stop about how next year they'll be seniors and then next fall they'll be out of here, even though they don't know where they'll be.

They don't need any more reminders of my youth. And it always seems like all the good stuff happens after midnight, all the stuff everyone endlessly talks about for the next few weeks, all the drugs, all the sex.

But I obey my parents and come home, hating them and hating myself. And I'm always too wound up for sleep. They can make me come home, but they can't make me sleep. I watch MTV for the rest of the night. I usually fall asleep around four, in front of the television, dreaming of dancing, singing, doing wild things.

This summer the videos have gotten much better. "Girls Just Wanna Have Fun" shows Cyndi Lauper bopping around, having a great time while her gross parents scream at her. She doesn't care and has a huge party right in her bedroom. I love Madonna too: she's tough and out for a good time, but even sexier than Cyndi. I love the video where this rich guy is all over Madonna. She likes him a little, but he gets pissed off when she spray-paints his Porsche.

It bugs me that most girls in the videos are having so much fun, while all the guys are getting pissed off or just acting stupid, but every now and then I'll see the video by Roxy Music that has a guy wearing a white linen suit and singing in a misty castle. It makes me want to dress up and smoke and do something chic and dramatic, but I don't get much of a chance to do that until late July, when Jeremy Scott's parents have a party at the country club.

Jeremy goes to private school, so I don't know him very well, but somehow Linda and Stephanie do and he's come out with us a few nights this summer. We seem to get along and I'm flattered that he's invited me to this adult party. Linda and Stephanie get to go to the dinner beforehand. I think Jeremy wants to go out with either one of them, but he's not that cute. He's a lot of fun, but a little too overfed-and-spoiled-looking.

I'm told to show up after nine, wearing a jacket and tie. I haven't worn either in years and nothing fits me anymore. But my mom is excited I've been invited to the country club and eager to help. She finds a white linen blazer my dad used to wear. Put together with my dark, pleated pants and skinny tie, it actually looks pretty cool. Not quite Roxy Music, but maybe Duran Duran on a good day.

Then we start fighting because she insists I come home by midnight. As charming and adult as I feel all dressed up, I still have a curfew.

While I'm putting gel in my hair, she offers to drive me over to the club. The sun is setting and I almost forget how pissed I am.

A guy in the lobby directs me downstairs and I follow the sound of music down a long hallway. The party's in a couple of large rooms with a live band, a dance floor, a bar, and a bunch of tables where I guess everyone had dinner.

The place is filled with people, but right away Linda comes toward me in a short blue dress that shows her tan arms and legs. Linda's Italian and sometimes tough, like Madonna. Tonight she looks beautiful. She takes my hand and kisses me on the cheek.

"Jimmy, you look so handsome. Come with me," she says, still holding my hand, leading me back out into the hall.

"But what about the party?" I ask.

"The real party's in here, baby," she says, taking me into the ladies' room. At first I'm afraid she's just going to molest me after I went to all this trouble to get dressed up. Nothing's happened between us since she kissed me last week, but I've caught her giving me funny looks, really serious, like she's studying me or something. I'm relieved to find that the large, mirrored room also contains Stephanie, Jeremy, and Steven McConnell.

"Hi guys," I say.

"Hi Jimmy," says Stephanie. "You look so cute."

She also gives me a kiss on the cheek. Her blond hair is pulled back and she's wearing perfume.

Jeremy says hi and shakes my hand. We're all acting so grown-up tonight. Jeremy's clothes look expensive, probably Polo, and remind me I'm wearing old stuff of Dad's, but it's his parents' party: of course they bought him new things to wear. And I'm cuter.

Steve McConnell says hello and gives me one of those looks that make all thoughts leave my mind. He's got on duck pants, his thigh muscles straining through the heavy white material, and no tie, just tan, hairy chest.

Steve's the tennis pro. Linda and Stephanie have been taking lessons from him all summer. They call him "the Pervert" because of the way he pats their butts and brushes their breasts while teaching them to serve. They pretend to think he's gross, but I can tell they're getting obsessed. I'm pretty sure the only reason Linda kissed me last week was because Steve happened to be watching. Watching me, actually, or at least that's the way it seemed.

"Does Jimmy like the things we like?" Steve asks Linda.

"I don't know," says Linda, giving me the serious, studying look that is not too different from Steve's. "You'll have to ask him yourself."

"Do you like the fast stuff, boy?" he asks me, showing me a vial of white powder.

"Cocaine?" I ask.

"Why . . . yes," he says, and everyone laughs although nothing's really funny.

"Sure, I guess," I say, trying to think up a story about having done it before, but Linda and Stephanie would know I was lying.

"Have some, we've already done a bunch," says Steve, coming very close to me in the crowded bathroom. I can smell his cologne and try not to stare at his ginger chest hairs. My dick gets hard as he shakes a little pile of the coke onto the corner of a golden credit card and holds it under my nose.

"Close off one nostril and take a big sniff."

I do what he says and the stuff flies up my nose.

"Good boy," he says, patting my back.

"I want to be a good boy too," says Jeremy, peeking over Stephanie's shoulder. He's got his arms around her waist and acting very frisky. She seems to be allowing it.

"Me too," cries Stephanie. "I want to be a good boy too."

Everyone gets another blast, then Steve lights a cigarette and Linda and Stephanie reapply their makeup.

Linda sees me watching her in the mirror.

"Do you want some too, Jimmy?" she asks, holding out her mascara brush.

"Get away," I tell her.

"Come on," she says. "Let me put a little on you. You'll look like Adam Ant. Guys in eye makeup are so hot."

"Yeah, I'm sure Jeremy's parents would think so," I tell her.

"They would," says Jeremy. "They're totally cool."

"Get away," I tell her as she advances toward me.

"Then somewhere no one can see," she says, and before I can stop her, she's pulling my shirt out of my pants and lifting it up.

"We'll make these stomach hairs a little darker," she says, laughing maniacally. "God, you are so tan. Look at this, Steven, he may be tanner than you."

I am proud of my tan and obediently hold up my shirt while Linda changes all my little blond hairs into black ones.

"No way he's tanner than me," says Steve, yanking up his own shirt and showing us his dark stomach, rippling with muscles and obscenely covered with black hair I'm dying to feel.

"Yeah, but look at Jimmy's tan line," says Linda, putting her thumb in my pants and pulling them down until he can see the white part of my skin that's never been exposed before. "He's had a much longer way to go."

Steve tugs his own pants down a little to reveal an equally white line and even more muscles angling down further, drawing me in deeper. His tan line is low and I can see a few curly pubes. He doesn't care at all. I try to imagine him in a bathing suit. It must be a little one.

Finally we go in to the party. The band's murdering a song by the Pointer Sisters that was already bad enough, but a lot of people are dancing. Jeremy has an older sister and brother and I think some of their friends must be here too. I can't tell which people are friends of which Scott family member. So many people are drunk and even some of the obviously old are sweating, shouting, and dancing around in ways I've never seen any parents act.

The coke's made me feel good, not really wasted, just warm and excited. Jeremy, Linda, and Stephanie must already be drunk because they start throwing themselves around the dance floor like everybody else.

Jeremy takes me over to the bar and orders us orange juice, with vodka, without any problem from the bartender. Then his parents come by.

"Mom, Dad, this is Jimmy Sweeney," he says. I wonder if I should hide my drink, but Jeremy's sipping his in plain sight. Maybe his parents think it's just orange juice. Then Stephanie comes up to the bar.

"Hello," she says, eyeing our drinks. "Yum, are those screwdrivers? Could I get one too?"

And Jeremy orders one for her too. His parents are smiling at us as if it's all perfectly normal. Then Stephanie lights a cigarette, which Mrs. Scott notices immediately.

"Honey," she says. "Could I bum one of those off you? I stopped years ago, but at times like these, I think it's best not to resist."

Jeremy was not lying when he said his parents were cool. They probably wouldn't have cared if I'd let Linda put eye makeup on. God knows, Mrs. Scott is wearing a whole tube herself. I bet Jeremy never has to worry about a curfew either.

"I love your haircut, Mrs. Scott," says Stephanie.

"You do?" asks Mrs. Scott. Her hair is black and glossy and very short. She's wearing big rings that sparkle as she runs her hands through her hair. "I just got it cut yesterday. It's so short, I'm still a little nervous about it."

"It's great," says Stephanie. "Don't you think so, Jimmy?"

"Yes," I tell her. "Very dramatic."

I'm not lying, she does look very glamorous and well groomed. Mostly I love the fact that she actually cares what we think about her.

"You're sweet," says Mrs. Scott. "Do you go to school with Jeremy?"

"No," I tell her. "I go to Carlisle High with Linda and Stephanie."

"Do you mind it very much?" she asks. "We were too worried to send Jeremy there. It seemed a little rough."

"It is, a little," I admit to her. "But there are a lot of fine people there."

Now that I haven't been there for over a month, I can say things like that. I love that the only things this woman knows about me is what she's seeing and hearing now. I love that she isn't a friend of my mother's or that she doesn't know only a few months ago I was a social reject.

A few friends of my parents are here and they're all very nice to me, obviously impressed that I'm here with them. I run into Mrs. Brennan, who used to be an art teacher when I was in grammar school.

"Jimmy, you always were one of my favorites," she tells me, squeezing me into her.

"Really?" I ask her. "But there were so many other kids who did the most amazing work, like Kenny Harrington. I always felt like such a failure."

"Kenny Harrington was such a kiss-ass," she exclaims. It's bizarre hearing those words come from her mouth. "I wanted to say 'Lighten up, kid, it's only art class for God's sake!' "

She laughs very hard at this and I realize she's a little wasted.

"You're not there anymore, are you?" I ask her.

"No way," she says and laughs very hard again. "It was fun for a while, but I got sick of dealing with Mr. Peterson. He was drunk half the time and didn't know what he was doing with that place."

"Mr. Peterson used to drink?" I ask her. I can't believe it. He was the principal, stuffy and ancient.

"All the time, " she says. "I used to knock back a few with him from time to time, you know, after a hard day with the little brats, but he was out of control. He'd be drinking in the middle of the day, and come into my classroom reeking of booze."

I search the room for Linda or Stephanie. I'm dying to tell them, but I want to hear what else this woman has to say.

"Listen to me," she giggles. "Cornering you and talking your ear off when you should be dancing with your friends."

"No, I love it," I tell her. "I'm the same way tonight, I can't stop talking. It must be—"

I stop just in time. I can't believe I almost told my fifth-grade art teacher I was on coke.

"What, dear?" she asks, leaning in closer like she missed what I said.

"Just the whole mood of the party, I guess," I tell her. For a second there, I thought she was on coke too. My mind is reeling at the absurdity of it. I came so close to saying it, and it would have wrecked everything. Instantly, I'd have become nothing more than a bad little boy and she'd be the adult who would have had to put me back in my place.

I actually like having to keep the coke a secret among the five of us. I like that we have to hide in the bathroom together and then reemerge pretending we're naturally so funny and excited and have so much to say. It's a big joke on the rest of the guests.

At high school parties, all the drinking and drugs are disgustingly obvious. Everyone's obsessed with getting some and makes a big deal out of doing them, but then they later blame the beer or the pot, pretending that's what made them do the things they were dying to do anyway.

Steve comes up and joins us.

"I hate to break up this charming teacher/student reunion," he says. "But the two of you are being very antisocial."

"No, you're not disturbing us," Mrs. Brennan giggles. "I've just been drunkenly talking this poor boy's ear off."

"Oh I doubt that, Nancy," says Steve, leaning closer into her, loudly whispering so I can still hear. "You can't be ignorant of the number of schoolboy crushes you caused."

"Steven McConnell," she says, beaming, "you are too, too much. The lies you tell!"

"I'm serious. . . . Can't you just imagine the number of first erections that occurred under those art tables? Perhaps it was partially that rush of creative juices, but one can't deny that the teacher herself had something to do with them—young James here has probably dreamed for years of this moment—when the two of you can finally meet as equals, both adults now, both a little drunk . . ."

I'm mortified at just how far Steve can push it. It's cruel and, of course, completely untrue. I'm speechless, but it doesn't matter, because Mrs. Brennan is no longer paying the least bit of attention to me. I go get another drink.

Later, Jeremy is off dancing with Stephanie and Linda and I'm alone with Steve.

"Can we do some more coke?" I ask him.

"So you like this stuff, huh?" he says, throwing his arm around me.

I look into his eyes and nod.

"But it wouldn't be fair to the others if you and I went off alone to the men's room and did some ourselves, would it?" he says. That's exactly why I want to do some more, but I don't tell him that. He's been totally reveling in the power his coke gives him. He made Linda and Stephanie each kiss him last time they wanted some. In the back of my mind I guess I'm hoping he'll ask something similar of me.

"I don't think they'd care," I say, trying to stay relaxed and casual about his arm that's enfolded me.

"Well okay," he says. "Since you're such a sweet kid."

We go into the men's room together. I'm sick with anticipation, but I manage to do some more coke. When we finish, neither of us moves. Steve leans back against the sink and stares at me with his arms folded and his legs slightly spread. Staring. Smirking.

I want to kiss him, or grab him and hold on, but I can't help feeling the way I did when I almost told Mrs. Brennan about the coke. I feel like I'm assuming way too much and if I act on this assumption, the whole scenario will come apart and I'll be just a stupid kid again.

But I am a stupid kid anyway, one who's done too much coke and drunk too much vodka, giggling and swaying around the bathroom while Steven calmly watches.

"Pervert," I say, saliva flying as the word bursts out of me.

"Why do you say that?" asks Steven, pretending to be hurt.

"I know all about you," I tell him, wagging a finger in his face.

"Takes one to know one, I guess," he says.

I just snort and roll my eyes.

He comes a little closer to me and speaks in soft, gentle tones.

"You may think you know all about me," he says. "But I know a few things about you too. I've been talking to your friends, they've told me about you."

"What?" I say, pushing away from him. "They lie. They don't know anything about me."

"Maybe they do, maybe they don't," says Steve, turning away to wash his hands in the sink. "Maybe they know more about you than you do."

We leave the bathroom and I realize I've blown it. The night is over. It's eleven-thirty and I have to be home in half an hour. But I'm relieved, glad to be going. I'll leave right now and walk home, trying to relax myself.

The dullness of this routine suddenly washes over me. This night had so much promise. Is this the way it's always going to be? Everything almost happening to me, but not happening, and then I walk home and relax? The party's not over for anyone else. The band's still playing, people are dancing, and I still want to be a part of it. I'm filled with energy, why should I use it to run away?

"I have to go," I tell them.

"No," says Stephanie. "You just got here."

"Come on, guy, stay," says Jeremy. "It'll be going on for at least a couple more hours. My parents have the place till two."

"I have a curfew," I say. "My parents will kill me if I'm late."

"Fuck it," says Linda. "What can they do? Kill you? They know where you are and that Mr. and Mrs. Scott are here. I'll drive you home later, it's no big deal. Call them and tell them you'll be a little late."

The thought of trying this approach with my parents is ridiculous, but for a moment I consider it. But I'd have to act sober and if I were really sober, I'd never dare call them.

"It's simple," says Steven. "Go home now, say good night to your parents, then wait about ten minutes and leave. I used to do it all the time. My parents never found out."

I'm flattered that even Steven wants me to stay. And it really could work.

"I'll try it out," I tell them. "Jeremy, where are your parents? I want to thank them."

"Oh no," says Jeremy. "If you're coming back, you don't have to say goodbye to them yet."

I walk myself home, calming a little. I say good night to my parents, slowly, innocently, while the inside of me races with the lies, the cocaine, Steven McConnell, and the rest of my night with him.

I keep on my clothes, even my jacket and tie, but get into bed. I close my eyes to see if I actually could sleep if that's what I decide I want. I can't. I open my eyes. I open my window and look out. I'm on the second floor, but the roof of the garage is right out the window and it'd be easy to climb out onto it and then jump the single story to the ground. It'd be easier to go downstairs and leave through the front door, but it seems more adventurous this way—the way it's done in all the videos and movies about fun, wild kids. Somehow I know that it's through this window that my night, my future, and my freedom lie.

I leave the window open and lie down a little, knowing I won't fall asleep. I sink into the bed while breezes from the outside blow over me. Just when I'm convinced I will stay at home and sleep, I find myself sliding out the window and into the dark night.

Slowly I walk back to the country club, savoring my freedom, this new world where I alone exist. I jump up and down in the empty street. I run the first few blocks. I start smoking cigarettes nonstop. I think the main reason I couldn't stay in bed is because I needed to smoke more cigarettes.

When I reach the club it's later than I thought. Cars are driving away. A couple I don't know are yelling at each other in the parking lot. Both of them are too drunk to drive and each blames the other.

"You're a fool!" the woman screams.

Downstairs the band has stopped playing and the lights are all on. Mr. and Mrs. Scott are saying goodbye to the last of their guests. Mrs. Scott takes my hand.

"Thank you so much for coming," she says. "It was nice meeting Jeremy's friends."

I contemplate leaving, letting it all end there. Then I see Stephanie and Jeremy by the bar. Jeremy's barely standing up, leaning heavily on Stephanie's back. She calls me over.

"Go out by the pool," she tells me. "Linda and Steve are hanging out there."

"Are you sure they want me with them?" I ask her. Maybe Steve is Linda's next conquest after all.

"Yes," says Stephanie. "Linda told me to tell you to go out there when you came back. She was sure you'd come back. I thought you were done for.

"I'm wrecked," she says. "Jeremy's got some of his mom's Valium. I'm going to take some and go home and try to sleep. I know, I'm a drag. Do you want some?"

I know pills and alcohol and coke do not mix. They create vegetables and I want to tell Stephanie not to take the pills, but I don't say anything. I want to tell her not to leave; I need her silly superficiality. I don't know if I can withstand the serious stares of Linda and Steven together. I want to ask her to drive me home, but she'll think I'm crazy for walking all this way and then just going back.

I say good night and walk out by the pool. Tiny lights are on in the pool and the bushes around it. The blue underwater glow swirls around everything like a dream. Linda's sitting in a chair, smoking and staring. Steven's lying back on a lounge. His jacket is off and his shirt is open. No one's talking and I approach them cautiously.

"Good," says Linda. "I knew you'd come back. Now we can play Steven's game."

"What's the game?" I ask.

"You put a line of coke anywhere on your body," says Steven. "And then someone else has to snort it off you."

"Sounds like a blast," I say.

"Not too perverted for you?" he asks.

"No."

"Well then you go first," he says, tossing me his vial.

I roll up my sleeve and tap a line out onto my forearm.

"What a wild man," says Steve, gripping my arm and quickly sniffing it clean. When he's finished, he licks the dust off. His tongue is hot and wet on my arm.

"My turn," he says, lying back and tapping a line out onto his dark chest, starting above a patch of hair and ending just below his Adam's apple.

"Who's up for it?" he asks, closing his eyes.

Linda looks at me and I look away. She goes over and snorts his chest, then licks her way up his neck. Then they start kissing. For a minute I stare, not really believing. I look away, back toward the clubhouse. The lights are out downstairs. Everyone's gone home.

When I look back, they've stopped. They're both looking at me. Linda's still sitting on the edge of Steve's chair and leaning into him.

"Do you think Linda's hot, Jimmy?" asks Steve, stroking her hair.

I want to laugh, it's such a rude question to ask right in front of her. I expect her to be pissed, or at least pretend to be pissed, but she just stares at me, like she really wants to know. It's pathetic.

"Yeah," I say.

"So how come the two of you never got together?" he asks.

"I don't know."

"Well I'd love to see you do some coke off her tits," he says. "Do you want to?"

"No."

"Do you want to suck some off my cock?" he asks.

"I don't want any more coke," I tell him. "I've already had too much."

"You're no fun," he says. "It's a party, remember? All you have to do is choose."

"If you don't choose, you'll never have any fun," says Linda. "You want to have fun, don't you, Jimmy?"

"Yeah, I guess so." I don't want to have any more fun and I never want to have sex.

"Why can't you choose?" asks Linda. "Don't you like me? Don't you think I'm hot?"

"I do," I say. "But . . . I don't know . . ."

"Or do you want Steven?" she asks. "He's a cute guy, I know. I wouldn't blame you if you wanted him."

"I don't," I say. I do, but not here.

"Maybe he doesn't want to choose," says Steven. "And why should he? There's no reason why any of us should have to choose and leave someone out."

"You don't want to leave anyone out?" asks Linda. "Is that it?"

"I'll be right back," I say.

I don't know why I said that, why I said anything. I don't owe them any explanations. I don't know why I don't go home except that I've done too much coke and I don't know what's going to happen to me. I don't think I'm going to throw up or pass out or have a heart attack, but sweat is pouring down my face and heat is radiating out of me. I can see the steam.

I go back inside, cross the dark dance floor, and go behind the bar to get some water. I plunge my hands into the leftover ice and the cold feels good. I open my shirt and rub pieces over my chest. I drop to my knees and lay my entire head on the bed of ice, slowly sinking into it as it melts.

I hear footsteps on the dance floor and I stand up, soaking wet, but cool now and a little more in control.

It's Linda.

"Jimmy," she says. "I'm sorry. I'm so wasted and—all this coke—it's turned me into a monster."

"You're not a monster," I tell her, but she does look kind of scary: sweaty, her eyes smeared with black makeup.

"No," she says. "I really am a monster. Before you came outside, I was telling Steven I thought I was plain evil and he was telling me that to be a good person I should do all the bad things I could think of and get them all out of my system and then maybe I could be good. Does that make any sense to you?"

I can't remember ever seeing Linda this wasted. She looks battered, but beautiful, and I wish I could hug her and hold her, but I can't now, not with Steven McConnell waiting to see it all.

"We should go home," I say. "But I don't think you should drive."

"I know," she says. "Steven already said he'd drive us home. I'll pick up my car in the morning. My father won't care, he knows all about these country club parties."

She walks back outside to get Steve.

Steve doesn't seem drunk at all and he drives fine. Linda's lying in the back seat, silent. Steve already knows how to get to our street. I tell him when we get to my house, but he doesn't say anything and drives further down the street to drop Linda off first.

I start getting all hot again and my dick gets hard and my thoughts and words form very slowly. I barely say good night to Linda but I don't think she notices. Steve drives back up to my house and parks a little before our driveway, hidden by a big fir tree on our neighbor's lawn.

He turns off the car and we sit in silence. I don't leave, he doesn't look at me. I'm trying not to shake, but my whole body shudders like I'm cold, but I'm very hot. I stare out the window and imagine Linda sneaking back up the street and spying on us. I know that's what I would do if she were in my place, but she's probably passed out in her bed by now, and even if she weren't, she'd never do a dumb thing like that.

Why am I here instead of Linda? Steve was supposed to be her next conquest, not mine. Who do I think I am, anyway?

My right hand goes to open the car door, but at the same time, my left hand has moved onto the thick white pants covering Steve's knee.

I leave my hand there for a second, then Steve moves it to his crotch. His dick is hard.

He unbuttons his pants and unzips his fly. He pulls down his underwear and takes out his dick and balls. He's big and hard. I take it in my hand.

He looks over at me and nods his head downward. He knows what I want to do. He puts his arm around me and I think he may grab my head and kiss me, but the hand is on my back and he's pressing me down with just the slightest pressure.

"Go for it," he whispers, and I lean over and put my mouth on his dick. I start moving up and down on it and he lets out a deep sigh, then runs his hands through my hair and presses me farther down. I come up, then take a little bit more each time until it's hitting the back of my throat. I gag a little. His dick is warm and thick and smells like he does, only stronger. And I keep wanting to gag.

"Oh, yeah, man," says Steve, breathing harder. It's great making him feel this way.

But, I don't know, after a while it gets kind of boring. For some reason I've got my eyes closed. I keep thinking I should open them. I should memorize every detail, finally getting to do what I've been dying for all these years. But I keep my eyes closed and keep thinking how different it is from when Chris and I used to do it.

I mean, it's not the first time I've done this. When I was a kid, Chris was my best friend and we tried sucking each other after seeing it in one of his dad's porno mags, but it was a completely different thing.

For one thing, Steve is a lot bigger and my mouth is getting cramped. And when Chris and I did it, we stopped whenever we felt like it. We were too young for any kind of dramatic finale, if you know what I mean. But Steve's a grown man and I know what's going to happen if I keep doing what I'm doing and it makes me a little nervous.

He keeps holding on to my head and now he's thrusting his butt off the seat to really go deep into me.

"Yeah! Oh yeah!" he starts yelling, and it sounds really loud to me. Maybe Linda's passed out down the street, but my parents are only a few yards away and they haven't been drinking at all tonight.

Then it happens. Steve shoots his load in my mouth, holding me way down on him so some of it spills down into his lap, but most goes down my throat and I have to swallow it.

I know what sperm tastes like from myself, but I've never swallowed so much of it before, and never when it was still so hot. I think I may puke, but I'm relieved he's stopped yelling and I can sit up. He zips up his pants and punches my arm, laughing.

"You little slut," he says. "How'd you learn to do that so good?"

"I don't know," I say. "Comes naturally I guess."

"Well you sure drained me," he says, starting the car. "I'll sleep easy now."

"Thanks," I say. "For the ride home, I mean."

"My pleasure, sexy," he says, then winks. "See you around."

He drives off and I walk down to my front door, forcing myself to take deep breaths. I look up at my bedroom window, still open. I consider climbing back in that way, but the front door's unlocked and it seems stupid not to use it now.

Home

JIM TUSHINSKI

Mother is painting stars. She thinks I'm asleep on the couch, wrapped in a heavy blanket, but I watch her as she paints, peeking out from a half-open eye, seeing her through a blur of lashes. She stands quite still for minutes, stands in front of a large canvas painted a dark blue that's almost black. Then she moves to a particular spot and stabs her brush. I fall asleep. When I wake up, galaxies have appeared.

Yesterday, I was in the hospital.

I was in a room, standing in the middle where they left me, looking at the blank walls, the metal frame bed, a desk, a piece of paper. *Dear Paul.*

Was this my room? I couldn't get my thoughts together. This place looked lived in. The sheets on the bed were in disarray. Did I leave in a hurry? Was I in the middle of something? A pen was near the piece of paper.

I sat at the desk, not aware of how I got there, unable to recall walking across the room, pulling out the chair. The piece of paper was too white, the ink too blue.

Dear Paul. I picked up the pen. Underneath the words I wrote:

Who are you?

I wrote it slowly and carefully, imitating the handwriting on the line above.

I'm in this room. Your name is written here. If this is my room then I wrote your name. I know who you are.

I looked up. The window was high in the opposite wall. The door had a little window as well, the glass there embedded with wire. I tried, for a moment, to imagine what was outside, but all I could picture was a flat, treeless place and an uneven sky.

Before I was in this room, before I sat at this desk and wrote the words on that piece of paper, I was walking down a corridor. I heard noises, people talking, things being moved around, but the noises didn't come to me all at once. They came in bits, selectively, weaving in and out of importance, balancing, then contrasting each other. It was nice in a way. I wanted to cry.

Next to me, a large man in white held my arm. I walked slowly, almost shuffling, and the man was there to help me. That made sense. I leaned against the man, who was warm and hairy.

Before I was walking down the corridor, I remember being someplace else. Another room, bigger than the room with the desk and the paper. I'm propped up on a bed, a hard bed with white, white sheets and railings on the side. A man leans over me, shaving my head with an electric razor. Was this the same man who helped me down the corridor? I can't be sure. The man shaves me with the razor and I think: How come he's shaving me? Why can't I move my arms and legs? The man takes a tissue and wipes away the saliva that runs from my open mouth.

All around me in this room I feel other people in other beds just like mine. I can't see them because I can't turn my head, but I feel them and hear them thrashing around, moaning or pulling on straps. I remember the sound of leather stretching.

I looked at myself in my mirror. My mirror. My room.

I was wearing a bright white gown tied at the back. My hair was black and thick and cropped close. My eyes stared back at me. Every so often I forced myself to close my mouth. I soon forgot, though, as I stared at my face. My mouth fell open again.

I mustn't be very old. That's not why I'm here. This isn't a nursing home. I'm younger than the man who brought me down the corridor. I'm a young man, really, but how young? Maybe twenty-three? Twenty-seven?

Looking at the room reflected in my mirror made me dizzy. I stepped back and lost balance.

In the reception area, I floated a few inches above the floor. It really wasn't a pleasant feeling. I had so little control—pushed around, and tethered like a balloon. The pills kicked in while I sat waiting in my room and now the air looked hazy. People had halos of light around them, like headaches made visible. The halos throbbed if I looked at them too long. If I looked at the people. At the halos, too. Through the foggy air, I saw a woman in a heavy wool coat. A tired, uncomfortable-looking woman. Her halo was gray, though I could see underneath the gray some wisps of black. She wore glasses with big, light blue frames that helped round her thin face. She smiled.

I knew it was Mother. People and things came back to me in no particular order and just as quickly left me, but she didn't need to remind me who she was.

"The doctor says there's no reason to keep you here anymore," Mother told me. We sat in the car. It was cold.

I didn't remember walking out the hospital door or across the parking lot. I didn't remember opening the car door. I could see the hospital from where I sat. I could breathe on the window and watch my breath condense. A gray layer of hardened snow covered the ground. The other windows started fogging up.

"He says with the medication and therapy you'll be fine. He has faith in you. Says you're a survivor." She pushed a button and a noise filled the car, followed by a jet of warm air. The windows melted before me and I could see the hospital again, a dark old building made of sweating stones. I thought about laughing, thought about reaching out to see if the windows might still be there. Then I thought about the act of laughing and the idea of the window. The air got warmer in the car.

She looked at me.

"We did this for your own good," she said, her voice trembling a little. "You needed help."

I wasn't sure how to respond, so I said nothing. She pushed another button, stepped on a pedal. The car moved.

"You don't look well, Michael. Did they feed you at all? You look so thin."

"Just tired," I said.

Mother stopped glowing as we drove away from the hospital. I looked at her—recognizing the tilt of her head, her gray and black hair, her knuckles straining from her grip on the car's steering wheel. These things seemed natural, familiar. Perhaps it was the pills, pushing me into a safe place. When I smiled, my mouth never seemed to stop moving.

"Your father couldn't come," Mother said, not looking at me, intent on the road ahead. I tried to watch the road as well, but felt myself rushing away from it as it moved toward me, one movement canceling the other and leaving the car suspended. Only when I looked at Mother did we seem to move.

"It's difficult for him to come home when he's touring," she said.

I can't picture my father or the places where Mother and I are headed, but somehow I'm soothed by the certainty that everything will become clear in time. The interior of the car, the cold feel of the deep red upholstery, the blue tinting along the top of the windows, the tan laces weaving in and out of the steering-wheel wrap—all these seemed as familiar to me as my hospital room.

"Yes," I said. "I understand."

She smiled, glanced away from the road for an instant, and looked at me. I understand. Yes. I understand what words to say so Mother will smile. She loosened her grip on the steering wheel. Her shoulders relaxed. Radiating out from the corner of her eyes, a web of wrinkles didn't disappear when her smile faded.

"You remember what it's like when he's touring," she said and I understood something in her voice, something hopeful and trembling, something transmitted to me at a frequency I couldn't quite hear. *You remember,* she said again, but her mouth hadn't moved. The heated air blew from the vent, hitting my face. I wanted to blink, but couldn't.

"Yes," I said. "Touring . . ."

I let out a sigh. Mother nodded, then shook her head while she smiled again.

This seemed so easy, like a game. Mother spoke and I replied. There was no need to say anything new. I reused her words and she smiled, and despite my numbness, I knew that to make her smile I had to choose my repetition carefully. I must choose and react—sigh, gesture, frown—and then listen.

I was confident now. Confident and numb.

I looked out the window.

The layout of Mother's house was unfamiliar. There seemed to be endless rooms opening off other rooms full of doors, stairs, and carefully arranged furniture. The walls were off-white, the colors coming from bold splashes of blue and red and yellow in the furniture's fabrics. I followed Mother as she walked and then turned toward me, to see if anything like recognition would appear on my face. I kept my face smooth. She spoke the names of the rooms as we entered them and made a spreading gesture with her arms, presenting the rooms to me.

"Living room," she said. "Family room, dining room, kitchen."

We climbed some stairs and I saw a hallway, more doors, and behind the doors—more rooms, more off-white walls, more gestures, more words. The carpet in the hallway was a different shade of plush off-white. I stared at it, focused on the twists of carpet fiber and the way light reflected. Mother bravely moved forward into another room.

"This is your room," she said.

Mother is painting stars.

"Mother," I say, and she stiffens, slowly putting her brush down on the small table. She doesn't turn around.

"This one's gotten quite large," she says, her tone clipped and a bit distracted, as if she's speaking to herself. "They've become larger over the last year."

For a moment, we're both silent. She stares at the blue-black night full of stars. I watch the back of her head, unsure what to say next, how to proceed.

"What do you do with them when they're finished?" I ask.

"Each one is different, you know." She turns around to face me, her eyes locking on mine. I can't look away. Something shifts and crackles in the air, then disappears.

"If I like them," she says, "if they're really good, I give them to my agent who sells them. But mostly I paint over them." She turns back to the canvas. "Until I get it right." She picks up her brush, dabs it in some deep blue paint, and touches a spot on the canvas.

It seems like a message, some kind of cue. I knew she wouldn't be talking anymore, that she had dismissed me. I get up from the couch and go upstairs.

"Michael," she calls, and it sounds almost like a warning.

"I'm thirsty."

It's my fault, really. She doesn't trust me, can't let me out of her sight. If I'm upstairs too long, she'll call for me again, then come up to see what I'm doing. It's my own fault. I should have known that lying and pretending to understand takes its toll.

I don't know how long I've been upstairs or when Mother came up. From where I'm sitting, at the kitchen table, I can see her holding a telephone receiver toward me, her hand covering the mouthpiece. "You have a phone call," she says. Her voice is flat and too polite. I don't remember hearing the phone ring.

I hesitate. I'm sure I've talked on the telephone before, though I don't recall when. I understand the principle, but the technique is elusive.

"It's Paul," she says.

I look directly at Mother, see her mouth move, but hear no sound. I read her lips, hesitate an instant more, then get up and take the receiver.

"Yes," I say, but choke a bit and repeat "Yes," afraid I haven't been heard.

"Mike," the voice from the receiver says, racing up the syllable of my name and sounding a little unbalanced. "How are you?" I imagine him from his voice, see him as dark and compact with a single, thick eyebrow and a full, reassuring mouth. The voice tries to sound casual, but I suppose the call is difficult for the voice—for Paul. I see him in a faraway place, a place with no background, no furniture, no sky. The air in that place glows.

"Tired," I say slowly, but putting a reassuring vocal spin to the word. "A little confused."

"When are you coming home, Mike?" Paul's voice asks.

The word "home" makes a sharp sound in my ear and I move the receiver away. Mother sees this and frowns. I want her to go. Even though I'm not sure who I'm talking to, I know this is private. I frown back at Mother and wave my hand at her as though she were a troublesome fly.

"I'm home now," I tell Paul without really thinking about it.

Paul says nothing for a while, then speaks my name very softly. "I miss you so much," he says.

His words make my heart pound and I'm not sure what I feel. I can't miss someone I barely remember, but I say what seems right, what Paul hopes for, and what I suspect is true.

"I miss you too."

I smile. The words are mine even if they don't make much sense.

Mother won't stop looking at me. She seems quite pale.

"I was hoping to speak to your mother," Paul says. "Is she there?"

"Yes," I say, and hold the receiver toward her. "He wants to talk to you too."

She hesitates. I can see her hand crumple a dishrag, then she moves a few steps forward and takes the receiver from me.

"Yes," she says, but looks at me. I walk away, across the dining room, into the living room where I sit on the sofa. Despite Mother's attempt to speak quietly, most of her words reach me.

"That's not really a possibility," she says, then after a pause, "Don't be ridiculous."

Paul seems to be doing most of the talking. Mother is quiet for a while, then she says abruptly, "I certainly can't stop you, but perhaps you should consider other people's feelings."

I can't hear what else she says. Perhaps she lowered her voice. Then I hear, "Yes, well that's what *you* say." She sounds bored and her tone is somewhat final, then she laughs and a chill shoots right through me. There's something so cold in that laugh.

When she comes back into the living room, nothing about her seems different, but the feel of that chill stays with me.

"Didn't he want to talk to me some more?" I ask.

She smiles a tight little smile and shakes her head. "No," she says.

"What did he want?"

The phone rings again, sounding too loud. Mother hurries back into the kitchen.

"Yes," she says, then lowers her voice.

When she returns, she says, "Wrong number. Let's go for a drive, shall we? You can help me get groceries. Getting out will do you good."

"What did Paul want to talk to you about?"

"I'm not even sure," she says. "He's a little odd."

"He asked me when I was coming home."

For a moment, she is absolutely still.

"That *is* odd," she says at last. "After all, he called you here." She stands there looking at me, then asks, "How well do you remember him?"

The chill runs through my shoulders, making them twitch. The hairs on the back of my neck tingle.

"Are you cold?" she asks, and I shake my head, managing a smile and a shrug.

"I remember him . . . very well," I say. I try to picture him but all I can conjure is a general impression—stocky with black curly hair. His face, though, is still blank. Everything's there—eyes, nose, mouth—but nothing's distinctive. "When I hear his voice," I say, "things come back to me."

"That's good." She seems to speak with conviction. "I'm curious," she says. "Do you remember more about Paul than you remember about . . . your home, say, or your father or me?"

I can't think fast enough and both Mother and I know my pause goes on too long.

"About the same," I say. "Things are getting a lot clearer."

Her smile sickens me.

"Your father will be so happy to see how well you're recovering. I think it hit him hardest. Not that we weren't all concerned, Michael . . . I certainly didn't mean that . . . but your father . . ." She stops and loses herself for a moment. "Well," she says, "shall we go for a drive?"

Mother bustles herself and me into coats, grabs her purse and keys, and as we're heading out the door, the phone rings again. I look at Mother, making a movement to go back and answer it, but she closes the door behind her and locks it.

"I'm not expecting any important calls. Are you?" she says. "The machine will get it."

As we pull out of the driveway, I imagine the machine never does pick up and I can hear the phone as it rings and rings and rings in the empty house.

"Michael," a woman's voice says. "Michael, wake up." Someone is shaking me, but I can't open my eyes very far and my head feels tender and enlarged. A woman with gray and black hair is standing next to the bed, her hand resting on my shoulder. "Karl and Amy are here. Sara, too. It's dinnertime."

"What?" I try to say. "Sleeping." I can't keep my eyes open, so I close them and hope she will leave. Just as I drift away into the darkness, someone shakes me again, this time almost violently. I open my eyes and the woman is still there, not a part of some dream, as I had hoped. She looks at me, annoyed perhaps or just concerned.

"You've been sleeping for hours," she says. "Everyone is here to see you."

"Go away," I tell her, but she won't.

My brother and sister are here for dinner. At least that's who Mother says they are. They come into the living room carrying several brightly wrapped packages, and I suppose the woman clinging to my brother's arm has to be his wife. Or is she his girlfriend? Mother didn't say. My sister Sara looks at me strangely, as if I've done something wrong or am emitting an unpleasant odor. She's older than me and her hair is unruly, falling away from her head in thick curls which she pushes this way and that. My brother Karl is taller than I am, maybe younger, with black shiny hair and blue eyes I can't stop looking at. When he talks to me, his eyes won't look away and won't let mine look away either.

"We brought your Christmas presents," my sister says. "A little late." She shrugs.

"You look wonderful," the other woman says. "So rested."

By process of elimination, she is Amy. She is blond and touches my brother too often.

Before we all sit down for dinner, I excuse myself.

"I have to wash my hands," I say.

"Karl, go with him," Mother says, but my sister laughs. It's a cruel laugh.

"Really," she says. "He's not an invalid, Mother."

"I have to wash my hands," I say and slip upstairs to navigate the off-white hallways until I find the room I woke up in. I close the door, sit on the bed. *Remember,* I think, *remember, remember, remember. Something. Anything.* I feel the panic slowly rising inside me, demanding that I scream. On the desk are a plastic orange bottle and an overnight bag. I get up and walk over to the desk. The label on the bottle says "Michael Van Dusen" and I know this is me, so I spill a little white tablet onto my palm.

"Michael," Mother calls from downstairs. "Are you coming?"

The pill goes down with difficulty, leaving me coughing and flushed. I sit on the bed again, close my eyes. My breathing grows steady. The edge of my pain softens and fades away. Is it the pills working so quickly or just my anticipation of them?

Someone knocks on the door. "It's Karl," he says. "Are you okay?"

"Yes." I put the plastic container away in the overnight bag and hurry to open the door. He's standing there, leaning against the wall, his hands in his pockets, with a casualness I can't help admiring since it's something I'm sure I lack. His face—it looks like my face in a way, but there's such a great difference, too. It's as if my face was modified, perfected. Memories and past experiences are beneath the features, not exactly visible, but sparkling out of those eyes. His hair is so black but the light, even the weak, unspecified light of the hallway, touches it with highlights of almost blue. His eyes say something to me, something I should be able to translate but can't. I want to touch his hair, his cheek, but can't.

"Mom's worried, you know how she is," he says.

"Yes." It seems the easiest response.

"Hell, we're all worried," he says, and then moves toward me. I take a step back, almost stagger. Karl stops and I see concern in his eyes, see a frown cross his lips. He holds out his hand.

"Mikey," he says, as though approaching a frightened pet. "Come on." He smiles and the smile is so sad. "Let's go downstairs."

I reach up to take his hand and when we touch, my fingers tingle. Suddenly he seems quite familiar to me.

Throughout the meal I hear the conversation from a great distance, realizing I'm being addressed directly only when the pauses between the sentences become too long. No one else seems to notice the amount of time between a question and my answer. Maybe for them it's as if no time passes at all. When Mother gets up to retrieve something from the kitchen, my brother leans over and pours me some wine. I notice a bluish tinge to his jaw where he shaved. I want to touch it, feel how smooth it is.

"Drink up," he says.

"Is that a good idea?" Amy asks. "Isn't he on medication?"

"A little wine won't hurt him."

He leans closer, speaks low in my ear. "Thickens the blood," he says.

His voice sends a warm shock through me. My brother is so close to me, close enough to touch. Should I kiss him? Instead, I reach for the wine and take a sip. I lower the glass, everything happening in slow motion, and again I watch my panic grow, as if I'm detached from it. The liquid slides down my throat, burning.

"Yes," I say in a whisper.

Mother comes into the room with a large box and puts it in front of me on the table. Inside are a number of smaller boxes, beautifully wrapped. The box is big. I know this, but now it seems so small and far away. The air begins to fill with the strange light. It envelops my family with a familiar and faint glow. I smile, a little frightened, and drain my wineglass.

"You shouldn't be drinking, Michael," she says. "Not with your medication." Then to my brother: "Don't give him any more."

"Open ours first," Karl says.

My sister stares at me from across the table.

I reach for the box Amy holds out, but it doesn't seem to have any solidity to it. My fingers pass right through and I watch it drop onto the table, upsetting the salt and pepper shakers.

"Goodness!" Amy exclaims. She picks up the package and looks confused, watching me.

"I don't think he even knows he dropped it," Sara says in disgust.

Pushing through the heavy glow, I reach out again and take the present, slowly, deliberately. I try to untie the ribbon and peel off the paper but my fingers won't move in the right way. They feel thick—bloated and soft. A string of saliva hangs in the air and drops onto the package. It takes me a long time to understand where it came from. I try to move my jaw, to stop the string of drool. With an effort, I succeed.

"Jesus," Sara says.

Now I start to cry. My words come out in an angry slur, but neither I nor any of my family can understand what I'm trying to say. Amy looks down at her plate, then takes the present and unwraps it. When she finishes, she sets it down in front of me. Inside is a small music box. She lifts the lid and a tune begins to play. A tinny, unrecognizable melody.

"It's your favorite song," Karl says, halfhearted.

I stand up, knocking my chair backward and surprising myself. I'm not sure where the energy comes from or why this anger makes it up through the glowing light. A scream sits inside me, waiting.

Mother looks terrified and beaten. She clutches the tablecloth, covers her mouth.

"Michael, please," she says.

"Just calm down," Karl says, touching me. "Take it easy." Then he turns to Mother and asks, "Does he need his medication?"

I stumble and fall forward.

A blanket covers me, pulled up around my neck. I lie in a bedroom. It's dark. The clock says 2:15. My head is clear, as if a large space exists there, an open window with a breeze blowing the curtains inward. A blue sky. No clouds.

I sit up.

I don't hear any movement, no sounds except the ticking of many clocks and a distant hum.

I get out of bed. The fear fills me up. Like a drop of oil on a clean white cloth, it saturates me.

Where am I? What's my name?

I walk to the hallway, grabbing on to the doorframe to steady myself. Nothing looks familiar.

As I move down the hall, I notice a bathroom to my left. I go in. Close the door. Sit on the toilet in the dark. And I breathe—rapidly at first, then forcing myself to go slower and slower. Taking air in, feeling it fill my lungs, pushing the panic out. Slowly, slowly. As suddenly as the fear comes on, it subsides, leaving behind the house, the bathroom, my name. This is my home, yet it is not my home. The people at dinner are my family, yet they are not my family. *Dear Paul,* I think, *who are you? Where are you?*

Inside the medicine cabinet is an orange plastic pill bottle. I remove the top and spill one white tablet into my palm, then pop the pill into my mouth. For a moment, I think about swallowing it, knowing the comforting numbness that will come, but at the same time I try to picture Paul and can only imagine a shadowy shape, can barely hear his voice. I cough the pill into the sink where it slips down the drain, enveloped in a glob of saliva. Paul is slipping away too. I hang on to the sides of the sink as if gripping them will keep him here.

I don't want to sleep.

Home Improvement

SCOTT ALLEN BOWLES

Maude Brewster sits in her kitchen with the phone tucked against her cheek, listening to her sister tell her about the floods. Her sister calls once a week to give Maude the latest catastrophe that has occurred to her town, now in its fourth week of almost continuous rainfall. Maude knows it pleases her sister that her county has been declared a disaster area, since it means that everyone who watches the news knows how miserable her life is. Now they understand what it's been like for her, everyone, even the President. She gloats that the brand-new Wal-Mart on the other side of the river was finally destroyed, after weeks of being surrounded by sandbag walls. "Those sandbags just burst open like acne and within minutes the entire store was knee-deep," her sister tells her. "Only been open less than a year. There's more people out of work. And these aren't rich people, you know."

"No, not working at Wal-Mart, I guess not," Maude says, crushing an imaginary cigarette out with her thumb. She can hear her sister inhaling deeply on her cigarette between disasters, which makes Maude crave a cigarette herself. She quit smoking a year before but still retains the motions that she loved most about smoking: lighting a cigarette and putting it out. Lighting one felt like a change of scenery, like seeing her life differently, as a smoker. Putting it out symbolized finality, declaring something bad to be over and done with, and then moving on. Occasionally she fantasizes that she could go back to smoking if she only partook in these two activities and omitted the breathing part that comes between them.

She checks the clock on the wall and pushes the imaginary ashtray away from her. She envies her sister's life right now; there's always something new happening: basements imploding from water pressure or lives ruined when a family business washes down the river. Maude lives in Skokie, where natural disasters rarely occur. She thinks she remembers a tornado years ago, before they built Old Orchard Shopping Center. She credits Old Orchard with putting Skokie on the map, giving it something to rival its neighbor Evanston with its Northwestern University. Now Evanston people, university couples with young children, drive over to shop at Field's and Lord & Taylor. Maude eyes them with superiority for finding out late what she'd known for years, that Skokie was a landmark waiting to be discovered, impervious to tornadoes or floods, because thanks to Old Orchard not even God would mess with Skokie now.

Her sister is onto a different subject, and Maude finds herself only half listening, focusing her attention on the television on her kitchen counter, where a home improvement show is teaching her how to install a heating system in a Southwestern adobe cottage. The host of the program is a rugged, bearded man whom Maude has developed an attraction to since she's started to pay attention to the show. She fantasizes about him coming over to shave the door to the downstairs bedroom which sticks, the muscles under his hairy arms flexing as he slides the plane up and down the wood.

Her call waiting clicks. "Listen, honey, I've got to go," she tells her sister. "I'm sorry about that Chinese family and their restaurant. Call you next week. Love you. Bye-bye." She clicks on the other call; it's her youngest son, Philip, calling from the hotel where he works as a waiter. "Are you still coming over for dinner tonight?" Maude asks him. "Your father's making bratwurst on the grill."

"Bratwurst?" her son says with a tone, then sighs. "Sure, okay. What do you want me to bring?"

"Whatever you want to drink, wine or something," Maude says, trying not to let her opinion that he drinks too much show in her voice.

He sighs again and she knows he heard it. "I'll just drink whatever you have," he says. "I thought I'd bring something for dessert. They have a great Italian sorbetto in the restaurant. Maybe I'll get some of that."

Bratwurst and sorbetto, Maude thinks, but she doesn't comment. She doesn't know where his fixation with desserts comes from, since it was never part of their meals when he was growing up, but she accepts it, considering it another way of proving himself more sophisticated than his mother, along with his expensive tastes and his big vocabulary.

She listens patiently while he fills her in on the details of his workday. Maude thinks at thirty-three he's too old to be a full-time waiter but she keeps that opinion to herself, still hoping that he'll change his mind soon and get a job in marketing or sales, or maybe go back to school and learn a profession. When someone asks, she tells them he's an actor in various plays throughout the city, which isn't a lie, although she doesn't tell the names of the plays he's in. She has gone to several of them, generally in questionable venues, not what most would imagine when they think of a theater. The plays she's seen have been either incomprehensible or depressing or both, and one had nudity. This upset Maude. Seeing her son naked as a boy she considered to be a sacred privilege of motherhood: to hold the child she carried and wonder at the perfection of his body. Watching him share that intimate knowledge with a roomful of people seemed to Maude to be vulgar; a betrayal.

His current play is a performance piece, which as far as Maude could tell means that it doesn't have a plot and he's the only one in it. She saw it in the basement of a bar, amidst cases of beer and broken furniture. She was so scared of being bitten by a rat that she sat through the entire play Indian-style on the metal folding chair, which she thought made her look hip enough to be there. The play was about sex, food, and politics, and again there was nudity. Before Maude could stop herself she saw that her son had shaved off all his body hair. She felt her face redden in the dark room and she kept her eyes focused on his forehead or above during the rest of the play. The two dozen people in the audience laughed and applauded at the appropriate parts, which Maude, again, didn't understand. She thought she was probably the only one there that night who wasn't stoned, and she left feeling very old.

"By the way, your home improvement guy is gay, so stop wasting your time," her son says suddenly.

Maude blinks and reaches for her invisible pack. "How do you know that?"

"Because he checked into the hotel today with another man and they shared a room together."

"So what?" she says. "Maybe he's just economical. He's always showing ways to save money around the house. He's probably just used to it."

"That's ridiculous," her son says. "He's on TV. He probably makes more than our whole family put together. Besides, you can just tell."

Maude doesn't question how you can just tell these things; she couldn't tell it about her own son until he told her himself over ten years ago. Now she realizes that the knowledge was there, but her unwillingness to admit what she suspected kept her from seeing it. She still feels her chest tighten whenever he talks openly about his lifestyle, as if daring her not to accept it, using terms like "sister" and "family" to describe other gay men. "Oh, she's a sistah," he'll say when they pass someone on the street. Maude thinks of the home improvement man as being economical and is pleased with herself for creating her own euphemism. She imagines herself whispering to the checkout girl, "He shares hotel rooms with other men. They say he's economical."

Her thoughts are interrupted by someone at the door. "Oh, honey, I've got to go," she tells Philip. "Come over around six. Bring whatever you like." Maude hangs up and opens the front door to the mailman, an angular black man whom she liked because he remembered her name, until she realized that he was just reading off the mail in his hand. She still likes him but wonders if he resents her for being white and not having to work and living in a nice suburb. She tries to find something to chat about that doesn't sound oppressive. "This rain is horrible," she says, taking the mail. "I wouldn't be surprised if we got a tornado, it's so dark out already." The mailman nods and smiles at her. She closes the door, worrying that her comment about how dark it was may have offended him. "It's not like I said that was bad or anything," she mutters aloud, then shakes her head and looks at the mail.

Two items stand out to her, one an invitation to join a retirement association, the other a subscription offer for a senior citizens magazine. How do these people know her age and what else do they know about her? she wonders. At fifty-seven she hates being reminded of what's around the corner, and she rips both letters up before discarding them. Among what's left is a television magazine; on the front cover is the home improvement man. She opens the magazine to the article and skims through it for references to his personal life. There is only mention of his daughter but no wife or girlfriend. That doesn't prove anything, Maude thinks, and he does have a daughter. He certainly didn't get that by sharing hotel rooms with another man.

At 5:20 her husband, Eliot, walks through the front door. Maude immediately feels irritated seeing him hang his jacket on the coatrack and she has to force a smile. Her husband still smokes, although not in the house, and he claims he doesn't smoke at all. She pictures him parking the car at the end of the block on his way home from work and puffing maniacally on his cigarette like a teenager, just to enter the house minutes later reeking of an ashtray and thinking she has no idea he just smoked. This is what makes her angry, being treated like she's too stupid to tell the difference. She takes one last look at the TV magazine and wonders if the home improvement man smokes, and if he does, whether he lies about it.

"Hi, honey, how was your day?" she calls, covering up the magazine with a newspaper. Eliot steps into the kitchen and holds up his hand in a semi-wave. A strong cigarette smell wafts off his fingers into her face and for a moment the craving to smoke is so strong that Maude is tempted to murder him. She wonders where he hides his cigarettes and makes a mental note to find out. "Philip is still coming over for dinner at six, so start the grill in a little while," she says, adding, "He's bringing sorbetto for dessert, so we won't have to worry about that."

Eliot stares at her, grunts the word "sorbetto," and shakes his head. He flips through the mail on the table, pulls the TV guide from under the newspaper and takes it into the bathroom. "A man of few words," Maude says, and she shudders, thinking of the home improvement man looking back at Eliot on the toilet.

Philip arrives at quarter till seven, and the meal is torturous. The bratwurst is overdone: dry and carbonized. Eliot refuses to touch the dessert that their son brought, which makes Philip comment loudly, "You can't get AIDS from sorbetto, Dad; you can't even get fat from it, not that you seem to care." Philip is more accommodating to his father, accepting a can of his beer, then a second, then a third, then a fourth. Maude is amazed at how Philip, with his high tastes, will down without complaint the cheap beer her husband buys. She wonders if Philip would drink Bactine if she poured it into a tumbler with some ice.

"I'm going home before the buses stop running," her son announces after dinner. "Spending Friday night in Skokie is a good reason for suicide." Maude nods, but doesn't say anything. She was hoping that he might want to rent a movie and stay the night, something he used to do occasionally. She knows that after he leaves, her husband will bury himself in his workroom in the basement and she will be left alone. At least Philip isn't driving, she thinks. The one saving grace of alcoholic waiters in this city is that they can't afford cars.

She kisses him good night and watches him walk down the sidewalk. At the corner, he stops, lights a cigarette, then turns the corner and disappears.

Maude turns back to the living room, scowling. It seems like the whole world is smoking, except for her. She takes her husband's jacket off the rack and feels through the pockets but finds nothing. She looks out the window at the car, tempting her in the dark. It's beginning to rain again, but to Maude this only makes it a challenge. She pulls the jacket on and runs out to the car.

She searches in the glove compartment and under the seats but finds nothing. The hood or the trunk would be too much work, she thinks, and she would see him closing it from the window. They have to be inside somewhere. She checks above the visors, feels the seams of the upholstery for tears, ransacks the cassette and cup holder between the front seats. By this time, she realizes how ridiculous she must look to anyone who might pass by; she also knows that with half the effort she could have driven to the convenience store a block away and bought a pack of cigarettes. She puts the key in the ignition and starts the car; the rains have begun pouring but the craving is all she can think about. The car backs out the driveway and starts down the street.

In the time it takes her to get from her car to the convenience store, she is drenched. The man behind the counter glances up at her and then returns to his magazine. Maude hopes it isn't pornography; she doesn't want to exchange money with someone reading a dirty magazine behind a counter. She starts toward the counter for cigarettes, then decides that looks too desperate, to go out in this weather just for cigarettes, so she looks around the store to see if there is anything else she needs. One entire wall of the store is made up of beverages in glass coolers. Maude crosses to the coolers and is overwhelmed at the magnitude of choices she has. Soda, beer, coffee, juice, cans, bottles, and cups cry to her for attention. She is so blinded by the packaging she doesn't notice the man approaching her from behind.

"Excuse me, can I get in there?" his voice says. Maude turns around. He is so close to her, her nose scrapes his beard and the sting lingers on her skin. He reaches past her and pulls a pack of beer out of the reach-in. "Thanks," he says, and then grins at her. "Five ninety-nine. You can't beat that." Maude stares at his beer, a six-pack of Guinness Stout.

"I wouldn't know," she says. "I've never tried that brand." She stares at his face and can't think of anything else to say. "You're the home improvement man," she says.

He doesn't seem irritated at all. "Actually, I prefer to be called Roger. And this," he says, holding up the beer, "isn't just a brand, this is what beer is meant to taste like."

He looks and sounds just like a beer commercial and suddenly Maude doesn't want him to leave. "I figured you would just buy whatever's cheapest," she says. "You always seem so economical." She could have ripped her tongue out. "Well, I mean on your show."

The home improvement man actually winks at her. "Don't tell anybody, but every now and then I like to splurge. You can't be economical all the time. It gets boring, right?"

"Right, it does!"

"I'm glad to know you watch my show," he says. "What's your name?"

"Maude. Maude Brewster. Oh, honey, listen, if anybody needs home improvement, it's me."

He raises an eyebrow at her. "Do you mean from a handyman or a family therapist?"

"I mean a really expensive therapist, but I can't convince my husband or kids to go see one." This earns Maude her first home improvement man laugh. "Am I right?" she says. "There has to be someone out there who knows how to retrain people, or at least keep them sedated."

"So that's what drives you to the liquor section on a Friday night?"

"Actually no, I came here to break my bad habit of quitting smoking, but if I'm going to do that I might as well indulge all my vices, right? I'll just clean out the candy aisle on my way to the register, pick up a *Playgirl* and be on my way."

"An average Friday night in Skokie, I take it?" he says, grinning.

"Hey, don't knock Skokie, it's a regular den of sin, we just make sure to pull down the shades first. What brings you here in this typhoon?"

"We were shopping at Old Orchard and just decided to pick up some beer for when we get back," he says. "I'm here in the city for a few more days doing some promotional things."

Maude wants to ask who "we" is but holds back. "What kind of promotional things are you doing?" she asks.

Before Roger can answer, a sound at the end of the aisle interrupts him. A tall blond man in a polo shirt and crisp white pants stands impatiently, glaring at both of them. "Really, Rog, were you planning on abandoning me here in this monsoon?" he says. "In another few minutes we'll need oars to get the car back to the hotel."

Roger looks at the man and smiles at Maude, embarrassed. "This is my friend, Lance. Lance, this is Maude."

Lance gives Maude a wooden smile. "Can't leave him out of my sight for a minute, although I must say the competition gets stranger every day," he says. "Can we please leave before we have to give the Professor and Mary Ann star billing? I'd swear the *Lusitania* just drove by."

Roger looks irritated. "I'm almost ready, Lance. I'm just having a conversation with someone. Don't get so bent out of shape."

Lance makes a hissing noise at him and says, "I'll just wait up at the counter and scratch off lottery tickets until you're done. That's actually my Friday-night fantasy. Maybe the guy working will let me read his dog-eared *Penthouse* and I'll really go wild." He spins around and disappears.

Roger looks at Maude apologetically. "Lance is impatient by nature. Don't take it personally. I guess I could use that therapist who retrains people too."

They return to the counter, where Lance is scratching on a two-foot-long piece of lottery tickets. He doesn't look up at either of them; Roger sets the beer on the counter. "You wanted cigarettes, right?" he asks Maude. "What kind?"

Maude glances at the magazine the man behind the counter was reading. It really is a *Penthouse*. "Never mind," she says. Suddenly Lance rips the chunk of tickets in half and holds half out to Maude. "Here," he says. In his brusque way, he is being friendly. He gives her a penny to scratch with. "Have you won anything?" Maude asks him.

"Four free tickets. I'm on a roll," he says. Roger finishes paying for the beer and turns to him. "Are you ready to go?" he asks.

Lance finally looks up from the tickets. "Do you mind?" he says. "I'm just having a conversation with someone. Don't get so bent out of shape."

"Ten bucks!" Maude shouts.

"What?" Lance says. "Hey, you're lucky! I guess we'll have to keep you. Come on."

"Come on?" Maude stares at him. "Where?"

"Anywhere we want, we're loaded!" He takes Maude by the arm and begins steering her toward the door. "Come if you're coming, Rog. I've got the keys." The three of them sprint to their van and pile in.

Maude feels exhilarated. "I can't just leave my car there. Won't they tow it?"

"They'll need to call the Coast Guard to do it, sweetheart," Lance says. "I wouldn't worry about it. The counter guy will still be on Miss July by the time we get back." Lance starts the van and pulls out onto the street with an immense splash. "By the time we get back" echoes in Maude's head. They turn and join the parade of cars rushing through the pouring rains.

They park in the hotel ramp and walk into the lobby. Maude associates the hotel with her son so much that she expects him to be there until she remembers he finished working already. "Where are we going?" she asks.

"We're starting with a drink, ASAP," Lance says. "Where's the nearest gin mill?" Roger holds up the six-pack he's carrying. "Better than that, after that drive down. Isn't there a restaurant-slash-lounge in this place somewhere?"

"Right there," Roger says, pointing. "I'll go up and put this away and meet you guys there." He walks to the elevators. "Should have known he'd know where the bar was," Lance whispers to Maude as they walk into the lounge. Maude has been here several times but tonight she sees it as if for the first time, noticing details and wondering what Lance would think of them. The entire room is decorated in the color cream: the carpet, the booths, the walls. Even the people seem part of the color scheme, their pale complexions blending into the surroundings. There is no noise in the restaurant except a television behind the bar where a baseball game is playing. Two men sit at the bar, and a dozen and a half people sit at tables or booths, mostly in pairs.

Lance and Maude exchange a glance. "Ish," he says. "I guess it'll have to do until Rog gets back. Belly up." He takes her arm and leads her to the bar. "Gin and tonic," he says to the bartender, a tall, sallow man. "Maude?"

"What was that beer that Roger bought?"

"Guinness," he says. The bartender nods without a word and gets their drinks. "What's with this place?" Lance asks Maude. "Nobody's talking. Look at all the people. They're just sitting at the table staring. I'm getting goose bumps just being here."

Maude looks behind her. Everyone is either eating or not eating in silence. They seem sad and old to Maude and their faces have an empty, resigned look to them. She whispers to Lance, "Part of the building is condo. Mostly old rich people. I guess this lounge is their big night out, or maybe they eat here every night and just aren't enthused anymore." She realizes that the restaurant is depressing her immensely. She turns back to the bar. In front of her is a tall glass canister filled with murky water. Inside she sees two tiny frogs sitting at the bottom of the water, motionless. "Are those frogs real?" she asks.

Lance squints at them, then taps the glass with his finger. One of the frogs flies to the top of the water slowly and gracefully. "They're some kind of African frog." It's the bartender who speaks, and both Lance and Maude jump from the sound of another voice. "I thought frogs needed air," Maude says. "Don't they drown, sitting at the bottom like that?"

The bartender stares at Maude coldly. "They haven't yet, ma'am," he says. Maude sees Lance eye her sideways and start to grin. He leans toward her and whispers, "The Undead never die, ma'am. Take a look around you and see for yourself."

Maude picks up her beer and tastes it; the thick brown liquid is soothing, like coffee. She lets it distract her from her surroundings, and takes a long swig from the bottle. Lance notices and grins. The frog that flew up flies back down and the other one flies up. They switch places again and Maude feels herself hypnotized by them until Roger suddenly appears between them. His presence breaks the funk they both feel descending upon them and they jump off their barstools. "Let's go," Lance says. Roger looks at him, surprised. "Don't you want to finish your drinks?" he says. Lance downs his gin and tonic and looks at Maude. She shrugs and starts to guzzle the bottle of beer until her eyes are watering.

"Attagirl," Lance says, patting her back. "Now let's get out of here before we can never leave." He sprints toward the door; Roger follows him slowly, confused. Maude turns to set the bottle back on the bar and her eye catches the frogs again. She leans closely to see them better. They are both sitting at the bottom of the tank, their noses touching the glass. "I know how you feel," she says. She catches the bartender staring at her, so she puts on her jacket and leaves the restaurant.

"That was the most depressing experience of my entire life," Lance says when she catches up with them. "I'm going to have nightmares about that for weeks. Those creepy people and that Twilight Zone bartender."

"It wasn't that bad," Roger says.

"Yes, it was," Maude says. "You couldn't tell because we got you out just in time."

"It's just a little suburbanite bar," he says. "I was there last night for a drink while Lance was getting ready."

Maude catches Lance's eye. "He's one of them now, Lance. Just put him behind you and go on. You have to save yourself."

Lance laughs. "There must have been a big pod in the room when he took the beer up. We wondered what took you so long." They walk down the sidewalk and hail a cab. "Let's find the happeningest place in town to undo the damage done by that haunted old haunt," Lance says, climbing in. An image of the restaurant flashes through Maude's mind, only the people are skeletons draped with cobwebs, and she shudders.

Roger directs the driver to a corner bar further north that he knows of. "Pool tables and good beer," he says defensively when he sees the look Lance has given him. "It's a nice place."

"'Nice' is not on our agenda, tool boy," Lance snaps. He catches Maude's eye in the rearview mirror. "We'll probably have to ditch him later."

Maude laughs, enjoying their banter. Her husband in his workroom comes to mind and she feels jealous. She wonders if Eliot has noticed that she's gone yet.

The cab stops in front of the bar and they get out. Roger starts for the door but Maude and Lance hang behind, looking at its facade. A pink neon sign advertises the bar's name and through the window they can see only a few people inside, each one sitting alone. Piano music can be heard through the door. "Double ish," Lance says.

"Are you coming?" Roger calls to them from the doorway.

"We're leaning toward 'no' right now," Maude says.

"This place is more depressing than the last one, and dirtier," Lance says. "Can't we go to a bar that doesn't drive us to drink?" Roger sighs in exasperation and looks up and down the street. Lance and Maude follow his look and they spot another bar down the block. From where they are standing they can see the word "Manhole" above the door. Two men dressed in leather pants step out of a cab and walk inside. "That's better," Lance says. "C'mon, Maude."

Maude hesitates. "I don't know how much of a hit I'm going to be in there," she says.

"Of course you will be," he says. "Underneath all that pigskin are raging queens who've probably built shrines to their mothers. They'll love you."

She starts to follow him until Roger jumps in front of them both. "You've got to be kidding me. A leather bar? We can't go there."

"Why not?" Lance says. "I've got leather shoes on. Besides, you're a construction worker fetishist's dream come true. Half the guys in there are probably addicted to your show. Take off your shirt and we'll be drinking for free all night." He pushes Roger to the side and steps up on the curb. Maude pauses, then follows him.

They enter the bar with Roger trailing, shaking his head. The doorman doesn't give them a second glance, and Maude is relieved. The bar is very dark and all men, mostly in leather or denim. Most of them stand alone with a drink in their hands, seeming to be looking at the art on the walls, all male nudes. Maude glances at one particularly lewd painting and decides not to dwell on any of the rest. They sit at the bar and the bartender approaches them with a curious look. "Car break down?" he says, looking mostly at Roger.

"Actually we came for a drink," Roger says. "Two Guinnesses and a vodka tonic."

"GIN and tonic," Lance pipes up. He is distracted by the art on the walls and begins a full turn to examine all of it.

"We don't have that," the bartender says.

"You don't have gin?" Lance asks incredulously.

"We don't have Guinness," the bartender says. "It doesn't sell here."

"Oh," Lance says. "What do you hairy, manly studs drink then?"

"Bud or Miller. Take your pick, buddy."

"I already took my pick and it was a gin and tonic," Lance snaps. "I still haven't seen it." He turns to Maude and Roger. "Okay, guys, how do you want to put hair on your chest? The Real Thing or the Real Thing Light? None of that fancy-ass nellie beer."

"Try not to get us thrown out, Lance," Roger says. "Miller's fine with me." The bartender looks at Maude. "Oh, I've got plenty of hair on my chest already," she says. "I should probably have a light." The bartender eyes Lance and gets their drinks. Maude looks around the bar. Across the room two men are talking, one a burly older man in leather, the other shorter and younger, with his back to Maude, gesturing extravagantly with his arms as he speaks. Maude recognizes him; it's her son Philip.

"Oh, holy shit," she says. Her remark interrupts Roger and Lance, who've begun to bicker at each other and they turn to stare at her. "What?" Roger says. They both look to see what she's looking at.

"Nothing," she says, turning to a drawing of two men having sex, which she immediately associates with her son, so she turns again to stare at the beer taps. "I thought I saw someone I know."

"Someone you know?" Lance says. "Here?" He steps toward her with a look of curiosity on his face. "So you do have a little history, after all. Was her name Bridget and did the gas company send her over to fix your furnace? Don't worry, we won't tell your husband a word."

"Not even close, Lance," she says.

"Her name was Kate and she coached your son's softball league."

"Ha!" Maude says. "No, her name was Cathy and it was soccer. You're getting warmer, though."

"Don't encourage him, Maude," Roger says. "You'll regret it later."

Maude takes a deep gulp on her beer. She can feel it starting to affect her. "My son's here," she says.

"What?" both men echo each other.

"Over there, talking to the guy in the hat."

"That's your son?" Lance says, squinting. "Did you know he was gay? This is so weird, mother and son cruising leather bars together. Hey, he's cute."

"Is he?" Maude asks. "I've always thought so, but I am his mother. He shaved off all his pubic hair. I can't believe I just told you that. Bartender, another round." She holds up one finger and circles it in the air.

"I can't believe you even know that," Lance says. "And don't tell me how. Are you going to go talk to him? God, where's a video camera when you need one?"

"I don't know," Maude says, thinking. "What do you think I should do?"

"Let's watch him and see if he gets lucky," Lance suggests. Roger gives him a look. Lance leans toward Maude. "You should wait until they slip into the back room together and then go in and call his name."

"What back room?" Maude asks.

"Lance," Roger says. "Enough."

"Oh, come on now, Roger," Lance says. "She's a big girl. Come, Maude, let's take a little tour." He gets up from his seat.

"Lance, I thought you said you weren't going to get us kicked out," Roger says.

Lance stares at him blankly. "I never said that," he says. "You said that. Besides, they can't deny us entry anywhere based on sex, race, or religious anything. There are laws, you know."

"I'm too old to be making political statements in a leather bar," Maude says. "Oh, shoot! Here they come." Philip and the man he was talking to circle the bar toward the exit, moving closer to Maude. When Philip sees her, he stops abruptly and stares.

"Ooh, is this juicy," Lance says. "Act casual. We're just out for a drink, after all."

Philip approaches his mother with an angry look on his face. "You followed me here?" he says.

His tone is hostile and the leather man is staring at her. "No, I didn't follow you, Philip. I didn't even notice you were here until a few minutes ago. I was just out with a couple of friends. This is Lance and Roger."

Philip doesn't say anything to either of them but his eyes linger on Roger. "Are you telling me we just happened to stumble across the same leather bar?" he says sarcastically.

Maude tries to placate him. "Well, isn't it nice to learn we have something else in common?" Lance coughs into his drink and Roger shushes him.

"Mom, I don't find this funny," Philip says.

The leather man looks at Philip. "This is your mom?" he says. Maude holds out her hand to him. "My name is Maude, but you can call me Mom if you like, since you and Philip are together." Philip blanches and Maude looks at him curiously. "Philip, what is the matter with you?"

"Nothing," he says. "I'm just not used to barhopping with my mother."

Lance sets his drink down and eyes Philip. "Well, maybe you should try it, missy. We have and she's a lot of fun." Philip looks at Lance with hatred but doesn't say anything.

"My gosh, Philip, settle down," Maude says. "It's not like I caught you in the back room or anything, although Lance and I were just heading in that direction." The leather man laughs and so does Maude but Philip only purses his lips coldly.

"I consider this my territory," Philip says. "Somewhere I can go without my mother invading it."

"Listen, sonny," Roger says, but Maude stops him. "I can't believe you, Philip," she says. "You just came to my house for dinner and now you tell me I'm invading your territory? Just because you're a regular at every gay bar in town doesn't mean you own them all. This isn't your territory any more than the city of Skokie is mine."

"Village," Lance corrects her.

"Okay, the village of Skokie." Maude says. "And frankly, Philip, it doesn't surprise me that the first gay bar I walk into in fifty-seven years, you'd be there, considering the odds." Lance whoops and the leather man raises an eyebrow and looks at Philip.

"I can't believe you said that," Philip says. His face is red with anger.

"Well, I can't believe how rude you're being," Maude says. "Look, Philip, I'm not just your mother, I have a life that has nothing to do with you. I'm not going to apologize for that."

"Does Dad know you're here?" Philip says.

For a moment Maude ponders this. "I'm out for a drink, Philip, it isn't like I'm having an affair at the Manhole. I don't tell your father every single thing." Philip smirks and Maude finds herself getting angry. "Don't be so arrogant, Philip; does Dad know you're here?" Philip is speechless but both Roger and Lance are laughing. "I'm just making a point, Philip. I'm not a total open book, so don't make assumptions about what I do when you're not around, and I won't make assumptions about what you do when I'm not around." Her eyes glance toward the door to the back room.

Philip's jaw drops. "I don't," he says.

"Like I said, Philip, I won't make any assumptions. If you're so embarrassed to be seen with your mother, why don't you leave? You were on your way out the door anyway." Philip is undecided for a moment, then he takes the leather man by the arm. "Come on, Stu, let's go," he says sharply. The leather man is hesitant, then follows Philip's lead, glancing back at Maude as they leave. Maude, Roger, and Lance are silent, staring at the doorway.

"Stu," Lance says. "Come on, Stu."

"Maude, are you all right?" Roger says, putting a hand on her shoulder.

"Oh, yes, no, I guess so," she answers, shrugging. "I'm angry at him, but that's nothing new." She swishes her beer and thinks for a minute. "Was he right? I mean, should I not be here?"

Lance snorts. "I wouldn't make this your new hangout, but you can be anywhere you want," he says. "He just had a brick up his ass. I think it would be fun to run into my mother at a bar." He looks around him. "Maybe not this bar, but a bar, anyway."

"He's right," Roger says. "Don't let what Philip said upset you. He was probably just embarrassed because he was on the prowl. I think getting caught by your mother is everyone's worst nightmare."

"Especially getting caught at the Manhole!" Lance says, laughing. "Can you imagine a worse scenario? The guy must be traumatized."

"Well, maybe we should get going," Maude says. "I still have three more children that I might run into somewhere. I don't want to alienate my entire family, at least not all in the same night."

They leave the Manhole and step out into the street. The rains have stopped momentarily and the sidewalks fill up with people. To Maude they all look content and purposeful, hurrying past her to destinations free of husbands or sons, and when Lance drags them into a dimly lit café, she doesn't protest. She sits together with two strangers and feels the weight of the night diminish by the comfort of their words. When they step outside, the glistening pools on the streets have almost dried, all traces of the floods almost gone, and they catch a taxi for the hotel.

Her watch reads 2:20 as she pulls into her driveway and the house is dark. When she gets inside she finds her husband asleep and wonders what time he noticed her missing. Philip's comment at the bar comes back to her and she thinks: No, Philip. Dad doesn't know I'm here. She lies down next to Eliot and closes her eyes. An image appears before her, the frogs, pressed against the glass walls, looking out at a world they can never touch. She pictures herself returning to the restaurant, taking the jar, and pouring the frogs into a lake. As their small bodies swim away in the black water and disappear, she slowly drifts off to sleep.

The next morning Eliot is up before she is. She sees him from the window, in the yard, clearing part of a tree that fell into their yard during the storm. Hours pass without them speaking to each other, Eliot in the basement or the garage, Maude cleaning the upstairs and cooking. When Eliot finally comes upstairs he is silent. She waits for him to say something, unsure of what her answer will be, vowing not to say anything until he does, but he never does.

At quarter past three the phone rings and Eliot picks it up. "For you," he says, holding the phone out to Maude. He leaves the kitchen but Maude can sense him around the corner. "Hello?" she says.

"So how's the head this morning, missy?" Lance says. "Did those two beers do you in?"

Maude laughs. "How did you find the number?" she says.

"Information," Lance says. "How many Maude Brewsters are there in Skokie?"

"One too many," Maude says.

"Uh-oh," he says. "Bad scene this morning?"

"No scene at all. He hasn't said a word." She can hear Eliot just outside the doorway. "I don't think he even noticed I went anywhere," she says, louder.

"Really?" Lance says. "Weird. Well, all the better. We're going out again tonight, so he shouldn't mind."

"Where?" Maude says.

"We'll find something," Lance says. "There's a party with some annoying TV people, but the food is free. Plus there's a couple of plays we've been talking about seeing. Legitimate theater. We probably won't see Philip there."

"You are mean," Maude says.

"Six-thirty. We'll pick you up. Lock the old man downstairs and sneak out." Maude contemplates how she will explain it to Eliot, then looks at her watch and decides she has hours to think of something. "Okay," she says. "Six-thirty." She puts the phone back and glances at the doorway but Eliot is no longer there.

The phone rings immediately after she hangs up. "Lance?" she says when she picks up.

There is a silent pause. "Philip," the voice on the other end says icily.

"Oh," Maude says. "Oops."

"Yeah," he says. "That seems to be the word of the week." A moment passes while they wait for the other. Philip speaks first. "Look, I'm sorry about how I acted last night. It took me by surprise and I didn't know what to do."

Maude lets her anger diminish. "Okay, Philip," she says. "I guess running into your mother when you're on the prowl is shocking. I suppose I understand."

"I wasn't on the prowl," Philip protests. "That's not what I mean."

"Philip please, you were at the Manhole," Maude says. "People don't go there for the beer. I didn't look in the back room but I can probably imagine what I would have seen."

"No, you couldn't," Philip says. "I mean, I've heard . . ."

"Philip," Maude says. "Change the subject. I'm still your mother, after all."

"Fine," Philip says, sounding relieved. "Well if nothing else, I was right about the home improvement guy. I told you he was gay."

Maude laughs. "His name is Roger," she says. "Well, he was still more interested in me than in you, so what does that tell you?"

"That sounds about par for me these days."

"What happened to the guy I met last night?" Maude asks. "He seemed like a nice boy."

"He was. That was the problem," Philip says. "We got two blocks away from the bar and he left me standing on the corner. He said he would never date a guy who was rude to his mother."

"I like that guy," Maude says, laughing. "What was his name again? Stu? Did you meet him at the Manhole?"

"Yes," Philip says, embarrassed. "Speaking of which, where did you meet Roger and his bitchy friend?"

"His name is Lance and he's a nice boy, so watch your mouth," Maude says.

"Sorry," Philip says. "I just figured somebody like Roger would go for someone more rugged. Lance was kind of a twink."

"Twink?" Maude says. "I'm not even going to ask. Look, Philip, I've got to get off the phone. I'm going out later and I want to have this place clean before I leave. You know I hate coming home to a dirty sink. I'll call you tomorrow." She hangs up the phone and turns on the faucet, squirting dish soap into the sink. "Twink," she says to herself, shaking her head, then she lights an invisible cigarette, exhales invisible smoke, and starts thinking about what she's going to say to Eliot.

A Pilgrimage of You

ALEXANDER CHEE

I want Ed to tell me how he scarred himself, and so on the morning of the 38th day we are together, I ask him.

He says nothing at first. He avoids my eyes, gets up out of bed and stalks into his workshop, a converted living room, leaving me alone in his bedroom. Today is as cold as San Francisco gets, a chattery 38 degrees, and we are in the drafty Victorian he rents at the foot of Potrero Hill. The heat hasn't come on yet and I shiver in the T-shirt and long johns I wore to bed. A closed-up gas station I can see out the window from where I lie advertises gas for 68 cents a gallon, as it has done for years.

I hear him turn on his blowtorch. Ed is a metalsmith and makes things out of silver, bronze, and sometimes copper. He usually makes animals he dreams up; none of them have ever lived in the flesh. If they did, the fossils they left behind are somewhere in Ed. In his house, the creatures peer out from on top of shelves, the refrigerator, the bathroom sink, the menagerie of a god, in miniature. He's begun working larger, though, and for the large pieces he uses scrap. He works quietly, clanking occasionally, so I pick up my copy of Shelley Winters' autobiography. I read the chapters about Marilyn Monroe and her, about their days together as blonde bombshells. They lived together when they were children, almost like sisters. They shared stories about their men, like girls with candy drops. Slowly, while I read, the salted smell of hot metals fills the room.

Ed comes back and stands in the doorway. I look up from my book.

In the dark, when I run my hands down his back, they raise up a little faster than the rest of him does: fifteen crosses, cut into his shoulders, chest, and back. Squiggly lines, barely able to keep their angles to each other. The older ones are white, the newer ones pink or purple against his brown skin. Like the way I drew stars when I was six.

He grins and looks away.

"Forget it. Forget I brought it up," I say. The radiators in the house start to whistle and they clank with a sound like spoons on cups.

"I don't understand what you want," he says.

"You do it to yourself?" I say.

"I did." He pulls up his shirt to show me his skinny notched belly. He slaps at it, smiling. Then he throws himself at me, knocking me back flat on the bed. He pauses for a moment, devilish, and thrusts his crotch at mine. "What do you want? You want to watch?" he says. "Is that what you want?" He rubs his stubbled face up against my own. I push up against his hands. "If you were going to watch me do it, maybe I wouldn't."

"What does that mean?" I say. He burns his chin against my throat.

"Maybe I would write your name. Would you like that?"

He lets go of my hands and they rise up around him, crossing over his back.

"The emperor Hadrian was so in love with this boy, Antinous, he made him a god when Antinous drowned one day while swimming in the river. He put statues up of him everywhere." He rises up and then comes down again, pinning me. "It's cowardly to wait until they're dead to worship someone, though—I want to worship now."

"You're calling the emperor a coward," I say. His smile widens.

He pushes up our shirts, pressing our stomachs together. "Here. I would cut your name here, on my stomach." I move nothing. He bites my ear, his tongue tugging at the silver ring there.

"There isn't even one for every year of your life," I say. "I just want to know why you do it."

"I haven't done it in years," he says, and he sits up.

I know how long it takes a scar to heal, the colors it takes with age. I know this is a lie. I wait for him to lie down again.

In the dark I'm often afraid and so Ed made me a ring. On the outside of the silver band it reads EDEDED and on the inside it reads ZZZCRSZZZ. This was on the 28th day. I'd told him it was already difficult for me to sleep without him and he smiled. A day later he handed me the ring and he said now I am around you in your sleep no matter what. These Z's here are for sleep. So sleep.

I am Ed's first boyfriend. He moved here three years ago, drove on his motorcycle all the way from West Texas, where the oil fields pump fire at the sky. I am here from Stockton. Nothing burns the sky there except for cigarettes and old tires, and when I moved here, I said goodbye to my mother and grandmother and took the bus with a suitcase full of tennis shorts at my feet.

Ed is far from my first boyfriend, but he is my first boyfriend to own his own motorcycle, and the nights we spend together, he chains our motorcycles together, the chain as thick as my wrist. His is named Ofelia; mine, Flipper. In a bag around his waist are tiny metal charms he made to keep them safe from thieves, and in fact no one steals them. In his house, we pull each other around on his single bed, silent, until we're warm and exhausted. Sometimes we lie still for hours, barely moving, awake in the dark, and I try to see everything above us inside my head, the air above us, the miles of sky, the engines of clouds and wind between us and the vacuum of space. I return, to Ed around me, the light grip he keeps on my arms. I can take his pulse on the vein that runs down his stomach.

The first time I saw Ed, it was sunset in the city. The sky hung down, coppery sheets of light off the roofs. He was standing, his bike resting against the inside of his leg, waiting in the early evening traffic. I didn't want to recognize him then but I did. I thought to myself: Oh. There you are. Soon after that we met, and I knew he recognized me from that day. After the third day, he showed me his notebooks, filled with drawings of my tattoos in the margins, done before he ever met me.

I sleep more now. On the nights we go back to my apartment, Ed waits for me at the bookstore where I work. After I get out, we ride side by side, not stopping, up and down Mission, Van Ness, Dolores, Valencia, the traffic lights all yellow and blinking, until, frozen and tired, we go to bed and I try to sleep. We talk about riding down to Big Sur or up to Seattle, but we never go. I rub the ring at night and wonder when it will be smooth. Ed wraps himself around me, all sharp bones and cold skin and he warms himself on me as he cools me down. One night he holds his hand up above my skin and he says, "Look. I can feel the heat coming off you."

Now he sends me a card, with a poem in Spanish. It says:

Si las paredes
no son tuyas,
Túmbalas con tus
proprias manos
El único que tiene
derecho a
tu vida eres tú
mismo
no lo d'gas—házlo

I sit on my steps after I get it, looking off down the hill. I turn it in my hands, as if there is some clue beyond it, but there isn't.

Later, I'm with my friends Josh and Darius. We hear explosions coming in off the bay, and we leave the café in the Mission where we've been for hours and walk out into the street. The poem is in my pocket. It's the early evening. We've been talking but I can't remember what about; I kept feeling myself move away into a place where I could only hear myself. I don't remember what it was I told myself there. All I know now is that we have to find out what these explosions are. The streets of the Mission are always the same, but the explosions may have changed this. We light cigarettes, look at boys walking by. There hasn't been any money in this neighborhood in thirty years, but people are still selling, the products and signs and people all yellowing in the constant sun.

"I think they're coming from over in SOMA," Josh says. He lies all the time, so in my mind I try to figure out if I agree. The explosions were gigantic and diffuse, like the sound of it was around us and not from anywhere at all.

We walk by a new gallery just as the door opens, and a blond dreadlocked man steps out.

"Did you hear the explosions?" says Darius. His hair is a blue streak rising up off his head, lighting up as the sun hits it.

"Yeah," he says. "Sounded like SOMA or maybe China Basin."

"We're going to go looking for them," says Josh. "Do you want to come?"

"Yeah," he says. "My wife and I were actually going to go look for them too. Let me get her."

They come out with a small child in a stroller. "Hi," the woman says. She looks at us like friends. She also has blond dreadlocks. The baby is blond and sleeping. We set off down the street, discussing how many explosions we've heard. We haven't heard any for a while. "Maybe they're blowing apart the overpass," I say, thinking of the dead freeway section near my apartment.

Josh and the man talk to each other, and I can tell already that Josh is lying to him. He introduces himself as Fred, and says he's from Palo Alto. Josh always tells people he's from the place where his newest crush lives. I watch the wife thrust her stroller out into the street, bumping it along from curb to sidewalk to street like it's a doll. I want to steal the baby away from her. I want to tell her to cut it out. I want to tell her she's a poor excuse for a mother and should go home and shave her head, because it is a stupid thing, a horrible thing for white people to have dreadlocks and dirty babies and art galleries all together at the same time.

I walk ahead, trying to see if the baby is upset. He's asleep, a smudge of dirt on his cheek. I resist the urge to wipe it off. His head bounces as he bumps along.

"I think it's artillery, Fred," says the hippie guy to Josh. Darius and I look at each other and smile. "I don't think we're going to find anything out this way," the woman says to no one in particular.

A group of guys sit under an overpass around a firepit, and we pass close by as we cross the street. "Hey," I say. "Did you guys hear anything?"

"A lion," says one. His skin is shiny dark, almost like an eggplant. "There is a lion down here."

"A lion," I say. "We heard something all the way back in the Mission."

"When a lion is angry, you can hear him from a very long ways away. Back at home, in Africa, I could hear lions for miles."

"That weren't no fuckin' lion," another guy says. "You *so* fulla shit."

Darius holds out a pack of cigarettes and they each take one. "We're going to head along," says the hippie guy. We wave at them as they continue off toward China Basin. Josh looks at us and we pretend we're mad at him for lying so much.

"What now?" Josh says. "Those people were fucking pathetic."

"Well," I say. "Let's head down toward the water and see what we find."

We find a warehouse a few blocks later, two blocks long, with a clock tower. The clock is unlit, no hands on the face. "Wow," Josh says, and slaps his hands together, as if wiping them clean. Darius and I go to the fire escape while Josh watches the streets. I hoist Darius up and he lets down the ladder, and then we all head up the eight stories to the roof. "I'm afraid of heights," Josh says from beneath us.

"Are not," says Darius. "Just don't look down."

The walls are faded old brick, and the rust on the ladder comes away on my hands. As I go by a window, I see a light down on the first floor. When we get to the roof, I see the center is gone, exposing all the floors down to the ground in various stages of completion. Beams, partial floors, lattices of metal and wire. Dead power lines curl up like vines, and unconnected pipes extrude, offer nothing. It's as if the building were fake, a mad scientist's ruse to hide his monster, now flying above us, in battle with exploding bombs.

On the edge overlooking Van Ness, a billboard perches unlit, the cigarette ad on it peeling off. We walk over to it along the catwalk edging the roof, and sit there looking down into the street and the city. From here San Francisco looks abandoned by the people who built all of these things, leaving them to us, who have no idea what to use them for.

"I really am afraid of heights," says Josh.

"What do you imagine?" says Darius.

"That I'll fall," he says. "What else is there to be afraid of about heights?"

"Why would you fall, though. What do you imagine?"

"That I won't be able to hang on. Keep my balance."

I light a cigarette and drop the match down off the outside of the building. "Don't look at your feet," I say.

"My feet? I have to look at my feet. I don't trust my feet," Josh says.

"They want you alive as much as you do," Darius says.

"Wanna bet?"

In English, the poem Ed sent me means this: If the walls aren't of your making, then break them down with your own hands. The only one who has a right to your life is you. Don't just say it—make it. I am running this over in my head while I smoke and watch traffic. It isn't the same in English. Translation is like somebody telling you about this meal they had.

I stand up. When I lived in Stockton with my mother, we dyed our hair the same blond. She wore these blue contact lenses and peaches-and-cream foundation. We smoked and watched TV evangelists and we pretended to be not-Korean. At my school I was avoided by the white kids and the other Koreans, the Chinese and the Vietnamese. But the Mexican kids understood, somehow. They knew about dyed blond hair and mothers and God. My mother sent money to the evangelists, and they sent us cards, magazines, newsletters. There were pictures of people talking about God. Don't think it's not a sin to play bridge, one said.

Here, a short ways away, I am natural—black hair, brown eyes, yellow skin. The parts of me that never see the sun are so white they glow blue in the half-light of city night. This is how I've always been but it feels new to me, like I've just been made. I don't know that I have a right to my life, though I suspect it.

My grandmother lives there with my mother now. She laughs at the TV, laughs at my mother when she sends them money. My grandmother laughs, and it's the bark of her life. As if each chuckle really said: Live, live, live. She calls my mother "the clown." And she does look like it, when Oma says it. She looks like a clown, as if the word had a little light in it.

"Chris," Josh says.

I look through the blue darkness toward his voice. The dark is easy on my eyes here, everything glows a little from inside, liquid.

"How do you like the view?" Josh says.

"Nice view," I say.

"I don't think I'm going to have an affair with that boy from Palo Alto," he says.

"Why not?"

"He just doesn't remind me enough of my father." Josh has been making incest jokes tonight, and Darius and I look at each other in the dark.

"He is pretty young," Darius says.

"I mean, I just want a father substitute."

"Sure," I say.

"I can't throw myself into his arms, wearing my terry-cloth bathrobe, yelling, 'Daddy.' I mean, he'd flip, probably. He doesn't know how to take a joke."

Darius and I nod.

We get up and take the stairs down to the entrance to the clock tower, walking in a line: I go first, Josh second, Darius third. "Baby, Baby, where does our love go?" Josh sings as we go down the stairs, and Darius slaps his arm. "Shut up," he says.

"What is that about?" Josh asks me as we pass by each other on the stair corner.

"It's for later," Darius says. "It's a mortgage on your bad behavior."

We find a spray-paint pencil, bright yellow, amid a heap of rope and old gloves by the clock-tower entrance. There are none of the recent animal smells of people; it all smells old, dried out. The dust films up my mouth. We take turns painting things, joyless. Josh and Darius paint swears, hearts, in a moment of utter boredom tic-tac-toe. XXO. OOX. OXO.

I don't want to paint anything. I lie down on the floor and close my eyes. Building is a kind of prayer, I think as I lie there. These cities are devotions. Each board both a shelter and a plea for shelter pointing up at the night.

What is it you fear in the dark? Ed asked me, when I first told him about my trouble sleeping. I didn't know. At the time, I remembered when I was a child and I wouldn't sleep for fear of dying. I lay awake nights then. I wanted to stay alive for every minute.

I fear death, I told him. And he laughed at me. He held me tightly. You can't squeeze it out of me, I said to him. When it's dark, I fear death.

You fear life, he said to me then. When you agree to live, you acknowledge endings. You acknowledge that there will be deaths. That life is a slaughter.

I open my eyes to the cold metal of the paint pencil pressed against my forehead.

"Wake up, sleeping beauty. It's a whole new world." Darius has painted his boots yellow. I can smell them near my face. "It's your turn."

It feels dumb, but I do it anyway and it feels like a spell. A dumb spell is still a spell. Dear God, I want to say. Stay away from my man. I draw fifteen crosses on the wall. It looks like the pattern to a bad tie. I throw the paint pencil back into the heap and we slink down the stairs, out the back. A security trailer is there, the light is on, and we do not look and we are not caught.

The next morning, Ed's at work on a kind of bird-man: wings from old oil drums, an engine block for a head, a body made from two shopping carts welded and bent. The whole thing will roll on the old wheels of the carts, a flightless, gaunt thing. Today, for a beak, he cuts an old megaphone into strips, sets them with hinges and he welds the hinged pieces to the face. The mouth will be able to open in many directions, though it's unclear how many right now. He is masked and so am I, in order to watch. The mask lets me watch as the welder's fire strings arcs: they go purple and then blue and then are gone.

"You read a lot of books," he says. "Tell me a story." He bends for the lower beak.

I tell him about some friends who went to Washington, D.C., with the ashes of another friend who'd died of AIDS. He'd asked them to throw his ashes on the floor of the Senate chambers and so they did. The guard who saw them come in did nothing, only smiling as they passed with the urn. The senators had for a moment not known what lay in front of them, and then they did: even as ash, flesh can see other flesh; like knows like. They rose up from their seats, shouting as they left the room. No one who was there tells me what it was they shouted; they could not believe that there was their friend, soon now to be swept up, and they were overcome with having given him what he wanted

"What happened to them?" Ed says.

"Nothing. They left quickly and without any other disturbance, and the guard who'd smiled at them before smiled again as they left. They were never caught."

"They gave him his due then, as a citizen," Ed says. "As a taxpayer, he was finally heard from." The flame lashes the metal together. "Okay. Another."

During the Korean War, I tell him, my grandmother buried all the family metals in the back yard: sewing machine, silverware, jewelry. They stayed there for the war, covered over by a plum tree, safe from the soldiers who were collecting material for bullets. If she'd been caught, they'd have killed her. She uncovered them at the end of the war, and the tree was there when she left. She traveled with a cutting, spliced now to an orangelo tree in my mother's back yard.

"Another," he says. The metal cools under his regard, the torch at his side, dark.

Once there was a town without a church. They were tired of a visiting pastor, afraid it meant God considered theirs a visiting faith. The rich men of the town built a beautiful church all out of wood taken from the forests on the surrounding hills, and the night after the day it was done, it burned to the ground.

"Bitterness," he says, smiling.

The next church they built with bricks made from clay from the river and roofed with the slate from the riverbed, found under the clay. The rich men of the town were now not as rich, and their wives were afraid of them, and their children sometimes went hungry. When the church was done, the river ran its pocked and barren banks and swept the church away.

"A crowd gathered the next day. There was no decision about how to proceed except to build again. And then a woman in the crowd came forward, and she told them that in a dream she had been told that there should be no church yet. And they called her a witch. And she said to them, if you cannot find God here," and I touch my breastbone, "you cannot visit him there," and then I gesture, as if to conjure the remains of a church basement. " 'All your building cannot aid you.' And then they killed her."

Ed is quiet at this. "A fairy tale from your evangelical days?" he asks, and keeps working. I leave the room and go into the bedroom, flopping onto the bed, where I pick up my book and read about Shelley Winters filming in water swirling around her ankles, bad catering, and how she is a superstar.

"It aids me," he says later, as I lie on his bed, reading. He stands in his doorway again. I feel like it's my room. "It aids me."

It seems normal to me to want to know how the people you love got hurt. You do this so at least if you do these things to them you know they will survive. You will not be the reason they die. You do not know people until they tell you what is the worst they can go through and live.

For ten more days he tells me nothing of the scars. It's trickier here because he made these marks himself. Darius had a boyfriend who gave him a T-shirt printed with blood from a cutting he had done to himself: a Celtic dragon figure, on the chest, above the heart, on the shirt as it is on the skin. It was inspired by love—if Ed did his for love, I want to know for who, then. Who saw the blood. Where he is.

Ed tells me this, first: "I had this Catholic thing. I had this idea that I could be a priest."

We are outside, on the sidewalk, near our bikes. It's morning and we've just eaten breakfast enchiladas on Twenty-fourth Street and Van Ness. Ed is getting ready to go to his job at the Scandinavian Designs warehouse and he tells me this as if it were a very natural thing to say before you go off to work.

I say nothing.

"I felt a calling to God," Ed says. "I thought then that what I was supposed to do was to go and be a priest. I even went to seminary, though I dropped out after a few months."

"You're not a priest," I say. "Did God stop calling?"

"He never stops calling any of us," Ed says. "It's like anything that happens all the time, though; it becomes invisible from being there always."

He leaves and I leave and we drive off in different directions, him to the furniture warehouse and me to the bookstore. The drive is the slow drive of day traffic, stoplight to stoplight, sunny and breezy. In the distance, clouds top the mountains like sun hats; on the hills it is dark, but here in the Mission, where it is flat, there is light.

I remember a time when I went to church. We cut felt-cloth figures and pasted them onto felt backgrounds and then these were hung in the church beside the felt works of other former children. I remember feeling nothing most of the time I was there, except that I was ugly, thin, aching to leave. Once, the reverend gave a sermon and the room seemed to shake with the presence of something enormous and invisible, like we were mice and the belled cat waited somewhere outside, almost a friend. And then my sense of this passed and it was another day, and ever since, it has been another day.

In the bookstore where I go to work that day, the naked fluorescent bulbs burn down on the best-sellers and remainders, and they look exposed, like drag queens caught out in daylight. The store I work at specializes in discounting the most popular titles and the least popular titles; there are three shelves of everything else. I think of how nice it is that they end up here together, the beloved and the ignored. The customers browse, and I wonder if they know the books here are not tagged, our inventory done by price, not titles. They could walk out with any of them and we wouldn't know, the cash register the only ritual that keeps these books from spilling out into the street. I ring the books in, sitting under a display for a gigantic and out-of-date world atlas. During the last earthquake, it fell, and as I had gone out for coffee, I was safe. Coffee saved me, I told people that day, and I thought it was really funny. I think of it differently now, as I hand the customers their celebrity biographies, their self-help books and adventure novels, covered in the gray plastic bags our company provides. It seems to me I might understand now what is meant when people say God is love. I don't know if I agree, but I know certain things: desire puts us in motion. We head out the door, we want something, somewhere, someone. And hiding under desire, somewhere in the laughing light desire veils, there is a bird trying to be half-man. There is a city in the night. There is the atlas crashing down to the place you might have been.

Ed picks me up at work. We ride around the city once. We stop down by the water, in China Basin, where there are only security lights, warehouses, building equipment. When we go home, we are wary of each other, as if we might spill open. The sex we have is always careful, but as we fall into the bed, there seems more care this night, the time we keep together collected inside of us and we are barely able to keep ourselves from bursting. Afterward, Ed asks me for a bedtime story. And so I tell him one.

There was once a one-armed boy, who lived on top of a far mountain that overlooked the sea. One day, as he took his bath, he saw his dogs out on the lawn, barking at the tall grass along the edge of his yard. He came down to investigate, and there in the tall grass was a fallen angel. He was the most beautiful thing the boy had ever seen, with feathers the color of black pearls and hair like spilled ink. He lay there unmoving, as if he was dead, and so the boy shut the dogs up in the basement and brought the angel on his back into the house, into his bed. Gradually, the angel began to breathe, and now he lay as if sleeping, and the boy climbed carefully into the bed beside the angel and watched him.

He wanted, after a while, to hold the angel. To see him out of his robe, to see where the wings joined to his back and the feathers turned to skin. The wings shook lightly, as if fighting a dream wind, and then, opening his eyes, the angel turned over onto his stomach, spreading his wings over the one-armed boy like a blanket.

"Who have you come for?" the boy asked, remembering the day he lost his arm.

"I can't say," the angel said.

"If I say their name, can you nod yes?" the boy asked.

"Yes," the angel replied.

The boy ran through the list of names he knew, of his neighbors and family, slowing as he approached the names of his parents. Still, the angel only shook his head, and the boy grew cold despite the angel's wings around him. And so he said his own name, and still the angel shook his head.

From the basement, one of the dogs barked, angry at being forgotten. The boy looked up and when he looked back to the angel, he saw the angel nod his head.

Together they descended the, stairs, and after saying goodbye to his dog, the boy stood in the yard and watched as the angel took the dog in his arms and flew away. He waved a last goodbye, and then went over to the spot in the grass where he had found the angel. He took the feathers up from the grass and sewed himself a pillow, where he rests his head every night.

Ed is asleep as I finish. I close my eyes, holding him as he sleeps, and I pretend that this is what night is, smooth skin, a beating heart, a few places where something has made you bleed and still you are alive.

The next morning comes with the flat light of a blue cloudless sky. I leave Ed asleep and go to a bar near the Valencia projects where I am earning extra cash that day doing makeup for porno videos. The bar is barely that, a long thin room with a pool table and a pinball machine. I set up my kit in the bathroom and the actors come in, take off their clothes, and I make them up. They aren't particularly beautiful but they are sleek like seals, muscular and willing. As they work under fake names, I can't remember them at all. I spend a half hour covering the back of one, and as I send him out, a new boy comes in.

"Take off your clothes," I say.

He looks like a soccer player. His teeth are white, his skin rosy and flawless. As his clothes come off, I can tell there will be very little for me to do. I wonder why he is here. He looks affluent and cared for, though this could have little to do with his parents.

"Any body acne I should know about?" I ask.

"Well . . ." he says. "Maybe." He turns around and bends over. A large red bump presents itself, on the inside of his right buttock, an ingrown hair surrounded by stubble.

"Hold still," I say. With a stick of Tattoo cover-up, I cover it. "Okay." I have him sit down on the toilet seat, where I shine him up with lotion and apply mascara to his eyelashes. He looks at my face as I do this. I try not to pay attention, but I can feel him examine the separate parts.

"You ever do drag?" he asks.

"Sometimes." I shrug.

"You'd make a beautiful woman," he says.

"You're done," I say.

As he opens the door, he smiles at me. I say, "Don't let them shave you there again." He nods his head at this, and I can tell he will try.

The name of the movie is *Blond Justice* and I'm there all day, because today we shoot the three-way, and three-ways are always trouble. I sit in the bathroom, out of sight, listening to music on my Walkman and reading the magazines lying around, all porn. A famous porno actor has died and the magazines are all full of pictures of him at every stage of his three-year career. My new friend the soccer player will live on this way. I find early pictures of him. His hair is shaggy and long, his skin pale. The man he is with, bearish and furred, holds him in place, like it's an assault. Surrounded by the pictures of the dead man, his own death seems close. I shut the magazine feeling as if I've betrayed him, and then there's a knock on the door.

"Touch-ups," says the PA when I come out. In the living room, the boys are slumped in a greasy pile, panting, and as I repair them, the hot light makes me wet. I leave paid in cash, my sweat cold on me and then gone as I ride my bike home.

Ed waits for me outside my apartment, sitting on his bike. "Horrible," I say to him as I walk up to him, and he stands up to hug me.

"But you got paid," he says.

"Everyone did," I say, smiling. He wrinkles his nose. "Come inside with me."

I turn the radio up loud as I walk into the apartment. "I have this need to play dress-up," I yell to him over my shoulder. He follows me into the bathroom and sits on the toilet seat, watching me as I apply base, lipstick, eyeliner, shadow. I pull on a blond wig. More lipstick. He smiles at this and I tell him all about the soccer player, how he thought I would make a beautiful woman. Ed laughs at this.

"He's right," he says.

"Where is the bird-man going to go?" I ask him.

"I hadn't thought about that," he says.

I think of the abandoned tower. How beautiful he would be there, his dark split beak a promise of menace. And then I remember the painting I did there as I left. I breathe a little faster. I can't bring him there.

"He'll find a place," Ed says. "If I made him he was ready to be made. He'll find a place." He walks out of the room and I hear the radio go off. The silence when he returns is like fresh water.

The soccer player is right. I do make a beautiful woman. The wig is a Barbie blond. I smile at myself in the mirror. I look like the Filipino prostitutes downtown. I look like my mother. I smile at myself in the mirror. Outside it's dark now, the sun setting sometime while I was drawing in my eyebrows. Ed reaches out for my hand and pulls me to him.

"Ever kiss a girl?" I say.

"Yes," he says.

"Like it?" I say.

"Yes," he says. And so I bend down and I kiss him.

"Where are we going?" I ask later. We've dressed. I throw the wig on my bed and wash my face. Out on the sidewalk, he unlocks his bike and relocks mine.

"Ride with me?" he asks.

"Where?" I ask. I'm hungry. I want coffee, the company of strangers eating and talking.

"Hush," he says, and I do. I climb on the back of his bike and wrap my arms across his chest. We float forward when he pulls out into traffic. The night opens up to let us pass and closes up behind us, and it does this all the way through North Beach's little sidewalk cafés and Chinatown's fish markets and noodle huts and the Marina's cheap motels and expensive houses. It does this all the way to the Presidio, where the naval base is, where the beach is, and we go to the beach even though we aren't supposed to be there after dark.

We get off the bike and the sea is black and the sky violet, the sand gray and giving off still a little warmth that I gather to me when I sink onto my knees beside a still standing Ed. I am shaking from the cold of the ride and I lie down to warm up. Here in the bay the sea is most like a river and I can see, in its small waves rush-rushing in, the sea is nervous, the sea feels us watching, all of us, we are helpless to the feeling that it knows something and is impervious and is yet still nervous. To my right, the bridge over the bay is a long arm reaching into the slim shadow that is Marin County, and I watch the cars slipping back and forth, heading from work to love to work.

"Don't smoke," Ed says. "Will you not do that?"

He goes to his knees beside me. I feel him hit the sand. "Why?" I say. "The makeup job was bad today?"

"It was kind of bad. I don't know how much more of this I can do." I'm not saying what I want to say, and so everything coming out of my mouth is false.

"There are other things you can do."

"Yes," I say. He is studying me, making my features out in the dark. As I light the cigarette I see him looking at me. "The bookstore, for instance."

"You make a beautiful woman," he says.

"You are never going to tell me about the scars," I say.

"I don't know."

"Just because I asked doesn't mean you have to tell me," I say. I throw a handful of sand up and stub out my cigarette.

"Yes," he says.

"Do you like me like this?" I ask. "Asking you questions you won't answer?"

"Yes." He puts his lips up against mine. He says it again. "Yes." He kisses me. "I like you like this." His upper lip is wet. Almost a groan, a sound comes from him. He presses me down into the sand. His hands run up under my shirt, stroke the lines of my ribs, pass down to my waist. He rests against my chest, not moving, just breathing. I put my hands in his hair. "You know why Hadrian put those statues up?" I say.

"Because he wanted to always be able to see him." Ed says this so close to me it feels almost like I'm saying it.

"Because he knew, if he couldn't see him, he might forget him," I say. "He might not have. He might have remembered everything there was to remember, always. But he might have forgotten him." Ed lies still, listening.

"But then all he is is a statue, afterward. A statue. Everywhere." I see him rise from the river where he drowned, the beautiful dead boy. The sea knows it can return nothing it has taken, but a river can be fooled, it hasn't yet become the sea. The river is a devotion for the sea, all hope and magic. The dead boy fools the river and walks. For the first moment, he is idle. Why has he returned? It's the middle of the night, and his lover, the powerful emperor, is asleep. He could go and the lover would never know. He could gather all the statues of him in the city and then leave, go back to the river, the city full of empty temples.

But he doesn't. The statues have survived to this day.

I want to say I know why he cut himself. I want to say he told me. Or that I figured it out. But it wasn't that way. That night on the beach, I want him to tell me a story. I want the gift of the part of him he is trying to get at with the knife. In the city behind us, people are taking off their clothes for each other. They are resting from building. They are praying. One more day, one more night pulled from desire into sunlight to sunset.

Wanting something, I pull an arm free to reach for another cigarette and I light it. He sits up off me quickly.

In the years that follow this, I will remember how angry I was. I will remember I was unaccountably angry. That I lit another cigarette. That later, Ed sleeps with someone else, and I sleep with the same someone else. And we sleep with so many someone elses that we go away from each other. And we are actually both so angry we don't talk for three years, until one day when I return to San Francisco, I call him at the apartment I've never seen, where he lives with his new lover, who is sick now. We both took other lovers after each other, had them both for years, and now I've broken up with mine and so I'm traveling. I want to leave them alone in their love, because it's what they want and what they have, except I have this thing I'm carrying around with me for him and it is still without shelter.

"It's Chris," I say, when he picks up.

"Hi," he says, his voice rising.

We're quiet. The silence between us hasn't changed. And then I tell him, "I just wanted to say, I want us to be able to see each other in the street and maybe, though I know we can't be friends, we could talk to each other."

He says, "I thought I'd never hear from you again."

"You really thought that?"

"I really thought that."

"The world is not so large." And then I give him my number, because I'm a coward, and I tell him I am in San Francisco for a few weeks before I return to New York. But I already know by now, he isn't going to call me.

I put the phone down when he hangs up. Everything I thought I had for him is for me. This is the only gift he can give and here it is, waiting for me to calm down. What I want to hear from him doesn't matter. It hasn't mattered in years. If God is love, and love sets you walking, then I say: Love takes you. I say: My God is the god of walking. I say: I am walking, walking, walking. Here I am. This is for you. Ed, this is for you.

Barrel Racers: El Charro

GARY BOWEN

I met Jo at the rodeo, which is where I meet all my women. I'm a cowboy and a winner and there is no shortage of women who will fuck a man just because he has a big shiny buckle. We call 'em buckle bunnies. Jo wasn't one of them. She stayed by herself, and I first noticed her as she was watering her horse, a big sorrel mare with dainty ankles. She herself was tall, about five-ten, which I immediately noticed. I prefer tall women; "ladies with altitude," as we call 'em around here. Her sandy brown hair was cropped short, which was the norm for cowgirls who compete—nobody wants to get hair caught and ripped out of their heads. She was tanned and lean, but not aerobicized. She was muscular, with broad shoulders that filled out her blue satin shirt. It was a bib front cavalry shirt, very masculine-looking, and very sexy, tucked into black jeans. She wore jeans with silver conchas down the outside, like a charro, and she wore them outside her boots, like a man. Black boots and big roweled Mexican spurs completed her outfit. Very flashy and very sexy, and not the denim and lace that barrel racers usually adopted to prove their femininity. Face it, it's not right, but folks often assume that if a woman is into a "man's sport" like rodeo, she must be a dyke. She can be walking around with a ring on her hand and a husband on her arm and some people will say the rudest things about her supposed orientation.

I climbed up on the fence and hung around. I love barrel racing, I'd do it myself if they let men do it. I love the horses especially. Power, precision, agility, and intense training, that's what it takes to produce a good cow pony. Barrel racing tests those skills. She lined up in the chute, her face intent, woman and horse melded into one. Then they exploded out of the gate, charged full gallop across the arena, and she laid the mare over like a motorcycle as she took the first barrel. That horse's head stayed inside a three-foot circle while the body churned full tilt 360 then sprang off to cross to the opposite barrel, wrapped around, clipped the barrel but it didn't topple—no penalty—yanked the reins hard to keep the horse's head up, and slammed around the last barrel, wider than the first, before rocketing home. She crossed the finish line and reined up hard, the horse skidding to a stop within inches of the arena wall. Applause exploded. Her time put her on top, and only the Devil himself would be able to dislodge her. Naturally I had to make her acquaintance.

The thought flickered through my head that if a winning ride like that made me antsy to meet a woman, then maybe I was a buckle bunny too. It gave me a twinge, but I decided to ignore it. I'd slept with barrel racers before, even ones who hadn't won. I wasn't a starfucker. So I walked up to her and said, "Congratulations! That was a great ride."

She looked me up and down with a long cool look. I couldn't tell if she liked what she saw or not; most women find me attractive. Six-six, bronze-skinned, black hair, brown eyes, and a powerful body. The men, now some of them don't like a brown man talking to white women, and I've been in a few dustups over it. But the ladies, they usually like it. And that's what counts.

"Thank you," she replied politely.

It wasn't exactly warm, but I wasn't exactly shy, either. I stuck out my hand. "I'm Jim. They call me 'El Charro.'"

She took my hand and gave it a bone-crunching grip. It caught me by surprise, and I winced. "I'm Jo. I've seen you ride."

Strength met strength and our eyes locked. I gradually increased the pressure, but she wouldn't break our grip. Her gray eyes sparked as she felt my strength surpass hers and her hand began to squash in mine. She didn't complain and didn't try to break away. I was afraid I'd break her hand and I let go. She smiled faintly, and I realized I'd lost, even if I was stronger. That nettled me; I don't need a dame who's into power games.

"Well, looks like first place is a sure thing," I said coolly. "Good luck."

"Looks like you've got second place sewed up in the bareback bronco riding," she drawled in reply.

I turned back to her. “Look, I don’t need attitude from you. I was just trying to be nice.”

“I don’t need you to be nice to my tits. You didn’t even look me in the face until I hurt your hand.”

That stung me. I yanked my eyes up from the level of her chest and flushed. “You’re an attractive woman, you should expect to get stared at.”

“You’re an attractive man,” she shot back. “How would you feel if everybody you met stared at your crotch?” She directed her gaze downward.

“I don’t think normal people stare at guys’ crotches,” I mumbled in embarrassment.

“Exactly my point,” she replied coldly. She turned her back on me.

I thought about the buckle bunnies. Yeah, they looked me in the face, but it was the buckle and what was under it that drew them. “Okay, you’ve made your point. But dammit, I like winners!”

I was telling it to the back of her head, but my eyes wandered down to her ass. Now that I was noticing where my eyeballs were ending up, I was embarrassed to discover how easily distracted I was by curvaceous parts. Sheesh, I was too old to act seventeen!

“You’re persistent, aren’t you?” she said over her shoulder.

“I wouldn’t be in second place if I didn’t see things through.”

“Maybe you’d be in first place if you tried a little harder.”

Damn, did she mean what I thought she meant, or was she just toying with me? I thought fast. “Can I buy you a drink?” I braced for rejection.

“Maybe,” she replied.

“Maybe what?”

“Maybe if you win,” she said, and sauntered off.

I had one more ride. Could I do it? I’d have to beat Pete Cochran, but then, I’d been trying to beat Pete Cochran all day. Now I had a little extra incentive. “I’ll hold you to that!” I called after her.

I was so wired that I strolled up next to Pete and told him, “I’ve got one more ride. You’re gonna lose.”

He looked at me in surprise and said, “In your dreams. You’ve got Godzilla.”

“You wait and see.”

The adrenaline was pumping like crazy and I could hardly wait for my ride. I didn’t know if she was out there watching or not, but it didn’t matter. If I won, she was going to make good. I mounted up.

We bounced across the arena, me spurring for all I was worth, hand held high, stuck to the back of that beast like I was glued to the saddle. It was a damn good ride. The pickup man suddenly appeared at my elbow, but I hadn't heard the horn, so I ignored him and kept riding. "You're done, man!" he yelled at me, and extended an arm. I let him pick me off then and he put me on my feet, black chaps flashing as I dismounted. The joke ran across my mind: "Why do cowboys make lousy lovers?" Answer: "They think eight seconds is a good ride."

I chalked up an 88. Grinning ear to ear, I walked back over to the fence and climbed up. Pete Cochran was standing there looking sour. I said, "Told you so," then jumped down and walked away, cocky as you please. When I found Jo, I said, "You owe me a drink."

She smiled slightly. "All right, Jim. You've got yourself a drink."

Several hours later I had dinner and several beers inside me, courtesy of Jo picking up the check. Women had picked up the check before, but they usually made a production of it. When I finally started wondering where the bill was, she just said, "I took care of it."

We went back to my room, and I was a little too beer-fuzzed to realize that usually it was the man who went to the woman's room. It's rude to throw 'em out, so the guy goes to the woman's place so he can simply leave when he's done. I let her into my motel room, and made a grab for her, but she put a hand on my chest and pushed me away. "You go too fast, cowboy. Why don't we get a shower?"

That sounded good to me. After a full day of rodeoing we were not fit company for civilized people; a shower sounded great. "All right. Gimme a minute." I used the john, brushed my teeth and used mouthwash, and started the shower. I stuck my head out. "Okay, join me?"

She had already peeled out of her clothes and walked naked across the carpet. She had small firm breasts, a flat belly, and long legs. She was uniformly tan and her nipples were brown. The black hair of her muff was trimmed short. "You're beautiful. Is it okay for me to stare now?"

She laughed. "Yes, you can stare now," she said. And she stared back at me, eyes raking over broad pectoral muscles covered with a little black hair, the line of hair swooping down across my belly to my groin, my well-endowed piece of meat starting to stretch a little. She put her arms around my waist and pushed me back against the doorframe and, standing on her tiptoes, met my mouth with hers. She kissed hard and I closed my eyes, more than willing to let her make the first moves. My hands cupped her softly padded but firm derriere, then her tongue was probing my mouth. I kissed back, then sucked on her tongue, letting her lead me. I hugged her tighter and her arms tightened around my waist. I ground my crotch against her lower belly, and she pressed back, keeping me off balance, leaning against the doorframe.

She broke the kiss. "Let's get wet, cowboy," she said. I followed her into the shower.

She soaped me up and ran her sudsy hands all over my body; I kept trying to wash her. Sometimes she would let me cop a feel of breast or derriere, but then she would pull away and push me around, washing my back or making me stoop so she could get my shoulders better. Her hands touching me all over made me hot, and the tantalizing little bits of her I got to touch made me hotter. But she had a definite plan of where we were going and when we would get there, and I wasn't allowed to backseat-drive. When she finally knelt to soap my legs I had a full hard-on. I really wanted her to suck me, but as her hands slipped up the inside of my thighs I figured I would eventually get it if I could just stand the suspense.

Then her hand was soaping the apex of my legs, massaging my full balls and lathering up my crotch. I watched her with dark eyes, and she glanced up and smiled. "You need something?"

"I sure do," I replied.

"Let me do it my way and I guarantee you'll like the results."

"I'm game."

She lathered my cock then, slowly pumping it with the soapsuds for lubrication. I threw back my head and let out a groan. More water, more soap kept me slick. Oh, the lady knew how to give a hand job! Her other hand slid up between my thighs and I spread my legs a little wider, letting my balls hang free. She caressed them with one hand while stroking me with the other. Then her hand slid between my legs and gripped my butt cheek. She let go of my dick and squeezed both my cheeks and I flushed a little. She guided me back a bit and let the water wash down my front and, holding on to my hips, turned me back and forth so that the water streamed on my crotch and washed away the soap. Then she grabbed my dick and pulled me forward.

She bent her mouth to my dick then, and as her lips wrapped around my foreskin, I let out a long sigh. Finally. Oh, that felt so good. She sucked the head gently, then more strongly, slowly increasing the pressure and the sensation, sliding her lips up and down on the first couple of inches. I was breathing hard, wanting her to take the whole thing. She was exquisite, making me wait, while she savored my flesh. Then her hand slid up between my legs again, and quested between my cheeks. I twitched a little as an accustomed sensation made itself felt between my legs. She was massaging my asshole and I didn't know what to do or think. What she was doing to my dick felt incredibly good, but I was uneasy about what else she might have in mind.

She felt my tension, because she looked up and said, "Relax. I'm gonna make you feel real good."

"Okay." I wasn't reassured.

"Maybe we should do this in bed," she said.

"Bed is a good idea," I agreed.

We turned off the water and toweled off, and I got my hands on both her tits and tongued them fiercely. She rewarded me by arching beneath my hands and moaning. Reassured, I picked her up and carried her to bed. I laid her down and stretched out beside her, whereupon she climbed on top of me and straddled me, my cock nowhere near her pussy. I looked up in surprise. She smiled. "I told you we were gonna do it my way."

Her hands caressed my chest as she spoke. "Now honey, I like a woman that knows what she wants, but there's a few things I want too."

"You'll get them. Just let me have my way first."

"Okay."

A warm buzzing was starting in my tits, which was traveling down my spine to my balls. Dammit, whatever she was doing to my nipples was making me horny! Nobody had ever played with my nipples, not like that. I started to squirm. She increased the pressure and I kicked and arched, breathing hard. "Shit!" I exploded. "Pardon my language, but—" She pinched hard and I about leaped out of my skin. I thought I had been hard before but that was nothing like what she was doing to me now.

She relented a little and I caught my breath. She continued twirling my nipples between her thumb and forefinger, and I started arching up again. She increased the pressure, I increased my writhing, and so it escalated until pressure became pain which only made me hotter which became too much stimulation and I said, "Ow!" She instantly relented.

"Just say 'yellow,' and I'll lighten up," she told me.

"Okay." I was aware that we had entered a different mode of being at that time, but I didn't know what it was.

"Can I please be inside you when you do that?"

"I have a different idea. Do you like eating pussy?"

"Yes." I brightened.

"Then why don't we sixty-nine? You can do whatever you want to me, and I can do whatever I want to you."

I had to think about that. "Anything?"

She laughed. "No permanent damage. But yeah, anything."

"Okay." I had it in the back of my head that I would do everything to her that she did to me. A little bit of anger was in the thought. She turned around and presented her lovely rear end to me and I immediately dove in. I do like to eat pussy. She had a big clit, at least an inch long, and it was erect and firm in my mouth. I sucked on it hard because a long time ago a woman had told me to "suck it until it breaks," and I had found that good advice with most every woman thereafter. She moaned and arched and shoved her mound against my face. I kept eating her, grinning to myself. What woman could resist what I was doing to her?

Then her hands cradled my thighs and pulled them up a bit so she could grip my butt cheeks, and her mouth closed over the head of my dick. She sucked my foreskin, which just about drove me out of my skin, and I tried desperately to shove my dick into her mouth. I lost track of what I was doing while she wrestled with me, then suddenly her finger plunged into my butthole at the same instant her mouth closed over my dick. I cried out and thrust hard, felt the hardness inside me and jerked back, but she braced her hand and I only impaled myself deeper on her finger. I cussed in Spanish.

She fingered something inside me while sucking my cock intensely and I was panting and rushing toward my climax. I started grunting and twitching, but she didn't let go of me. Then I was humping and thrashing, pressure boiling over into the most intense orgasm of my life. I fountained into her mouth while my butthole clamped tight on her finger. I kept coming and coming, letting out a long groan, then suddenly collapsing. She withdrew her finger, then looked over her shoulder at me.

"Any complaints?"

I shook my head silently. After I caught my breath I asked, "What in the world did you do to me?"

She turned around and grinned like the cat that has eaten the canary. "Oh, just a little something men always like."

"But I'm not gay," I said.

"You don't have to be gay, stupid. It's a muscle. If you use it, it gets stronger and more flexible. It feels good to use it." She ran her hands over my abs. "Doesn't it?"

"But I'm not wired that way."

"Yes, you are. Every man is. Look, lots of men like their girlfriends to do that to them. If you were gay, you would want a man to do it to you, not a woman. See, sex is just sex. Orientation is who you want to have sex with."

"Um, I see what you're saying, but it's messing with my head."

She lay down beside me with her hand on my belly. "I don't usually date straight men. I prefer a man who knows his body and is comfortable with it."

"Well . . ." I wanted to claim I was comfortable with myself, and, in point of fact, up until about five minutes ago, I had been. I thought.

"I know what I want. The question is, are you interested in learning how to give it to me?"

"This sounds like a long-term project."

"It is." She was looking past me into space.

"Jo, I would like to spend more time with you. But I'm on the rodeo circuit. So are you. I don't think we can make commitments."

"No, of course not." She sounded disappointed.

"I wish I could. Where do you live? Maybe this winter."

She gave me her phone number, reluctantly I might add. I could tell she didn't think I would call. She got up and reached for her shirt then.

I grabbed her. "Hey, wait. We aren't done."

She waited. "What did you have in mind?"

I hated to have to ask it, but I had to ask it. "Did you come?" I burst out.

"No."

I felt my face flush. "Well, come back to bed and let me finish you off."

She dropped the shirt and climbed back into bed. I immediately dove between her legs. I cradled her hips in my hands and tongued her big clit, sucking and chewing on it until she thrust up and smeared her juices across my face. I settled in to eat her for as long as it took, while she thrashed beneath me and began to make noises. She got louder and louder and I began to fear my tongue wouldn't hold up long enough, but suddenly she thrashed violently and cried out, "Enough!"

She collapsed with limp legs and I grinned in triumph. Only problem, I was hard again. I lay down beside her. She took one look at what I had, then rolled onto her side and spooned up next to me. "Got any lube?" she asked.

I racked my brain. "I've got some hand lotion. That should work."

"Get it."

When I came back she lifted her ass and crouched on her hands and knees. I lubed my cock up good, then crawled over on top of her like an animal. I pressed the tip against her smaller hole and she began to breathe hard and moan. Her hand in her crotch rubbed her clit, and I slipped an inch inside her. She moaned louder, and her hole tightened on me. I held still, letting her struggle with me, then finally her hole relaxed and she said, "More."

In this manner I gradually worked the whole length inside her until my balls were slapping against her wet pussy. I wrapped one arm around her waist and held her tight while I began to slowly rock. Her hand was busy in her pussy and her breathing and moaning both got louder. I fucked her harder, taking longer strokes inside her, trying hard not to lose control and just start hammering away. She reached between her legs and grabbed my nuts, squeezing hard. "Harder!" she yelled.

So I obliged, braced both hands and banged inside her, wanting to come myself, because I have rarely had such a tight sweet hole to play with. She was howling and shuddering then, and I felt the spasms as she came. I gave myself permission to come then and jackrabbited inside her until a few moments later I was spurting for the second time. This time was not quite as intense, but was longer and more mellow than the first time. Both of them were very, very good. We collapsed.

"Oh Jo, you are so hot," I told her, cradling her in my arms. "That was fabulous."

A few months went by and I saw her again, up in Cheyenne. I blinked and looked twice. Yes, it was her. But she was bulking out, her shoulders even bigger than I remembered. She must have been working out with weights. Her jaw was squarer too, and she'd cut her hair all the way down to a buzz cut. Now she really did look like a dyke. She was wearing a red bandanna print shirt tucked into blue jeans and her waist had thickened. She'd put on some weight. She didn't look as good as she used to. I was disappointed but it would be rude for me to pretend I didn't see her, either.

"Hey, Jo! How's it going?"

She looked up in surprise. "Jim! Long time no see."

"You been lifting weights? You're getting big!" I tried to make a joke of it.

She smiled that same old half smile as if I wasn't exactly funny. "Yeah, I've been working out."

"You look like a bull dagger," I said thoughtlessly.

"I'm not a lesbian. I like men."

"I know. I'm sorry, I shouldn't have said that. It's just that, well, it isn't fair, but you know how people talk."

"Did they send you over to say that, that I'm not feminine enough to be a rodeo queen?" Her voice was hoarse, like she had a sore throat or maybe was trying not to be upset. "Do I embarrass them? I keep winning, you know. Maybe that embarrasses them."

"Jo, I didn't say that."

"It's okay. I'm switching rodeo circuits as soon as the season is over. I'm fed up with the crap. I know damn well I could ride as a man and I wouldn't get a tenth the bullshit I put up with here."

"Where you going to go?"

She didn't answer, just glanced sideways at me. "Buy me a drink?"

"Sure, Jo. I can do that."

In the beer tent the server said, "Can I see some ID, sir?" to Jo. She handed over her driver's license. Jo was almost as old as me, at least twenty-seven, though I didn't know for sure. The server handed back her license and a beer. I got mine, but he didn't ask me for ID. Something wasn't computing, but I didn't know what. She led us to the opposite side of the tent, far away from the occupied tables. "You think I'm too butch, don't you?"

"Well, I got no objection to women bodybuilders. But you need to be careful, otherwise people will think you're a man."

She laughed without humor. "I like it when they think I'm a man. They treat me better."

I drew in the beer circles on the picnic table top. "What's wrong, Jo?"

"I wanna ride bulls."

"Sheesh, Jo, even I'm not that crazy!"

"I'm sick of being Miss Fancy Pants barrel racer. I wanna rodeo like a real cowboy."

I took her hands between mine. "Jo, don't you ever let anybody tell you barrel racers aren't real rodeo. Heck, I'd barrel-race if they let me."

"Would you?" She seemed surprised.

"Yeah, I would. I like horses and I can't rope worth a damn."

"You can, you know."

"Oh sure, exhibition. But people would think I was funny, you know?" I waffled my hand. "Light on my feet."

"So? I have to put up with people thinking I'm a dyke to barrel-race. Why should you have it any easier? If you wanna do it, that's what you should do. Or don't you have the balls to stare down guys who would snicker about your chosen sport?"

That stung, that really stung. "I'm Chicano. I get all the crap I want already."

"What if there was a place where there wasn't any crap?"

I smiled. "I think you and I would both go there."

"It's called IGRA. International Gay Rodeo Association. Men and women compete equally in all events." I froze. "I'm not a lesbian, but I am a transsexual. I figure if anybody can deal with me, they can. I don't have many options, so next season I'm mounting up with the queers."

I didn't know what to say. "This stuff about being a man, you're really serious. I mean, it's not just the usual women's bitching, is it?"

"Yes, I'm serious. All my life I've felt like a man. But people could never see anything except the body and nobody would believe anything different than what a pair of tits told them. So I'm changing my body. I don't like having to do it, but it's the only way I know how to get people to see me as I really am."

"Were you, ah, doing this, back when we, um, that is?"

"Yes. I'd been on the testosterone about four months at that time."

"Oh. And it, uh, does what?"

"Makes me look like a man."

I looked her . . . him? . . . in the face. "So how far does this go? Is there like, surgery or something?"

"Yes. As soon as the season's over I'm having breast reduction surgery. I'm changing my name, going over to IGRA. As far as anybody over there knows, I'm just some gay cowboy."

"I thought 'gay cowboy' was an oxymoron," I joked.

"Don't be stupid, Jim."

I rested my chin on my hand and reviewed our previous encounter in an entirely new light. "So you're trying to tell me that when we were together, it was like I was with a gay guy."

"Yeah, that's what I'm telling you. Though I realize it didn't look that way to you at the time." She sounded apologetic, something I wasn't used to.

"Shit." She shrugged. "So, uh, what do I call you now?"

"Jo. Nobody knows yet. Just you. So let it lie. I'll disappear quietly. You can talk about me after I'm gone, okay?"

"I wanna sleep with you before you go."

She looked very surprised. "Why?"

"Why are you doing what you're doing?" I countered.

"Lot of reasons."

"So you have your reasons, I have mine."

I lay between her legs, thrusting hard. My senses told me I was in the body of a woman, but my brain said, "Don't you believe it." The contradiction between sensation and perception screwed with my head and though I was hard as a rock, I couldn't come. Finally I rested. "I need help," I said quietly.

"What do you want?"

"Do what you did to me the last time. With your finger." I was blushing.

"Okay." I rolled off of her, and she loomed over me. She still had her T-shirt on, restraining her small breasts. The burly shoulders looked like a man's shoulders, but the rear end was well rounded still, though smaller than it had been. Conflicting signals alternated in my brain. Man, woman, gay, straight, something else.

She slipped her finger inside, and I groaned and arched. I needed to come, I was ready to come. Two fingers worked inside of me. She settled between my legs and leaned over me and now there was a broad-shouldered young man leaning between my legs. I squeezed my eyes shut. "I am not gay," I told myself. I didn't want to come, not like that. Not with a man between my legs. My head was royally fucked over, then my legs tightened around him. I opened my eyes and looked at us. He was there, bracing against the pressure of my legs as they tightened on him as I thrust deeper onto his hand. I needed to come real bad.

"Oh shit," I said, then my resistance collapsed. I started bucking wildly, wanting him to climb into me and do it right. Then I burst into a million pieces.

He lay behind me and one gentle arm wrapped tentatively around me. "What the fuck am I?" I whispered. "I like women. But I like-hate-love what you just did to me."

"Do you like me?" he asked.

That was not the answer I expected, but it deserved a serious answer. "Yeah, I do."

"Maybe your orientation is Jo," he said. "Who says you have to be gay or straight? Maybe there are as many orientations as there are people in the world."

I relaxed then. He snuggled against me and it was a feminine kind of snuggling. I smiled. Parts of Jo were still there. Had always been there. "I didn't know you very well before," I said.

"Nobody knows me well."

"Well, I think I know you better than anybody else now!"

"Yes, I think you do. But that's not saying much. I've never even discussed this with other people. I tried to raise it, but it would always go down tangents, or just not go anywhere at all. You're the only lover I've had that knew."

"The only?"

"Yes."

I was disquieted. What did it say about me that I had sex with a transsexual? I groaned. "This is too weird for me."

Her arm tightened around me. "Don't you chicken out on me now," she whispered fiercely. "I'll hate you if you do." That was the old Jo talking, the one that had told me to get my eyeballs out of her cleavage. Ah, lightbulb.

"No wonder you were so pissed about me staring at your tits."

She—he—almost laughed. "Yes, well, after this winter it won't be possible anymore."

I winced. "That sounds like it would hurt."

"I imagine it will."

I rolled over to face her. Him. "Do you really have to do this, Jo? Is it really that bad? I mean, I could marry you, then people would have to quit with the lesbian crap, right?"

"I've been in the closet all my life. It hasn't helped. I don't mind being called a lesbian. What I mind is being called a woman."

Suddenly, I got it. A couple of things clicked into place, and I rolled over on top of him and kissed him fiercely. "I wasn't joking about marrying you," I told him. "Let's get married now, while it's still legal."

"Are you serious?"

"Yeah, I am. I'm crazed, but yes, I'm serious."

A host of emotions flitted across his face. "You want me because I'm transsexual?"

I flushed and looked away. "It seems so," I finally said. "I never even knew what that was until now, but now that I know it, I want it."

"Well, damn. You surprise me, cowboy."

"My name is Jim."

"Jim. Okay. Look. In six months, ask me again. I won't do anything about my ID until then. If you change your mind, well, you gave me a fair chance. If you still think you want me, then I'll marry you."

"I won't change my mind. Can I borrow your horse?"

"Why?"

"Why? I wanna barrel-race, dammit. No point in being shy now."

He laughed quietly. "Okay, Jim. I'll show you how it's done."

Blood Brothers

MICHEAL SKIFF

Kevin parted the black leather drapes of the bar and stepped into the night, leaving the pounding music behind. A marine layer cloaked the sky, reflecting the pink of the Los Angeles city streetlamps from its belly. These lamps were spaced apart on the sidewalk by the shadows of trees that hung overhead as Kevin walked to his home, just a few blocks away. Traffic was sparse, only cars cruising to make a pickup or looking for a spot to park before going in the bar.

Ahead, in the shadow of a tree's canopy, was a male figure leaning back against a wall, one leg propped up and arms folded across his chest. Kevin slowed his pace out of caution, though it probably came across as a cruise. As he approached the figure, Kevin looked into the baseball-capped face of a kid who had come on to him back in the club. They had locked stares as the guy palmed Kevin's crotch. But Kevin had got the feeling the guy was tweaking. Something about his stare was a little too intense. Now the kid was looking back at him with recognition. And hope. He looked like he could be fun, Kevin thought, but it was getting late. Kevin preferred to do his tricking on the weekends, when he could take some time to play. He nodded at the kid, giving him a "What's up?" while passing him quickly enough as to not encourage him.

Kevin crossed the street, and as he did, he glanced back over his shoulder. The kid had left the wall and was also crossing the street.

"Hey, wait up," a voice called, and the kid came trotting up alongside Kevin. "You leaving already?"

"Yeah. I'm a working man. Can't party tonight," Kevin replied.

"That's too bad. You live around here?"

"In the neighborhood," Kevin said, trying to remain evasive, though he could see his porch light not too far ahead.

"What's your name?" the kid asked.

"Kevin."

"Mine's Billy," and he stuck out his hand to shake Kevin's, disrupting their stride.

"Not a Bill?" Kevin asked.

"Huh?"

"You're not a Bill?"

"No, just Billy."

"Cool," Kevin said, glancing at Billy for the first time under a bright light. Dressed in white tank top, gray sweats, tennis shoes, and a dark baseball cap with the Nike swoosh emblem embroidered in white, the demeanor was boyish, but Billy was not. He was probably a few years older than Kevin's thirty-one. They walked past several houses in silence. Kevin considered walking past his own place.

"You want some company?" Billy finally said.

"Thanks, but not tonight."

Billy came up close to Kevin, bumping against him. He lowered his voice, as if to keep any passing cars from hearing him. "I'd really like to suck your cock. It felt nice . . . back in the bar."

Kevin felt a rousing in his jeans. They'd arrived at the base of his stairs. "Listen, Billy, I'd like to get into something with you, sometime. But it's late."

"We don't have to do it all night. Just a little while, until you get off. Then I'll go."

"It's too bad they walled off this fireplace," Billy said as he looked over Kevin's living room. "At least you still got the hardwood floors."

The apartment was a boxy stucco and wood frame guesthouse, circa 1940s, built over a garage.

Kevin was busy clearing a dinner dish and glass from the coffee table, placing them in the kitchen sink. "Do you do poppers?" he called to Billy.

"Yeah."

Kevin grabbed a bottle from the freezer and put it in his pants pocket. Passing back through the living room, he excused himself for a moment as he went down the hall into the bedroom. There, he pulled off his tan workman's boots and tossed them in the closet. As he was leaving, he noticed his Rolex watch he'd left on the dresser earlier after work. Kevin opened a drawer and buried the watch beneath several rolls of socks. When he returned, he found Billy squatting in front of his bookcase.

"I think you can tell a lot about a person just by looking at their bookcase. And their music collection," Billy said. Kevin's shelves held mainly theater texts and plays. "Are you an actor?" he asked as he flipped through a script.

"No," Kevin said, coming up behind Billy. "I'm in accounting. Never made it as an actor. Those are from college."

Billy stood and studied a collection of photos on top of the bookcase. Prominent in front was a photo of Kevin with his arm around an attractive younger man. "Is this your lover?"

Kevin stood behind Billy and looked over his shoulder. "That's my little brother. Well, not so little now."

"You guys look like you're real close."

"We're probably closer than most. Never tried to kill each other," Kevin joked.

Billy looked at the other family photos that captured Kevin and his brother at various ages. "I wish I had an older brother. I only had sisters," he said, looking at a picture of a teenage Kevin and Billy, swimsuit-clad at some summer lake. "All older. I bet there isn't a single picture of me with any of 'em." Turning to face Kevin, he began to stroke Kevin's chest. "Did you and your little brother ever . . . mess around when you were growing up?"

"No."

"Did you ever want to?" He toyed with Kevin's nipples.

"If you were my little brother I'd want to."

Billy let out a quick gasp.

"You want to be my li'l bro', Billy?"

Billy peered up at Kevin sheepishly.

"You like that?" Kevin drawled.

Billy nodded slightly.

"Climbing in my bed, after the folks have gone to sleep?" Kevin continued. "Let you fall asleep at night with your head on my chest?" he said into Billy's ear, putting his arm around Billy's shoulder and guiding him into the bedroom.

Billy reached down and rubbed the hardness in Kevin's pants as they walked. "I always wanted a big brother. Someone to look up to. Maybe worship a little."

He seated Billy on the edge of the bed and stood before him. Looking down at him, Kevin removed his T-shirt and displayed a body found on those who do their worship in the gym.

Billy caressed it with his hands. "You're so big. Strong."

Kevin pulled off Billy's tank top, knocking the baseball cap to the floor, and revealing a bald spot. Billy quickly bent to pick the cap up and returned it to its place on his head, with the bill turned backward this time. Then he buried his face in the crotch of Kevin's pants. Reaching in his pocket, Kevin pulled out the bottle of poppers. He twisted the top off and placed the vial under Billy's nose.

Billy inhaled, then began to mouth the front of the jeans, turning them a dark blue.

"Does my little brother want to suck his big bro's cock?"

Billy's eyes widened as he stared into Kevin's. He answered with a stream of "yeses," all muffled into Kevin's crotch. Kevin reached down and unbuttoned the first button of his fly. Then the next and the next, until a patch of musk brown hair was inches in front of Billy's face.

"You have to ask for it, Billy."

"Oh, yes! Would you please let your little brother suck your dick? I'll make you proud of me, Kev. You can teach me just how you like it and then I'll take care of you. Whenever you tell me to. Please?"

Kevin reached in his pants and pulled out his hard cock. "You better be good to this."

Billy paused for a moment, looking into Kevin's eyes, then impaled his face on the cock. Kevin groaned approval, as he breathed deep the bottle's vapors, his body going flush with the rush of his pulse. Billy pulled the front of his sweats down and began to stroke his own cock. Kevin paid it no notice. He was busy reaching behind Billy to finger his butt.

"One of the duties of a big brother is to show his little brother how to take a cock up his ass," Kevin said. He pried Billy off his dick, forced him onto the bed, unlaced Billy's tennis shoes and pulled his sweats off.

"If you're going to fuck me, you gotta use a condom, okay?"

"No problem," Kevin replied, taking off his own pants and socks. "I'm clean, and I plan to stay that way."

"Good." Billy then added, " 'Cause your li'l bro' was a bad boy a few years ago."

Kevin grabbed lube and a condom out of a nightstand. "Now the secret to this is," he said as he tore open the condom and rolled it on, "you got to be real quiet because Mom and Dad are sleeping in the other room." He applied lube to Billy's butt. "Now this may hurt you at first." He lowered himself onto Billy. "If you make any noise, Mom and Dad will hear you, and then you won't be able to come and spend the night in your big brother's bed anymore. Understand me?"

"No, I'll be real quiet. I promise. Even if it hurts." Billy wrapped his legs around Kevin's waist. The head touched his hole. "I want my big brother," he said, and Kevin was inside him.

Kevin bucked and Billy received. They touched each other's faces with their hands. Kissing lips. They did more poppers. Billy's baseball cap rolled onto the mattress. Sweat dripped off Kevin, bathing Billy.

"You're the best big brother," Billy moaned. "I know you'll protect me and make sure nothing bad happens to me. Holding me tight at night in your bed. Do whatever you want. I'll let you."

Kevin turned to look at their reflection in the mirror above the dresser. He watched the intensity with which he fucked Billy. The rhythm of his body's motion. The way his ass dimpled with each thrust. How his triceps rippled as he clasped the pillow behind Billy's head.

"Oh, Kev, I can feel you coming," Billy moaned from somewhere beneath him.

Kevin lay in bed dozing until Billy woke him by nuzzling his nose into Kevin's armpit. Kevin opened his eyes only to stare into the glare of the ceiling light. He propped his head up on the pillow to get a glimpse of Billy. "You gotta go. I'm falling asleep . . . and I have to get up for work in"—he looked at the clock on the dresser—"oh, shit . . . three hours." After a moment, Kevin reached out and tousled Billy's hair. "Okay, bro'?"

Billy gave Kevin's chest a kiss. "Not a problem." He got off the bed and grabbed his sweatpants from the floor. Kevin, not moving from the bed, watched as Billy stepped into each leg and pulled them on. Billy pulled his shirt from the tangle of sheets. Kevin began to fade out again until Billy brought him back with "You wanna exchange numbers?"

Kevin believed the phone number thing was pretty pointless. He had hoped that Billy would leave quietly, maybe doing him the favor of locking the door behind him as he went. "Yeah, sure," he said, picking himself up out of bed. From the dresser drawer, he grabbed a pair of boxers which he slipped on, put the lube back in the nightstand, snatched up the condom and poppers, leaving Billy to finish dressing.

Kevin stopped in the bathroom and dropped the condom in the toilet. Stepping up to the bowl, he began to piss, chasing the floating mass around in the water with his aim, then flushed. In the kitchen, he deposited the bottle in the freezer door. Kevin grabbed a pen and tore off two pieces of paper from a pad next to the phone.

Kevin returned to the bedroom as Billy sat on the bed tying his shoe. Kevin set the paper on the dresser and wrote his number. As he did so, he told Billy, "I don't get in 'til seven. And please don't call after ten. I won't answer that late." Kevin held out the paper to Billy.

"Okay," Billy said, taking the number from him. Billy bent to lift the pant leg of his sweats. Reaching into his sock, he pulled out a small brown leather pouch, unzipped it, and put the phone number inside. Then he tucked the pouch back into his sock. Billy stood up and took his cap, which had gotten wedged between a pillow and the headboard, and faced the mirror. He positioned the cap on his head.

Kevin sprawled back onto the bed.

Billy bent over the dresser and started to write down his number, telling him, "You can use my number anytime you want," when the dresser began to tremble, then lunge at Billy. The mattress shook beneath Kevin. The earth exhaled with the hacking of a violent rumble, as the room became the chamber of a jackhammer applied to its surface. Kevin saw a look of perplexity on Billy's face.

"It's an earthquake, baby!" Kevin grinned at him.

The look was replaced by fear as Billy was jolted off balance as the dresser drawer smacked his leg. On the wall behind Billy, Kevin noticed the mirror bouncing.

"Oh, shit . . . Get away from the mirror," Kevin shouted above the deafening clamor of the apartment's contents. Grabbing Billy's arm, Kevin pulled him toward the doorway. The mirror captured the image of the two of them being pursued by the nightstand, when suddenly the room went black, and a smash of its glass called out over the pounding, as Billy collided against Kevin in the darkness. A sharp pain shot through Kevin's bare feet. They collapsed together in the bedroom doorway.

Billy clung to Kevin as Kevin pulled him into a huddle within the arch. "What the fuck?" Billy muttered.

"It's a big one. Just hold on to me. We'll ride it out here." Kevin felt Billy strengthen his hold. Kevin struggled to keep wedged in the doorway. "Relax . . . they usually last just a few seconds," Kevin said, when he too jumped from the sound of a thundering crash which ripped through the living room.

"What was that?" Billy asked.

Kevin, unable to see in the darkness, could only reply with a hesitant "I don't know." He remained solidly braced, trying to counteract the earth's motion and Billy's flinching at each picture that landed from the walls around them.

Then the rattling ceased.

The pounding apartment settled into a twisting sway. The rumble faded into the night. In its wake, the earth inhaled the screams of alarmed cars and barking dogs.

"Are you all right?" Kevin asked.

Billy was shaking. "I think so. I got smacked by something. Is it over?"

"That was it," Kevin said. Then the ground shuddered for a brief moment more. Billy gripped Kevin. "Except for the aftershocks."

"We should get out of here," Billy said, loosening his hold.

"Stand up, it's okay now," Kevin said, and started to rise to his feet. "Ow, fuck!" Pain stabbed up from his feet and he froze, then fell back to the floor, dragging Billy back down with him.

"What's wrong?"

"My feet. Shit!" Kevin cried out. He touched the sole of his left foot and felt several pieces of glass embedded in it. The right foot throbbed too. "I got glass in my feet from that fuckin' mirror. I need to see to get it out. I've got a flashlight in the kitchen. Can you go get it?" he asked.

"Isn't it too dangerous? The place may have collapsed somewhere. And I don't know my way around your place."

"Let me get this glass out my feet, then we'll go," Kevin pleaded. "So you saw where the kitchen is, right?"

"Yeah."

"The flashlight is in a utility drawer across from the refrigerator. The top one. If it's not, it's on the floor with everything else. Let's hope the batteries are good. Just move slowly, Billy. Shit's gonna be all over in there, but I'm sure the place isn't falling down."

Billy untangled from him and lifted his leg over Kevin in the darkness. Billy stepped into the hall. Glass and frames from the pictures that once lined the walls crunched under his tennis shoes. Kevin remained with his back supported by the arch of the door. He listened carefully to gauge the damage to his home as Billy trekked to get the flashlight.

"You doing okay?" Kevin checked.

"So far," Billy returned.

The sound of the broken glass stopped. Kevin figured Billy must be beyond the hallway. "Can you see at all?"

"Very little . . . but, man, you've got a big hole in your roof."

"Oh, shit. Well, stay away from that."

Kevin could make out Billy's feet slowly shuffling on the carpet. Then there was a thud and Billy mumbled something.

"What happened?"

"I just stumbled against something. I think it was the bookcase."

For a moment, Kevin didn't hear any sound. "You all right?"

Then more glass broke. Billy probably was stepping on the photos which had been arranged on top of the bookcase, Kevin figured. He envisioned Billy moving into the kitchen. Instead there was silence. Then he heard the twisting of a doorknob. "Billy?" Kevin cried out. It sounded as if Billy was trying to get out the front door, struggling to force it open. Kevin pleaded "Billy! Don't go . . . please! Stay and help me!"

Giving up on the door, Billy called back, "I'm not leaving. I was going to see if there was someone outside who could help us. This door is jammed shut."

"Relax, okay? Just get the flashlight so I can do something about my feet. Then we'll be out of here."

Billy made his way into the kitchen as metal pans clanged on the linoleum. "I think you might have busted a pipe somewhere . . . I'm kinda wet."

Kevin didn't hear any water, but the thought only added to the mess of food, appliances, and utensils that Kevin imagined was now his kitchen. He heard Billy fumbling with a drawer and fishing around in its contents. Then he saw a section of the living room illuminate with a bright light.

"Thank God, it works!" Kevin yelled.

"Your place is really trashed. Damn . . . it looks like it was your fireplace that collapsed. Must be why it's so cold in here."

When Billy turned down the hall, the beam blinded Kevin. He couldn't make Billy out behind its brilliance. Kevin took a look at the bloodied bottoms of his feet. Light reflected back from pieces of the embedded glass. From all the blood he saw on the floor, Kevin figured he was hurt pretty bad.

"You gotta get to a doctor," Billy said, squatting across from Kevin.

"Just hold the light. Let me try to pull this glass out." Kevin's breath quickened as he considered the task at hand. Kevin held the top of his left foot with one hand and carefully grasped a piece of glass with the other, took a deep breath, and pulled it from the flesh. He grimaced. Kevin felt for the next piece. "Your first earthquake?" he asked. Billy remained quiet behind the glare of the flashlight. "You'll get used to them. Usually they're little things. You hardly notice them."

He felt the sole for more glass, then positioned his other foot into the light. Kevin could see two embedded shards, one in his big toe, the other near the heel. "When we were kids, there was a pretty serious one that scared us bad. Though . . . you would have liked this . . . my little brother just *had* to sleep with me every night for weeks afterward."

Kevin waited for a reaction from Billy, but didn't get one. He held his toe still, about to pull, when the beam quivered. "Could you hold the light steady?" he said, then picked out the glass. "I think this is the last piece." Kevin twisted his foot into the light which continued to tremble. "Don't be so nervous. Where is it you're from, anyway?" Kevin asked, looking up into the beam's white glare as it suddenly fell through the air and hit the floor next to his foot.

Kevin picked up the flashlight and aimed it at Billy.

The shimmering red of blood down Billy's front greeted the light. Squatting against the wall, shivering, Billy stared vacantly upward. Little reflections of light glittered from his hair and shoulders as he twitched. The blood was flowing from the side of Billy's head. Another aftershock shook the room for a moment, setting off a car alarm outside. Billy was startled back to attention and tried to grasp the situation. "So . . . did you get the glass out?"

"Most of it, but . . . Billy you've been hurt . . ."

"I have? Where?" Billy asked, in the same moment looking down and seeing his red shirt. "What happened to me?" he asked slowly, meeting Kevin's eyes with a lost boy plea. "Where?! Where am I hurt?"

"Somewhere . . . it looks like your head, maybe your neck, I can't tell. Just try to stay calm . . ."

"We gotta do something . . ." Billy began to panic.

"I'll get us help," Kevin said, standing, pain surging through his feet. Billy feebly tried to do the same. "Don't move! Stay there. I'll take care of this." Billy sank back down. Kevin went into the bedroom, flashlight aimed at the floor ahead. When he pulled at his closet door's handle, it resisted, then slid open. He dug through a pile of shirts, suits, and ties, seizing the first pair of shoes, some canvas sneakers, that he came to. Ripping out the laces, he balanced painfully on one foot and then the other, putting each sneaker on. The shoes' cushioning felt slightly better than the hardness of the wood floor. Finally, he snatched a dress shirt from the top of the pile in the closet and returned to Billy in the hall. When Kevin looked at Billy, he couldn't tell if it was the glare of the flashlight or whether Billy was turning pale.

Only Billy's eyes moved, following Kevin as he squatted in front of him.

Kevin carefully placed the shirt on the side of Billy's head, trying to avoid actual contact with the injury. "Here, hold this in place. I'm going for help. I'll be right back."

Billy grabbed Kevin's arm. "Kevin, please . . . stay with me."

"You're going to be okay, Billy. Just apply pressure with the shirt."

Billy raised the shirt to his head. "Like this?"

Kevin nodded. "Yeah." Then he turned the light from Billy and went into the living room. Bricks covered much of the furniture and piled up against the door. A draft swirled in the room. Through the gaping hole in the ceiling, Kevin could see a darkened night sky. Dangling plaster revealed exposed wood beams. Kevin aimed the light toward the kitchen. Under several layers of expelled refrigerator contents, Kevin found the cordless phone's receiver. It was covered with a cold stickiness that smelled of orange marmalade. He pressed the "Talk" button, but nothing happened.

Billy began to stir in the hall, breathing heavily.

Kevin put the phone and flashlight on the dining table and tried to pull the door open but gave up after several tries. He opened a window and yelled out into the darkness, "Help! Somebody! Please, help!" But his pleas were swallowed up by the squawking of a car alarm down below which hadn't reset.

A pounding came from the hallway behind Kevin and Billy's voice echoed, "No! No! No! No! Noooo!"

Kevin grabbed the flashlight and rushed back to where Billy was thrashing about, kicking at the floor and wall, mumbling, "Not like this . . . no. . . . Please, God!"

Kevin dropped to the ground and struggled to pin him in place. "Billy! Billy, calm down! Stop moving, you're just making it worse."

Billy's twisting weakened, then stopped. Billy's back was wedged to the wall. Kevin lay on top of him. In the stillness of the flashlight's beam, Kevin watched their panting oversized silhouettes cast on the wall.

"Is someone coming to help?"

"The phone's not working. The door's jammed 'cause the chimney collapsed . . ."

"I'm safe with you, Kev."

Kevin released Billy and sat up.

"Don't go," Billy said, reaching to take Kevin's hand.

"I'm not."

Then Billy dropped his gaze from Kevin's face, sat up slightly, and raised his hand to point at Kevin's chest. "I'm sorry. I didn't mean to . . ."

Kevin looked down at himself, his bare flesh now glistening red. A faint, knowing smile came over his face, then passed. "I guess this makes us blood brothers," Kevin said flatly.

Billy began to tearfully apologize again.

Kevin took Billy in his arms. "Shhh, I know you didn't mean to."

"I'm scared," Billy quietly whispered.

"I'm sure you are. But I need you to be strong for me and hang in there until we can get some help. Okay . . . li'l bro'?"

Kevin could feel Billy's head on his shoulder nod yes.

Billy reached up with his hand and rubbed his scalp. "I think I lost my cap," he said, weakly patting his head. "Don't let me forget it."

"No. I won't," Kevin said softly, and held Billy tighter.

Early morning light revealed a web of cracks on the hallway wall in front of Kevin. Billy's head rested on his shoulder.

"Hey, Billy," he said.

Billy didn't move.

"Come on, buddy." Kevin jostled him gently. Billy's head swayed stiffly. Kevin tilted Billy's head up. His skin was cool, his face blanched. Billy's eyes remained closed. Hair had begun to mat with drying blood. "You're still with me, man . . . Billy, come on! Wake up!" Billy's head jerked back and forth as Kevin frantically shook his body. When Kevin released him, Billy slumped back against the wall.

Kevin took Billy's wrist to check for a pulse, repeatedly probing the flesh to find if he had missed the vein. He dropped that arm and tried the other. Failing there, Kevin began to press around Billy's neck, all the while shouting Billy's name. Finding no signs of life, Kevin gave up.

He painfully rose to his feet. Kevin stared for several moments at the wall behind Billy, smeared red, before figuring he should try to get help. At one end of the hall was a heap of bedroom contents. Kevin limped the other way, into the living room. A patch of sky now existed where the toppled chimney opened the roof. Morning sun had begun to burn off the clouds, revealing some blue. In the daylight, it was obvious that not only was the door blocked with a substantial pile of bricks; the doorway itself was askew. Kevin went over to the phone lying on the dining-room table. When he pressed "Talk," there was a beep and the number pad began to glow. He listened for the hum of a tone, and then dialed 911.

The phone buzzed with a busy signal.

Kevin hung up, then dialed again, still receiving a busy signal.

He gave up after the third try. Kevin remained there, slightly seated atop the table, wondering what he would say to the operator if he got through.

"We're very busy here. What is your emergency?"

"I'm hurt, I'm trapped in my apartment, and there's someone here. I think he's dead."

"What kind of injuries have you sustained?"

"It's my feet. I stepped on some glass."

"Lots of people stepped on glass. And why do you think this other person . . ."

"Billy . . ."

". . . is dead?"

"I couldn't find any pulse. He doesn't seem to be breathing."

"And how long has he been this way?"

"I don't know . . ."

"Who is he?"

"I don't . . ." Kevin stumbled on the thought.

"Do you know him? Is he a stranger? A friend? Does he have a last name?"

"He's some trick I picked up last night and now he's dead!" Kevin yelled in his mind, walking back to Billy in the hallway.

Kevin looked at Billy's blood-soaked sweatpants and tank top. Setting the phone on the floor, he bent to search around Billy's waist for pockets, or a wallet, but didn't find either. He paused in frustration, then remembered the pouch. Kevin tugged the elastic legging back up Billy's ankle to reveal a lump inside his sock. He grasped the top of the sock with both hands and peeled down until the pouch fell to the floor. Unzipping the top, Kevin found a small glass vial with some white powder inside, a few dollars and change, and Kevin's phone number. Kevin threw the pouch and its contents to the ground, stepped over Billy, and walked into the bedroom to find the paper with Billy's phone number.

Kevin attacked the heap, pushing the mattress aside, pulling the dresser up from the floor, and hurling its drawers across the room. He tossed handfuls of clothes over his shoulders until he came to the shards of the broken mirror. Crouching low, Kevin picked through the pieces, feeling the occasional cut of glass in his hurry. He found the pen Billy used. Then he noticed the brim of Billy's cap, peeking out from under the nightstand. Kevin shoved the stand against the wall and picked up the cap. Under it hid the white slip of paper. Kevin snatched it up and read "Billy," then the area code, followed by the first two digits. And nothing more.

"Oh, fuck me!" Kevin sobbed.

Stunned, he stood and shuffled his way back down the hall, still absentmindedly holding Billy's cap. He stopped above Billy. Billy rested to the side, inches above the floor, on his awkwardly crooked arm. Kevin knelt to put the cap on Billy's head. Holding only the bill, he tried to put it on him like Billy had worn it, but Billy's head moved about and he slid further to the side, his head making a resounding thud on impact with the wood floor. Kevin let the cap fall, landing on the side of Billy's face.

He picked up the phone and dialed 911.

Hating Yourself in the Morning

DREW LIMSKY

When Celeste's father was dying of cancer, hair began to take root on his chest, where there never had been any, as if his body had finally recognized its misstep and had an idea to start all over from a revised blueprint. As though this nascent covering, however feeble or belated, might somehow shield the speechless, oxygen-tented body beneath it.

Celeste thought of this, to torture herself, as she stood at her bathroom mirror, staring at the single black hair that had just that day—Thursday—gotten long enough to curl in the hollow of her neck. She put her thumb to her throat, but instead of pulling out the hair, she rubbed until the skin below her larynx was crimson and raw. She sold cosmetics at Bloomingdale's and knew how to cover almost anything; therefore her self-destruction was halfhearted, ineffectual. She disgusted herself.

Celeste was using up her sick days. It had been snowing for three straight days and she hadn't gone out during that time. Celeste despised the cold. She couldn't locate her gloves. She smelled a fetid, fruity odor coming from her armpits and, oddly, from the webbing between her fingers. But it was not for these reasons, compelling as they were, that Celeste chose to remain housebound. These problems, after all, could be easily surmounted. She could shower. She could throw on one of the thick fisherman's sweaters Tad had left behind and then her long army surplus coat with the drawstrings. The broken drawstrings. Once outside she could keep her hands inside her pockets. Or she could lick her fingers and risk frostbite just for the fuck of it. Since she was never going to touch a man again, she wouldn't be needing her fingers.

No one had ever walked out on Celeste before; she felt it was a lot like having an undiagnosed allergy and finding out that something, a peanut or a wasp, for example, had been lying in wait all her twenty-nine years, ready to upend her. Tad had called her a whore, then had left. Tad's departure—his leave-taking, she liked to call it—was why she had allowed herself to fall into such staggering disrepair; the other part, being called a whore, she didn't mind so much. In fact, she rather enjoyed that part. Of course, she hadn't slept around in some time, but then Tad was hardly known for scrupulousness in his choice of epithets; he was careless with language. Being a musician, he seemed to select words more for their sonorousness than for their meaning, and then he proceeded to assign definitions all his own. So when he'd called Celeste a whore, he may well have meant "liar," or, if he was stoned, "chair."

Whore. She'd heard how inexperienced girls, innocent of the city and strapped for cash, could be lured into prostitution. But to Celeste, it didn't seem as easy as it sounded. She wondered what concrete steps had to be taken in order to become a whore. Would one have to apply to an escort service, or learn how to lean into car windows with a certain finesse? Was there a particular language, a code prostitutes knew that protected them from arrest? Did it involve only responding to, and not making, offers? But this was simply a mental exercise; something told Celeste that she would live her life without the experience of taking money for sex, that she could think of herself as a whore aspirant, and let it go at that.

Celeste's hair fell in clumps over her eyes; it was her preferred way to look at herself—half veiled. Fuzz from a never washed blanket dotted her head. It did not become her. With her tongue she picked a piece from her lip and spat it into the bathroom mirror, where it stuck on her reflection like an exploded beauty mark. Even her lint signaled violent undoing, termination.

She refused to go out because she didn't trust herself to appear in public without eliciting questions like "Are you okay?" and, more urgently, "Is something happening to you?" Even through her hair Celeste could see that her eyes were alarmed, fevered, panicked enough for strangers to notice and comment upon, at least with their expressions.

She could hear the television coming from the next apartment. It was loud enough that certain air-emitting consonants penetrated the wall and vibrated the water in her toilet bowl, yet individual words were difficult to discern. She stood very still, with her forehead against the mirror—her crisscrossing bangs felt like a wire mesh cutting into her skin—and heard the word "earthquake," and a couple of seconds later, "tent city."

Celeste wanted to live in a tent city; she was tired of her apartment. She wasn't exactly sure what a tent city was, but she felt confident that she looked appropriately traumatized for one. People still might ask her if everything was okay, if something was happening, but it seemed to Celeste that everyone would be asked those kinds of questions in a tent city. She would just shrug and say, "Earthquake," in response to such inquiries. She pulled her head back from the mirror with some satisfaction. From three overheard words she'd constructed a life for herself, one that seemed a considerable improvement over the one she was living—as she liked to think of it—against her will.

Like the people in the tent city, she felt as if she were awaiting instructions. She didn't know from whom these instructions would come, but she hoped that they would be helpful.

Friday, Celeste decided to take a bath. Her friend Victor had stopped by the day before and strongly suggested "a tan, a schtup, and a bar of soap." He had taken a whiff of her T-shirt, adding, "and not necessarily in that order."

So she prepared. She found a candle and a single bath bead. She unfolded a towel. She regarded this as an outing.

She set her boom box on the toilet and played her favorite tape of Tad's, a soundtrack from a movie she'd never seen. She would shave her legs with Tad's shaving cream, the squat can with the ring of rust around the bottom. She'd do that.

The tub took a long time to fill. She sat in a half inch of water and flicked the drain lever every thirty seconds or so, because she couldn't detect which position would allow the bath to hold water. When she was finally confident that the stopper was in place, Celeste began to cry: she had no bubbles.

By the time the tub was full, Celeste realized that the sound of the spout and her own sobbing had made her miss the first song on the tape—the windy, whooshing cut that was perfect for the bath. Now the second number was on, the annoying one that sounded like chattering teeth and bones knocking together. "Skull music," she said aloud.

Tad's shaving cream was coming out liquidy in her palm, and as she smoothed it along her calves, covering herself in a thin, unsatisfying coat, she read, too late, the instruction to Shake Well. So she shook the can belatedly and replaced it on the ledge, because that was how she did things: backward. She believed, sometimes, in a parallel universe, one that righted our missteps and exchanged our inharmonious actions and put them into proper sequence. In this other world, a girl exactly like Celeste turned on the music after the tub was full and shook the shaving cream before using it. She had pretty, airy melodies to accompany her bath, and foamy clouds on her legs instead of dribbling marshmallow soup. And in this perfectly catalogued world, Celeste left her boyfriend before, not after, he left her.

She tapped out her razor on the side of the tub and leaned her head back, looked at the ceiling. The peach-pink paint had cracked, was curling away from itself in a swarm of V shapes, like pairs of knife slashes, or, Celeste admitted with some hesitation, women's exposed genitals. She looked down at her parted thighs—when Celeste realized she could only see herself because she was lacking the insulation of bubbles, she almost cried again—and then looked back up. Laughing crotches, she thought, closed her eyes, and dropped her chin below the waterline.

She must have stayed that way a long time, settled in quite comfortably, because it took two identical right hands to pull her shoulders out of the water. The hands were calloused from lifting weights and tanned from Miami Beach; they belonged to Victor and Robert, Australian twin brothers from the nicer, more expensive building across the street—the one with the fat doorman who looked like an opera star and always seemed to be sleeping standing up.

Celeste drew her knees up to her chest and whisked water from beneath her eyes. She must have inhaled some bathwater through her nose; her brain felt like it was burning. The sensation reminded Celeste of her childhood, of her father trying to teach her the crawl with his hoarse, coaxing voice and Celeste failing at something called rhythmic breathing.

Victor moved to drain the tub. "You fall asleep? I only suggested a bath, Miss Ophelia."

Robert lit a cigarette from the wick of Celeste's candle, then blew the candle out. "This is bad," he said, invoking his favorite line from *Titanic.* He looked at Celeste. "Is this one of those cries for help that everyone ignores?"

Celeste leaned over and reached for her towel on the toilet seat. The twins were talking too much. Victor, who go-go danced and tended bar at a gay club downtown, was burlier than his brother and more somber. For a dancer, his movements were stiff, like G.I. Joe, but his voice was deep and lulling; sometimes the sound of it made the skin beneath her ears tingle. His hairdresser brother, Robert, the allegedly straight one, was effeminate and more animated—his jaw didn't seem as securely attached to his head. He opened his mouth wide when he spoke; Celeste could see all of his fillings.

She stood up in the draining bath, shivering, holding the towel against her chest. Robert turned on his heel and left the room, shutting the door behind him. Shouting from the kitchen, he offered to make some tea; he was fascinated by her well-stocked pantry and liked to fuss in it. Celeste loved Victor and Robert, but they confused her; when she was with them, she always had to remind herself of things.

Victor rolled up his sleeves past his heavy, tear-shaped forearms and started drying her hair with the hand towel she had used to clean the sink; she didn't protest. "Enough is enough, Celeste. He was an asshole. The kind you fuck and forget. You'll do better." The twins had never liked Tad much; they said he was "untalented," but this seemed to be a euphemism for something Celeste couldn't quite put her finger on.

"A year of my life down the drain," Celeste muttered, glancing at the draining bath despite herself.

Victor smirked. "Oh, the metaphor of it all."

"Victor, I loved him. It embarrasses me, but I did. Just because you've given up on all that—"

"Oh, I believe in love. And I also believe that Tom Cruise and 'Nick' Kidman have sex. Together."

Outside, Robert started to beat on the door. In a stage whisper he said to his brother, "Tell her she's a goddess!"

Celeste stepped out of the bath, wiped steam from the mirror, and saw Victor laughing in the glass. "People no longer ask," he said, "if I've ever thought of sleeping with my brother."

The possibility disturbed Celeste, but her discomfort was not based on moral grounds; to have sex with your twin would require a kind of self-love she didn't want to contemplate. For a moment she became dizzy, as if the room were coming to a point, like a tepee.

Victor flipped the tape over; it started playing fast violins, like the chase music from cartoons. This is my life, she thought, scored to the soundtrack from *Road Runner.* "Come out with us tonight?" he asked.

"Right," Celeste said, glad he'd changed the subject from fraternal incest. When she pulled her hair behind her shoulders her breasts became visible.

Victor was staring intently at a point above Celeste's head. "I can't talk to you until you put those away."

Victor helped her into her robe; it had an odd, powdery surface and once it was on, Celeste saw Victor look into his hands as if he were afraid something had come off in them.

Celeste stroked her widow's peak absently. "Maybe I should try to become a lesbian again."

"You'd be a terrible lesbian," he told her. "There are no lesbian makeup artists. Besides, I thought we decided Robert was the lesbian."

Celeste grabbed the edge of the vanity and looked into the sink. "Can't do it tonight," she said.

"You're talking yourself into being a basket case, you know that." He put a hand on the back of her neck and squeezed. "You know that, you know that," he repeated softly, like an incantation.

She held herself; the sound of his voice made her eyes burn and water. She loved the sound of men's voices, some of them. She'd lost her virginity to her English teacher while still in high school because he'd told her things she was always afraid others would hear. "I wake up fucking you, Celeste," he'd said, "I wake up making love to you." He'd spoken to her in the pockets of bright yellow hallways, protected by a hundred teenage voices, between bells; he told her things in a low voice that wavered into a whisper, the way Victor's was doing now.

And Tad. Warbling pieces of songs he was working on, covering her face with his bong-warmed, pot-flavored breath. "Like a river," he'd sing, "like a stone. Like a handful of lightning bugs, a poem." It had given her a chill, even though she knew there wasn't a thing on earth like the four he'd mentioned.

And then he'd left, but not before releasing that puzzling accusation of prostitution into the air.

Voices. Her father had stopped speaking to her when she was nineteen, a year before his throat cancer was diagnosed, when she'd announced she was moving to New York with the New Jersey Bell repairman. The guy's name was Van—she'd always been attracted to men with one-syllable names—and he'd wanted to open a coffee bar in SoHo, and call it "Coff, Coff." She closed her eyes, briefly, in a wince, remembering.

"Please, Victor, I don't want to hear it. Not from you, with the twenty-four-year-old model you have to play with." She looked away from him and made an angry throat-clearing sound that was self-directed; she heard herself becoming spiteful and shrewish, and to Victor of all people, who loved her and thought of her as a roll-with-it party girl.

"For now, Celeste. You want to know where Kenny is this weekend? Visiting his ex in San Francisco, a man old enough to be his father. If the guy would have him, Kenny would go back in a heartbeat. I'm everybody's terrific second choice, everybody's coverage."

"Which just proves my point."

"It proves exactly nothing. C'mon Celeste, if I thought of every guy who took a walk, the tricks who said I was incredible and then didn't return my phone calls, I'd never leave the house. You know what Marianne Williamson says. It's time to get back on the horse, baby."

"Marianne Williamson talks about a horse?"

"No, she talks about life as a process. The horse was mine."

Celeste turned to Victor. His lashes were long and black and his eyes were so blue that when she first met him, she was sure he wore colored contacts. His neck was strong and finely contoured—it was an important-looking neck, appropriate for the voice it encased; still, someone, if he could be believed, had gone looking for something else—bluer eyes maybe—or, not having her thing for voices, had grown tired of the soft vibration his words made.

He wrinkled up his forehead and leaned against the towel rack, waiting for her answer. The jeans he bought were often too large in the waist because he had to buy a size that would accommodate the muscular sweep of his thighs, sometimes he had them tailored, but now they were gathered up by a wide silver belt. He nodded toward the shaving cream on the bathtub ledge. "What is that?"

"It's Tad's."

"How did I know that? Could it be because its bottom is all brown and crusty—so reminiscent of its owner's? Now what can I say to get you to leave this hovel?"

Celeste scowled, tensing her stomach muscles self-consciously; she hadn't done her aerobics videos in weeks—even at her most energetic, she could barely make it through the tape intended for pregnant diabetic women—but then, she hadn't eaten much either. She would look good and skinny in her club clothes. She met Victor's Crayola eyes. "Tell me you won't take no for an answer."

"Why?"

"Just," she said, "do it."

Victor rolled his lovely head around on his shoulders. "I won't take no for an answer." It sounded better than she thought it would, more convincing; she tingled.

"I'll need to wash out some underwear," she said.

At Limelight, they left a small, hot room and went upstairs to another room—indistinguishable from the first except that it was smaller and hotter, and upstairs. They made their way to a pair of overstuffed, cracked-vinyl period armchairs (though Celeste couldn't identify which period) and put white tablets under their tongues. By the time Celeste had removed all her rings, lined them up on her black-stockinged thigh, and replaced them on her fingers, the tablet had dissolved and Victor or Robert or perhaps their friend Noel, who looked nothing like them, was introducing her to a handsome man with a blond swoop of hair and a goatee that reminded her of an upside-down tent.

"I'm Ed." It was a tough, solid name, Celeste decided; but you wouldn't know from the way he said it. He made the most of that one syllable—his name became a hungry, chocolate breath with a melting consonant. Even in the dubious light of the club, she was sure she could spy Ed's tongue gently licking the roof of his mouth to end the word.

He asked her to dance. She held out her hands, and when the twins pulled her from the depths of the retro chair, they struggled; she imagined herself as a mother being helped off the ground by her children after a picnic. She was long-necked and thin-legged, but she was deadweight and she knew it. She steadied herself on thigh-high boots and brushed away a soggy cigarette butt that had become affixed to her miniskirt.

"Did you say something?" the man named Ed asked.

Back on the horse. "At some point," said Celeste.

It was too early in the night to be dancing so hard. Ed's eyes were shut and his hands were suspended in the air at waist level, palms down, as if he were pressing the heads of invisible midgets. His sideburns were wet with perspiration and the neck of his T-shirt was soaked through. It was just after midnight and the club's flashing spotlights were hitting as many patches of empty dance floor as people. It was too early in the night, Celeste thought again, to be dancing so hard.

The hit wasn't making her feel anything; she was beginning to suspect she'd paid twenty dollars for a Tylenol. She was anxious, first, because she didn't really like Ed and, second, because Ed didn't seem to be looking at her. Her feet made little baby steps and she kept swatting her hair in frustration. She was lacking in inspiration and tried to approximate the steps of a black girl on the dance floor who had full hips and short legs and therefore a lower, better center of gravity. The girl held one arm stiffly in front of her, bent at the elbow with her thumb and forefinger almost touching, as if she were holding a teacup. The girl's body seemed to follow her hand in a peculiar, protective way Celeste thought was sexy and tried to copy, until she was reminded of carpal-tunnel syndrome. At one point Victor grabbed her, put his face against her ear, first asking if she needed to be rescued; then inquiring how she had injured her hand.

"I'm fine. I'm hitching up my saddle," she told him.

"Well, put your hand in your pocket or something. People are going to think that you and your horse fell into a thresher, aren't they?"

Ed wasn't looking at her, and yet there was this creepy inevitability about him. She looked at his jeans, snug and almost white with wear in the thighs, and knew that she would see them crumpled up on the floor that night. She imagined asking him to stand on her bed and make a tent by pulling up the center of her comforter in a fist, and letting her get inside. She wanted to be safe and guarded, but still alone. She wasn't sure if she could ask a total stranger to do such a thing. Perhaps if she fucked him first . . .

Boots, black coat, she felt very sexy stepping off the curb on Sixth Avenue with Ed walking ahead of her. The snow had turned quickly to ice, and the city was shiny and brittle, like hard candy. She slipped on a metal grate, and had to throw her weight in the other direction to avoid catching her heel between the slats. She recovered herself and took two ambitious strides to keep pace with Ed, but he was already well past the midpoint of the intersection with his shoulders hiked up in protection against the cold.

She thought she'd had plenty of time. But two pairs of headlights were coming fast in the two lanes she still needed to cross. Horn sounds: one high-pitched and unbroken, the other staccato. They were racing. Boys. No one was slowing down. She felt cars whizzing by behind her, flapping the skirt of her coat. "Shit," she said, because she thought it appropriate to show her disapproval of the situation, but actually a calm had settled over her like thick liquid. She had no decisions to make, she had nowhere to go. She saw a vision of herself flying in the air, silent, in slow motion, a movie; the word "paralyzed" popped into her head, then burst like a bubble. She had done something backward again, and now she was going to die; it surprised her how easily you could surrender control.

The car in the lane farthest from her crossed over, overtaking the car that was going to kill her. At first this didn't seem to improve anything, but something told her to move, not a lot, but a little, and then she was in the free lane; then, somehow, safely on the curb. She felt her feet inside her boots again. Ed hadn't looked back.

When she caught up with him, he was staring straight ahead. Her lungs, all her organs, seemed to be fibrillating like the time she'd eaten nothing but SweetTarts dissolved in Diet Coke for four days straight. "Shit," she said again, to acknowledge that she'd almost died.

"You shouldn't have hesitated," Ed said, in a pleasant, patient voice that told her she was making too much out of it, though she was sure she hadn't made anything out of it at all.

"Mmm," she said, in something like agreement. He asked her where she lived.

"Where do *you* live?" she responded. Celeste's expectations for the evening had diminished considerably, and she wanted the option of a quick exit. Though she knew it was probably safer to take him to her apartment—particularly if he turned out to be a rapist/murderer as well as insensitive—she didn't care, she didn't want him pulling a tent up around her, didn't want him in her bed. Besides, if he were a rapist/murderer, she reasoned, he would have been far more attentive to her almost becoming roadkill, if only for the missed opportunity.

She looked ugly in his bathroom mirror. She was bent over the sink in her bra and skirt; the skin on her stomach looked blue. She found a bar of translucent orange soap, and washed her hands because their sex had left the odor of latex on her fingers; Ed had only been intermittently aroused. But even in its listless state his penis had retained its slight upward curve, as if the skin of its top side had been pulled too tight, like in a bad face-lift. He'd kept spitting into his palm and massaging himself; he'd enlisted her help. Ed seemed to have an unlimited capacity to salivate, and kept producing strands of spittle that hung from his lower lip to his hand, and from his hand to wherever he touched her body. It had caused her to feel slightly nauseous and detached; she didn't like to think of Silly String at sexual moments.

It had been so easy to come home with him, so easy to get him into bed. She wondered if she were starting a promiscuous period, as she was wont to do after a breakup. If tonight was any indication, she thought, she would have no trouble picking up men who wouldn't look back to see if she'd been struck by oncoming traffic. Perhaps she could work her way up.

She heard him outside the bathroom door. "Cecily, everything okay?" *Now* he was asking if she was okay.

Perhaps the girl in the alternate universe who looked like Celeste and did things in their proper order was named Cecily; Celeste felt a rush of goodwill toward this other girl, hoped she'd had a good time tonight, prayed she'd found some good drugs and a dehydrated sexual partner who'd caught her name.

She turned off the water and dried her hands on her skirt. "Incredible, Ed."

It occurred to her that tonight she and Ed had entered a tacit conspiracy, a conspiracy to see her life as shit, to acknowledge it as such. If he knew this, he wasn't talking. Back in her dingy apartment, crotches were still laughing at her, deservedly so, yet Celeste felt the night had been a meager triumph, just surviving it. She imagined herself as a commuter detained at a way station between this world and the other, orderly one; she needed to be here in order to get to the next, good place. She closed her eyes and leaned back slightly, picturing herself falling through the slit in her father's hospital curtain and into the transparent folds of his oxygen tent.

Several minutes later, Celeste got up from the floor with a renewed sense of purpose.

In the hallway she found a stereo magazine and wrote out a fake home number and a fake work number composed of the most implausible chains of numerals she could think of. The "work" number she left had eight digits. Below her imaginary numbers she wrote, "Just for tomorrow—Cecily." Then, jangling her keys inside her coat pocket, she slid back the bolt on Ed's door. She left him standing there, naked, staring at the magazine, the dripping, rolled-down rubber holding on to his penis like an upended stocking cap.

On Eleventh Street: snow. Her ankle felt tender inside her boot, from her turn in the gutter outside Limelight. Beneath each streetlamp fell a skinny pyramid, a tent of light and swirling white dust; finding herself inside one of them, she listened to the early morning winter.

A beat-up yellow cab was moving up the snow-covered, ice-covered street, too fast, rattling. She watched its approaching tire treads churn up snow, then saw the taxi swerve to avoid the suddenly opened door of a parked car. The cab cut a hard diagonal to the other side of Eleventh, slowing all the time, then skidded into a mountain of frosty, discarded Christmas trees piled high in a warehouse driveway just ten feet from where Celeste was standing. ("Avalanche," Celeste said under her breath.)

The driver opened his door and looked back at his cab in a perfunctory way, too quickly to assess any damage; he glanced at Celeste and clicked his tongue, reminding her of how she'd cursed after almost getting hit by the racing cars on Sixth Avenue. It was a fitting, if not a felt, gesture, an acknowledgment that you were supposed to behave as if you cared about things—send some audible signal—whether you did or not.

The driver shut his door, and Celeste heard him gear into Drive. The cab passed in front of her and continued down the street. Spring will be better, she thought, and began her walk to the corner. In the plate-glass window of a restaurant she caught her reflection—a tough city girl with hair over one eye, and no reason to smile—stepping backward to humor herself.

Dann

MICHAEL ANTHONY GOLD

It's a Wednesday night near the end of January and I'm home alone, lying in bed in the dark, but I can't sleep. At five past eleven the phone rings. I make no move to answer it, so three rings later the machine switches on in the living room. "Mike and Angela can't come to the phone right now," our greeting announces. "We're so hung over, we can't even get out of bed—and we sure as hell can't deal with whatever you were planning to tell us. But don't hang up! Talk to the machine, and we'll call you back once we recover—it might be a few days, but we will call you back . . ."

"Bukowski!" someone shouts after the beep. "I know you're there. Pick up the phone. Bukowwwski? Craig and I are with Angela right now. She told us you're at home, so we know you're there—"

I bolt out of bed and grab the phone. "Dann! What's up?"

"Maybe I should be asking you what's up," Dann says cheerfully.

"What do you mean?"

"I mean you're panting so loud . . . like maybe I interrupted—"

"An orgy?"

Dann laughs. "Is that what's going on?"

"It's true," I agree, "but I wouldn't say you interrupted anything. They're all carrying on just fine without me."

"Good, so they won't care when you leave the house in five minutes, will they, Bukowski?"

"Why would I be leaving the house in five minutes?"

"Because you're coming to get drunk with us," Dann explains.

There's a mirror on the wall by the phone; when I focus on my reflection, it occurs to me that I'm nodding—this despite the fact that

I just finished off half a bottle of Robitussin and two shots of NyQuil. This despite the fact that I promised myself I was going to stay home tonight and get some rest for a change. "Who's us?" I hear myself asking. "And where are you?"

"Us is me and Craig. At the Balboa Café. Wise Monkey's playing tonight. So get your ass over here, we demand that you show up!"

"The Balboa Café . . . where's the Balboa Café?"

"Bukowski! What do you mean, where's the Balboa Café? You've seen it a thousand times—it's right across the street from our work."

"It is?"

"Yeah, come see for yourself—pretend you're going to work and then look across the street and go there instead."

"Okay," I tell him. "I'll see you in twenty minutes."

"I'd better see you in twenty minutes, Bukowski, or else I'll be left with no choice but to come over and forcibly kidnap you," Dann says, and I laugh into the receiver even though he's already hung up.

The Balboa Café is crowded and loud and there's a three-dollar cover to get in, due to the presence of the band Wise Monkey. Besides being responsible for the cover charge, Wise Monkey is also creating the majority of the noise in this bar. I hate paying a cover to go anywhere, and I hate crowds, and I hate noise. I prefer quiet bars with cheap drinks, no attitude, and not too many people, the kind of place where you can sit in the corner and talk quietly and smoke too much and pass out on the table if you feel like it without being hassled. If you passed out on the table at the Balboa Café, the bouncers would undoubtedly either beat the shit out of you or call the cops. The Balboa Café is definitely not my kind of place, but it hardly seems to matter; I'd go anywhere to be with Dann.

Dann's full name is Dann "E" Williams. I know this because I've seen his birth certificate; his middle name really is "E," quotation marks and all. I've known him for two months, ever since I got hired as a waiter at the Spaghetti Company Restaurant on Mill Avenue in downtown Tempe, Arizona. Dann waits tables there too. I've been in love with him since the first night we worked together, which was also my first night on the job. I got to follow him all over the restaurant—he was training me and I was supposed to be observing him take orders and deliver food—but the only thing I ended up observing that night was his butt. Dann is beautiful, cool, charming, and straight. He's a year older than me—twenty-five—six inches shorter than me, and he plays the conga drums in a band. We have nothing in common except the tendency to drink too much and too often.

Dann and Craig are standing very close to the band. We spot each other at the same time and they beckon me over. Dann hugs me and says, "Bukowski, I can't believe you actually showed up!" His grin is enormous and genuine and I marvel at the fact that I'm the cause of it.

"I told you he would, Dann," Craig says. Craig is Dann's best friend and roommate, plus he plays lead guitar in their band, which is called Polliwog and is actually pretty good. They do shows about three nights a week, mostly in Tempe but sometimes Phoenix, Mesa, or Scottsdale; on the nights they're not playing, they hit the bars anyway as part of the audience.

"You were right," Dann agrees, "So hey, let's go buy our brother a beer."

I try to protest and offer them money, but they either ignore me or don't hear me because of the band. A minute later they return with six bottles of Sam Adams. They give me two, one of which I chug immediately.

The Balboa Café is normally your typical yuppie bar, patronized by clones with their tucked-in, freshly ironed and neatly pressed Polo shirts and oxfords, short hair perfectly coifed, jeans impeccably faded to the proper shade of blue. Tonight, however, due to the presence of Wise Monkey, there's another group here as well: guys with long unkempt hair, flannel shirts, glazed eyes, predominantly black T-shirts promoting bands like Stone Temple Pilots, Pearl Jam, Alice in Chains. This mingling of yuppies and wannabe Seattle grunge types is both comical and potentially inflammatory. The two groups' mutual contempt for one another is obvious; if it weren't for the steroid-popping bouncers crawling all over the place, we'd probably be watching a fistfight right now instead of a band.

The band is really into the show tonight, all seven members working up a sweat on their instruments and jamming hard. Their style is some odd mixture of jazz and funk and reggae, mostly instrumental and definitely hypnotic if you give yourself up to the music. I let my mind wander, enjoying the feeling of the Robitussin and the beer coursing through my veins, enjoying the sight of Dann who's now dancing in a slow, trancelike groove, perfectly in synch with the wail of the sax and the beat of the drums.

Before I know it, he's beside me again, chugging a beer and then draping an arm around my shoulder. "You know something, Bukowski," he says. "I haven't known you that long, but I have to tell you—I really love you. I guess it must sound weird for me to say that, but it's true—I really love you. You're a great guy."

"Thanks," I say shyly, wondering if it's dark enough to hide the fact that I'm blushing. "I love you too, Dann. Obviously. You always make me smile."

"Smile now, Bukowski," Dann says, grinning. "You look like I just sentenced you to death row or something."

I smile. Dann's hand slips away from my shoulder and I wish I had the nerve to put it back. "Bukowski needs more beer," he announces to Craig, who immediately heads to the bar.

"I would pay, you know, if you'd give me a chance," I say.

"We don't want you to pay, though," Dann says. "Craig and I think you're cool. Plus"—he pulls me toward him conspiratorially—"earlier we bought four beers, and they were eight bucks, right? So we gave the bartender a ten, and guess what? He gave us back twelve dollars. So don't start thinking we're really generous or anything."

"Okay." I laugh. "I won't start thinking that."

Someone taps my shoulder from behind. I turn around. "Angela!" I say, grinning at my roommate and best friend. "What are you doing here?"

"I knew I'd find you here," she says.

"How?"

"I was at Long Wong's earlier. Dann and Craig showed up and asked me where you were. So I told them how you were home because you're on the verge of getting sick and I said how you were adamant about not going out drinking tonight. Of course Dann laughed and tried to bet me twenty bucks that you'd show up here once he called you."

"Did you bet?"

"Of course not, Mike! Why would I purposely throw away twenty dollars?"

"Hey, sister," Dann says to Angela.

"Dann!" She smiles and they hug each other. "Listen, I need to get a drink."

"You and Bukowski," Dann says, laughing.

"What?" Angela says.

"Yeah, what?" I repeat.

"I've never met anyone who drinks as much as you two," he explains. "Except maybe for Craig."

"No, except maybe for you, Dann." Craig laughs.

Angela goes to the bar. When she comes back, she starts up a conversation with Dann. I try to listen in but it's impossible to hear what they're saying so I give up. Instead I look at Craig and ask him what he's thinking about; he tells me he's thinking about Janesville, as in Janesville, Wisconsin, and how he might have to hitchhike there sometime in the near future and although I'm certain he tells me all the reasons why, none of his words stick; all I can concentrate on is Dann.

I'm still concentrating on Dann a couple minutes later when he turns to Craig and whispers in his ear. Craig cackles like a madman; Dann says they'll be right back and they disappear into the crowd. As soon as they're gone, Angela grabs my arm and pulls me in the direction of an empty booth in the very back of the Balboa Café, where it's impossible to see the band and therefore a lot less crowded. We sit down across from each other.

"Dann really likes you, Mike," she says in a low voice, leaning close to me like she's divulging some deliciously scandalous bit of gossip.

I adopt her demeanor, leaning forward so that our faces are almost touching. "He does?" I whisper as my heartbeat quickens. "What do you mean?"

"He told me he thinks you're amazing. He said he thinks about touching you all the time! He also said he digs being around you because he loves the way you always smile."

"He said all those things?"

"Yes! All of them!"

"When?"

"A couple hours ago, at Long Wong's. And guess what else he admitted? He's made out with a guy before!"

"Yeah, actually he told me that a while ago—but he also said he didn't like it."

"No, he said it was weird, Mike. As in strange, unusual, different. He did not say he didn't like it. Trust me; I was sober when we had this conversation."

"Was he?"

"No, of course not," Angela says. "But that's not the point. The point is that he obviously has some kind of interest in you, Mike!"

"But what kind of interest?" I wonder.

"That, my friend," Angela says, grinning, "is what you need to find out."

I nod and take a long swallow of beer.

"By the way," Angela says, "did Dann mention to you that he was the one who set it up?"

"Set what up?"

"The night he got together with his best friend. Dann said he was curious what it would be like to make out with a guy—but not just any guy, it had to be a guy he really liked as a person. So who better than his best friend, right? Anyway, apparently Dann purposely got him really drunk, and he pretended to—"

"Check this out," Dann says, swooping down beside me in the booth so that our shoulders and legs are touching. Craig is carrying a round server's tray that's loaded with cocktails, some half gone but many nearly full. He sets the tray on the table and slides in next to Angela.

"Where'd you guys get these?" Angela asks.

"We stole them from the yuppie scum in the other room," Dann explains.

"We love stealing from yuppies," Craig says. "We figure they deserve it."

Angela extends her hand in Craig's direction. He shakes it. "When Mike and I used to live in LA, I had this huge bumper sticker on my car and guess what it said. It said 'Die Yuppie Scum!' They definitely deserve it!"

"So what do they drink?" I ask.

"Scotch," Dann says flatly. "This one's a scotch and soda, I tried it already. And this here's a scotch and water, I tried it too. Actually, I think I've tried all of them. There's one gin and tonic, plus two more scotch and sodas."

"Scotch," Angela says. "How typical."

"Hey, I think this was a truly considerate gesture on their part," Craig snickers. "After all, what could be better than complimentary scotch laced with yuppie germs? Who could ask for anything more?"

"I could ask for Dann," I say quickly, wishing immediately that I could retract the words.

"You mean ask for my hand in marriage?" Dann asks me, smiling enigmatically.

I feel myself blushing.

"Dann would marry you, Bukowski," Craig says. "Trust me, I've known him for years. He loves you, man. We both love you."

"Too bad gay weddings aren't legal," Angela says. "Just think, I could be the maid of honor."

"And I'd be the best man," Craig adds.

"Okay, Bukowski, I accept your proposal," Dann tells me. "As soon as they legalize gay marriages, call me and we'll do it. Even if I'm married to a girl by then, who cares, we'll get married anyway. I've always fantasized about being a bigamist!"

"I propose a toast," Craig says. "To Dann and Bukowski's gay wedding."

We raise our glasses in salute and everyone drinks. A few minutes later, one of the overbuffed bouncers announces that it's nearly one o'clock so we have exactly three minutes to consume all beverages and leave the premises.

"Do you guys want to come over?" I ask Dann and Craig, trying my best to sound nonchalant.

"Sure," Dann says. "As long as you've got something to drink."

"We always have something to drink." Angela laughs.

"I figured as much," Dann says, then: "Hey, Bukowski, did you drive here on your scooter?"

I nod.

"Cool, I want to ride on the back."

"As long as you won't sue me if we wreck."

Dann puts his arm around me. "I won't sue you, Bukowski," he says. "But I might have to kill you."

We walk to my scooter arm in arm, and Dann holds on to me tightly the entire way home. His elbows press against my sides and his fingers dig into the flesh around my belly button and every time I step on the brakes he rests his head on the back of my right shoulder—and even though it's barely 40 degrees outside, even though my teeth are chattering uncontrollably and the chilly wind is numbing my hands and ears and face, if I knew of a way to make six blocks become sixty miles, I'd do it in a heartbeat.

Later, after Craig and Angela have gone to bed (together) and after Dann and I have had a few more beers and after I've shut off all the lights except the one in the kitchen, where Dann is sitting on a barstool, I tell him, "Dann, I've got to pass out now, I'm really fucked up. You can sleep on the couch if you want—we've got a huge thick warm blanket and I'll give you a pillow and it'll be—"

"No, man," he says. "I want to sleep in your bed."

"You do?" I say dumbly.

"Yeah, I do. So is that cool with you?"

"Of course!"

I start cleaning the kitchen, unsure of how to proceed. As it happens I don't have to worry about it, because Dann stands up and trudges toward my bedroom. A couple minutes later I do the same. My room is dark, but after a few seconds my eyes adjust and I can see Dann. He's curled up on my bed, on the side away from the wall, eyes closed. I take off my jeans and climb over him. I'm wearing boxers and a T-shirt. Dann's wearing jeans and a sweatshirt. Only inches separate us but I'm afraid to touch him. I don't want him to think I'm coming on to him. I have no intention of coming on to him—even though I think he's beautiful and smart and charming and funny and there's nothing in the world I'd rather do.

Dann touches me. I jerk away, assuming it's an accident. "Hey brother," he says.

"Yeah?"

"I don't want you to misread this, I'm not trying to lead you on or anything, but I really want to touch you right now."

"You do?"

"Bukowski!" Dann's voice is suddenly stem. "If you ask me that one more time, I swear I'm going to laugh at you and say no, just fucking with your head, brother, that's all."

"Sorry," I say.

"Don't be sorry," Dann says. "Just accept—I mean just—come here."

He tugs on my arm and we move closer to each other so that our legs and our sides and our arms are barely touching. I feel at once tense and euphoric, realize I've been holding my breath for a long time and exhale audibly. Then Dann says, as if he could read my mind, "Bukowski, what I really want is for you to just hold me."

I manage to swallow the words "You do?" as I put my arms around him. He takes hold of one of my hands and squeezes it tightly and says, again, "I swear, Bukowski, I'm not trying to be some kind of tease or mess with your mind. It just feels good to be with you like this."

"I know," I agree. "Don't worry, Dann. You have no idea. This is fine. No, better than fine, it's perfect. It's all I ever wanted—to sleep with a guy I like and hold his hand and feel him next to me and know that there's no expectations, nothing to worry about, nothing to—"

I stop talking when I realize I'm about to cry and maybe Dann senses this too, because he grips my hand even tighter and leans closer into me. This night couldn't have been better if I'd planned it—except I know that if I'd planned it, none of this would be happening right now. But it is happening; this charismatic guy who makes me laugh is here with me, holding me, and all these things make me love him so much that I can't help it, I start crying.

"What is it?" Dann whispers.

"Nothing," I tell him. "Everything's perfect. Just ignore me. I'm happy, I'm fine, I swear. Really, don't worry, I'm fine."

"I wasn't worried, Bukowski," Dann says softly. "I know you're fine. I could tell that right when I met you—it's why I like you so much. I just don't want you to be sad."

"I'm not sad," I tell him. "I promise. Not sad at all."

It's a long time before I sleep, but that's how I want it. There'll be plenty of time for sleeping, plenty of nights in the weeks and months to come filled with nothing more than solitary dreams. But this may be the only night like this—the only night I can synchronize my breathing with Dann's, trace drawings on his palm with the tip of my finger, listen to his heartbeat, and imagine how nice it will be in the morning when I wake up and he's still here beside me.

Series

DAVID PRATT

Peachy held on by planning for the next event—just get to Halloween, Thanksgiving, Kevin's memorial service, Kevin's lover Chris's memorial service, get to Christmas—which was easy because Peachy had seen Martha Stewart on *Today* wrapping presents in tulle and he was, pardon the expression, dying to try it.

We knew better than to tell him, "Get to Valentine's Day." That was not his strong suit. I told him near the end that he could know he was loved, and he said, "I was not loved. I've always been a woman who arranges things." I wondered then what I'd ever meant by "love."

Peachy died on a warm Saturday in January. His mother insisted on a priest. Peachy hadn't given a sign in hours, but when the white collar walked in he opened his eyes and said, "Well! God's judgment we deliver!" That fast-forwarded me. What might I die believing?

The parents abandoned the apartment. Our friend Mona and I split up the meds ("meds" is a word you toss off to sound like an authority in the middle of all this) because we had friends who were still alive who could use them. No one we knew wanted the holistic stuff, but we took it anyway. I still have Peachy's bee pollen. I go to the fridge for a midnight snack and I take out the pollen. I study the smiling bee. I read the directions. I read the directions again. I put it back, for one more day. I do this night after night and I never get my snack.

Jimmy went first, in July '95. He was forty-three. We'd known each other since NYU. We weren't lovers, but one of us might call the other on a

January or July night to trade the rack of isolation for some timeless play. Afterward, not having to deal fully with the other created relief, and sadness.

With Jimmy near death and his parents coming to visit for the first time since he'd moved here, he tried to sit up in bed and he croaked, "In . . . the . . . closet . . ." I went in and dug till I found a cardboard box from the liquor store, full of paperbacks with black-and-white covers and titles like *Pledge's Cherry* and *Milking Baby Brother.* Could've knocked me over. Jimmy tried to sit up again but couldn't. Trapped on his back like a turtle, he rasped, "Take them . . . away . . ." So I lugged the books to a Dumpster five blocks away and heaved them up over the edge. Jimmy lapsed into a coma before his parents came, and died three days later.

Then Mario went in August, at forty-one. He'd been Jimmy's lover for six years, during which Jimmy hadn't called me as much. Mario and Jimmy had split up in August '93, after Mario found his first KS lesion in his mouth.

For the sake of the benefits, Mario had worked at a place where you charge theater tickets. But he really lived to make movies—first Super-8, then video. We had "premieres" with gowns and red carpets and coke. The most fabulous one was for Mario's AIDS conspiracy thriller, this kind of Mary Higgins Clark thing called *Fuck Me Dead.* Mario's *Citizen Kane,* however, was a forties-style melodrama called *Forever Rectal.* I have it on tape but I can't watch it now. And yet, as with so much stuff left to my guardianship, I can't throw it out.

Back from Fire Island September 24th, I found it on my machine: Brett was gone. Brett had played all Mario's heroines. He wouldn't let anyone tell him how to do drag, though—and Mario wouldn't either, so as to preserve the "purity" of Brett's performance—so in one called *Police Harlot 2000,* Brett played this transsexual cop who held our friend Danny at gunpoint and said, "Up against the wall and spread 'em!" while he kept trying to straighten his wig with the other hand. And then there was Brett's one straight role, in *Forever Rectal,* where he got to say, in a none too masculine voice, "My God, Professor! They want our women!"

I must take care not to reminisce too much.

In the end Brett grew too sick to perform, and Mario abandoned mainstream entertainment for cinema verité solos in which he detailed each pill and each new lesion (the best of his Late Period was a ten-minute video called *Tape of My Last Crap*). Brett hadn't changed his will since Mario died, so his costumes were all left to Mario. We gave them to Mario's widowed father, who spoke almost no English and who had never met Brett. He clutched the wigs and spike heels to his chest, said "Thank you" over and over, then asked me something in Italian. Danny translated: the old man thought his son had had a girlfriend, and he wondered where she was.

I felt as though someone had liposuctioned out my soul.

Kevin and Chris died in December, within days of one another.

Last of all (I promise) was Howard. Howard lived to see protease inhibitors sashay down the runway at Vancouver, but he refused to take them. For fourteen years he'd been planning to die, and so he did. His guru said it was his "path."

AIDS has shattered the vessels of memory, like lamps unto our feet. When I see a friend who is still alive—when he can spare a moment between pills—our conversation drifts. Did we really know people named Peachy, Jimmy, Brett, Mario, Howard? Did they make movies, wear dresses, wrap presents, read porn? I'm negative-as-of-eighteen-months-ago-and-haven't-done-anything-other-than-oral-sex-without-ejaculation-with-people-I-basically-trust-who-say-they-haven't-done-anything-other-than-oral-sex-without-ejaculation-with-people-they-basically-trust-who-say etc. I may live another forty years. For what? To plant marigolds? Read *War and Peace*? Have sex?

Wesley comes over and we watch Nick at Nite. Wesley is my boyfriend, for lack of a better word. I can't imagine myself having such a thing.

Nick at Nite has back-to-back Mary Tyler Moores. These are our dreams: Mary's French windows, Rhoda cracking wise at weird, harmless Phyllis. Things changed after Mary moved to the high-rise. She was getting ready for the eighties. Rhoda and Phyllis had their own series. They were getting ready for the eighties too. Wesley backs up into the harbor of my legs. I put an arm around him and imagine I am a fireman carrying a child from a burning building.

If I show less interest in sex now, Wes, it doesn't mean I don't care for you. You belong to my life—your back curving in the light as you floss, the way you make signs and call restaurants to eradicate all Chinese menus from our life. The way you put your juice glasses in the sink without washing them. I put my arm around you like in high school wrestling, the sweat and uncertainty, but we never speak of it to one another, barely look one another in the eye when it's over.

Wesley is a composer but he hasn't composed anything in over a year. Once in a while he'll shut himself up with his keyboard and play ten minutes or so. But when I say that the simple act of doing so is good, he gets angry. He says he has nothing to say that hasn't been said, so he has a moral duty not to compose. Glasses pile up in the sink. We're at a party hosted by a composer friend who's won a fellowship. Wes proclaims, "The paradigms are moribund." To me this sounds like something from *Masterpiece Theatre:* "Cook says the paradigms are moribund." / "Lovely! We'll have Freddy to lunch Tuesday week!" Wes ignores me, which gives me my strongest desire for him in weeks. He says that artists who refuse to make art are the real winners. He says we should all stop creating, then honor the dead on World AIDS Day, by having a "Day with Art." On the way home Wes says he pities the "poor fools" out there still composing. "Oh, yeah," I say, "poor Philip Glass!" "Oh, right!" Wes says. "Who can't make four hours out of someone counting? 'One-two-three-four-five-six! One-two-three-four-five-six!'" "All right, all right!" I say. "How about . . . John Corigliano?" Wes stares. "*The Ghosts of Versailles? The Ghosts of Versailles*??? All the ballyhoo, I wanted some kind of big *Parsifal–Boris–Don Giovanni* catharsis and what is it but *Figaro* with dead people!" He looks out at the city passing by and says, "*The Ghosts of Versailles* . . . Huh!" Back home I kiss him and pull his tie off. In bed he marks time, playing with his dick. His sudden sense of duty is attractive. When I come he holds me and whispers, "Yes, yes," then rolls onto his side. I reach for his dick. He removes my hand and squeezes it briefly. " 'S okay," he says.

Wes does word processing at a bank. The bankers love him because he's figured out stuff about Excel that even Bill Gates doesn't know. He leaves for his shift with me still in bed and I think: Where do I want to go today?

I'm seized with a desire to clean. I go on a rampage—living room, bathroom, bedroom. I vacuum desiccated roaches. I dig slime from the soap dishes and soak charred oatmeal from burners. I throw out the shower curtain, which once was clear but which, without our ever noticing, gradually clouded with gray dots.

Then at three o'clock I'm on Lafayette Street, walking past antiques stores, past the Keith Haring souvenir shop, past boutiques so conceptual I don't know how to approach them. I'm thinking: What a fertile age we live in, while I'm cruising this boy in drooping jeans, who stares at an orange trash thing filled with burning books. Aristotle, Chaucer, Shakespeare—classics by the yard blowing away. I ask: Is he a literature buff? No. Where is he from? Barnstable, Massachusetts. He works for an insurance company. Red rings circle his eyes. I ask him what he does for the insurance company. He says it involves an adding machine. I ask if he'd like to go do something. Like what? He snuffs back mucus. Gold hairs corkscrew from his chin. His name is Rick. We shake. He studies his gray and blue Sauconys, snuffs back more mucus. We take an uptown R to Forty-second Street and change to the 1.

Rick admires my house: it's so clean. He wants a beer. I get one and check the time: Wes comes home in an hour and a half. Suddenly I know Rick will not leave. Wes will come home and see him but not see him. He'll say nothing. We'll become a *paralysie à trois*. Rick scratches. I think he carries a disease more terrible than AIDS. When you have Rick's Disease you believe that at any minute you could die. In fact you don't die, you never will. The disease is that, because you think you could, you won't touch anyone, for fear of communicating the disease.

Rick has been locked out of his room on Twenty-second Street. If I give him twenty bucks and a token, we could maybe do something. But there's nothing I want to do. Why are we here like this? The thought that we might do something was so compelling. I can't tell if it still is. I wish this had never happened, but if I think about asking Rick to leave, I feel I'll die. He eyes my grandmother's candlesticks. In the end I give him five bucks and the token. He snuffs back mucus. As he shuffles to the door I ask: How old are you? He says sixteen. *Madre!* And he really works in insurance? He glares at my nineteenth-century watercolor of an empty bandstand with red, white, and blue bunting. "So," I say, "my boyfriend'll be back soon with the Dobermans, Himmler and Goebbels!" Rick edges out with a last snuffle. Once again, Irony triumphs over Need.

Wes comes home and starts dinner. He bought goat cheese and red leaf lettuce at the Fairway. I wait for him to notice something. He doesn't, and this devastates me. I come up and I put my arms around him. He pats my forearm, not turning around. He remarks how clean the place is. He hopes I didn't tire myself out. This afternoon, Wes, I brought home a bum and I don't know why. But goat cheese awaits. It helps the conversation: it's good goat cheese, but not as good as the goat cheese from Zabar's . . . This takes more energy than cleaning a thousand apartments. Ten-thirty at last. Wes backs into the harbor of my legs. Mary makes everything okay. Spunky, unexceptional, giving in to what others wanted—no one reassured us like Mary. You could have stepped into Mary's world and been gay, but you never would have "gotten sick" (as we say). Mare just gosh darn wouldn't have allowed it.

After Rick, I proceed not to straighten up. I don't want to do any of this, but . . .

Scottie, an NYU film major, cruises me at a deli on Eighth Street. We go for lattes at Starbucks, and he tells me David Lynch has redefined the parameters of American cinema. We have sex in the laundry room in his dorm. The next and last time we get together he brings deli flowers to my place. I have to throw them out—out out, as in on the street. I could have told Wes I bought them for myself, but I never do that. On my way down I wonder: What would Jimmy or Mario or Brett or Peachy say about this? We came of age in the hedonistic seventies, Source of All the Trouble, yet I think my dalliances look pathetic to my dead friends. They wonder why I don't stay home with the nice man I found. While I trash the flowers I explain to them that, if I were single, I'd find this slutting around pathetic too, and I wouldn't do it. But with Wes, I need a fount of hope.

Next comes Maurizio—nineteen and kisses like trash on fire. He has a thing in his eyebrow and has what Jimmy used to call NFA—No Fixed Address.

You don't remember which one Jimmy was, do you?

Maurizio lived in Tompkins Square Park—which he mentions when the conversation allows, or even when it doesn't—and now he lives on Madison Street with the family of a woman he met at Gray's Papaya and with whom he struck up a conversation based on a shared interest in Malcolm X (the woman is black, Maurizio is white). He takes the carved jade from around his neck and tries to put it around mine. I remind him about Wesley. All I want is to own Maurizio's slender, hairless body and copious ejaculations. He pops three or four times a session, winces and cries out in Italian as he shoots on my chest. My thinner, grayer fluid follows.

Just when we have this routine down, Maurizio wants to talk. He wonders where Wesley is in all this, and he wonders why I seem not to wonder this. (Maurizio belongs to what Peachy used to call "the feelings mafia.") I say Wesley is none of Maurizio's business. I apologize for this and say I was just tired. Maurizio smiles sadly, chin on bare knee. He drops the other bent leg onto the rumpled sheets, and traces his toes with a fingertip.

Maurizio moves out of Madison Street and into a shanty at Ninth and C, next to an old man with a duck. This does not race my motor the way it races Maurizio's. I do not find the guy with the duck to be a cool piece of found art, but I do give in to Maurizio's insistence that I meet him, because after the howdy-do I want to have Maurizio come on me.

The old man's duck is named Gertrude. She nests in a wheelchair. To make her lay eggs, the guy plays seventies soul. The O'Jays in particular make Gertrude groove, eggwise. "Smilin' in your face, all the time they wanna take your place . . ." Gertrude lets out a quack, and voilà! But instead of getting naked, now Maurizio wants to show me the organic market on Sixth Street, where he buys mushrooms to put in a duck egg omelet the three of us share. Then Maurizio videos the guy telling stories.

Any day I will tell Maurizio I'm too old for this. But before I can he moves out of the shanty. He leaves a note with Gertrude's keeper, promising he'll call me.

I can't decide what to hope for.

In the *Times* they review a novel—by a Serb or a Croat—in which cabbages sprout all over the hero's body. The reviewer says it ends up like watching someone else's nightmare. Nightmares, however, tend to be disjointed and autistic, the dreamer only acted upon. The critic said he thought he'd stop reading if he weren't being paid. Then he decided he wouldn't; he'd keep going no matter what, because he believed the author was actually daring him to stop. If he did, the author would win. So he kept reading, as page after page the author offered more absurdities, more cabbages, in lieu of any traditional ideas of love or order. Maybe, the reviewer concluded, withholding transcendence was the point. Maybe transcendence could come only by plowing through cabbages without end.

The end comes in the basement of a porn store on Eighth and Forty-third. There's a boy with Jesus-gold hair. He bats His eyes so bluntly it jolts me. I follow Him back to the booths. Our quarters drop. I punch my button and unbuckle as the curtain goes up. There is Jesus, staring at the video screen, pulling His dick. He holds up a piece of a cardboard box, black Magic Markered: "Fifteen years old. HIV negative. For $5 I suck your dick or you suck mine." Video kills the Bible star. Here I am: the only living boy in New York. Peachy on Gay Pride day: "On this Day of Days there are a thousand kids cringing and naked in basements in this City, all desperate for some prick in a uniform to come over and piss on them so they will feel valid! And there's another hundred people. Right now in fucking Normal, Illinois, there's a six-year-old at the dinner table with his father sneering, 'Don't put your hand like that, it's queer!' and the kid sits there feeling doomed, utterly and completely doomed, at six, and later he's lying awake and Daddy comes in and fucks him and tells him it'll be 'our little secret'! And now the kid wants the uniform prick's number. Jesus! Any fag wants love in this City should find a straight woman or a dog!"

The world goes to a hot, wet blur. I will not die thinking that! I refuse!

I bash the red button. My icon zips up, folds his sign, and leaves with the video still going. I stumble out of my booth and take the stairs two at a time up to the main level. I plow past videos without end, past women gagged and bound, past Great Danes with bubble-gum dicks sniffing vaginas. The sunlight hits. I can't go back underground to the train. I can't be with a cabdriver. So I walk home. On the way I buy a T-shirt for Wesley with the Mary Tyler Moore logo, from the opening when her name fans out and comes at you and you enter her world. "Love is all around." At home I shower—can I get all the cabbages off?—and collapse on the bed.

When I wake up, Wes sits caressing me in his new T-shirt. We watch Nick at Nite.

I don't know what Wesley or I want. The kid in the porn booth wanted money and maybe love. Scottie wanted to be right about David Lynch. Maurizio . . . That guy with the duck meant more to him than I could fathom. What do I or the man I share my life with want? We stay together, the once clear future becoming a snowy screen. But like that reviewer, I'll keep going. Not because I don't want the author to "win."

Life—that is to say, death—always wins. I'll keep going because, even after Jimmy, Mario, and Brett, even after Peachy and Howard, I'm still the kind of moron who believes, in spite of all evidence to the contrary and in spite of the overwhelming Thanatos in this world, that this time he will pull the big Harvey rabbit out of the hat—no matter how empty the hat looks and no matter how arthritic his hand has become.

You see why Wesley won't compose. An audience brings him that kind of hope and it paralyzes him. But it's all predicated on that hope, Wes. It's why you took up composing in the first place! You also see why Wes and I will probably never break up. Wes backs into the harbor of my body and we watch Mary. Maybe he is boring. Maybe neither he nor I can give or receive love. I thought I loved Jimmy, Mario, Brett, Kevin, Chris, Peachy, and Howard. Now I don't know what people mean when they say "love."

Maurizio writes: "You probably don't want to hear from me. I know what I did to you was shitty, but I figured cutting you off would make you mad enough to get over me and go back to Wes. He is better for you than I could ever be. You deserve that. I still think of you. I hope we can be friends. I would be happy if we could get together and talk. I really hope to hear from you, but I will understand if I don't. Love, Maurizio."

"Love." People did love once. From about the end of the Black Plague to the start of trench warfare. That was the Age of Love.

Wes, you have become a part of my life—leaving glasses in the sink, explaining why the WordPerfect macro editor was better in DOS than in Windows, getting a "No Menus" sign made in Chinese, putting your Mary T-shirt on every night . . .

And when I tell you . . . Wes, hit the mute button a sec (and you do, but continue to stare at the TV)—when I tell you that last month for a total of about fifteen seconds I went down on a boy named Maurizio, but-his-name-doesn't-matter-and-I'm-sorry-I-don't-even-know-why-but-maybe-we-should-y'know-not . . . do . . . certain stuff till I . . . you know . . . again—you stare at the TV like a boy whose parents are struggling to say "I love you" while the boy just wants to fly his imaginary airplane around the ceiling. You massage my forearm till just enough time has passed for me to feel the depths of dread, then you say, "I guess everyone does." Mary's name appears, one-two-three, for the next episode. You hit the mute button again and squeeze my arm and I want to say, "You don't," but I'm afraid. This is a later episode, with no words to the theme song. "Who can turn the world on with her smile?" By 1975 we'd stopped believing. Rhoda and Phyllis had spun off, leaving Mary in her high-rise. I still want them all back together in the house. I want one more Mario premiere. With love all around. Nearly everyone from those premieres is gone, and I take it personally. I have to, just to hang on. I squeeze you in return, and thank you. Your thumb keeps going. In the commercial break I add, "I just . . ." You straighten your spine, turn partway to me, and say, "It's okay." I pause. I put my closed lips to the back of your neck, but I do not know whether your skin is warm or cool.

The Black Narcissus

REGINALD SHEPHERD

The meditation
On the signs and sacred images of desire
Must have an end.
—Allen Grossman, "The Recluse"

The endless parade of manicured bodies canceling out mine (four in the morning on Halsted Street, middle of July) must have an end. And so it will, but not today. Some day, some hour, afternoon, and soon, but not today. Recluse that I am, I still have things to do with desire. Like tell myself a little story.

My mother always told me, "White people, they stick together, but a nigger'll just as soon stab you in the back as look at you." But what did she know about white people, trapped in that tenement apartment until the night she died? And where does that leave me (a long way from the Bronx by now), wanting you or to be you, to be your friend at least? You said you wanted to be mine. Watching you casually drape your arm around some other man's chair, your gray eyes smiling into his, I see that she was right after all. The white men always leave together. (What does capitalism have to say about that, busily extracting surplus value from a crowded smoky room, overpriced drinks and cigarettes, and cocaine in the corner bathroom?) What does their matter matter, and why? By the end of the night (*Hurry up, please, it's time*) a pretty white guy's cheekbones matter more than all my clever discussions of dialectical materialism, especially to me.

You might call me bitter, and you'd be right. Just grant that I might have cause. But you came to hear a story. Let me think of one.

This is the way it never happened. His name was Fabrizio, but that was too many syllables to call out across the street between classes, so everyone called him Fab. I called him that too, wanting to be part of "everyone." We were best friends that year.

Fab threw the best parties in town, the latest music and the latest people wearing next season's perfect outfits, laughing in French and Italian in the hallways. I never liked those people, because their lives weren't mine, but I always loved the lilt of foreign causerie. Fab had the kind of downy, tawny skin the teeth want to leave marks on, apricot, new peach, brown hair whose tips turned gold in the sun, and hazel eyes flecked with gold. He never would have slept with me, not in a million years, not for a million dollars. He already had that.

I remember the first time I saw him, pulling up to the curb on his expensive motorcycle (everything in this story costs money), his hair falling careless yet so artful across his unlined brow, at noon even. No, that wasn't the first time. The first time was at a party, 1 a.m. or so. (Who'd even worn a watch that night?) I didn't know he'd thrown it until days later: it was one of those parties you hear from down the street and say, "Sounds like someone's having fun, I think I'll go and watch," the best kind if you're not popular. That's the way college was, standing around hoping no one noticed I hadn't been invited. He was dancing on a chair beside a speaker singing along with a song about brotherly love. "Solitary brother, is there still a part of you that wants to live?" When you find what you want, it always belongs to someone else.

Fab belonged to no one but myth and his own kind, but I can keep his picture here in three thousand worthless words. I carried that party inside me for months, long after the honey-gold boy who took me there (and afterward stuck his perfect finger up my ass while he waited a little impatiently for me to come) had dumped me for some more original sin (a white man from Boston I wanted too: he wanted to be a writer, now he's dead). I spent months looking for that song, took it as a kind of promise: there's still beauty in the world, even if I can't touch it. Who wants to see his fingerprints smeared over beauty anyway, to smudge its perfect skin?

The second time I saw Fab, then, he was pulling his motorcycle up to the curb with his roommate Dylan the Welsh ale heir (the biker boys, we called them, my small group of friends brought together by what we lacked, being people-who-were-not-popular), throwing his bangs back from his forehead and lightly wiping his brow with a dirty linen handkerchief. He never wore a helmet. I followed him around for weeks (he walked sometimes too, as if he were a mere mortal, sat in the dining hall and ate polenta: shat too, probably, but I wasn't there for that). One afternoon he turned and said, "What do you want from me?" He didn't mean it as a challenge. All I ever wanted was everything, but Fabrizio wouldn't even give me his ass, just one overcast afternoon before he went to photography class. (It would have been warm there, inside his body.) "We'll have coffee, okay? You're a strange one." Fab always meant what he said. "I like people who aren't afraid. That's why I decided to meet you." What Fab didn't understand is that I was so afraid of my needs I wore them like a winter coat in May. My fear was all outside me: that's what I called Fab. I guess that's what he meant: I was more afraid of myself than I was of him.

This is a list of the ways in which we were different: Fab was beautiful, Fab was rich, Fab was tall, Fab was confident, Fab was popular, Fab was from Milan, Fab was white. This is a list of the ways we were the same: we both loved to ride around campus on his motorcycle (marking the boundaries of a territory, his), my arms wrapped around his waist, but not too tight. We dismounted the bike on opposite sides.

This is the way it never happened. He turned around on the street in his black cashmere overcoat, asked "What do you want from me?" I told him, and he gave it to me on the living-room rug (plush, white of course) of his third-floor apartment with "Property is theft" stickers on the kitchen cabinets. His ass, I mean, doggy style, pale and smooth and pulling me farther in, not far enough. We listened to Billie Holiday sing "Lover Man" while our bodies did things they wouldn't repeat. "Satisfied?" he said, and went into the white-tiled bathroom to shit me out.

It wasn't what I wanted after all, but it was better than the nothing I had. I wanted to be him, to know how it feels to be so real. My baggy jeans would never fit that way, not my skin either.

Four things he never said to me:

Fuck my ass, nigger stud.

Give it to me, you black son of a bitch.
Make me cum with that nigger cock.
Shove that big black cock up my tight white cunt.

What would these things sound like in Italian? More words I wouldn't understand.

This is the way it happened. There was a boy when I was a graduate student at Brown University, learning how not to write poems. We never met. He was beautiful, clear beer-bottle-brown eyes and burnished olive skin. Aren't they all lovely, and don't I hate them for it? They mean too much to me, those men and boys meaning nothing but themselves, striding across the too-walked-over world as if they owned it. At Brown (Camp Bruno, shining city on College Hill) they did, had men to floss their hair and shine their skin, had men anytime they wanted, in any position. They shone in the September sun, gold of early autumn. Who wouldn't wish to do the same, to own such excellence, or break it if he couldn't? All power and no substance, exactly like gods.

He was one of the cool people, the beautiful who live beautifully and at a distance. I bought a pair of black suede Doc Martens because I'd seen him wearing them, thought they would make me more like him, someone you'd want to watch cross the street, or need to brush against in passing in a library doorway. *Excuse me, I was just* . . . I imagined his thin pale lips pressed to my darker, thicker lips ("blow job lips," my friend Paul called them), or wrapped around my cock, my cock swimming deep into his smooth white ass. I always imagined his ass as smooth, my tongue lapping at it like vanilla ice cream on an August afternoon, sweet and just starting to melt.

Burnt from the Notebooks, Spring 1991:

Last night (*ah yesternight!*), Wednesday, at the Underground ("Night Out at the Underground," "Alternative Night": our night, but who's the us? to what is this all-white scene alternative?), two guys so beautiful I could cry. But why? "A grace not much involved with merit." Why is it that sheer, ephemeral physical beauty holds me so in thrall when worn by a man wearing white skin, no more than a paisley shirt or a pair of two-tone saddle shoes, nothing to do with him: "no whiteness (lost) is so white as the memory / of whiteness." No matter what I (merely, compensatorily) *do,* they *are:* no matter but their matter, nothing matters but them. "In the way that music is more absolute than literature, beauty has more authority than intelligence." It seems silly, really, and when not laughable, infuriating: who are they to me, why should they be anyone? Of course, I'm no one to them: the truly enraging part.

I wrote a poem to him, for him, about him (*I wrote a letter to you, my friend, so many letters I never send:* I listen to too much silly music, making up emotions for myself), the Euroboy of my dreams and nightmares: affectionate, a bit malicious, utterly sincere, sincerely uttered. "At him" might be more accurate.

ANOTHER MOVABLE FEAST

Tawny skin the teeth want to leave marks on, down
of peaches just past ripe, apricot, russet
and gold. He says his light brown eyes
are green. It seemed to me then that beauty. *He sucks*
the stem of his sunglasses through pursed lips, or slowly
moistens with a facile tongue the upper, then the lower
lip, head slightly tilted to the left. Why
is the eye so caught? It seemed to me that beauty
(scanning the room to be certain he is seen)
was the one thing everyone wanted to have
(he brushes a carefully combed fall of hair
from his brow) or to be *(his small teeth even*
when he laughs with friends, whiter
than his metaphorical skin) or, failing
that, destroy. *And where to keep it*
when he leaves the three o'clock café, what
to do with it? The teeth want to
bite into ripened fruit, to tear
the skin and let the juice run out.
He rides
his foreign-made motorcycle helmetless, perhaps
into an afternoon where he'll be splayed
across the asphalt and the rusted chrome
of the car in question, a summary of all the virtues

pressed to the pavement's page. (People gather
in nervous clumps or walk more quickly, the other
driver quietly cries.) I grow hard and strange
-ly formal at the thought of it (or,
failing that, destroy*), the ceremony*
of his unperjured body tangled in corruptions, skin
sallow in late-light and tinged with green, the black
and purple marks the teeth have left.
He doesn't get to keep it.

Fab's not dead, of course, just on another continent. He's in Rome for the summer with his grandparents (important people who own important things): dating the right sort of girl, riding down to Naples to meet his English boyfriend on the sly. That's what I need about him: the life I imagine him living. I graduated from Brown years ago. I'll never pine on the fringes of that world again, and I miss that lack. I'll never walk among those privileged terms again, a smudged blank on white paper. I can't want him without wanting to tear his perfect skin, opaque screen of my desires: as if I wanted to know what's behind it. I can't want him without wanting to be hurt. Wanting him hurts me, because it isn't him I hate. I can't humiliate myself forever. *The meditation on the signs and sacred images of desire must have an end.* An end is also a goal; a melody has a conclusion, but no goal. Good night, Friedrich Nietzsche.

If this were an opera the goal would be clear. We all know how the story ends: someone always dies for love, music making drama shapely. No one dies, no one cries, though sometimes I wish I could cry, wish I could feel those things, like love, could hear those things, like music. I wanted to write about the feelings I have while waiting to fall in love and not translate them into words that betray them: "I am in love with him." Because I never was: not with Fab, not with anyone who looked like him. Not with anyone who didn't, either, not with myself, for sure.

This is a story about pain. I was only ever interested in feeling pain (that is, in feeling), and I only feel that about men, preferably men I don't know. I only feel pain (call it desire) about men I want to be. I like to think pain makes me interesting: it makes me better than him, whoever he is this week. It gives me something to write about, something to do when I'm not writing. (I'm *collecting material,* you see.) It gives me something else with which to bore myself. I call it safety, wanting him without knowing him.

This is a story about bodies: they take in food and make shit. This isn't a story about bodies at all: they're its occasion, but not its meaning. Those Platonic virtues dancing under strobe lights at Roscoe's, or strolling shirtless through a summer street fair sucking Popsicles like cocks, aren't bodies, just afterimages matter in motion leaves behind, reflected like the Mediterranean summer sun I've only read about. I call it beauty. Perhaps this isn't a story at all (you've thought of that), just a series of events occurring near the body, sensations and impressions the mind makes meanings of. Proximities and failed connections.

The body is this thing that stands between me and other people, my black body, their white bodies, my black body I try to make mean something different from all the other black bodies it's confused with, my black body I try to redeem with my sharp mind and good taste in shoes, blithe spirit trapped in a brown-skinned mortal coil. I'm not like those other bodies, the ones that commit crimes and speak bad English, mere body with bullet holes, knife wounds, track marks marring it. I'm not the man you think I am. I'm not the man, I think. But the body joins me to other people: those men dancing shirtless at Manhole on Saturday night, would their white flames draw me mothlike if they gave off no visible light? Without the body there'd be nothing to touch, so how could I be lonely? (No poetry there.) My black body I try to get their white bodies to touch: maybe it will rub off.

I'm more real than my too-real body (it stands in the way of the world I want to call mine), but his white body makes him real. His body makes sense in a way mine never can. This is my body, this is not my body at all: but he's his body *and* its meaning. He's nothing but olive skin and brown eyes just like mine. On him they look so different.

The body means nothing, but riding on the subway with a white policeman leaning against the door, in a car full of black people I was not like. I knew what this black body meant to the gun humming patiently in his holster. I sat reading a book about the bodies of black gay men (their lives), trying to make my body different from those black bodies around me by sheer force of will. *Men make their lives, but not in circumstances of their own choosing:* Karl Marx wrote that. Only black people ride the subway, after all, and white policemen don't read books. But they know a nigger when they see one.

This is the way it happened. Fab? I made him up. There was a boy named Duncan Sheik, from South Carolina, a sophomore or junior. I watched him in a diner on College Street, a café on Waterman. I found a picture of him in the freshman face book: he'd remade himself since then. His tan skin my white teeth wanted to tear pales in my memory (he runs away again), but I'll always remember the party where I didn't meet him, and the foreign motorcycle he rode around campus, marking the boundary that kept me out of his world, the border that kept him in.

Now he's a pop star, barely breathing. I bought his album, listened to it every day, named a poem after a song. It's not dedicated to him. He did an in-store performance one Friday afternoon at my local Borders and I almost went: tried to, but he was late and I got restless, bored at Borders. Besides, I'd told an acquaintance who worked there that I went to college with Duncan Sheik, and he'd told Duncan, who was curious, wanted to meet this person, reminisce perhaps. I didn't want to be embarrassed by the revelation that he hadn't the vaguest idea who I was. I remember little hands around a water glass, white smooth fingers curling.

Here's a flower for a world made safe for imagined white men and me. I can't possibly recall its name.

Little Murmurs

HENRI TRAN

The first notion I had of my mother as a real person came sometime after I had been brought back from Hong Kong to live with my father and stepmother. It was during my preschool years. We were living in Cholon, Saigon's Chinese quarter. Our house was situated behind the Binh Tay market, not too far from my father's factory. My kindergarten was only a few blocks away. Late one evening just when we were getting ready for bed, the doorbell rang. It was a police sergeant under the command of one of my father's friends who was a sheriff deputy. The sergeant informed my father that my mother had been arrested by a warrant from the Foreign Visitors and Immigrants Administration Office. She was being held in the district jail, waiting for deportation, her tourist visa having long ago expired. Without asking for further explanation, my father jumped into his clothes and drove to police headquarters. He arrived just in time to have a few words with the deputy in charge and was allowed to get into the back of the jeep which was escorting my mother to the Tan Son Nhut airport. He stayed there until she boarded the first available flight out.

When my father returned and told us of the event, it did not occur to me to ask where my mother was sent to or why she had been deported. I was concerned with another matter closer at hand. An aura of something exotic and mysterious had always enveloped her, but until then she had only hovered around my life—and our lives—like a face outside the window. The sudden visit from the police that evening, plus the fact that she was put on a plane and flown out of the country against her will, had brusquely unfolded that aura to reveal something tangible, and vulnerable.

As a small boy I knew I had a mother. However, the woman whom I called Mom and who tucked me into bed every night was someone very devoted to me—my welfare depended on her love and generosity—this person was not her. My mother lived somewhere else. She would sometimes show up for a short visit, only to disappear again. She might be living in another town, another country. She might be traveling around the globe, I knew she took a lot of trips on airplanes. As far as I was concerned, the fitful occasions when she put in an appearance at our house during my early childhood years did not convey the impression of another life related to mine. She was a stock figure: it was her that I referred to when the need to proclaim my origins arose: "Me too, I have a real mother!" I used to think of her the way I might have thought of a benign relative who skipped in and out of the family circle—a long-distance aunt, for example—and whose existence belonged solely to an era that I was still too young to regard as my past.

I remember a visit to a villa in the outskirts of Gia Dinh, the French quarter of Saigon. Some adult figure walked me through a shaded patio, then I found myself in a large bedroom. There was an air conditioner humming in the background. My mother was in bed, not fully awake, in her silk pajamas. I noticed the shape of her breasts: they were full. There was a pair of black wing-tipped shoes of extra-large size sitting on the lid of a steamer trunk placed at the foot of the bed. A tall wooden cradle stood by the window. The curtain was not drawn, revealing a cloudy afternoon. There might have been a dark-haired, pink-cheeked infant sleeping inside the cradle. I was told to take a look at my half sister Elizabeth, born in Saigon but soon to be taken to Paris. The cradle might have been empty and it is possible that I had merely imagined a sleeping infant in it, since I never saw my sister again.

When I learned that my mother had been deported from Vietnam because she was a French tourist with an expired visa, and that even my father could not have saved her, I burst into tears. Suddenly my mother became real, she was alive. Almost as quickly the realization came upon me of something being too late, something being terribly wrong. Her existence was thrust into my present—and my world. Her relation to me was no longer shrouded in mystery, but dipped in a sense of doom.

As I grew up I began to keep tracks of my mother's whereabouts. Her sojourn in France lasted two years, the duration of her marriage to her French husband, Elizabeth's father. After their divorce, by which she lost custody of the girl—but retained her French citizenship—she returned to Hong Kong in the late 1960s. In the meantime, my family had moved into the high-rise on Hung Dao Street, and I was going to grade school.

My mother made frequent trips into town during this period. She was no longer at an age at which she could go back and work in her old haunts, the dance halls and nightclubs around town. Even though no one put a title on what she did for a living, she passed as a small-time jewelry dealer—a shady, underground business at best. My suspicion was that she smuggled her wares around Southeast Asia. She might be coming in from Hong Kong or taking off for Singapore or on her way to Bangkok. Whenever she came to visit us, she would unwrap some trinkets of diamonds or jade from a handkerchief and show them to my stepmother.

I often accompanied her to the airport to see her off. It would be a hot, dusty afternoon. I remember her wearing a loose summer dress and a pair of cork-soled platform shoes. Her wavy black hair was tied up in a ribbon. Her porcelain skin glowed when we stepped into the shade; I could feel a spell of coolness as I watched her put on the cherry lipstick she always used. She had her sunglasses on, and her click-clack jewelry. If there was a long stretch of waiting, she would light a cigarette and puff away distractedly. Sometimes it amused her that I observed her so intensely. She would feign embarrassment with a smile and playfully give me a little slap on the cheek. To my already quizzical eye, she appeared on one hand too continental to be taken for an Oriental lady and on the other too provincial to pass for a jet-setter. She looked girlish and casual, almost petulant. My father used to joke that she was a fake Parisian—that, indeed, she was *une dame de vignerons,* anxious to go back for harvesttime in some vineyards in the South of France! In the cab that drove us to the airport my mother would tell me the same thing I had heard so many times before: "You're a big boy now, be good to your parents . . . I'll be back soon . . . what do you want me to bring you next time?" I would reply with something equally insignificant, knowing that next time might be next month or next year, and soon means some unmarked spot on the calendar. I would tell her to take care of herself and not to worry about me.

Inside the terminal, after she had checked in at the ticket counter, we would take seats in the lobby. The feeling of urgency normally evoked by flight departures had long been replaced by something more familiar: we might as well have been sitting at the breakfast table, blabbering about what we were going to do for the day. The long stretches of time I spent with my mother waiting for her flight, which always ended abruptly by an announcement over the PA system, were brief fragments of our life together. When the passengers were allowed to board, I would hug my mother and kiss her goodbye, then look on as she walked through the customs gate, turned around, and waved at me one more time before hurrying down the corridor with her makeup kit in hand and her carry-on suitcase in tow.

The next time my mother was back in town, she would come and visit us, usually on a weekend morning. My stepmother would sit with her in the living room and they would chat for a while. I would be at my desk nearby doing homework. Sometimes my father would be home too. But there always came a final moment when I had to join them on the sofa, sitting between the two women who appeared to be the best of friends. My father used to tease me that I acted like a chicken with a rubber band stuck in its throat—a Vietnamese expression describing the state of someone caught with his pants down. I remember differently. I remember that my stepmother would be telling my mother how independent I had become lately, how I sided with my father so that I would not have to listen to her, and that I had begun to come up with excuses for staying out more.

"Just like his dad." She then ended her sentence with a pained smile. But my stepmother was not really complaining, because she expressed her grievances to my mother in an amusing way. Her words were all very casual and lighthearted; indeed it would seem that she was trying not to show her annoyance at raising an unruly child. It was only the burden of responsibility for my behavior which was getting out of her control that was wearing her down. She certainly could have, would have, done a better job, had it not been for her poor health. And if only my father would stay home more, and pay attention to what was going on, etc. The underlying message, even I could tell, was the thankless task of a parent who knew that one day this child, he too, would leave her; and no amount of love and devotion in the world could make him stay. She was saying to the other woman that no, it has not been a holiday raising this boy, he takes after his father, he knows how to break your heart.

I smiled at my mother to let her know that it wasn't so, then at the other two to warn them not to stray too far from the truth. The reason I behaved like a chicken with a rubber band stuck in its throat was that I had to act in a peculiar way to reassure everyone that I was not as unruly a boy as I might appear to be. After all, they had been bragging about my grades just a minute ago. It was like I had to send the same message out on a different wavelength to each of them, that in spite of whatever had transpired, the "lucky bastard"—a term of endearment my stepmother was especially fond of—was as good and wholesome an offspring as any parent could hope for. (They really had no choice, you see, I was their only child, the only child.) I was also the living, thriving proof that all faults had been forgiven, misdeeds redeemed, and yes, their best efforts under the circumstances had not gone unrewarded. I was the one who had to swallow the rubber band so that my father, the ringmaster of our family circus, did not have to. And he could just sit there and laugh.

When my mother took her leave, I waited for my stepmother to say, "Darling, walk your mother down the stairs." She would lean on the balustrade in front of our condo and look on as my mother and I walked the length of the balcony which led to the stairway. We walked side by side, trying to appear unhurried and at the same time keeping a guarded distance between us, watching our steps as though mother and son were parading down some big boulevard, Finally we came to the top landing and began to descend the two flights of stairs.

Nobody could see us now. As I bounced up and down the steps, my mother would make some overture so that she could reach out and touch me. "When are you going to get a haircut?" and she would run her hand through my hair. "What happened to your elbow?" and she would stroke the back of my neck down to my shoulder to my upper arm. I had a chance to take a good look at my mother and truly smile, all the while commenting how pretty she was or how little I cared for her new hairdo. When we got to the bottom of the stairs, I would linger and my mother would stall, for she knew that I had been waiting for this opportunity to give her a kiss. It was usually the hollow between my nose and my upper lip that landed briskly somewhere on the lower part of my mother's jaw beneath the earlobe. It was a stolen kiss, if ever there was one, because I was afraid that some neighbor coming down the stairs might catch me in the act of kissing my mother. I was also afraid that my clumsy show of affection might ruin her makeup, and worse, that it would leave its trace on me. As she stepped out to the street and I turned around to head back, I would brush the palm of my hand across my mouth, sucking in the lingering perfume before wiping it off on the seat of my pants. Then I would rush upstairs. My stepmother would still be waiting at the front door. There was always a worried look on her face, as if I had been gone for a dozen years.

Sometimes it was suggested that my mother take me out for dinner or a movie. These were special occasions: I would put on my white shoes and wear my leather belt and button up my shirt collar. I was proud of having such an attractive lady for a mother, and in return, I wanted her to be proud of me. It might be a Sunday and we would sit through a double feature in a noisy theater somewhere in Cholon to pass the afternoon away. I remember one time it was a James Bond movie—*Dr. No,* I think—paired up with a scintillating pseudo-travelogue titled *Orient by Night,* in which a group of geishas danced together in a big production number under twirling umbrellas and drifting blossoms, then one by one each performed a striptease or a magic act. After the show we would come back out in the street under the waning sun and go someplace to eat. If there were still time because it had not been a double feature or because the electricity had gone out in the theater, then my mother would take me back to her place, a garret somewhere.

It did not matter where, because the kind of place she could afford nowadays was always at the top of a creaky wooden staircase on the second floor of some cramped quarters of Cholon. It could have been Hong Kong, or Paris—as it had happened some time before when I was still in the care of my grandmother and again in later years when I went abroad. It really did not matter, the way our lives came together only to drift apart. In a little nook in the corner of her room, my mother would cook something for us on a hot plate, most likely noodles because they were quick to prepare and there were always a few strips of barbecued pork and some wilted green onions left in the cupboard. I would dawdle quietly around a half-folded table between a narrow window and a thin curtain, carefully lay out the plastic spoons and chopsticks as if they were the finest china, fold the paper napkins the way waiters did with real cloth ones in fancy restaurants. But after a while I would stop making believe and just sit and stare at the small, sticky bottle of soy sauce, its shadow slowly stretching toward the edge of the tabletop; or gaze at a speck of lint hanging lifelessly in the dusty shaft of worn-out sunlight. A soft breeze would sneak up behind me and whisper that the afternoon was drifting down the alley, and soon another day would have gone by.

We would eat in silence. There was an impatient air about my mother as though she could not wait for me to grow up so we could talk. Or since I was becoming a young man, she would rather that I lead the conversation. Or maybe our being alone together in a room somewhere was not the most natural thing in the world and my mother was afraid of what I might be expecting of her. In any case it came almost as a relief to both of us when it was time for me to go home. At the foot of the stairs at the entrance to my building, we would say goodbye. A furtive kiss from me on her cheek, a brush of her hand through my hair, then we would part. Halfway up the stairs I would turn around and watch her get into a cab or a cyclo; when she was gone I would feel fine. We had not done anything that could be construed as a betrayal. I had come back to the home of my parents, and I had not squandered anything precious—such as love, for example—upon my mother.

After I started high school, my stepmother's heart condition took a turn for the worse. She began to have fainting bouts. Those flights of stairs that led to our floor became torture for her. Sometimes I came home from school in the afternoon to find candles burning in my parents' bedroom, the shutters drawn, my stepmother lying facedown, half undressed in her bed; and Auntie Wah or Auntie Ba from next door would be doing all sorts of things trying to revive her. They would dip a coin in eucalyptus oil and scrape my stepmother's back until there were long welts along her flanks and around the back of her neck, as if lashes had been doled out to her. And poor Sue, our young maid, would have to stay up all night, crouching by her side, trying not to doze off while continually pounding her fists as if she were beating drums on my stepmother's back and arms and legs to help the blood flow. Watching Sue meekly perform her massage, one was inclined to think that the girl was doing her best to hammer life into an unwilling body. For it seemed that my stepmother was dying.

Toward the end of my second year in high school, my mother happened to be in town for a long period of time and to my great surprise she was staying at the Rex Hotel uptown, where my father dropped me off for a visit. This time there was not a pair of wing-tipped shoes but a man in her room. I was introduced to Uncle Lu, a big, portly Chinese man with shiny bald pate and narrow eyes behind thick glasses. His stature was imposing as if he were the strictest teacher at school. When he spoke, I was disappointed because his Vietnamese was fluent, with nary an accent, and therefore I could not poke fun at him behind his back. His clothes were plain and somber, though carefully styled, like that of an executive—which he was of a Taiwanese shipping company as I later found out. But his manners were mild and he was a soft-spoken man. When he smiled and shook hands with me, I felt rather amused and could not help but smile back.

We went out for dinner at the Majestic near the harbor. I ordered a *salade niçoise* without the faintest idea what *niçoise* was supposed to be, but Uncle Lu was impressed. A week later the three of us went to a restaurant-nightclub in Dakao where a singer in miniskirt and push-up bra belched out "Love Potion Number Nine" while we dined by candlelight. I had ordered a *loup de mer,* which turned out to be a fish—another shot in the dark—and was gulping down some smooth Beaujolais, which impressed Uncle Lu even more. He was sitting between my mother and me, looking smug because my mother was so beautiful—"With those diamonds twinkling in her ears, your mother looks like Liz Taylor," he remarked, shaking his head as though disbelieving his good fortune—and because I was such a smart boy. Uncle Lu looked almost handsome, for his eyes also twinkled, his bald pate shone, and his gold-rimmed eyeglasses were bathed in pink. He was well scrubbed, he was in love, he was rich. And I almost wished he were my father.

The next time my mother got back in town it was neither a garret nor a hotel room where I came to see her. This time it was a small house in the affluent suburbs of Phu Tho, an extension of Cholon to the east. It was not quite a house, a town house rather, at a corner of a quiet side street facing a small cemetery. Uncle Lu had bought this house so that they both would have a comfortable pied-à-terre when they came to town. If nothing else, I was grateful to him because later this house would be the place where my grandma came to die. For some long years she had not been back from Hong Kong to visit us, and we were too busy with our own hectic lives to be bothered. Furthermore, I was harboring some hope that there would come a time and place where my mother would settle down and then I could see more of her and my grandmother.

Uncle Lu was a member of Club Sportif on Hong Thap Tu Street. It used to be a country club for the French community in Saigon. But now the French were leaving and the Americans coming, bringing with them a myriad of foreign correspondents and diplomats. Club Sportif had a casino and swimming pools and endless rows of tennis courts. French and English were spoken there. There were guards at the gate. On Sunday mornings a steady stream of cars, mostly Peugeots and Mercedeses, would roll through the wide cobbled driveway past the admission booth and unload their passengers at the foot of the steps that led to the ornate front of the casino. One would wander through the marble-floored lobby and come out on the other side, descending upon grassy turf which ran between sections of tennis courts.

At the end of the walk stood the aquatic complex, a big sprawling building with its facade decorated with portholes to resemble the flank of an ocean liner, and three swimming pools spreading across its terrace. On the deck surrounding the pools, waiters in white uniforms circulated among rows of lounge chairs serving drinks to the guests. On one side there would be tanned, *far niente* European matrons wearing big sunglasses and wide-brimmed hats, stretched out in their bikinis with the straps down, sipping umbrella cocktails and lazily fingering their tricots. On the other side there would be clusters of American officers, big hairy bodies in dark trunks and sunburned skin, who would not go near the water but stay glued to their spots for hours like a herd of walruses. They chewed on their cigars, tried to keep their eyes from wandering too far from the pages of *Time* or *Newsweek,* whose bloody battlefield pictorials were getting soggy with tanning oil and fading away under too much sun. Now and then the men would comment loudly in their twangy accent which nobody but they themselves could comprehend, poking the air with their cigar stumps. The women would show their annoyance by swatting an imaginary fly, or impulsively unraveling their knitting.

Outside the aquatic complex, there were pathways crisscrossing the interior park, paved with white gravel and stretching all the way to the foot of the thick walls that encircled the compound. These walls were laden with drooping wisteria and covered with bright patches of bougainvillea. When the sun stood still, they shimmered like huge macramés of smoldering fires. Up close, they were pockmarked with holes that the swallows and robins had used for their nests. The walls were barely high enough to prevent the awkward, leprous plumerias from reaching over with their blistered branches, seemingly to offer bouquets of intoxicating white flowers to passersby in the street. High above, tall jacarandas loomed over the long walls, dappled the white gravel, lulled the fierce sun, and, drenched the noisy landscape in their purple bloom. Beneath this canopy, cicadas sang through the heat, while here and there a gecko lizard in the deepest hue peered down from the crook of a tree branch, from the glass-embedded top of a guard tower, or amid the broken shells inside a looted bird nest, smacking its tongue in regret, as its tail—so brittle as to be dryly snapped off by a sudden turn of its unwieldy trunk—tumbled down and lay wiggling on the parched pavement.

Uncle Lu took me there, and for whole Sunday afternoons I was free to roam while he played sets with his business friends. My second time at the Sportif, I ran into Philippe, a schoolmate from my French junior high. He was a Vietnamese-speaking French boy whom previously I had simply adored from afar. Not only did we go to the same school but we also had the same birth date, albeit a year apart—I was thirteen, he was twelve. Here on the aquatic terrace, there were no parents or teachers or classmates to come between me and the object of my affection. I had Philippe, and the infinite blue of a summer sky, to myself.

"Philippe, petit garçon aux pommettes!"—young boy with blushing cheeks—I would tease him, while he tried to say something naughty in Vietnamese. Young boy with downy limbs and perky loins, young boy with a head of golden hair and limpid eyes that make you want to drown in them. Young boy whose innocence is deceiving.

"On va s'embrasser au fond de l'eau!" I whispered to him that we would dive under and exchange a kiss at the bottom of the pool. Philippe pretended not to understand and started to swim to the other side so that I would chase him and push him down and we would thrash around. At last we went down, descending through a world of crystal water and sunlight and bubbles that sparkled without sound. I tried to kiss him with my puffed-up cheeks and puckered lips like a blowfish, but Philippe swallowed the air in his mouth and held his breath. Without warning, he planted his lips upon mine. I was startled when I felt his tongue darting inside my mouth. I thought he was playing a trick, so I kicked him away and quickly came to the surface. When he came up, Philippe accused me of cheating and swam off. "Cheater, cheater,"

he yelled back in his stilted Vietnamese from across the pool. I waved, making a sign for him to return to my side. He wrinkled his nose and refused to come near me. But later when we were in the locker room, as I was drying off and occasionally flicking the wet towel across his white buttocks, Philippe got me to chase him behind the shower stalls. I thought he was going to show me a quick erection. But no, he was leaning against the wall, waiting. When I came around, he grabbed my arm and drew me close. Breathlessly he whispered, this time in his mother tongue, *"Henri, embrasse-moi!"*

I obliged because we were no longer at the bottom of the pool and I wanted to try the same trick he had played on me earlier. But being a gentleman, and being thoroughly infatuated, I did it with much grace and tenderness, though I had never done it before. I closed my arms around him, so softly, for fear that something would break, trying to convince myself that this was not a dream, that we were not fooling. We were not—Philippe, for once, was standing still. His dark lashes swept a sidelong glance at the thin trickle of water on the white-tiled wall. He was waiting for me to make the first move, and all I could do was hold him tight, pressing his cheek against mine, my nose burrowing into the peaches-and-cream softness of his skin. He turned his face to me. His beautiful eyes loomed, but I was afraid of staring into them. Trembling, I let my hands fumble alongside his body. My head slumped on his shoulder, my mouth stranded helplessly upon his neck.

His legs were brushing against mine. The towel fell at our feet. I had not yet learned to surrender, because when he reached down and fumbled at my crotch, I yanked his arm away. I did not know how to make love; at this moment I only felt that something had come over us like a tidal wave and engulfed us, and I wanted to make sure I had him secured in my arms so that we would not lose each other when we were finally swept away. Philippe stared at me wonderingly, his face flushed, his mouth open. I myself could hardly breathe, we both seemed gasping for air. . . . Yes, I can feel your tongue dabbing at my cheek, your lips grazing upon my eyelids. Just one more whisper, I promise, but only for the chance of saying your name one more time—"Philippe!"—before we kiss. Before I drown.

It was not quite the kiss I had always dreamed for a certain lady. It was much more than that. It was the shrill cry of a caged bird that suddenly finds itself teetering on the ledge of an open door. "Philippe,

Philippe—" I kept whispering, as if to hush the wild, frantic clapping of the wings. Then I closed my eyes. So once again we would fly, through a sky of waters as iridescent as your eyes, while the sunlight wove its molten gold through your hair, and strings of clear bubbles, bright and wondrous, wrapped around us like another embrace, and sparkled without a sound, like the murmurs of my heart.

Lost Time

DECLAN MEADE

It will be April soon, another winter all but over. Walking home the other day—Friday—carrying his few bags of shopping, John was looking at the trees along the roadside, noticing the tiny green buds and thinking to himself how great it was to have the long days of summer to look forward to, when Sheila Courtney pulled up in her fancy car and told him to hop in.

"It'll save you a bit of a walk," she said as she lifted her own shopping off the passenger seat and put it into the back. She never asked if John wanted a lift. If she had he might have said no, thanks, Sheila, you're grand, I like to walk and it would be a shame to take a lift on a beautiful day like this. But she'd have insisted anyway or she'd have offered to at least take his shopping for him and drop it off up at the house. He didn't want that either so he got into the car and prepared himself for the worst.

Sheila sat staring over at him for a couple of seconds before she started up the car. Her eyes rested on his face, then moved down to the plastic bags he was holding on his knee.

"How are you, then, John?" she asked, and her voice was all kind and soft. People ask him that question all the time—always using that same tone of voice—and they watch him while they ask it as if they expect him to break down in fits of sobbing at any time and the only thing that's preventing this is their kindness and softness.

"Oh, I'm fine, Sheila, thanks."

"And how is your poor Nan?"

"She's grand," he says, and then Sheila sighs as if to say oh, John, of course your Nan's not grand, how could she be and don't I see for myself what a poor state she's in when I bring her the Communion on Sundays. Sheila's sigh says all this and then she adds: "You're a good man, John."

"Have you thought about what I said to you last Sunday?" is her next question, and he has been waiting for it.

"I need to talk to Nan about it," he replies, and even without looking at her he knows she's thinking that he's a complete head case but she doesn't say anything more because they're nearly up at the house. He has the door open before the car has fully stopped and he has said thanks for the lift and goodbye to her and is walking through the gate. He knows she'll just sit there looking after him until he's inside the house, so he doesn't turn back.

"You're a good man, John." He's heard that one before too. He used to be a good boy and now he's a good man. In the beginning John was a good boy because he never had a father. Of course John had to have had a father at one time—there are three photographs of a tall, thin man in a dark gray suit—but the one he had got himself killed in an accident at work before John was even born. Then John was a good boy because he'd stood so calm and quiet beside Nan at his mother's funeral after they put the coffin in the ground and everyone came shuffling past with their long, sad faces. Nan had told him not to cry. Any crying he wanted to do could be done later and at home—not there in the church or in the graveyard or in the house while people were still milling around after the funeral.

"Neither of us will shed a tear in front of them," Nan said, "that's where your mother went wrong." So he waited until the pots of tea and the plates of sandwiches were all gone and everyone had disappeared back into their own lives but by that time he was too tired to cry and he just wanted to go to bed and have Nan read him a story. Nan didn't seem to want to cry either. She read two stories and before he went to sleep she told him that his mammy was much better off up in Heaven—she'd never really managed to be happy down here at all—and he knew that Nan was right.

He had never known his mother to be anything but sad. She spent most of her days in bed or lying on the sofa. She was always crying and shouting at him and Nan to stay away from her. Then sometime in the afternoon she would head down to the town, coming back a few hours later with a bottle in a brown paper bag which she took off up to her room. She'd want to see him then all right, wanting him to play cards with her or to listen to her singing but he always told her he was too tired and Nan would tell her to leave him alone, could she not see the child was upset. That's when Mammy would go mad altogether and start screaming at Nan that she was trying to turn her own son against her and that she had never given Mammy any chance at happiness whatsoever and that one of these days she'd throw herself into the River Boyne and then we'd all be sorry. Go ahead and jump, Nan would fire back at her, don't let us stop you. And maybe one day his mammy would have thrown herself into the river but they'll never know that now because she was killed instead by some driver who didn't see her coming along the dark road swinging her brown paper bag.

Sheila Courtney drove off after he'd gotten inside the house but he still needed to give himself a couple of minutes down in the hall before going up to check on Nan. She was sitting exactly as he'd left her on the big brown armchair beside her bed—a special chair that was supposed to be good for her back and where she spent all her days now.

"Fierce busy in town," he said as he walked over and sat down on the edge of the bed. "Fierce busy altogether."

She looked up at him as he took her hand in his but her eyes were completely empty and after a few seconds they fell away. She was like this all the time now, not like Nan at all but like some stuffed toy that could do nothing for itself—nothing except sit in her chair and stare at the floor and dribble from the corner of her mouth. He didn't mind of course. How could he when Nan was the one who had always looked after him? He made sure she wanted for nothing. He brought her a cup of tea in the mornings, placing the cup on her night table while he raised her up onto the pillows, then holding it while she sipped away at the strong sweet liquid. When she'd finished he helped her out of bed, got her to put on her dressing gown and then helped her into the chair. He was terrified of bedsores, checking her legs every day for any sign of them even though he wasn't sure what they would look like—they just sounded awful. He spent as much of the day as he could sitting on the bed beside her, not wanting to think of her being lonely or afraid.

He had come home one Friday morning last October to find Nan lying unconscious on the kitchen floor. That had been a terrible day altogether. An ambulance came and he had to go to the hospital with her. All kinds of doctors and nurses flying around, asking all these questions, and then there was a long, long time when he was just left sitting in a little room and he didn't know where Nan was or what they were doing to her.

"Your grandmother is a very lucky woman, Mr. Murray, very lucky indeed," the doctor said when he finally came in to talk to John. "The stroke she suffered would have killed most people."

Three weeks they kept her in the hospital and then they told John that Nan's condition was stable but unlikely to improve.

"Do you mean she won't be able to talk again?" John asked.

"It's likely," they said.

"Poor thing," Sheila Courtney said last Sunday after she'd given Nan her Communion. She says this every Sunday when she comes back downstairs, her head bowed and her fingers clasping the little silver box.

"I don't think she even recognizes me."

John says nothing because he just wants to get Sheila out of the house as quick as he can. Off on your way now, Sheila, there's a good woman, don't let me stop you. But she doesn't budge.

"Still and all, John, I know she looks forward to receiving the sacrament. Your Nan was always a devout woman. She never lost her faith," she says, glaring up at him. John stares right back at her, determined to ignore the when-was-the-last-time-I-saw-you-at-Mass look that's sitting smugly on her face and thinking to himself how he'd still be going if it wasn't for the sight of hypocrites like her poncing round the altar Sunday after Sunday. Then he moves to the door to open it in case she's forgotten the way out..

"Yes, yes, I suppose I'd better be going. Time to get the dinner on," but a few steps is all she takes, before she turns and starts up again. "I was just saying to Gerry the other night how my heart goes out to you living up here in this old house, looking after your Nan, and I was thinking how you'd be much better off moving into town. The houses in the new estate are really lovely, John. One of the two bedroom ones would suit you and your Nan down to the ground. You'd be in town with all the shops and everything close at hand." She's on a roll now, no stopping her even if he tried. "And Gerry said you'd have no difficulty selling this place. The house itself might not be worth much but Gerry said the land it's on is a prime piece of property. Those are the words he used." She pauses then and looks at John, wondering if he's heard a word she's said. "Sure, I'll leave you to think about it anyway."

John thinks about it all right. He imagines packing up all his and Nan's belongings in boxes and arranging for someone to transport them to the estate. He sees their new house: freshly painted and with new carpets; central heating; a fitted kitchen; a place devoid of memories and shadows. Then he thinks of Nan waking up in a strange room, not knowing where she is, and not having all the familiar objects, sounds, and smells around her. He thinks of himself walking out through the front door, standing on the doorstep, and being caught in the full glare of twitching curtains and neighborhood watch. He sees bulldozers tearing away at Nan's old house, removing every trace, and he sees the bright new bungalow—or perhaps there'll be two of them—that will be built on this prime piece of property.

Fifteen years ago bungalows started to spring up all over the place. At first one, then another and then another. Now when John walks the two and a half miles to and from town he has to pass eleven white rectangular boxes with their aluminum windows, their garages, their flat green lawns. Initially, Nan had taken great interest in each new neighbor, making it her business to find out who these people were, where they had come from, and what they did for a living. The Farrells were the first to build. Tom Farrell was the second son of James Farrell, the solicitor. He was an engineer with the County Council and had just married a girl from up above Slane. The Hennessys came next: Margaret and Brian. They were both from town. Margaret's family had had a shop and a pub for years. Brian was one of the auctioneers. Then came the Fallons, the Balfes, and the McNallys, but after that it became more difficult. Connections with the town were not as clear; families began to blur. John no longer knows all the names. Some people moved away; others came to take their place. Cars get changed all the time. Little children have grown up.

John's up early when Sunday morning comes. He stands outside Nan's door, listening for the sound of her breathing. She'll sleep for another while so he decides to take a walk. Outside, it's warm and the sky's a cheerful blue in between the friendly white clouds. Plenty of time before Sheila comes with her head bowed; her lips pursed. Plenty of time to wake Nan and prepare the room: to lay the white cloth over the night table; to place the crucifix on the cloth; to light the candle; to wrap Nan's rosary beads round and round her bony fingers. But John is only a couple of hundred yards from the house when he hears the car. He knows it's Sheila, an hour early. He turns and runs though he's sure Sheila will see him galloping up the road and into the house.

She's standing on the doorstep by the time he gets back downstairs and opens the door: not a hair out of place; a colored scarf, knotted at the neck, draped over the shoulders of her long navy coat.

"You're early," John shouts.

She is holding the little silver box—her precious cargo—in her outstretched hands and glances up as if to say now, John, you mustn't raise your voice before the Lord.

"You're too early. Nan's not ready for you."

"But this is the time I always come at."

"It is not. We're not ready. You'll have to come back later."

"Did you forget to put the clock forward, John, is that what it is?"

"Will you just go?"

His voice has risen to a yell. Sheila steps back, reaching for the door of the car.

"I'm going, John. It's all right."

She eases herself into the car and bangs shut the door. John raises his hand as the engine starts but he's not sure if he's waving Sheila on or calling her back. He watches while the car reverses out through the gate. Back inside, he returns quickly to the top of the stairs, into the room where Nan's breathing has stopped and the silence is complete.

The Bank President

DAVID EBERSHOFF

Many years ago, when I was a young man living in New York, I took the train home to bury my father. The mayor of Nice, which in Indiana rhymes with spice, was waiting for me at the station, his bald head gray and damp. "What? No wife?" Napoleon said, his hand falling painfully on my side, on the rib Joseph cracked the previous night in a bright red burst of jealousy. I winced, and brought to my mouth Joseph's linen handkerchief, the one with his monogram stitched in gold.

Napoleon and I were driving in his Mack Jr. pickup across fields of soy and corn, past muddy watering holes and silos crammed with cob. Each time the truck hit a rut I gasped delicately. "Seems you got yourself too used to pavement," Napoleon said, his little German mustache twitching. "I'm just tired is all," I said, ashamed of my rib, and how I broke it. As we entered Ripley County, Napoleon gossiped about the farms along the white dirt road; this was in the mid-thirties when it'd been so long since anyone had made any money that most people had forgotten how. "Your daddy was just about to take away old Mifflin's farm because of one bad investment in hens," Napoleon was saying, his teeth as gray as grain.

My father owned a Merchants and Farmers bank, and hundreds of people from all over Indiana and a few dozen from Kentucky came to the funeral. In the graveyard Lesby sat with me, her pie-shaped face turning syrupy in the heat. Her arms were doughier now, and she was slower in the eyes than when she took on raising me after my mother died when I was baby. Whenever a breeze ran up the graveyard hill, her chiffon skirt with the black roses would flutter up into our faces, causing a hiss of giggles from her baby niece Francine, who was dangling from the pitched iron fence.

Afterward Lesby set up a buffet of roast and bratwurst in our backyard beneath the ash. Francine crushed cherries for the bowl of Eden Punch. It was nice, the wake was. I was standing in the shadow of the old pony barn, greeting the guests, shaking their comfortless, damp hands, feeling for the first time what it was like to be my father. "I don't blame him much," one bankrupt woman was saying, the poverty showing in her loose skin. "Not anymore." "He was in a hard position," another man said, his watery eyes trying. The ache of the blue bruise on my left side grew as one lady after the next hugged me, as farmer after farmer slapped my back.

Napoleon was already trying to find me a wife, but not just anyone. "Now, watch out for this cross-eyed one," he would warn. "She's an orphan."

"Dr. Davenport tells me this one can't have babies."

"Look real hard, this girl's got some Negro in her. See the curls?"

The little square photograph of Joseph was in my breast pocket; I could feel it in there, its tiny weight, the slightly startled face in the picture—a face white and sharp-eyed with the guilt of a child—tucked against me, nuzzling. I wanted to look at the picture with its brown shadows but didn't dare, for surely somebody would turn his neck and ask, "Who's that?"

I continued hugging the hot mourners, staring out blankly at the farm. Beyond the yard sat the tractor shed and the henhouse with its little ramp. Then the fields. As I was gazing out there, the heat wavy above the soil, a huge figure appeared on the tide of the corn. With the western sun behind, it was a black silhouette, massive and slow. It lifted its arm to scratch, and I realized it was a man, a man with a head like a prize-winning pumpkin, a man with a stooped body strangely resembling cattle. And then I knew. It couldn't have been anybody else. Only he. Chester, with eyes as brown and slick as pelts. Chester, who fled Nice when we were boys—running away from the wrath of my father on a yellow summer evening not entirely unlike tonight.

The mourners in the yard were looking to the sky. A dry-smelling rain was beginning to fall. I dashed into the old pony barn; nearly everyone followed. Inside was the heap of the Juliet, the balcony-like apparatus constructed each Christmas for the Pageant of Glass Balls.

The Juliet's white two-by-fours filled the pony barn, a cage of planks and gangways. It looked like a scaffolding wreckage I once saw on Madison Avenue; or the collapse of a great roller coaster. The mourners were pressing me against it, the splintery edge of a two-by-four poking my side. Over their limp humid hair, through the barn's open doors, I could see Chester standing in the field, the rain leaping off him, the stalks of corn bowing demurely as he slowly lifted his arm and scratched his neck.

"I have to lie down," I said to Lesby. "Help me lie down?"

"So long," the guests began to say, their mouths stained punch pink.

Lesby led me out of the barn, toward the house. But she dropped my arm when she saw Chester. "My big dumb boy!" she cried, and then began to run to the corn.

"Who would've thought this old slow giant boy could keep himself alive?" Lesby kept saying later in the kitchen. She was fixing her hat onto her plate of tight, snail-colored curls; then the generous pats of apricot pancake, especially around the eyes. Outside, Francine was pirouetting in the hail, her yellow dress clinging like flesh, her wet braid heavy as a mop.

Chester was sitting on the porch, muddy and crushing crab apples in his pail. When we were kids, my father would never let him in the house, and Chester would sit on the porch and wait and wait through dinner until I could leave the yellow-oak table to go out and slingshot rabbits.

"Doesn't look much different, does he?" Lesby was saying. "Only huger." She was tucking her day's pay deep into the neck of her blouse, into the pink piggy banks of her breasts. She was hitching her chiffon skirt. "Now you sure you're all right, Will? I'll stay if you want," she was saying, twisting Chester's wet collar and pulling him and Francine off into the calm clean night.

The old white house fell still.

The phone's receiver had the dirty mint smell of my father's Evansville cigars. I asked the operator to dial New York, and then shut my eyes.

"Buckaroo!" Joseph said. "You all right?"

"Will be," I said. I thought about Chester, wet and silent on my porch, his glowing eyes like a raccoon's in the window.

"I miss you, Buck. When're you coming home?"

"Shhh. The operator might be listening," I said. "Lela Bullard. Town gossip. She might be—"

"Hey, how's your rib?"

"Sore," I said. "All those old ladies today probably gave me a bigger bruise than you." There was a silence that reminded me of troubled sleep. I was tired; the morphine couldn't bury the pain, the tight pain from Joseph socking me after he accused me of looking at another man. Now I considered telling him about Chester but didn't know where to start. "The bank's going to need me sooner than I thought," I only said.

Joseph's breath was puffing through his small duckish mouth; I could hear a police whistle below his window; I could hear the nicks and scratches of the telephone line, the cough of connection, the clicks and shuffles of someone probably listening in. Maybe Lela Bullard was still on the line, her headset snaking through her bush of red hair, and just as I was going to tell Joseph to hang up, that I'd wire him in the morning, Joseph said quickly, almost too quickly, though it didn't seem so at the time, "Well, I'm coming too, Buckaroo."

Mattie Killion's farm out on the Switzerland County border was my first foreclosure. Look hard into their eyes and tell 'em to kindly move on, my father once said, his white-veined hands gripping my shoulders until I thought they'd crack. But I didn't have it in me, I feared as I walked around the farm. With Mattie Killion watching me from her doorframe, I was worried that she'd see something in the way I was cautiously stepping through her tractor shed and poking around her sties—something flimsy and weak that would tell her and the whole town I wasn't much of a man. From here I was going to drive up the long road to Indianapolis, where I'd meet Joseph's train from New York. Only Lesby knew he was coming, and I'd lied to her, saying he was staying no longer than Christmas. Even so, I was convinced that Mattie Killion and Napoleon and everyone else knew about me, about what kind of man I was; they could see it in the grumpy way I shut myself up in the big white house, could hear it in my voice cracking when a decision had to be made, could read the pink in my cheeks each time someone asked what I thought of a pretty gal. Folks' eyes would creep over me as I walked from my farm at the edge of town to the bank, their worn fingers tipping their hats slowly. If I didn't own most of the damn county they'd probably run me out of town, or worse. They'd probably do it anyway, I told myself each morning as I snapped my bow tie at my father's long-face dresser.

Mattie Killion was eyeing me from her doorframe, fingering a pillowcase with a crocheted fringe, shivering in the hot wind. I was looking more at her freckled face and her scabbed legs than at her land, looking at the sharp, almost Chinese eyes of her children pressed against the dirty windows. The sun was hot, no clouds, not even a thin white strip. It was just Mattie and me, and her children in the window. And the cluck of her hens. But then a snorting noise came from the corn, as if a little one-man locomotive were pulling in. We turned our heads, and there, as if coming from nowhere, Chester was stepping out of the cornfield, his boots crushing stalks. His shirt was stained, and he looked like he might be about to howl from the heat. He was such an unexpected sight that I moved toward him, as if being pulled, and ended up walking straight into a pushcart, recracking my rib.

Mattie Killion ran to me and split open the crocheted pillowcase to wrap my chest. "I'm so sorry, Mr. Covington," she kept saying, her little slanty eyes blinking back tears, her panicky voice shooing away her children. "Run along," she was saying. "Don't get near Mr. Covington. Mr. Covington doesn't want you near." And then, "You, too, Chester. Leave Mr. Covington alone."

Chester's eyes were moist, his open mouth a black hole. His hands reached to cup my head. "You need me, Will?" Chester said, his fingers stroking my hair. "Can I help you, Will?"

"Go home," I said. "Get on now," and I lamely swatted away his giant warm hands, as if to show all of Nice, and especially Chester, that I'd grown up and no longer would let another man cradle my head.

The only thing Dr. Davenport could do for a cracked rib was a good tight gauze wrap. I drove to Indianapolis holding my breath with every bounce; I was thinking about the private life Joseph and I led in New York during the past few years. We found a building on West End Avenue with only two apartments on each floor. That way no one would ever think we were living together, no one could see me slip into his apartment at night in my flannel nightdress and out again in the morning. Joseph said it was silly to buy two apartments when we only needed one, but what else could we do in those days? "We could tell the world to leave us alone," Joseph would sometimes say, the gambler glimmer twinkling in his eyes.

Joseph's train arrived late. When it pulled in I was so anxious to see him I began to imagine hugging him right there on the platform. Sometimes I think I was lucky to have loved another man back then because we were forced to squeeze so much emotion through the tiniest daily gestures; our handshake on the platform was hard and long and as intimate as tongue kissing.

Driving back to Nice in the night you couldn't see much of the land—just flat black stretches of bean fields that looked like neat, square ponds. Joseph kept closing his eyes. His small hand crawled over to my thigh. "Let's pull over," I said. The night was blue, the nearest farmhouse a couple of miles away. There was a cluster of poplars in a dry creek where I thought I could park the car.

"Why stop now?" Joseph asked.

"It's just that—"

"Is it your rib, Buck?"

"No, it's just that I think I'm going to feel funny being with you in my father's house. What if his ghost is hanging around? And I'm sure you'll want to—" I plucked his tiny hand from the pool of my lap and held it like a starfish. "Maybe we could lie down in the back seat and get it over with."

Joseph thought about this. "You're never going to forgive me, are you, Buck?" He was looking out the window, his neck hairy and buckled with a dull silver scar.

"Already have."

"Then keep driving." Part of me wanted to ask him to leave, to go back to New York that very night, but I stopped myself from thinking that.

I showed Joseph to my father's dressing room, where he used to take his Saturday afternoon naps. I moved to open the linen closet, but the little stabbing feeling in my side twisted. "And now we're home," Joseph then said, pulling me toward the narrow step-up bed. "It's our home, Buckaroo," he was whispering, but as I lay down on the balled chenille spread, my damn old rib was hurting so much that Joseph could only stroke my hair as I whimpered toward sleep.

Dr. Davenport couldn't believe it, but my rib healed in a week. "Must be the heat," Lesby said. "Humidity's good for fusing."

"It's because I'm here to take care of you, Buckaroo," said Joseph, who talked me into naming him the bank's vice president. It didn't seem like such a bad idea. No one else in town I could hire. The first thing Joseph did was turn the linoleum-floored secretary's lounge into an office for himself. "Just want to be near your office," he said one day, his arms full of peppermint-green ledgers. He added, "For decision making, that is." Then he kissed me, right there in my office with the Kurdish carpet and the lion-dog andirons perpetually looking at each other and the oil portrait of my father mounted on his horse, Missie Lee.

"Not in the office," I warned. The sun through the windows was slanted and hot.

"But if the door's closed, why not?" Joseph said, and before I could answer he put one salty hand over my mouth and the other in my lap, and I sat back in the buttoned-leather chair and watched my gray-faced father gaze distantly from his mare.

"I don't know about you, Buck, but I want to become the biggest bank in the southern counties," Joseph declared one day at my desk. I could smell him next to me, his birchy summer smell as he leaned over my desk. When we were apart, I liked to lie down on my father's day bed with one of his ribbed undershirts over my face. Once when I was young, I came home from school and walked in on my father doing the same thing with one of my mother's ivory silk undergarments. The red-faced shame that flooded him disgraced me as well, and both of us were embarrassed to know that the emotion of longing had found its way into our house.

"You ever lend beyond corn and soy?" Joseph said one day. "I mean into something other than a few pigs and chickens?" He was holding a pamphlet from the Tool and Die Association over in Danville. "There's money in barley and black walnut wood, money in sorghum grain and natural gas. Hell, there's money in racing dogs and glove manufacturing. I want to grow. You want to grow, don't you, Buck?"

"Nobody's growing these days."

"We will," Joseph said, shoving his arms through his junior-sized seersucker coat. "Come with me."

The bank was in the center of town, on Cayuga Street, across from the square where the Juliet rose each Christmas week for the Pageant of Glass Balls. Mattie Killion's farm was twenty minutes east, past the Grain Exchange and the barbershop with the Cuban-style haircuts painted on the front window, beyond Shelton's slaughtering house with its hosed-down brick facade as red and moist as meat, way out beyond Antoinette Street where Lesby lived with Chester and Francine in a little brown house that had never been painted, its side planks shifting and rotting like teeth.

Mattie Killion's yard was empty except for an old sow roped to a weeping willow. Chickadees were pecking loudly at a patch of sunflowers. Joseph walked to the edge of the spotty cornfield. He was such a small man that the frail, tired stalks made him look like a child surrounded by grandparents. He scooped some soil into his hands. "How bad is this dirt?" he asked.

"Cuts the yield by about a quarter," I said.

"Not so bad," he said. "And she's got Chester helping her out. You like him, don't you, Buck? You think he's a good guy, don't you? He says you were friends when you were kids."

One of Mattie's Chinese-eyed boys appeared at the screen door. "But what if the bank gave her more money to run this place?" Joseph said. "It's all about how you value risk, Buck. You see risk and say it's worth a penny. I see risk and say it's worth a dollar." He spread a piece of paper across the Pontiac's humped hood. His pencil formed a column of figures: 12,000 . . . 9,000 . . . 9%. "What if we were to give old Miss Mattie money to hire a couple of hands and a few extra bucks to expand into honeybees."

"Honeybees?" I said.

"Or something. Give the old girl some money to make money."

A little girl with pale green veins in her temples walked out of the barn. "Is that the bank man?" she asked the pig.

Joseph slapped my lapel. "Come on, Will. I bet there's a way." I was staring down at his sheet of calculations; Joseph had the sloppiest handwriting I'd ever seen and sometimes I felt I shouldn't trust a man whose letters and numbers looked like a very young child's.

"Here we go, Buck," Joseph said. "Let's put a bigger time factor into how you value this farm. Why not? All Mattie needs is time." Joseph's pencil stabbed out the numbers, dividing and multiplying by interest rates and number of years. "You're kicking her out because of accounting, not because she can't run a farm. Conservatism killed the cat."

"Where'd you hear something like that?"

"Hey, Buck, who lost his load in the crash? Who had to go begging to his Indiana daddy for a second trust fund?" Joseph stood on the balls of his feet, rocking softly. "Not me, Buckaroo." He walked close and whispered in my ear, "If we were alone, I'd kiss you right about now."

"Let's talk about this in my office," I said, worried that the greasy air was carrying his words.

"You've got no balls." Joseph walked around the yard in a circle, his buck saddle shoes yellowing with dust. He was studying the house with its steep green roof and limestone chimney, surveying the patchy field of flapping corn, ears peeking through their husks like babies waking from naps.

Mattie Killion stepped onto her porch, a nursing bib over her shoulder. "How's your rib?" she called, her hand visoring her eyes as if politely hiding their red-rimmed hatred. Behind the house, the corn trembled nervously. Chester walked toward the house, dragging a hoe. His undershirt was so damp that his pretty nipples, round as cherry tarts, were there for everyone to see. I don't know who was looking more, Joseph or me.

"Just the person I wanted to see," Joseph said, shaking Chester's hand. "Was Will always this much of a scaredy cat when he was a kid?"

"Not that I remember," Chester said.

"Say, Chester, do you know anything about honeybees?"

Chester looked to me, his long face seeking an explanation. He used to look at me the same confused way when we were kids when I'd tell him I no longer wanted to be best friends with my fat old maid's son. He'd mope away, his feet raking the dirt, but the next day he'd return to the backyard and whistle "My God Is So High" beneath the swishing ash until I'd come out and say, "Hey, Chester, you want to help me catch a rabbit?"

"I know it's about the time of year to set up their hives," Chester said. An arm lifted and scratched his stomach. Mattie's little girl screamed.

Something about the thick humid air made me think there were tiny stars of electricity swirling around out there in Mattie Killion's yard. Joseph looked so wound up that I thought if I touched him he might spark. An old anger was coughing itself up inside me; an old phlegmy feeling of hurt. Chester was standing a few feet away, but I could feel his ripe heat on my face, sinking like sunlight into the poplin of my suit. And there was Joseph, bouncing on the balls of his feet, offering a candy wrapped in bright yellow foil to Mattie's little girl. For some reason, I wanted each of us to go his own way. For some reason, I thought that would be best for all. In those early days of my return to Nice the whole town watched everything I did, and I could tell Mattie and her two papery-skinned kids were looking at how Joseph and Chester both were leaving me mute and hot and, to tell the truth, a little bit excited downstairs.

"I've been thinking, Mattie," I finally said. "There just might be a way. A way for the bank to help you out."

Joseph worked his way into Nice's habits. He'd drive out to the mortgaged farms, walking the crops with the farmer, eating the baked caramel ham of the farmer's wife, playing tetherball with the pointy-eared children. He'd spend a little time in most every merchant's shop, helping with the receiving of paint cans down at Frederick's Hardware or the horse washing over at Peter Roll's, the last livery in the county. "Money comes from relationships," Joseph would say in the dark of dawn, pushing back the bedclothes and leaping naked into another day of deals. Although the nearest house was a half mile away, every time his girl-sized body stepped past the window I'd convince myself for an hour after that Napoleon was on his way to lock me up in the cold jail of sodomy, snatching away the bank forever; but then Napoleon would never arrive, and each day in the furrowed flat of Indiana would advance as ever before.

One evening Joseph came across Francine lying in the gully along the town line; a bull had charged her, and now she lay unconscious, a neat black hole stabbed into her side, her dress with the little brown sailboats shimmied indelicately up her waist. Had Joseph not come along and *noticed* the girl in the rut, why she could've *died,* Lesby told the whole town, over and over, always sinking her soft jaw into her milk-white fist. "He *saved* her."

"He's more one of us than some folks," Napoleon would say, trying, as a member of the board of directors, to understand the bank's new accounting procedures. "Of course I know a hundred dollars this year isn't worth a hundred dollars next year. But what does that have to do with—" But Napoleon would stop because he didn't really know what to ask.

"I was thinking about hiring Chester as a security guard," Joseph proposed one morning, walking onto the stage of the open window of my bedroom, and then off.

"I don't trust him," I said, still in bed, a little sick from a summer cold.

"Why not?"

"When we were kids he'd steal things from me," I said.

"Like what?" Joseph was tying his bow tie in the mirror. He was such a small man that sometimes an urge to beat him up, to throw his featherweight body against the wall, would swell up in me—not because I wanted to, but only because I could.

"Things," I said. "He left town when I was fourteen because Dad caught him doing something, caught him red-handed. Dad said he'd die before Chester could come back to Nice."

"What'd he catch him at?"

"You'll have to ask Chester," I said. "As far as I know, Dad never told anyone." Power is a funny thing. It's an awkward day when you realize it's sitting in your lap. Your instinct is to protect it like a child, but you hardly know how. "Leave Chester alone," I said.

Joseph hired Chester anyway. "It's the least you can do for Lesby," he said, ordering up a special-made security uniform from Indianapolis. "Shoot, is he a big boy!"

Joseph was the smallest man in town but he'd propose a ball game or a wrestle anytime. I once found him and Chester shredding each other's shirts on the checkered kitchen floor, Lesby cheering them on with some mighty strong language. "Pin his little ass!" Things like that. Good grief. Joseph and Chester stood up and apologized boyishly, though they weren't really sorry. Chester's voice was so low and solemn and lovely that I had to sit on the three-legged stool Lesby used for cleaning the chandeliers, catching my breath, waving Chester out of the house.

It was the same bass voice that I once overheard at the bank—the type of man's voice that thumps in a wall. "Will will never know," Chester said, to someone. And then, "We'll sneak through the side door. I know how to get past them all." A huge hand squeezed my heart, paranoid that Chester was now seeking revenge, ruining me like my father ruined him. I defensively opened the door to the file cabinet room. Inside Chester and Lesby were blowing up party balloons. "Oh, you ruined it," Chester said, a Happy Birthday balloon balancing in the bowl of his palm.

Even so, every once in while I found myself saying to Joseph, "Just keep your eye on Chester."

"Will do!" Joseph would reply, bouncing on his toes, checking his watch, faithfully kissing me goodbye. He'd add, "But Chester's working out real well. Besides, he likes you, Will." My father used to say the same thing when I was a boy and he'd hire Chester to help with sacking the grain or slaughtering a hog. Chester would sometimes take me along, showing me how to do things you'd think my father would have taught me. Seeding corn, cutting alfalfa, fetching eggs, baling hay. That was my favorite, watching the mouth of the machine with the six-foot whirling belts spit out bales of hay like yellow, rotten teeth. Chester and I'd haul them into the old pony barn's loft with the pulley because the old white Juliet took up all the space down below. Every year it was a little bigger and more complicatedly constructed, and if you saw it in the pony barn never in a million years could you guess what it was used for. My father would warn me not to play on the Juliet, but Chester and I would climb over the heap, splinters slipping into the meat of our thumbs. He was slow, but I never thought of him that way, his sprawling body somehow seeming like a special gift. I'd follow the shanks of his legs over the apparatus, deeper into its cage of two-by-fours, careful of stabbing nails, careful of brittle wood.

One day, deep inside the Juliet, Chester showed me his thing. He told me to touch it, but I said no. "You're gonna," he said, shoving me against a row of planks. I saw his gold patch of hair and the plum-head of his penis. A thin tiny nail sank softly into my chest as Chester pushed between my legs. I thought about screaming but couldn't. Chester proceeded clumsily, piercing me while the nail remained lodged beneath my sternum, its tiny silver stem looking no more odd or painful than a piece of lint dangling on a sweater. When Chester was done, he left me tacked to the two-by-four—split open, teary, and gently calling his name.

The next day I found Chester helping Lesby tie up the tomatoes and asked him to take me back to the planks. And again the next. Although I knew enough not to talk about it, I didn't quite figure on the trouble I was creating for myself. And for Chester. I'd never known any real misfortune, hardly would have recognized it. Until one day when it swept in with the swiftness of a stock market crash, when my father found me naked and pinned to the wood that brought the Pageant of Glass Balls to life, my barely adolescent body red and dented and desperate for more. Two days didn't pass before a steamer trunk was packed and my father was driving me to the train that would haul me away to a boarding school high up in flinty New England where any sprouting passions, the headmaster promised, would be treated with cold showers and the glassy New Hampshire wind.

Christmas came. Chester shyly asked for a job on the crew I hired to haul the Juliet out of the pony barn the week before the Pageant. "I don't think it would be a good idea," I said. "What with children being involved."

"I'm not sure why you're being like this," Chester said. We were on the back porch, Lesby humming in the kitchen. The winter sky was smudged. The ash tree was trembling in the wind. "Your father's dead, Will," Chester said. "He's not here anymore to tell you how to live."

His hand fell on my shoulder, its weight crushing and warm.

"What's going on out here?" Joseph said, stepping from the kitchen.

"Will won't give me work on the Juliet," Chester said.

"Give the boy a job," Joseph said. He smelled like dinner, like pimply chicken skin.

"It'll take a week to put up the Juliet," I said. "Evenings too. What about his guard job down at the bank?"

"It's Christmas week, Will. The bank is safe. You're there all the time. I'm there all the time. It'll be fine." Joseph and Chester shook hands, Chester's hand swallowing Joseph's, their hands linked and swaying for what seemed all night, the whole icy night.

The next day the crew arrived and began pulling the pieces of the Juliet out of the barn. "It's like one of those museum dinosaurs," Chester said. "Like we've got to piece together the bones." I was on a ladder, organizing the dismantling, when I slipped, smacking against a piece of the Juliet and then hitting the ground. A short, sharp *crack!* rang out in the brittle air. My little helpless yelp echoed in the barn. Chester cried, "Oh my Will!" He jumped from his ladder and was holding my head almost before it hit the straw.

"I've got your head," he whispered.

"No, let me be," I said. "Where's Joseph?"

"He isn't here," Chester said, his thumbs rubbing behind my ears.

"Find him."

"I was looking for him earlier. Don't know where he is."

"Find him," I said.

"But I'm here," Chester was saying. "I'm here."

Dr. Davenport ordered me to stay in bed till after Christmas. "Can't," I said.

"But you will," Joseph said. He and Lesby and Napoleon were standing above me, their nostrils dark and trembling. Napoleon had already kicked Chester out of my bedroom. Now he sent Joseph and Lesby to the kitchen. My father's pale blue nightshirt was still hanging on the brass hook behind the door, thin as a ghost.

"Something funny about Chester," Napoleon began. I tried to shrug. "He's at the bank more than you think. One night round eleven I walked by and saw him through the window waxing the floor." Napoleon lifted a photograph of my father sitting in his office holding a gold brick. "He supposed to be waxing the floor?" Napoleon said. "At eleven? And another thing. Get the boy a new uniform. That one's too small."

Joseph's head appeared in the doorway. "Need anything?" he asked, his smile brighter than the snow beginning to fall outside. "I'm headed down to the bank. Might be a while."

The crew continued hauling the Juliet from the old pony barn, tapping together the two-by-fours in the square. From my bed I could hear the lumber crack and creak as they loaded it into a truck, and I could imagine the small precise pecks of the narrow-neck hammers nailing the Juliet together across from the bank.

"Mattie Killion's expanding into honeybees," Joseph would say each day as I lay in bed, handing me loan papers to sign. Or: "There's a tract of land down in Switzerland County that just might have oil underneath. And if it doesn't, it's fine for tobacco. Sign here." He'd come into the room at night and hold my hand with his small fingers and say, "Shoot, everyone's complaining about not making money these days. They don't know where to look." Then he'd turn out the lamp and we'd be there in the dark, me lying beneath the chenille spread and the old horsehair blanket, Joseph curled in my father's smoking rocker, our hands suspended and cold in the night.

The Juliet rose until Christmas Eve, when at last the Michigan spruce was surrounded by a net of white wood. Dr. Davenport told me not to, but I took my place on the bandstand for the Pageant of Glass Balls. Napoleon was there in a raccoon coat, pumping the hand of the governor. Joseph was on his toes, telling the mayor of a Kentucky border town about the honeybee business. The bank's managers were on a picnic bench, a row of nervous blue-wool humps. Red glass balls were hanging from the bandstand's eaves, tinkling in the breeze.

The square was full, the sky pale. The folks from Antoinette Street were in the corner under the campanile, swapping wives under a twig of mistletoe. Farmers had driven their buckboards into town, and mothers were passing babies down from the carriage seat. The Negroes had walked up from Hoosier Creek; they were huddling beneath the elms with baked potatoes in their pockets, milk and ginger ale in their jugs. A thirty-man band formed an arc around the Juliet, their music tinselly.

At noon the Presbyterian Redeemer's church bells began to ring. The church's double doors with the little steel studs opened and the first child of the pageant emerged. It was Francine and she was wearing a green papier-mâché globe, like a Japanese lantern. Single file, other children followed in their glass-ball costumes. A huge ball of wax paper sprayed gold. An old barrel painted red and hung on suspenders. Padded felt engulfing Mattie Killion's youngest girl. The children walked carefully toward the Juliet, trying not to smile or look at their parents, for that isn't what a glass ball would do.

O pretty little ball of glass
I will hang you upon the tree
O pretty shiny ball of glass
Should you shatter
so shall we!

Fragile! Fragile! Fragile!
Who's more fragile, you or me?

The glittery children dreamily strolled up the Juliet's ramp, hanging a glass ball on an open branch of the tree. Then they'd descend in slow loopy steps that Lesby, the pageant master, must have choreographed. From a pine crate stuffed with straw the children would pluck another glass ball and ascend again, so that there was a steady line padding up the Juliet and back down, ball after ball, like ants carrying off a doughnut's sprinkles.

Fragile! Fragile! Fragile!
Who's more fragile, you or me?

Lesby was running around in high heels and bobby socks and a thin bib-front blouse. "The pageant's going well, don't you think?" she was asking. "I know I'm not supposed to say this, but Francine's the best ball. Don't you think she's the best ball out there?"

"How's the rib holding up, Buckaroo?" Joseph asked, his face pink, the tip of his nose raw. "See, Chester did a fine job with the Juliet."

"Where is he?"

"Over at Mattie Killion's. He's building her hives." I could tell Joseph wanted to rub my cold hand in his palms. "He's a good kid, Will," he said. "He likes you."

"He likes you," I said.

"Now what's that supposed to mean?"

The children began to wonder who held the place in line that would get to clip the spun-glass star to the top of the tree. They were cautiously watching one another, their small eyes screwed up. The crowd in the square began to pay attention to the decorating, all their bodies lined up and turned to the tree as if posing for some class photograph. Francine was dancing and singing in her papier-mâché ball.

Fragile! Fragile! Fragile!
It's going to be me!

"They're waiting for you to hand out the star, Buckaroo," Joseph said, swinging the hand-blown star around in its blue velvet sack. "Don't drop it, Buck," he said, tossing it to me.

Then I coughed; it felt like a small shard of glass fluttering in my throat. I wiped my lips with Joseph's handkerchief, and blood blotted the linen next to his gold monogram. A salty and warm taste pooled in my throat. As warm as fever.

"I'm going home," I told Joseph.

He was singing along with the children. When I said this, his mouth pinched. Something in the way he suddenly became pale made me grab his elbow, my fingers twisting his camel's-hair coat, clutching him right there on the bandstand.

"Anything wrong?" he asked.

"Stay and give out the star," I said. "Someone from the bank should give out the star." And then, to Napoleon and everyone else: "So long. Business to tend."

Cayuga Street was empty, the windows at the Versailles Hotel bright and gold and quiet. Inside, Lela Bullard was at the town switchboard, her dreamy red-maned head resting on her hand; she waved lazily. The pain was lifting from my side to my upper chest, as if it were a little beast trying to crawl out. I coughed again, and blood spurted brightly onto a patch of old snow.

From my office window I could see the children mounting the Juliet; I could see the little white bandstand; I could see Joseph's dark head, his black hair flipping up in the wind like a small dog's tail. Francine was dancing around the bandstand, her legs milk blue in the cold, her glass ball costume denting as she ran excitedly into an elm. The children's singing was lifting higher, to the point of quivering glass. Joseph was holding the blue velvet bag with the gold drawstring, and part of me expected him to drop it, to drop the glass star, shattering it inside the velvet bag.

Then I coughed again. This time it was like a rip inside my chest, and I thought of Mattie Killion tearing through her crocheted pillowcase to wrap my rib. Inside I could feel something deep detach from something else, a slit opening. I was caught in the long instant after the injury but before the pain. All of Nice was refraining the song of the glass ball, and I began to bleed.

Then I fell. The Kurdish carpet was as hard as cement; its pale wool fringe mixed with my hair. My head was lying between the two lion-dog andirons, their bronze paws on their bronze balls. Blood was sloshing in the tank of my chest. My desk was hiding me from the door, and I could see nothing but the rib-molding ceiling and the black-stained mouth of the fireplace. It was dark in the office, becoming darker. My red cry was like a call lost in a cave.

There was a cheer from the square and a shot from Napoleon's silver-plated pistol. I knew the last ball was sitting pleasantly on the tree. A child was chosen to hang the spun-glass star.

Fragile! Fragile! Fragile!
I told you it would be me!

Then it was quiet. Then again another cheer. I could hear the gravelly scraping sound of the crew pulling the Juliet away from the Michigan spruce.

About now I imagined Joseph would begin to worry about me. With the star hung, he'd go home to check on me, find no one, and return to the bank. Fifteen minutes, that's how long it would take. And I shut my eyes and thought of Joseph at our old bank jobs in New York, his office near my desk, his voice lifting over the heads of everyone in the department, "Buckaroo!"

It was dark in the bank now, and I shut my eyes.

Later something woke me up. Outside, it was dusk. The town was silent. Outside my office at the clerks' stations there was a scraping sound like the slow dragging of feet. Why hadn't Joseph come for me? The room was a rose color from the sinking winter sun, the shadow behind my desk deep. Someone was walking aimlessly around the bank. Someone was opening drawers, pencils shifting in the pencil drawers. A paper clip fell delicately to the floor. Papers crackled, an abacus clicked.

I could tell it was Chester, his huge feet stubbing the clerks' felt-padded stools. He was stealing from my bank, and I wasn't surprised. A key scratched at Joseph's office next door, the brass lock clicking open. Joseph had cheerfully given the bank's key to the giant of my youth, to huge-limbed Chester, who hung in the memory of my childhood like a heap as big and brittle as the old Juliet.

A huge hand reaching into my rib cage and squeezing the wet sponge of my heart—that's what it felt like, lying there on my office hearth, my head between the andirons my father bought from the German in Chicago who'd said to my father and me, "You sure must be important people in Indiana." "Hell, I *own* Indiana," my father had replied, meaning it, and I nodded calmly, as if it was the most natural thing in the world for a man to say. Now I was lying like a bog—flat and damp and oozing; I was lying behind a desk that made money faster than anything else in the state, with Chester groping my bank, his hand reaching inside files and drawers as it once reached inside me. I couldn't move, or become angry, because something in me had given up, something in me was defeated years ago, shattered like bone, bruised like spleen. I wanted Chester to rob me and leave so I'd never again have to feel guilty about the way my father had ruined his life.

There was a heavy snap, and the door between Joseph's office and mine unbolted. My wet heart slipped into my throat. The office was gray, the portrait of my father hidden in shadow. I knew Chester was standing in my office. I could hear him here—my father's former office where I was now meant to rule and Chester was never meant to enter, and how had things become so turned around? How was it that I was no more visible than a stain on the Kurdish carpet and Chester filled the room, his body drawing air? And just then the pain spread wildly, as if leaping a fire wall, and I seemed to feel my left lung collapse, and I didn't know whether I would live or die, was less certain of that than anything in my life. I was about to call out, "Chester, please help. Chester, I need your help," but just then I saw Joseph's tiny feet step around the desk's pedestal legs. His hands curled into balls. His little purple mouth shook. "Buckaroo," he whispered, and I realized at that moment that the bank was also collapsing, that the granite walls were cracking, that in another second Joseph would run out the bank's side door and across the dormant gray fields without ever looking back, and that the only thing that could save me now would be Chester showing up for his night shift, happily humming, "Fragile! Fragile! Fragile! Who's more fragile, you or me?"

Sharing Hale-Bopp

DAVID WATMOUGH

I've got to tell you some things that maybe you'll find quite boring. In any case I don't much like spilling out a whole lot about myself. The reason for that is part of the whole business—as some of you brighter ones will understand right off the bat when I tell you I was born in 1912.

That means not only that I'm an old gent—eighty-six to be precise—but that I came into a world that had one thing very much in common with the one I shall surely soon be leaving. A world that World War I was about to turn into something unrecognizable to all those after my parents' generation. I'm not just talking about the impact of the auto and the airplane, the telephone, radio, and TV—which all those heaped and rat-mauled bodies from guns, gas, and exploding bombs on the Western Front were never to know as we have known. But the sense of later horizons looming as the century gathered momentum, exciting for some, scary for others.

Like now, that is. "Now" being a burgeoning test-tube world of cloning, invitations to outer space, and electronic buddies on the Internet that we get to know better than we ever knew our parents but will never smell, see, or discover whether they are tenor or baritone.

But that earlier, more hushed world into which I was born was one in which you were taught to keep quiet about a whole bunch of things that nowadays you blurt out in front of every camera and microphone. Crying in public, I was taught by my physician father and Sunday-school-teaching mother, wasn't just unmanly for a son and vulgar for a daughter, it was a disgrace to one's family. *We Gordons didn't do that.*

Now the lachrymal glands have been developed by TV interviewers to the point that if you have trouble with a loose denture on-camera, you automatically burst into tears! Lost cats, autistic kids, three-way sex, and hurricanes all get the same treatment. I wouldn't join those facile snivelers if it was for my own funeral!

So now you know where I'm coming from. Or rather where I chronologically came from. You might as well also know that I was born in Victoria, British Columbia, Canada, The British Empire (yes, as kids, that's what we wrote out fully in our schoolbooks after our names). The year the *Titanic* sank and Captain Scott reached the South Pole.

Well, I shall save you the gory details of my coming out as a gay man—slap bang, incidentally, into the dismal unemployment days of the Depression yet! I'll just say that a bearded hobo had his pleasure of me against the wall of a freight car in the beautiful Rockies, coming through Kicking Horse Pass on the Bow River—between Winnipeg and Vancouver. I remember all that because I was staring frantically out of a crack in the wooden car while he was busy hurting me up my crack.

By the time I was working as second cook in a logging camp outside Port Alberni I was almost back in the closet! I certainly kept myself to myself—when I wasn't fighting off the attentions of those sex-starved lumberjacks. I saved my sex for whenever I could get to Vancouver. And by then I'd forsaken sodomy for fellatio. It was quicker and safer, and was equally available in the Greyhound bus depot, the movie theaters of Granville Street, or the blissful bowers of Stanley Park—the latter truly a cocksucker's sylvan dream.

The year 1939 and World War II found me aged twenty-seven volunteering for the Royal Canadian Navy, where after a year as a regular matelot I went to Officers' Training School—emerging as a sublieutenant and finishing the war in London attached to Canada House as full lieutenant.

I don't doubt for a moment that others had a more interesting Depression than I did, others a more exciting war. But then comes a sequence which was a lot more to my liking. In London, during the flying bombs and rocket raids on that already blitzed city, I met my lover.

He was also a young naval officer—a kind of opposite number to me—stationed at the nearby British Admiralty. For me it was love at first sight when I spotted him at what I thought was cruising around the Cenotaph in Whitehall, although he denied it to his dying day.

Whether it was that shaky start or not, I don't know, but Neville took a hell of a lot of wooing. I didn't feel safe until, with the war over, I watched him step down from the train at the Canadian Pacific station in downtown Vancouver. In his hand he had the Penguin copy of Shakespeare's sonnets which we had read aloud to each other on Hampstead Heath, watching the buzz bombs zip overhead. I wanted to hug him, kiss him, for bringing the sole literary testimony to our attempt at a honeymoon. Instead we shook hands.

He joined me at UBC, where on my service grant I was headed for law school. I guess we were the first two gay lovers who went through UBC law school together. Mind you, in those pre-GayLib days, no one ever knew that. I gather things are different up there nowadays. Or so the gay gossip goes: hardly a straight law prof in sight! For the next forty years—he as a practicing barrister and I as a legal counselor employed by my old prewar boss, Macmillan Bloedel, where I used to be a cook—we lived together in an old wooden house, now demolished for a high-rise, in the city's West End. Until he died on me, that is. Of colon cancer in 1985.

That left me as "Widow Ian Gordon," aged seventy-three, shattered of heart but strong of body, facing the unknown challenges of age in protracted health and bitter loneliness.

I guess I thought for months and months after Neville's funeral that everything was now over. But the reality was that everything was about to begin. For one thing, there was an excess of energy devoid of interests. Oh yes, I read many books, I inherited the sole care of our Burmese cats, Ying and Yang, until they too went their way. I husbanded two flower boxes of nicotiana and salvia and several pots of geraniums and petunias on the balcony as if they were the Van Dusen Botanical Gardens. I kept the classical record industry flourishing locally, dutifully making the switch from thousands of LPs to a proportionate number of CDs. I was rarely out of book or record stores by day or restaurants by night.

But these things and diligent attendance at plays and concerts throughout the season, and dinner invitations and occasionally playing host, failed to nourish me, failed to wake me from deep spiritual sleep.

In fact it wasn't until this past spring, when I was exercising my little pug, Godfrey, which Joan and Larry had given me for my eightieth birthday, that big chunks of reality fell into place for me. A world, albeit an unknown one, came alive and prodded me to do likewise.

March 31 to be precise. It was a warm evening, unseasonably so, and I was wearing just a white wool short-sleeved shirt and slacks. Sandals probably. Godfrey was on a leash but foraging ahead as he invariably did as I took him on his favorite nocturnal walk around the park side of the ornamental lake named Lost Lagoon. I enjoyed the multicolored fountain as well as the view of the prowlike conglomeration of West End high-rises whose windows flickered like tinsel when reflecting the sunset and whose cement towers were bathed white when the moon took over.

There was a bench I liked to rest on briefly, halfway around. It was dedicated to a friend of Neville's and mine who had succumbed to AIDS and bore a plaque in his name. Godfrey was more into the quacking of ducks and other waterfowl bobbing safely a few feet offshore, and excited by the tantalizing scent of raccoons which lurked all about us in the dense bushes. But this is my story, not his.

There were several other associations for me. Some of them have even more poignant meaning in the light of what I am about to tell you. This was the part of Stanley Park that my lascivious youth had claimed in prewar days. It was also the spot I had witnessed a onetime mayor of Vancouver cruising and seen—or thought I saw, through a screen of rhododendrons—a gay orgy taking place, with a uniformed cop distinctly involved as well as someone I'm prepared to swear on a stack of Bibles was the boy movie star of an earlier era, the East Indian, Sabu, of *Elephant Boy* and *Jungle Book* fame.

That, of course, was no longer mere yesterday but ancient history. There were few left who could dispute my memories or fancies of such louche goings-on in distant days. But sitting there, tugging on Godfrey and reining him in all the time lest a raccoon attack him, I relived that past as if I were seeing it all through the inverted end of a telescope, it was so tiny and distant.

Then suddenly everything became large and immediate. I was being addressed. Nothing at all unfamiliar about the preamble. "Do you have the time? Oh, isn't it a beautiful evening." Then the gears changed. The young man asked whether he could sit down too, and did so before I could respond. It was still light enough to see he was no Quasimodo. Adonis more like. Like me, he was wearing a short-sleeved shirt. Unlike me, he was wearing shorts.

"Do you know what tonight is?" he asked.

I remained silent. At my age it takes time to sort out replies to strangers—especially beautiful strangers.

"It's the eclipse of the moon," he announced proudly—rather as if he were responsible for it.

"Mind his face," I cautioned. "Godfrey doesn't like his face touched. You can stroke his ears and, better still, scratch him just above his tail."

In fact the youth had already begun to do just that. Worse still, my faithless pug was wiggling his fat torso with pleasure, quite prepared to offer the same solemn-eyed fidelity and protection to this utter stranger as he vouchsafed me every time I put his piled dog bowl down before him.

"It's not just the moon," the young man persisted, stretching down now to serve Godfrey's scratching better. "It's the comet Hale-Bopp. The partial eclipse of the moon means the comet should be seen better tonight than any other time. Well, at least on this visit. None of us will be around for the next one, I guess! What is it? Four hundred, five hundred years from now? Fantastic!"

I finally unearthed words—though I couldn't hurry their individual birth. I don't think I had used my voice box that day except for one brief conversation early that morning and a few remarks to Godfrey like always. "I suppose you want an old man to remember other comets up there. Meteorites maybe?"

He seemed impervious to my tone of slight testiness while picking up on my actual remark. "I saw Halley's, you know. But this one is something else. I mean a tail and all!" I let that go. I watched Godfrey instead. He was progressively pissing me off with his stupid flirtation with my bench neighbor. I wondered if the guy was about to call me "gramps" as some of the kids in the neighborhood do. But they are usually the under-twelves or so. This guy could have been an old thirty or young twenty—just like so many gays for whom nature has composed a dissembling mixture of tender years and emotional immaturity more effective than any woman's facial or careful makeup.

"I've seen you out here before, haven't I?"

Godfrey had stopped licking, was resting back on his comfortable rump, eyeing the guy with his phony expression of sadness over the untrustworthy human condition. He had obviously decided there was no food potential in Mister Hairy Legs and was therefore ready to go. But I wasn't. Not quite. The guy's question would have an answer—even if it wasn't one he might be expecting.

"You might have. Let me see, I've been coming here for about fifty years. I think I should add that during that time my motives for being here have changed. Changed quite a lot."

It was his turn to surprise me. "Fantastic!" he said—it seemed to be one of his favorite words. "You must have seen some incredible changes. Boy! You've had experiences some of us would give our eyeteeth for!"

I wanted to tell him that my eyeteeth, like the others, had long gone—though not as a result of a quirky offering for the sake of an experience. I don't think it was that nervous imagination of mine, but from the corner of my watery eye I saw he had snuggled an inch or two closer. I turned and faced him head-on—then took the plunge. "It isn't so much the experiences, it's the person that has had them who has done the changing."

For the first time I noticed freckles. Neville had had freckles. They had been one of his most endearing facial features. Those on this boy's nose didn't move me at all. I think it was at that precise moment that things began to fall into place.

"I'm so glad we've met," he said. "I think I can learn so much from you. Are—are you into any kind of relationship?"

My sandal gently touched Godfrey. "With him," I said.

The kid laughed. "I meant with—well, another guy."

I said nothing.

The silence seemed to rattle him. "My name is Marvin and I come from a broken home," he said suddenly. "I never really had a dad. I guess that's why I prefer mature men—if you know what I mean."

I leered at him, only sore I'd taken the trouble to insert my dentures. "With me, Marvin, you're beyond 'maturity.' Beyond even grandfathers. You are flirting with geriatrics!"

He looked a little hurt. Then I guess he wasn't much used to rejections from the graveside.

His pretty lips pouted. "I don't think age matters, really. It's just the person that counts. And we all come in different packages, don't we? That's what makes life so fantastic."

I fought to still look impassive as I spoke. "I see you are a philosopher, young man. But there's one thing I don't think you've fathomed yet. You may not think that age matters but this old fella thinks it matters a hell of a lot. For him, that is."

"I don't understand."

I too strove for honesty. "I don't think I do either," I told him. "At least not very much. But for one thing, Marvin, you think I'm gay, don't you?"

Then he really did look startled. "Aren't you?"

Very slowly I shook my head. "Not anymore."

He didn't shake his curly head, it was rocking—presumably with disbelief, not Parkinson's. "You make it sound like yesterday's fashion style."

"The clue is the 'yesterday,'" I informed him. "I was gay for a thousand yesterdays and that included having a permanent lover for forty-odd years and almost as many sex sessions as meals during the Depression. World War II was made for the likes of me. Imagine being stationed in London and having sex-starved male servicemen arriving from all around the world, and more and more of them, day by day. And then meeting your lifetime lover right in the middle of it! After bringing him back here after it was over, my lover and I in due course with our combined incomes were more social gay than you could shake a stick at. Party . . . party . . . party!

"There must have been twenty or thirty couples in our circle and a good number of singles. You know, it was us postwar gays who invented brunch, influenced fashions, rescued restaurants from bankruptcy, reinvigorated ships' cruises, and even brought real death back into fashion in a relatively war-free world with too many medical soaps on TV.

"And now none of it means a fucking thing to me! I am no more interested in sex with you than with Godfrey here. Safe or otherwise. I have far more woman friends than men, and politically correct gay newspapers who think all cocks lie comfortably to the left, louts in leather with bad breath, and ass-wiggling comedians all bore the tits off me. As for lining up before a smoke-filled environment to have your eardrums raped while you watch silly queens who think sequins a form of sophistication . . . Need I go on?

"Of course, a lifetime's practice leaves little flakes in my existence. I'm still color coordinated and women's plumbing problems can revolt me, as do the commercials for them on TV at breakfast time.

"But all that is superficial, empty stuff. No, Marvin, for all intents and purposes you can say I have resigned my gay membership, turned in my queer card and become just another sexless old man. That may be hard for the likes of you to believe—it's contrary to all the contemporary clichés about dirty old men still getting it on. Then when isn't reality duller than wishful thinking would like it to be?"

I finally shut up. Not just to collect further thoughts but because, frankly, I'd exhausted myself. Must be five years since I'd given a speech that long. Probably when I'd had the row with Mrs. Zindfeld next door and told her to fuck off with her brute of a lab who had growled at Godfrey, who was then a recklessly intrepid puppy.

I needn't have worried about my silence, though. I'd certainly got my neighbor on the bench started. He erupted with a further flood of "pure" thought uncontaminated by the disconcerting nuts and bolts of razor-sharp realism that increasingly deflates my hopes and dreams.

"Oh, you must have been so HURT! Such bitterness can mean nothing else. Do you know what I think? You have INVENTED the death of your friend! I think what really happened is that he just crept away in the middle of the night. He could not live with such a heavy weight around the house. And this age business . . . Know what my mom used to tell me? You're as young as you think you are, Marvin. She was a simple woman in some respects, my mom, but she sure could come up with the answers! Well, I tell you frankly, I'm envious of all your long experience. So few of us have had sustained relationships. How many can say they met the light of their life in the dread horrors of war. And lots of us can't stand our trivial gay newspapers, or the worship of youth they promote. And you know, sex isn't everything. There's way more to life than just that."

(I wanted, oh how I wanted! to tell him that for me now sex was nothing. Take the SEXUAL out of homosexual and what have you got? But I didn't. There was too much distance, too much misunderstanding for any bridges between us. I just rested my mildly aching backside against the seat in a more comfortable position and let him carry on.)

"I just know I could bring rich things into our life." His voice quickened pace, gathered in volume. "I'm not just a pretty face, you know! I not only do windows—I do toilets! My friends will tell you Marvin isn't afraid of hard work. But I think I can say I'm more than a homemaker. Like you, I hate loud music and I just can't stand cigarette smokers—I've walked out of a room when someone has lit up. And I like real intelligent conversation. And I don't mind telling you that too many of my generation don't go in for that. Then I read, you see. And I don't just mean the comic books either. Do you know what I do? Now this is especially when I don't have too much money. And sitting, talking here, I think I can be honest and say that's a lot of the time. Well, I get hold of the Sunday paper, turn to the book pages, and write down all the books reviewed that week. And because—like my mom says—I have an old head screwed on young shoulders, I have learned patience. I just wait until those hardback books come out as paper. That can sometimes mean a year, or even more. But I keep my book clips in a drawer at . . . well, where I live, and then check them out. Oh yes, I also keep a diary and I jot down important things. Like the eclipse of the moon tonight."

I sighed with relief. Or it could have been my breathing. I've been having slight respiratory problems this past winter. Anyway, I decided I had an out.

"Marvin," I announced, "it's dusk already and darkening by the second. Our time has come." (I also felt it was time to move lest the raccoons that frequented the bench came looking for a handout at their favorite time of the evening and take a swipe at Godfrey, who would stupidly retaliate. But I spared Marvin the nature tips.)

"Let us step out by the edge of the lake and observe your partial moon. And if we are lucky we will catch Hale-Bopp too."

And that is what we did. We did not stand alone. A scattering of dimming strangers craned their white faces up at the eclipsed moon. A woman said she was surprised at how stark the shadow over it proved to be. Another wondered whether the eclipse would increase throughout the night. A third said it was awesome, while Marvin declared it fantastic. Then someone spotted the comet further to the west and heading out to sea. Godfrey yapped. But then he doesn't like a lot of human legs crowding him. I decided he was too heavy and we'd be there a shade too long for me to pick him up, which I knew was what he wanted. I would have handed him to Marvin but that would have protracted things afterward and I was already aching for home and a decent chair to rest my aching bum.

At first the brilliant comet with the fiery tail so prominently extended evoked silence but I didn't doubt the clichés would follow. For the third evening—the others from my apartment window—I drank in the eerie visitor and felt again the utter relief that it was unconcerned with our species and that, unlike the human world of the late twentieth century, it would not be coming our way again—at least for a hell of a long time. Not like the instant replays of sports shots, or murder sites heaped with bedraggled flowers, which were the regular fodder of the TV I saw all too much of in my healthy but purposeless years.

As the silence my civilization hates was finally broken, and audible sighs of relief joined the oohs and aahs of our straggly assembly, I made to break away from the circle. As I feared, Marvin fell in immediately at my side. I let a now home-obsessed Godfrey tug me a few paces before I frustrated him and relieved Marvin.

"Before we say goodbye," I began firmly, "I want to say something about what we've just seen. Standing there, I felt quite close to you—closer than on the bench. Looking at Hale-Bopp, we did have something truly in common. Then the whole human race has something in common when a Hale-Bopp heaves into sight. I even felt close to that motley bunch tasting the night air."

"I felt we were all so very close," said my young acquaintance. "Sailing along at light-years of speed and light-years away from us on Earth . . . well, it makes you think, doesn't it. Fantastic!"

I had one last try. "Do you know what *odium humanitatis* is, Marvin?"

He shook his head. "Look it up when you get home," I told him. "But in a way I'm glad you don't. It's an unpleasant affliction I've suffered more and more since living on this excess of time I've been handed. It's another of those things that blemishes life for excessively healthy ancients like me. My alternatives being kept from their coffins are just the opposite. They long for human company, would do anything to see the face of a kind stranger who will only spare a moment to listen to them."

Marvin shook his curls before me for the last time. "I'm sure all that could be put another way—be given another interpretation."

I shrugged. "Say good night to the nice man, Godfrey," I said, and went home—not yet to die.

La Tortuga

CHRISTOPHER LORD

Not until late their last full day on the beach in Puerto Vallarta did Tom realize that Brett, asleep beside him, was no longer the same young man he had met in the spring. The precise moment was just as the waiter brought him his second margarita at the restaurant of the "blue chairs." Tom pressed his glass against his forehead, giving small relief from the headache that lingered from last night's experiences at the bar. He was suddenly aware of his own body, wet and soft like clay in the heat of the Mexico sun, moist gray hairs curling out from the open neck of his beach shirt.

Tom's eyes followed a line from Brett's tan smooth face down to the cleft in his sternum separating the large flat nipples, to the twist of hairs at the top of his black Speedos that pointed toward the coil of his balls and cock, semi-hard even now.

Lewis had been dead almost a year when Tom purchased the time-share week in Puerto Vallarta, intending to use the time to read and unwind before making the trek for Thanksgiving dinner with Lewis' parents. That was in March; in May he met Brett. Reading the personal ads in the free weekly newspaper was a clear sign that Tom had been thinking about dating—placing an ad was undeniable evidence of it. Brett's was the first serious response to the ad.

Tom, at forty-five, had wondered whether he would find another partner. After Lewis' death from a cerebral aneurysm Tom had gone into hibernation until spring when, spurred into activity by the demands of the neglected yard, he realized that he would survive. That realization had led to the personal ad. And it had led to Brett who, at this moment, turned his head away from the sun.

He was a mouth breather. It was one of the first things Tom had noticed that night they met in a neighborhood restaurant. But Tom had paid more attention to Brett's square twenty-two-year-old face with its sense of wide-eyed wonder and immaturity, and the lean, well-muscled torso under the black T-shirt.

When Tom invited Brett back to the house that first night it really was with the intention of letting him borrow some books Tom had mentioned during coffee, but a tender kiss led to unexpectedly passionate lovemaking. And Brett called the next day, and the next, each time managing to charm Tom from his suspicion and reluctance to consider himself "dating" again. Brett read the books Tom had recommended and many more since.

Tom took a sip of his margarita. The "blue chairs" restaurant was the place gay men went in Puerto Vallarta. Blue-painted wood and canvas sling chairs dotted the beach from the restaurant halfway toward where the water slapped the sand. Most of the men on the beach were Americans in their thirties, although from time to time Tom heard German and French as well.

Farther down the Playa de los Muertos local families played in the surf, the children's squeals and laughter occasionally drifting toward Tom. Beyond, in the crescent of the big hotels, a lone parasail drifted toward shore from above, the parachute collapsing silently around its passenger as she landed. Brett slept, although he now had a full erection, outlined through his swim trunks. Tom laid a magazine across it.

At first Tom considered that Brett might be a gold digger. As unpleasant as it was, he had to recognize that the combination of his age, economic independence, and loneliness might make him a target for predatory types. Brett, however, proved not to fit that bill. He was scrupulous about paying his own way and honest when one of Tom's suggestions was beyond his means. Their relationship had moved quickly, if not to intimacy, at least to familiarity. The more activities Tom suggested, the more he discovered Brett's ignorance of the things Tom had learned to take for granted—calamari, a fine Merlot, chamber music, the local repertory theater. Tom was the first man Brett had spent the night with, all of his previous encounters being anonymous safe-sex episodes at the nude beach.

In spite of his general inexperience Brett was a tender, exciting lover, coaxing Tom into a level of erotic thought that he had forgotten he was capable of, one not present in the last few years with Lewis.

Tom's close friends had a bemused response to his "taking up" with Brett, as one had put it; curiously, he didn't care much about their reactions. And while Brett, on his first introduction to Tom's circle at a small Sunday brunch, hadn't demonstrated any of the scintillating wit of the "snap queens," neither had he been tongue-tied or socially inappropriate. Tom thought his friends had made a bit too much of Diane Schuur's recording of "Teach Me Tonight" while they sat around at coffee after the eggs Benedict, but concluded afterward that Brett hadn't understood the joke.

The thought of breakfast reminded Tom of their arrival in Puerto Vallarta. After checking into the condominium hotel they walked past the pool behind the hotel to a concrete walk along the beach. Brett noticed a square section cordoned off with mesh fencing. A sign posted on the fence stated "Nido de Tortugas—Prohibida la Entrada." Below, in English, it had been translated as "No Trespassing—Turtles Nesting." They approached the fence to look inside but could see nothing but sand, slightly lumpier than the surrounding terrain. Nearby, standing under a large palapa with a shelf around it, was a handsome Latino man wearing a crisp white uniform.

"Señores! Did you arrive at Las Palmas today?"

"Yes," Brett answered.

"Is this your first trip to Puerto Vallarta?" The Latino's accent was thick, insinuating. He began pulling maps and brochures from a display on a shelf. "We hope you'll join us in the morning for a welcoming breakfast."

"That's really not necessary," Tom said.

Brett began asking questions about restaurants and clubs.

"No problema," the salesman said. He put his arm around Brett, pulled him in close, then began circling locations on the map. "These are places the locals go. My favorites. And for late at night try this one." He wrote down the name of a gay bar.

"Thanks," Brett said.

The salesman again offered the welcoming breakfast, but Tom scooped up the map, took Brett by the elbow, and pulled him back toward the hotel.

"I'd been warned how predatory these people could be. I should have said something to you sooner."

Brett slept on. He turned in his sling chair, the magazine falling onto the sand. A banana boat flew past, bobbing as the riders bucked deliberately up and down. The blue chairs were multiplying.

Tom ordered another margarita and looked around for the middle-aged gay couple he and Brett had met a few days earlier. The couple, a Spaniard with a Castilian accent, and his partner, a retired Navy captain in his early fifties, had entertained them with an intimate knowledge of gay Puerto Vallarta and had invited them home for an afternoon fiesta with some of Puerto Vallarta's permanent gay residents. But the couple hadn't shown up again to cement the offer.

From the Spaniard they learned that a local entrepreneur sponsored a gay nude version of the "booze cruises" Tom had heard about from straight friends. So Tom and Brett had made sure they were on the cruise which, along with the visit to the gay bar, had occurred the day before.

They arrived at the Playa de los Muertos the previous afternoon and saw the catamaran anchored a quarter mile off the pier. After being ferried there in a skiff Tom watched the town recede from view, dirty white buildings stacked like blocks up the tropical mountainsides behind the main city streets. The captain was a buff redheaded man named Gerry, who, as soon as the catamaran was underway, handed out frozen bananas topped with strawberries which, dipped in chocolate and coated with shaved coconut, resembled erect penises.

Most of the dozen passengers lay on the bow of the catamaran, spread out on foam planks. Brett, stripping immediately, started talking with two young men who were swing actors in a Las Vegas version of *Starlight Express.* They were about Brett's age, handsome and slender, and wore string bikinis that showed their shaved buttocks. Tom stripped down to his swim trunks, his white ceramic skin notwithstanding, and let the sun warm him through the sunscreen.

Tom could hear Brett talking with the actors, their voices low, slightly metallic, on topics like movies and music. Some names they mentioned Tom had never heard of.

Not long after passing the rocks of Los Arcos the catamaran slowed and Gerry called out that they were about to disembark. Tom, Brett, and the rest of the passengers were helped into two skiffs that headed toward a cove and came to shore.

"We'll be here about an hour," Gerry said as he removed sandwiches, chips, fruit, and more drinks from a cooler. "This is a private beach. You can go behind the big rocks by taking that trail behind you."

After they finished eating, Brett took Tom's hand. "Let's explore."

They climbed twenty feet up the hard dirt-packed trail from where they could see a more secluded cove several hundred yards away. Tom followed Brett, occasionally using his hand to help him maintain balance on the uneven trail.

When he caught up Brett was resting, studying a rock with hundreds of brown crabs darting over its surface. Brett turned around and kissed him, Brett's mouth warm, tasting of beer and mustard.

Brett moved one hand down toward Tom's crotch.

Tom pulled away and took a breath. "Here?"

"Why not?"

I don't think so—"

"Consider it a new experience—like calamari."

When they were finished Brett wiped his mouth with the back of his hand and smiled. Tom looked away at the surf, at the crabs scuttling over the rocks. He heard voices coming from the direction where they had landed. Tom put his swimsuit back on and waited for Brett to dress. They headed back to the cove, where the rest were assembling for the return to the catamaran. The actors smiled, first at Brett, then at Tom.

On the trip back Tom fell asleep. When he awoke, Brett moved toward him and put his arm around him, kissed him on the forehead. "A great day, wasn't it?"

Not until they were back at the pier did Brett say that he had agreed to meet the actors for a drink at one of the gay bars that night.

At dinner Brett's attempt to order his meal in Spanish was diverting to the handsome waiter whose English was reasonably good but the effort irritated Tom, and he interrupted and completed the transaction in Spanish.

As Tom considered it now, the next day, he wondered why he had stayed so long at the bar. At first he and Brett sat talking, insofar as that was possible over the pounding dance music. When the actors joined them, Tom, unable to hear much of the conversation, drifted into a reverie. He watched as Brett danced with each of the actors, then with several young men from a gay tour who were staying in the Conchas Chinas area.

Tom had never enjoyed the bar scene but Brett was having a good time, and when the drag queens paraded in sometime around one o'clock in the morning, and then the nude dancing started—not the kind of stripping Tom had seen at home, but totally nude men taking tips in the cracks of their asses and in their mouths since there were no G-strings to hold the bills, only their erect cocks writhing in time to the music—Tom didn't want to interfere.

Those few older men who were in the bar stayed to themselves at a few tables as far from the dance floor as possible. One of them, an American, walked up to where Tom was sitting and tapped him on the shoulder. The American, about Tom's age as he guessed in the lurid light, bent down and pointed to Brett on the dance floor while speaking into Tom's ear.

"Such young beauties, don't you think?"

Tom looked over his shoulder; the American's boozy breath gamy and stale. Tom said nothing.

"At least we can imagine," the American continued. "Can I buy you a drink?"

The meaning in the American's words made Tom shudder. "No, thank you," he replied. "I'm about to leave."

Tom told Brett he was taking a cab back to the hotel. He encouraged Brett to stay.

"I'll go with you," Brett shouted above the music.

"Really, no," Tom answered. "I've had too much to drink and I just need to sleep."

Brett kissed Tom on the cheek. "Don't wait up," Brett said.

Tom returned to the hotel and went to bed. He awoke enough when Brett returned to see that it was after four o'clock in the morning. Brett tumbled into bed, slid over next to him in spoon fashion, and went immediately to sleep.

Now the afternoon sun was dropping, forcing Tom to push his chair farther beneath their palapa. Brett stirred in his chair. He sat up, rubbed his eyes, his elbows out like a child, and looked around him. He scratched his flat stomach and ran his hands down his legs.

"I suppose it's time to go back," he said. "I haven't been good company today."

Tom smiled. "We came here to do nothing. That's what you've been doing. You must have needed the sleep."

"I'll miss this beach," Brett said. "But we can come back—next time."

They walked to the corner and caught the bus for *los hoteles.* Brett started talking to two Americans in the seat in front of them who had turned around to ask him a question. They were Brett's age, one with huge brown eyes, his dark hair under a Lambda baseball cap, the other a stunning example of a California blond with large teeth white as mirrors. Tom rubbed his shoulders, testing for sunburn.

In the lobby, Brett stopped at the desk to check the exchange rate. Instead of coming back with cash he gave Tom a colored piece of paper.

"They're going to let the guests free the turtles," he said as Tom looked over the flier. "Let's go see."

They walked through the gate to the beach. The palapa where they had been approached by the condominium salesman was empty, all of the brochures and pamphlets tucked away. A line of people stretched along the water where a young woman stood in front of a large white bucket. Beyond the people the sun was low on the horizon, sending deep pink, orange, and vermilion blurs of color across the sky.

"These turtles were hatched on hotel property," the young woman said in perfect American English.

Brett joined the line, Tom standing behind him.

"We're going to ask each of you to take a turtle and hold it carefully until we give you the signal to release it. We'll wait until it's dark so the birds won't be able to see them."

A woman with long red fingernails stood next to Tom. "I'd hate to see them eaten," she said.

The young woman and an assistant began reaching into the bucket and handing a small object to each person.

Brett moved forward. "Come on," he said, taking Tom's hand. "It's another new experience."

The young woman's treble voice carried from one end of the line to the other. "When the water comes in we'll give the signal for you to place your hands in the water and let the turtle be carried away by the waves. If the water moves behind you, don't move your feet until we tell you, or you might step on the turtles."

The young woman handed a turtle to Brett. She offered one to Tom, but he shook his head and she moved down the line.

"Look at it," Brett said.

It wasn't the kind of turtle Tom remembered seeing in the dime stores when he was a child but larger, a dirty brown color, with small thick flippers that moved in a continuous haphazard fashion at its sides. The turtle raised and lowered its head, moved its flippers across Brett's hand, and opened and shut its mouth, large in comparison with the size of its head. Brett held it gently by the edges of its shell, letting it stroke the air.

"Do you want to hold it?" he asked Tom.

"No, you're doing fine."

"We're almost ready," the young woman announced as she stopped at the end of the line. Tom estimated that at least sixty people now stood along the water, the waves touching their toes. "Don't do anything until I give the signal."

Brett's eyes were brown and moist, his youthfulness never more obvious to Tom than now, excitement lighting his face. Brett watched the turtle waddle in his hand and up his arm, redirecting it with his fingers so that it wouldn't fall.

"Is everyone ready?" the young woman called.

Tom put his hand on Brett's shoulder, feeling Brett's warmth through the thin cotton shirt.

The waves came in at ankle level, just as the young woman shouted "Now!" and everyone bent down and released the turtles.

"Look!" Brett said, rising from his crouching position, reaching back and putting his hand on Tom's.

Tom scanned the water, seeing the turtles as they bobbed on the surface. The next wave came up to Tom's ankles; as it receded, it carried the turtles farther out.

"Swim, little guy!" Brett called as Tom felt Brett's grip tighten around his fingers.

The woman with the long fingernails looked over. "How long are they gone?" she asked Tom.

"I think they come back here to lay their eggs, eventually."

"I wonder how they know where to go?"

Tom turned his head back toward the horizon.

The sun had gone down enough to make looking at the water difficult, but he could still see the small heads at the surface. Each wave swept the turtles farther away until they were no longer visible against the darkening undulations of the waves. People were moving away now, breaking up the line.

Brett turned around. "That was cool."

"Yes," Tom said, removing his hand from Brett's shoulder.

They went to the room to shower and change clothes, then returned to town for chicken quesadillas and drinks. After dinner they decided to stroll along the kiosks and booths near the bridge that divided the old part of town from the new. It was late, but some kiosks were still open for business. Brett and Tom separated for a while, and

Tom purchased a blanket, thinking that he would use it as a wall hanging in his guest bedroom. He found Brett a few minutes later completing a transaction.

"I wanted to remember tonight," Brett said, holding out the object to Tom. It was a wooden turtle, several times the size of the one he had seen earlier, but not a bad likeness.

Although Brett had expressed interest in sex when they got into bed after returning to the hotel, he didn't make any comment when, by gentle pressure, Tom let him know that he was more interested in sleeping.

During the flight home Brett mentioned that he had given his number to the actors from the cruise, who were planning to spend a few days in the Northwest soon and wanted to get in touch.

Turning away occasionally from the flat clouds that obscured his view, Tom looked at Brett to see him dozing or reading the airline magazine.

It was inevitable and obvious what would happen next—if not immediately, then within a few weeks. The arc of their experiences would split, one curving sharply upward, the other returning to a more sedate trajectory. Pain would be minimal on either side, tempered by the benefit each had derived from the other, from the growth in confidence that had occurred. These months hadn't been about love or commitment, but about the preliminaries that make those things possible with other people at other times. On his side Tom realized that he would, if not immediately, then soon, seek someone with a darker patina, someone with whom he could explore a deeper range of emotions. He thought then about the impending visit to Lewis' parents, knowing that it was the last trip there he would make. They would ask so many questions. He began thinking about his answers.

Inside the gate Tom was jostled several times as he and Brett made their way through the crowd toward the baggage claim area.

"Why don't I go get the bags," Brett said. "I'll meet you at the parking lot pickup sign."

"All right," Tom replied, putting his hands at Brett's sides. It was unfair, he thought, that he couldn't kiss him at this moment.

Brett walked into the crowd up the wide low ramp leading to the terminal. His carry-on bag was slung over his right shoulder and his elbow was out, his forearm moving haphazardly to steady him as he moved. Tom, standing still now, lost sight of Brett momentarily as passengers arriving from other destinations merged with others trying to maneuver their way through the long wide aisle.

After a moment Brett's head and shoulders appeared. He was looking around, trying to find his bearings. Then the crowd surged as new people entered from the closest gate and, in a large, swift undulation, swept him forward and away.

Notes on the Contributors

Gary Bowen

"As a gay transsexual man, I've found that there isn't much erotica that is written either for or about us; and so I've been writing stories drawing on my own experiences in an effort to eroticize and publicize the gay transmale body. To further this goal, in 1997 I established *Roughriders Erotic Ezine* on-line to feature fiction by and about gay transmen. In addition, I have also served as a judge for the Lambda Literary Awards Transgender category, and have published three books, as well as a great deal of short fiction, poetry, nonfiction, and other works. I can be reached via my Web site at: www.netgsi.com/~fcowboy."

Scott Allen Bowles

Scott Allen Bowles sneaks writing time in at work when he thinks nobody's looking, and when he gets caught he pretends to be writing deadly exposés about his co-workers in order to keep Corporate America nervous. "Home Improvement" evolved from musing about families, the ones we choose and the ones chosen for us, and from watching too many *Home Improvement* reruns late at night. He currently resides not too far from Skokie.

Alexander Chee

Alexander Chee has an M.F.A. from the Iowa Writers' Workshop in Fiction. His stories, poems, and personal essays have appeared in *Interview, Big, The James White Review, Out, XXX-Fruit, Hope,* and the anthologies *Boys Like Us* (Avon, 1996) and *Literature of Tomorrow* (Holt, Rinehart & Winston, 1990).

"I wanted to write a love story as complicated as I knew love to be. And not bitter. So I waited, and then a teacher said something about the *Oresteia* that reminded me of Chaucer, and I thought, Oh, right, and then wrote this over three years."

David Ebershoff

David Ebershoff's first novel, *The Danish Girl,* will be published by Viking in early 2000, followed by a collection of short stories. In addition, he works at Random House, where he is the publishing director of the Modern Library. About his story he writes:

"I decided to write 'The Bank President' after driving from Boston to California a few years ago. The flat, quiet stretch of Indiana brought back memories from when I was a child and I visited a small town there, where my great-uncle ran a bank. I only met him once, and he died before I entered the second grade, but the memory of his porch, and the light at dusk on his stairwell, and the walnut-faced bureau in his hall with who-knows-what in its drawers; all this caused me to imagine how one—someone like you or me—would have lived in his day."

Philip Gambone

Philip Gambone's collection of short stories, *The Language We Use Up Here,* was nominated for a 1991 Lambda Literary Award. His essays have appeared in a number of anthologies, including *Hometowns, A Member of the Family, Sister and Brother, Wrestling with the Angel,* and *Boys Like Us.* His latest book, *Something Inside: Conversations with Gay Fiction Writers,* is forthcoming from the University of Wisconsin Press. He teaches at the Park School in Brookline, Massachusetts, and in the creative writing program at Harvard Extension School. Of the story in this anthology, Philip writes: "In 1996, I had the great fortune to teach for a semester in Beijing. 'The Singing Boy,' one of a series of stories I'm writing about those four months in China, is loosely based on an experience I had while on a field trip with my students."

Michael Anthony Gold

Michael Anthony Gold grew up in Southern California and received a B.A. in Creative Writing from UCLA in 1992. Since that time, he has lived in eight cities in four different states and has worked as a bartender, construction worker, substitute teacher, bill collector, busboy, housekeeper, and proofreader. His current home is in San Diego, California, where he is a part-time secretary at an engineering firm. He is actively seeking more meaningful employment.

Reginald M. Harris, Jr.

Reginald M. Harris, Jr., is an information technology support specialist for the Enoch Pratt Free Library in Baltimore, MD, and co-editor of *Kuumba: Poetry Journal for Black People in the Life.* His work has appeared in *The Baltimore Gay Paper, The Baltimore Review, The James White Review, The Harvard Gay and Lesbian Review, Obsidian II,* and in the anthologies *The Road Before Us: 100 Black Gay Poets* (Galiens Press) and *Men on Men 7: Best New Gay Writing* (Plume). "'Haram' is part of my continuing interest in getting inside the heads of people different from myself, and illuminating the lives of normally voiceless, 'ordinary' men and women."

Drew Limsky

Drew Limsky was educated at Emory University (B.A.), New York University (J.D.), and American University (M.A.). Currently a Ph.D. candidate at NYU, he has taught writing at American University and Brooklyn College. His work has appeared in the *Washington Post, Philadelphia Inquirer, Atlanta Journal-Constitution, Baltimore Sun, Christopher Street, Genre,* and *His*^{2}. "Every time I try to create a strong, together character, by page two they dissolve into a complete mess—I guess messes are more interesting. But what I like about Celeste is that she's both a mess *and* a survivor. 'Hating Yourself in the Morning' is my bid for the next Julia Roberts–Rupert Everett vehicle."

Christopher Lord

"I'm a native Oregonian and live in Portland with my partner, Evan, and our papillon, Sky. 'La Tortuga' is based on experiences that Evan and I had while traveling in Mexico to celebrate my fortieth birthday. Not long afterward I began writing, and I haven't stopped since. My stories have been accepted by *Men on Men 7: Best New Gay Writing* and by *Amelia.* I've completed one novel (currently in search of a publisher), enough short stories for a collection, and am hard at work on another novel.

"In one life I'm an insurance executive; in the other I long to be Henry James."

Declan Meade

Declan Meade lives in Dublin. He is a facilitator with Outwrite, Dublin's lesbian and gay writing group, and editor of *The Stinging Fly*, a literary magazine. He says, "'Lost Time' is about the place where I grew up. Even though it is only an hour away from Dublin, the short journey home often feels as if it involves a certain amount of time travel. John is back there, living a life that I could never live."

David A. Newman

David A. Newman is a previous award winner in the Hemingway Short Story Competition. His stories have appeared in *His^2* and *Men on Men 7: Best New Gay Writing*. "I sat down to write a story about religion and a killing at a Kentucky high school and 'Good News and Bad News' came out instead, specifically the first paragraph. Laney's house serves as a sort of purgatory where Kevin is pulled between hope and hopelessness, trust and fear, and, ultimately, living and dying." Newman lives in Los Angeles, where he is at work on a novel and a collection of stories.

Robert Ordoña

Robert Ordoña is gay, Catholic, and Filipino-American, not necessarily in that order. He studied Creative Writing at San Francisco State University, where he won the Herbert Wilner Memorial Short Story Award. His work has been published in *Fourteen Hills*.

"I would like to thank Sister Cleta for allowing me to interview her about her work in San Francisco's gay community. She made only one request—that my character 'in no way resemble Julie Andrews.' Alas, Sister, the temptation may have been too great.

"This story would not have been written without the constant harassment of Rick Bacigalupi, Shannan Summers Bacigalupi, and Elsa Dixon—to them I dedicate this story."

David Pratt

David Pratt has published stories, essays, and poetry in *Art & Understanding, The James White Review, Christopher Street, Genre, The Chiron Review, Excess Compassion,* and other periodicals. His essay "To Be Loved" appears in *Men Seeking Men* (Michael Lassell, ed., Painted Leaf Press). He lives in New York City, where he is finishing his first novel and working on a second.

"In 1996 a friend of mine lost five friends to AIDS in almost as many months. That situation, fictionalized, became the opening of 'Series.' The rest developed (in a way that follows, I trust!) out of bits and pieces of things that happen to us here in the nineties."

Lawrence Reilly

Lawrence Reilly now lives in Brooklyn, but grew up in suburban New Jersey. "Looking back, one of the most significant realizations about growing up was not so much all the sex and drugs that everyone was doing, but how much they all wanted to hear about it: who was doing what and with whom. It was not only gossip about other people, you had to let them know about yourself as well or else they'd drive you crazy with their wondering. The closer you got to your friends, the harder it was to be an innocent bystander. They wanted you to participate, to make choices and state preferences. There was something appealing about people's curiosity, but something scary too. People would give you what you thought you might want, you just had to admit to wanting it. '1984' attempts to address some of these feelings. It is an excerpt from my almost completed novel tentatively titled *One Way or Another*, which covers one year in Jimmy Sweeney's life in which he goes from a hate-filled introvert very in touch with his sexuality to a popular boy-about-town increasingly ashamed of his differences. His friendship with Linda Marino effects many of his changes and ultimately saves him from himself."

Rick Sandford

Rick Sandford learned to read at a school called Peter Pan. Until he went blind from CMV he never stopped: "That pastime is the primary component of my happiness." Among the things Rick never did were drive a car, have sex with a woman, possess a checking account, and smoke cigarettes. However, he had been an usher, a busboy, a waiter, an actor, a porno star, a film extra and stand-in, and a writer. His autobiographical novel, *The Boys Across the Street*, will be published by Faber and Faber in the fall of 1999. He died of AIDS in 1995.

Reginald Shepherd

Reginald Shepherd was born in New York City in 1963. He's lived in Chicago for several years and currently is an assistant professor of English at Northern Illinois University. His first book of poems, *Some*

Are Drowning, was published by the University of Pittsburgh Press as winner of the 1993 Associated Writing Programs' Award in Poetry. Pittsburgh published his second book, *Angel, Interrupted,* in 1996; it was a finalist for a 1997 Lambda Literary Award. His third collection, *Wrong,* is due from Pittsburgh in 1999. "When I was a grad student in creative writing at Brown University, home of the hip and trust-funded, I spent a lot of time wishing those cute, rich white boys would notice me and almost as much time thinking about all the reasons they wouldn't. What I think about, I tend to write about: thus this story, which is fairly self-explanatory, not to mention self-involved. On the topic of gay writing, my only thought is: if it's not *writing* first and foremost, it's not anything."

Micheal Skiff

"My first-year anniversary of living in Los Angeles was celebrated in the early morning hours with the Northridge earthquake—my first earthquake. My boyfriend happened to be up, getting a glass of water, when it struck. I woke up, slightly nauseous from the motion, and began to move to where his voice was yelling 'Earthquake!' But he raced into the bedroom faster, pulling me back onto the bed in the darkness, and said in the sexiest drawl, 'Where do you think you're going?' He held me tight as we bounced about on the bed. He remained very calm, so I never really felt in danger. It will always be one of the most romantic moments in my life.

"But besides being queer, my muse is darkly morbid, so the product of the experience is 'Blood Brothers.'"

Henri Tran

Henri Tran is a West Coast writer living in Southern California. One of the early contributors of *His,* he now makes a second appearance in the series with "Little Murmurs," which was meant as "a eulogy to that lovely background to my most cherished childhood memories, Club Sportif. Sadly, during my first visit home in 1992 I found it still standing but crumbling, being used as a public playground and left in complete disrepair, overgrown vines and all. Incidentally, my mother drops in uninvited at the opening of the story, and stays on for a great length. All the more ironic since she disowned her only son when he came out to her, via a transcontinental phone call no less. 'How could you do that to me?' was the last thing she said. Since then I have run into her once, in Paris at the Gare d'Austerlitz. The encounter lasted less than a minute, during which about five words were spoken, all by me, before we went our separate ways. 'High drama,' according to my dear friend Carole." Upon the publication of this work, the author renews his resolution to send out more submissions, and not to look back when in Paris.

Jim Tushinski

Jim Tushinski's short fiction has appeared in *The James White Review, Prism International, Pen and Sword,* and in the anthologies *The Gay Nineties* and *Quickies.* He was born and raised in Illinois but is now a longtime San Francisco resident. "'Home' is an excerpt from the opening of my novel-in-progress, entitled *Ecstasy.* The genesis of the novel was an interview with an anonymous gay man in Jonathan Ned Katz's groundbreaking *Gay American History.* Fascinated by the implications of re-creating one's life from scratch and with the terror one feels in the grip of amnesia, I wrote a very heavy-handed short story set in the early 1960s that dealt with forced institutionalization and homophobia. Over the years, however, I kept coming back to the character of Michael and found that he was more comfortable and interesting living in the present day and being an out gay man. The reasons for his breakdown and hospitalization grew more complex as the idea for the novel percolated, with homophobia rearing its ugly head almost as an afterthought, which is much more insidious because it's easier to dismiss and excuse."

David Watmough

"Born in 1926 in London, England, of Cornish ancestry and upbringing, in the early 1960s I moved to Vancouver, where I have written all ten volumes of my fiction.

"'Sharing Hale-Bopp' arose from successive sightings of the tailed comet Hale-Bopp in the spring of 1997. It somehow united in my mind (largely because of its chronological indifference to human life spans) both the crucial constituents of growing older for gays, when the sex drops out of homosexual, and the winding down of our paradoxically sordid yet idealistic century when we are tempted to think excessively of the uniqueness of our planet in the galaxy."

About the Editors

Robert Drake is the author of *The Gay Canon: Great Books Every Gay Man Should Read* and the novel *The Man: A Hero for Our Time.* He is co-editor of the anthologies *Indivisible: New Short Fiction by West Coast Gay and Lesbian Writers, Gay Fiction at the Millennium, Lesbian Fiction at the Millennium,* and the Lambda Literary Award-winning series *His: Brilliant New Fiction by Gay Writers* and *Hers: Brilliant New Fiction by Lesbian Writers.* From 1986 to 1998 he earned his living as a literary agent, finding time to serve from 1993 to 1998 as Book Review Editor for the *Baltimore Alternative* and teach writing at community colleges in the city of Philadelphia and Anne Arundel County, Maryland, as well as The American University and St. John's College, where he received his master's degree in 1993. Born in Portland, Maine, and raised in Charleston, West Virginia, he presently makes his home in Ireland.

Terry Wolverton is the author of *Bailey's Beads,* a novel, and *Black Slip,* a collection of poetry. Her fiction, poetry, essays and dramatic texts have appeared in numerous literary publications, including *Zyzzyva, Calyx,* and *Glimmer Train Stories,* and been widely anthologized. She has also edited several acclaimed literary compilations, including *Blood Whispers: L.A. Writers on AIDS,* and, with Robert Drake, *Indivisible: New Short Fiction by West Coast Gay and Lesbian Writers, Gay Fiction at the Millennium, Lesbian Fiction at the Millennium,* and the Lambda Literary Award-winning series *His: Brilliant New Fiction by Gay Writers* and *Hers: Brilliant New Fiction by Lesbian Writers.* Since 1976, Terry has lived in Los Angeles, where she's been active in the feminist, gay and lesbian, and art communities. In 1997 she founded Writers At Work, a center for writing workshops and individual creative consultations. She is currently at work on two books: *Embers,* a novel in poems, and a memoir, *Insurgent Muse,* to be published by City Lights Publishers.

Acknowledgments

The editors wish to thank Linda Rosenberg, Marcela Valdes, Valerie Cimino, and Betsy Uhrig for their considerable efforts on behalf of the *His* and *Hers* series. We also offer our considerable gratitude to Robin Podolsky, E. Scott Pretorius, and Gwin Wheatley for their editorial assistance.

Once again we extend thanks and kudos to Susan Silton for her striking cover designs and to Valerie Galloway for her remarkable photography.

It is a privilege to work with the talented writers whose works appear between these covers. To them, most of all, we offer our gratitude.

All stories are printed by permission of the authors.

Permissions Acknowledgments

"Barrel Racers" by Gary Bowen: copyright © 1999 by Gary Bowen

"Home Improvement" by Scott Allen Bowles: copyright © 1999 by Scott Allen Bowles

"A Pilgrimage of You" by Alexander Chee: copyright © 1999 by Alexander Chee

"The Bank President" by David Ebershoff: copyright © 1999 by David Ebershoff

"The Singing Boy" by Philip Gambone: copyright © 1999 by Philip Gambone

"Dann" by Michael Anthony Gold: copyright © 1999 by Michael Anthony Gold

"Haram" by Reginald M. Harris, Jr.: copyright © 1999 by Reginald M. Harris, Jr.

"Hating Yourself in the Morning" by Drew Limsky: copyright © 1999 by Drew Limsky

"La Tortuga" by Christopher Lord: copyright © 1999 by Christopher Lord

"Lost Time" by Declan Meade: copyright © 1999 by Declan Meade

"Good News and Bad News" by David A. Newman: copyright © 1999 by David A. Newman

"World Without End" by Robert Ordoña: copyright © 1999 by Robert Ordoña

"Series" by David Pratt: copyright © 1999 by David Pratt

"1984" by Lawrence Reilly: copyright © 1999 by Lawrence Reilly

"Manifest White" by Rick Sandford: copyright © 1999 by the Estate of Rick Sandford

"The Black Narcissus" by Reginald Shepherd: copyright © 1999 by Reginald Shepherd

"Blood Brothers" by Micheal Skiff: copyright ©1999 by Micheal Skiff

"Little Murmurs" by Henri Tran: copyright © 1999 by Henri Tran

"Home" by Jim Tushinski: copyright © 1999 by Jim Tushinski

"Sharing Hale-Bopp" by David Watmough: copyright © 1999 by David Watmough